DEVIL'S NIGHT

ALSO BY TODD RITTER

Bad Moon

Death Notice

DEVIL'S NIGHT

TODD RITTER

Minotaur Books New York

This is a work of fiction. All of the characters, organizations, and events portrayed in this novel are either products of the author's imagination or are used fictitiously.

Printed in the United States of America. For information, address St. Martin's Press, 175 Fifth Avenue, New York, N.Y. 10010.

www.minotaurbooks.com

Library of Congress Cataloging-in-Publication Data

Ritter, Todd.
Devil's night / Todd Ritter.—First edition.
pages cm
ISBN 978-1-250-02853-2 (hardcover)
ISBN 978-1-250-02854-9 (e-book)
1. Women police chiefs—Fiction. 2. Murder—Investigation—Fiction. I. Title.
PS3618.I79D48 2013
813'.6—dc23
2013009831

Minotaur books may be purchased for educational, business, or promotional use. For information on bulk purchases, please contact Macmillan Corporate and Premium Sales Department at 1-800-221-7945, extension 5442, or write specialmarkets@macmillan.com.

First Edition: August 2013

10 9 8 7 6 5 4 3 2 1

To Sarah

DEVIL'S NIGHT

It was dark.

Too dark for Kat's liking.

Windows were few and far between, and those she did pass were so small they offered nothing more than narrow slips of moonlight. Rather than lighting the way, they only made it harder for her eyes to adjust to the blackness pushing at her from all directions.

Kat had a flashlight, but she didn't dare use it. The beam might reveal her presence. And the element of surprise was more important than visibility. Other than her gun, it was the only weapon she had.

Her trusty Glock was clenched in her right hand. Her left hand was just below it, supporting her outstretched arm at the wrist. Walking that way slowed her down, which was good. She couldn't risk moving too fast. Like the flashlight, sudden movement would give her away. Kat couldn't have that happen. Her life likely depended on it.

So she skulked through the darkness, trying to fight the exhaustion that clouded her mind. Thoughts came slowly, taking twice as long as normal to piece information together. For instance, she should have known that she was nearing the stairs, but her brain was too sleep-addled to realize it. Instead, she ran right into them, slamming her big toe against the bottom step. The pain was so sudden and jolting it almost made her yelp. She caught the sound halfway up her throat and gulped it back down.

Swallowing hard again, Kat began her fumbling, cautious ascent. She paused at each step, resisting the urge to sprint up them two at a time. Despite her utter exhaustion, part of her wanted to just get to the top and see what awaited her. But another part of her already knew, and it terrified her.

Pausing halfway up the stairs, she leaned against the railing and listened for sounds from above. She heard nothing. Not for the first time, she wondered if she was wrong. About her destination. About what was being planned there. But everything she had learned in the past day pointed to this place. This moment. This hour.

Kat's thoughts suddenly slipped away from her. It was happening with alarming frequency now. Her train of thought would derail and she'd suddenly find herself blank and aimless, wondering where the hell she was and what she was doing. Severe sleep deprivation did that to you.

She couldn't bring herself back with a slap. Although it had worked earlier that night, it would be too noisy in that echo chamber of a stairwell. Instead, she pinched herself. Hard. Right on the back of her upper arm, where it hurt the most.

It did the trick.

Alert again, she pushed on. Up the stairs. Heart pounding. Trigger finger flexing at her Glock.

Soon she was at the top of the stairs and rising into the room. There were more windows there, massive ones that let in enough light to see by.

Taking in the room, Kat realized she would have preferred darkness.

The first thing she saw was a body on the floor. It was a man, slumped on his side and facing the far wall. Blood matted his hair and oozed from beneath his head in a circular pool that crept across the floorboards.

Even without seeing his face, Kat could identify him. She rushed to his side and, despite already knowing that he was dead and gone, checked his wrist for a pulse. When she didn't feel one, a heaviness flooded her heart. Yet another casualty in a day that was full of them.

"Who did this to you?" she whispered. "And why—"

She stopped speaking as her gaze flicked to the dark corner nearest the body. Something was there, shrouded in the shadows.

A propane tank.

It was small, just like the one hooked up to the gas grill in her backyard. The cap had been removed, replaced with a grease-smeared handkerchief that soaked up the liquid inside. The gas that leaked out was a noxious vapor that made Kat dizzy.

She glanced in the opposite corner. It also contained a propane tank. As did the room's other two corners. Each tank was the same. Caps off. Stuffed with rags. Waiting to be ignited.

A mere spark on one of the rags could make an entire tank explode. That would set off a chain reaction. Explosion after explosion after explosion.

The whole room had been turned into a bomb.

And Kat was now standing right in the heart of it.

24 HOURS EARLIER

1 A.M.

Kat was dreaming about Henry when she heard the sirens. She had no idea why. It's not as if she dwelled on him so much during her waking hours that it invaded her subconscious at night. In fact, it had been weeks since she thought about Henry, months since she had heard from him, and a full year since she last saw him.

Yet there he was, front and center in her dream. They were in a nondescript room so dim and vast that Kat wasn't sure if it was a room at all. Dreams were like that. Ceilings not supported by walls. Floors as malleable as wet sand. The only thing concrete about their surroundings was the table in front of them—white Formica as bright as a smile in a toothpaste commercial.

On the table were two large sheets of paper, thin and translucent. Henry, staring at his swath of paper, frowned.

"I don't know how to do this."

"It's easy," Kat said. "I'll show you."

She lifted a corner of her sheet to the center, cementing the fold with a crease. Henry followed suit. They did it again, this time simultaneously, with an upper fold.

"See," she said. "I told you it was easy."

Then the sirens started, so distant and muffled that Kat at first thought they were just another part of the dream. But they continued, even after Henry, the table, and the paper all vanished. That's when she knew they were real.

Kat listened without opening her eyes. Although they were far away, she could tell the sirens belonged to the fire department and not her police force. The ones on the fire trucks were louder and deeper—the baritones to her patrol cars' tenor.

Sliding out of bed, she went to the window and saw the reason for the sirens—a fire, glowing orange and eerie in the distance. She couldn't tell how large it was or pinpoint its exact location. All she knew was that she needed to be there, no matter how much she wanted to crawl back into bed. Pausing only long enough to yawn, she started to put on her uniform a mere hour and a half after taking it off.

She was mostly dressed by the time her phone rang. As expected, it was Carl Bauersox, her deputy, sounding much more energetic than she did. On the night shift, he was used to being alert at this hour. Kat was not.

"We've got a fire, Chief."

"I know," Kat said. "I hear the sirens. What's burning?"

"The museum."

He was referring to the Perry Hollow Historical Society and Exhibition Hall, a collection of documents, artifacts, and photographs that dated back to the town's founding and beyond. Because of its unwieldy name, and because most of the town's history resided within its walls, people simply called it the museum.

"Is it bad?"

"Looks like it," Carl said. "It's a big draw, too. We're

going to have a crowd control problem on our hands in a minute."

This didn't surprise Kat. Fires weren't common in Perry Hollow, and she was sure a good portion of the town would come out to gawk. They certainly couldn't sleep. Not with all those sirens echoing down the streets.

"Hold them off as best you can. I'll be there soon."

When she was finally on the road, her own sirens blaring, Kat noticed that the fire was visible from all over town. Even from six blocks away, she could see the licks of flame flashing over the rooftops of neighboring buildings. A thick column of black smoke, rising straight up into the night sky, punctuated the blaze like an exclamation point.

Crossing Main Street, she noticed plenty of residents staggering along the sidewalk in tossed-on sweatpants, sneakers, and robes. All of them were headed in the same direction she was, drawn mothlike to the flames. Crowd control problem, indeed.

She brought her Crown Vic to a stop a block away from the museum, parking sideways in the middle of the street. It wasn't much of a roadblock, but it would be enough to keep any cars from trying to come through. Plus, it was easy to move out of the way to let in fire trucks from neighboring towns, if it came to that.

Kat hoped it wouldn't.

Leaving her patrol car, she hurried down the street, finally getting a good look at the blaze. It wasn't as big as she first thought, but still bad by Perry Hollow standards. It looked to be contained to the front of the building, a three-story Queen Anne with all the frilly trimmings. Fire ate away at the steeply pitched roof and munched swiftly toward the ornate turret in its center. Flames leaped from the front windows and curled in the crisp autumn air, making Kat think of Satan's fingers beckoning a group of sinners to Hell.

Filling the street in front of the museum were two of the Perry Hollow Fire Department's three fire trucks. A ladder truck and a standard pumper, they formed a wide V on the lawn. In the center, members of the volunteer squad—all five of them—had already unfurled their hoses and were now blasting away at the blaze. The jets of water rose high into the air, arching over the front lawn before diving into the flames.

The squad's third truck, trusty Engine 13, was a 1973 Ford used for brush fires. Despite its age, it was the truck that saw the most action. Brush fires were the norm in Perry Hollow. House fires were not—a fact made noticeable by the sheer amount of onlookers standing on the other side of the street. While Kat had overestimated the force of the blaze, she had underestimated the size of the crowd. Half the town, it seemed, was there, huddling together and gazing at the flames.

Carl tried his best to keep them at bay, but they were an unruly lot. The young men and teenage boys in the crowd were especially eager to get closer to the fire. Kat intercepted two boys, the same age as her son, who had slipped past Carl and made it halfway across the street.

"Where you headed, boys?"

One of them—a freckle-faced kid with a snide smile—answered. "To see if the firemen need our help."

"They don't need anything but for you two to keep at a safe distance."

Kat ushered them back to the curb, yelling to get the attention of the rest of the crowd. "Everyone take a step back and stay there. This isn't a basketball game, people. Courtside seats are not available."

She sidled up to Carl, who was visibly relieved to have reinforcements.

"Just in time," he said, wiping sweat from his perpetually clean-shaven face. "They were starting to overrun me."

"They're just excited. There hasn't been a fire in town since—"

She cut herself off. Not that it mattered. Carl knew what she was going to say anyway. The last major fire in Perry Hollow was at the sawmill the town had been built around. Abandoned for more than a decade, it had gone up in flames a year earlier, with Kat and two others still inside. One of them had been Henry Goll, the unexpected costar of her dream. He and Kat almost died in the blaze. The person with them perished, although that wasn't such a bad thing, considering that he had been trying to kill them.

Feeling the heat of the current fire on the back of her neck, Kat realized that it was the one-year anniversary of the mill blaze. No wonder Henry had been in her dream. Her brain was trying to remind her that it was now October 31. Exactly a full year since the great Halloween fire that destroyed a piece of Perry Hollow history.

Kat faced the burning museum. Although she hadn't been inside it since grade school, seeing yet another part of the town's past go up in flames saddened her. At least she wasn't trapped inside this time. If there was a silver lining to be found, that would be it.

Another bright spot was the fact that the blaze already seemed to be under control. The fire on the roof had receded, leaving the museum's grand turret untouched. The flames at the windows, those devilish fingers, had retreated indoors, allowing the firefighters to march closer and focus on the hot spots.

But as the fire got smaller, the crowd on the other side of the street grew larger. There must have been fifty people there, with still more on the way. They stood in a tight pack, eyes on the fire, murmuring to each other with a combination of concern and excitement that always seemed to occur at scenes of public chaos. Kat spotted a lot of familiar faces in the crowd and nodded or waved. She saw Burt Hammond, Perry Hollow's mayor, sporting a black suit and a face so pale it made him resemble a wax statue. Standing with him was Father Ron, who had been the priest at All Saints Parish for as long as Kat could remember. Nearby were Jasper Foxx and Adrienne Wellington, both of whom owned stores on nearby Main Street. Dave Freeman, whose lawn bore the brunt of the onlookers, passed out Styrofoam cups to the crowd. His wife, Betty, followed, filling the cups with coffee she poured from a thermos.

Pushing past them was a tiny woman with a big perm, a parka thrown over her pink nightgown. Kat recognized the parka—not to mention the hair—as belonging to Emma Pulsifer, vice president of the Perry Hollow Historical Society. Seeing Kat, Emma rushed forward with a manic energy that verged on hysteria.

"Chief Campbell, have you seen Connie?"

Kat knew of at least four Connies who lived in town. "Could you be more specific?"

Emma sighed with impatience. "Connie Bishop."

"Constance?"

"Yes," Emma huffed. "I've been looking for her everywhere."

Constance Bishop, a prim but eminently friendly woman, knew everything there was to know about Perry Hollow. Accordingly, she served as president of the historical society. Kat wasn't sure what that entailed, but she assumed the museum fire was something that would concern her.

"I haven't seen her," she said. "Have you tried calling her?"

Emma held up her cell phone. "Four times. No answer."

She looked up and down the block, head bobbing wildly. With her puffy hair and unfortunately pointy nose, she brought to mind an exotic bird, like something from South America you'd see on the Discovery Channel. The resemblance was only heightened by the way she flapped her arms helplessly.

"I don't know what to do. I thought Connie would be here and have a game plan."

"For what?"

"Saving the artifacts, of course," Emma said. "There are priceless items in that building. We can't just watch them burn."

Kat told her they didn't have much choice in the matter. As long as there were still flames inside the museum, no one but members of the fire department would be going inside. That didn't sit well with Vice President Pulsifer.

"But the deed for the land Perry Mill was built on is in there," she said. "Signed in 1760 by Irwin Perry himself. And rare photographs of the town. And maps. We have items dating back to before the mill. Before the town was even called Perry Hollow. If we don't do something right now, all of it could be destroyed."

Kat looked to the museum again. Two firefighters had used the ladder truck to climb onto the roof, which they sprayed down with foam. Two others were in the process of knocking down the front door. When it gave way, they had to jump back to escape the flames rolling out of it. But they recovered quickly and ventured inside, hose blasting. Next to her, Emma Pulsifer cringed, no doubt imagining all that water damage.

"There's a back door," Emma said with noticeable desperation. "I know the fire's not out, but the town's entire history is in there. If we go through the back, we can try to salvage something."

"This is a tragedy," Kat told her. "It truly is. But I can't let you in there until the fire is completely out. I'm sorry. It's too dangerous."

Emma replied with a short, sad nod, the distant firelight reflecting in the tears that formed at the corners of her eyes. Quietly, she dialed her cell phone, pressed it to her ear, and turned away from Kat.

"Connie? It's Emma. Where *are* you? Call me back immediately."

Kat looked over Emma's shoulder, checking to see if the crowd was still behaving. They were, although one man near the back was on the move. He towered over the rest of the crowd, showing less interest in the fire than in getting past those who were watching it. Kat only caught a brief glimpse of his face—as pale as a full moon—but it was all she needed. She'd recognize those scars anywhere.

"Henry?"

The man didn't hear her. He continued working his way through the crowd, carrying what looked to be a small suitcase. Kat tried to follow him, practically shouting his name.

"Henry Goll? Is that you?"

She was in the thick of the crowd now, surrounded by people far taller than her five-foot frame. Kat cursed her shortness while squeezing between the two boys she had forced back onto the curb earlier that night.

Exiting on the other side of the crowd, she looked in all directions, seeing no sign of Henry. If it was even him. Kat had her doubts. The last time she had heard from him, he was living in Italy, making it unlikely he'd be walking the streets of Perry Hollow at one-thirty in the morning. Perhaps she had spotted someone who merely looked like him. Maybe it was a trick of the fire-lit night. Or maybe she was simply seeing things. It was late, after all, and her dream had put Henry back into her thoughts.

Concluding that the dream was to blame, Kat whirled around, ready to return to Emma Pulsifer. She instead collided with a man standing on the edge of the crowd.

For a brief moment, she again thought it was Henry. The man was as solid as she remembered Henry being. Bumping into him felt like smacking into a brick wall. Kat almost said his name again, so certain was she that the man she had collided with was the long-lost Henry Goll.

Yet when the man spoke, she immediately realized her error. Henry's voice was deeper and more halting. The voice of the man she had bumped sounded high-pitched and startled.

"Whoa," he said. "Sorry about that."

"It was my fault." Kat wiped a strand of hair away from her face. "I should have been watching where I was going."

"Look before you leap, right?" the man said.

"Exactly."

Kat studied the man a moment, certain she had never seen him before. Since she knew practically everyone in Perry Hollow—if not by name, then by sight—she assumed he was a recent arrival. Or else a visitor. He had the appearance of someone who didn't belong. Although his voice contained no hint of an accent, he looked vaguely foreign, with deep-set eyes the color of coal, sharp cheekbones, and blond hair pulled back in a ponytail.

His clothes, too, were out of place in a jeans-and-T-shirt town like Perry Hollow. His collared shirt was buttoned all the way to the neck. His black pants were too tight and too short. An extra inch or two of white socks poked out from the cuffs before vanishing again into pointy shoes fastened by silver buckles. Over it all hung a black trench coat that was slightly frayed at the sleeves.

Kat introduced herself, hoping the stranger would do the same.

He merely nodded politely. "Nice to meet you, Chief. Have a good night. Don't stay up too late."

He departed, his trench coat fluttering behind him. Kat watched him walk toward Main Street, still unable to shake the feeling that something wasn't quite right about the guy. And it wasn't just because he refused to give a name. It was the whole package—his face, his clothes, his whole manner—that unsettled her. Had the circumstances been different, she would have tried to follow him, just to find out where he was going.

Behind her, the crowd on the Freemans' front lawn erupted into cheers and applause. They were clapping for the firefighters, who had started to emerge from the cloud of smoke still pouring out of the museum.

The fire had been conquered.

Kat waited to approach the ladder truck until the firefighters had peeled away their turnout gear, their cast-off boots, coats, and helmets littering the grass. She then thanked each of them, doling out a few high fives in the process. She was in the midst of being taught an elaborate handshake by Danny Batallas, the youngest member of the squad, when the fire chief beckoned her over.

Even in his younger days, Boyd Jansen had looked so much like a fire chief that it was inevitable he'd become one. Strong upper body. Thick around the middle. He kept his mustache neatly trimmed, although, like his sandy hair, it gathered more gray with each passing year. Joining him at the front of the ladder truck, Kat greeted him by his nickname.

"Great job, Dutch. You and your boys knocked that fire out in a hurry."

The chief waved away the compliment. "It was a birthday candle—quick to flare up, easy to snuff out."

"That's a good thing, right?"

"You'd think," Dutch said. "But my gut tells me that fire might have had some help."

And Kat's gut told her she was about to be served some bad news. She was proven right when Dutch pulled her to the far side of the ladder truck, where they were out of earshot of the others.

"That fire went up quick," he said. "Never seen one sprout so fast."

"It's an old building," Kat countered. "Not exactly fireproof."

"You're right. But I've seen enough fires to know that this one makes me suspicious."

Suddenly, Kat longed to be back at home, in bed, fast asleep. Because if she understood Dutch correctly, she wouldn't be getting any sleep for a very long time.

"You think someone set the museum on fire?"

"Maybe."

"On purpose or by accident?" Kat asked. "It's the night before Halloween. A few kids could have been bored and decided to get creative on mischief night."

She was grasping at straws. In Perry Hollow, mischief night never got more dangerous than a few egged windows and a generous toilet-papering of front yards. Very rarely did it escalate into setting something on fire. If it did, that something was usually a paper bag full of dog poop.

"You don't know too much about fires, do you?" Dutch asked.

"Not really," Kat said. "How'd you guess?"

"Because if you did, you'd know that a flaming bag of shit couldn't do this kind of damage."

"Do you think we should get an arson investigator out here? Maybe find out just what we're dealing with."

"That," Dutch said, "would be a fine idea."

"Chief?"

Both Kat and Dutch looked to the front of the ladder truck, where Danny Batallas now stood.

"Sorry," he said, blushing. "My chief."

Dutch straightened. "What is it, Danny?"

"Did you give the all clear to enter the museum?"

"Hell, no. Why?"

Danny jerked his head in the direction of the still-smoldering museum. "Because I think someone's about to."

Kat was on the other side of the truck in an instant, although it wasn't fast enough to catch the face of the person rounding a burned-out corner of the building. Not that she needed to. A flash of pink fabric flaring in the person's wake was enough.

"It's Emma Pulsifer," she said. "Help me drag her out of there."

Dutch and Danny both grabbed helmets before joining her in a sprint across the museum's lawn. Kat felt them behind her as she hopped over the fire hoses still sprawled in the grass. Then it was through a wall of smoke that drifted languidly from the building. Small bits of ash swirled in the air, clinging to her face. She swiped them away as she moved along the side of the museum.

Reaching the back of the building, Kat saw the door Emma had mentioned earlier. It was open and creaking slightly back and forth on its hinges. Smoke escaped from the doorway, but not as much as from the front of the building. Back there, it was merely a trickle. Still, it was enough to make Kat want to cover her nose. It smelled like the world's biggest ashtray.

"She's already inside," Kat told the two firemen behind her.

"She shouldn't be anywhere near this place," Dutch hissed with annoyance. "God knows how unstable it is. The whole thing could crumble with one wrong step."

Hearing that did nothing to put Kat's mind at ease as she leaned in the doorway. It was dark, of course, the gloom made even worse by the smoke that hovered like a stubborn fog. Kat tugged the flashlight from her duty belt and flicked it on. Then she stepped inside.

Emma Pulsifer was just beyond the doorway, standing in what appeared to be a cramped hallway. She bumped against the walls, fumbling blindly in the darkness. Kat placed a hand on her shoulder—a small attempt to calm her.

"We shouldn't be in here," she said. "It's not safe."

"I know." Emma looked up at her with tear-filled eyes. "But please let me try to salvage at least a few things. *Please.*"

Kat liked to think she was too tough to be swayed by tears. She was wrong. The fire had left Emma devastated. Letting her try to save a few items was the least she could do.

"Okay," she said, stepping in front of Emma. "But let me go first."

Dutch entered the museum. Gripping his own flashlight, he aimed the beam at Kat's face. "Not a chance," he said. "*I'll* go first."

Behind him, the voice of Danny Batallas rose from outside. "I'll stay right here, if you don't mind."

"Go back to the truck," Dutch instructed. "Tell the others what we're doing. If we're not back in five minutes, send in a rescue team."

He waved his flashlight back and forth between Kat and Emma. "You got that? Five minutes."

Dutch handed each of them a helmet and demanded that they put them on before going any farther. "You'll thank me if the ceiling caves in," he said.

Kat did as she was told. The helmet was heavier than she expected—a weight pressing down from the top of her skull—and did nothing to aid in navigation. It obscured her peripheral vision, forcing her to twist her head to the sides if she wanted to see anything that wasn't directly in front of her.

Not that there was much to look at in the hallway. Inching through it, Kat saw only a few administrative offices and a meeting room. Still, she could tell that this section of the museum wasn't nearly as fire-ravaged as the front. Other than the smoke and some puddles of water, everything seemed to be in decent condition. It wasn't until they reached the end of the hallway, which opened into the main gallery, that Kat saw the extent of the damage.

The gallery, a large room packed floor to ceiling with displays, had been obliterated. Sweeping her flashlight across the room, Kat saw that portions of the floor and most of the ceiling were badly charred. The walls were, too. The one facing the street had been so severely gutted that she could see right through it to the thinning crowd outside. Whatever had been hanging on the wall was now gone. Only warped and blackened frames remained.

In fact, most of the displays in the gallery had been destroyed. Those that weren't consumed by the fire had been ruined from water damage. Display cases that might have withstood the flames had been knocked over by the pressure of the hoses. The floor was covered with glass shards and water, which combined to make a crunching and sloshing sound that reminded Kat of a pebble beach at high tide.

Roaming the gallery, she noticed random objects among the detritus, some of which she still remembered from her childhood visits. A pocket watch. A woman's shoe. A blade saw from the mill's early days. In the corner, a wax figure wore the remains of a Union Army uniform from the Civil War. Drops of water fell from the sleeves, and large holes that resembled cigarette burns marred the fabric. The figure's face had melted, its misshapen nose oozing down to what had once been its chin.

She looked to the wall opposite the front door. Still hanging there, safe in its frame, was the deed Emma had mentioned earlier. Roughly the same size as a newspaper and written in florid script, it stated that Mr. Irwin Perry now owned a hundred acres of land outside an unnamed village in southeastern Pennsylvania. A year later, the Perry Mill opened, flooding the village with workers. To mark this surge, the village was officially named Perry Hollow. Of all the pieces in the museum, the deed was the most treasured. Seeing that it had been spared made Kat breathe a sigh of relief.

Emma, however, was downright overcome with emotion. Sniffing back tears of gratitude, she hugged both Kat and Dutch.

"You helped save history," she told them. "You really did."

"I'll take it down," Dutch said. "Then we've got to get the hell out of here. I don't want to press our luck."

While he removed the frame from the wall, Emma took off her helmet and whipped out her cell phone one more time. "I have to tell Constance. She'll be thrilled to know the deed survived."

She dialed and held the phone to her ear. A second later, Kat heard a muffled trilling coming from somewhere inside the museum. It chirped three more times before abruptly going silent.

"She's still not picking up," Emma said, flipping her phone shut.

Kat also removed her helmet. "Call her again."

"Why?"

"Just do it."

Once again, Emma tapped in the phone number. And once again, Kat heard the electronic trill. She edged to a corner of the room. The sound was slightly louder there, though still muffled. When it chirped again, Kat realized the noise was coming from beneath the floor.

She turned to Emma. "Does the museum have a basement?"

"There's a crawl space under the gallery. We sometimes use it for storage, although the rest of the collection is up in the attic."

"How can I get down there?"

"A trapdoor," Emma said, confused. "You're standing on it."

Kat took a step backward, finally seeing several gaps in the floorboards that formed a square. A nickel-sized hole—easy to miss if you weren't looking for it—sat on one side of the square. Kneeling, Kat jammed an index finger into the hole and raised the trapdoor until she could slide a hand under it.

Seeing what she was doing, Dutch handed the framed deed to Emma. He then knelt next to Kat, aiming the flashlight into the crawl space as she removed the door and peered inside.

What they saw was Constance Bishop.

She was slumped over a wooden chest, her generous rump raised in the air. Her legs were bent slightly, knees pushing against the wooden chest, and her lifeless arms dangled forward. One of her shoes was missing, revealing the sole of a foot blackened with dirt.

Dutch moved the flashlight beam over her body, which hadn't been able to escape the fire hoses despite being beneath the floor. Beads of water dotted the pale skin on the back of her legs. Her blouse and skirt, darkened by moisture, clung to her body.

When the light reached the back of her head, Kat saw a

flash of crimson. Blood. Just behind her right ear. Tiny bits of white stuck to her hair. Bone fragments, Kat surmised. Or maybe brain matter.

"Sweet Jesus," Dutch muttered.

"What's down there?"

It was Emma Pulsifer, stomping toward them with the deed tucked under her arm. Kat stood, trying to block her, but it was too late. Emma peered into the crawl space, spotted Constance, and choked out a strangled cry.

"No! Dear God, no."

She clamped a palm against her open mouth, the deed slipping from her arms. The frame shattered when it hit the floor—Perry Hollow's founding document smashed into a hundred pieces.

The noise snapped Kat into action. Returning to the floor, she lowered herself into the crawl space. It was a tight fit, especially with Constance there, but she managed to squeeze herself inside. For once, being short was an advantage. Still, wiggle room was nonexistent, forcing her to stand behind Constance, straddling her lifeless legs.

As Dutch held the light steady from above, Kat leaned forward until her chest was pressed against Constance's back. She placed two fingers against the side of Constance's neck, feeling for a pulse.

There wasn't one.

Not content with the results, Kat pivoted as much as space would allow and reached for Constance's left arm. Although it was as heavy and unwieldy as wet cardboard, she managed to raise it enough to slip two fingers against her wrist. No pulse there, either.

"She's dead," Kat announced.

She swallowed hard, suppressing the sob that threatened to bubble up from deep in her chest. Part of her sadness was, of course, for Constance Bishop, a kind woman whose life had been cut short. The rest of the grief was reserved for her town. She thought the violence had died with the Grim Reaper killer. She was wrong. Murder had once again visited Perry Hollow.

Above her, Emma's sobs grew louder. They blasted through the hole in the floor and echoed into the smallest recesses of the crawl space until they became tinny and faint. The light above Kat shifted as Dutch apparently turned in an attempt to comfort Emma. The new slant of the flashlight's beam illuminated the left side of Constance's head, her shoulder, and part of the arm that Kat was still holding. It also, Kat noticed, shed light on a series of black marks on Constance's hand.

"Don't move," she shouted up to Dutch. "Keep the light right where it is."

"Why?" he called back.

Kat didn't answer. Instead, she leaned forward even more, staring at the dark lines on chalky flesh. They were letters, she realized, scrawled in what seemed to be black marker.

Someone had written on Constance Bishop's hand.

Kat twisted the wrist until all of the words were visible. Fear poked her ribs as she read what had been written across Constance's skin. It was a fear she had last experienced a year ago. A fear she had hoped to never feel again. But there it was, jabbing at her with an insistence that made her want to scream. It stayed with her as she read the words on Constance's hand a second time, then a third.

A mere five words long, the message was simple but agonizingly clear.

THIS IS JUST THE FIRST.

2 A.M.

It was the longest journey of his life, if not in distance then in actual travel time. Sixteen hours total. Most of them containing at least one headache.

First was the maddening cab ride through rush hour in Rome—a gridlock of Smart Cars and scooters and curses shouted in Italian. Next came the interminable wait at the airport as his flight was delayed. Twice. Once onboard, it was ten hours in coach, trying to sleep as the college kid sitting next to him exhausted an endless supply of gadgets: iPad, iPod, iPhone.

After they landed in Philadelphia, it took an hour to get through customs, although he was still an American citizen. He chalked that up to his face. People tended not to trust a face like his. As annoying as it was, he couldn't blame them.

He considered every roadblock an omen, telling him to turn around. He certainly had considered it. Many times. The words *I shouldn't be doing this* ran through his mind more often than not. It was a bad idea, clearly. Anyone could see that. Yet he pressed on, exiting the airport and stepping once again onto American soil.

Since he didn't have a driver's license, in the U.S. or in Italy, he had to plead with a cabbie to drive him forty-five minutes into the middle of nowhere. When begging didn't work, cash did. An exorbitant amount that he had to pay up front before he could even open the passenger door. Reaching town, he found a very familiar police car blocking the street his hotel was on, forcing him to carry his luggage several blocks on foot, through a crowd, in front of a fire.

A fitting end to his journey, really. And, he thought, yet another reason why he should have stayed where he was. But now it was too late to turn back. Now he couldn't blame the traffic or the delayed flights or the snide jackass at customs.

Now, whether he wanted to be or not, Henry Goll was back in Perry Hollow.

He was staying at the Sleepy Hollow Inn, a three-story bed-and-breakfast that was the only game in town as far as hotels went. His room was on the top floor, and while surprisingly large, it left a lot to be desired. It was too antique, too flowery, and smelled too much like cheap soap. All that pastel and potpourri was suffocating—like being hugged too tightly by an old woman.

As he unpacked, Henry considered finding another place to stay. His options, though, were limited. He knew exactly one person who would put him up for the night, and she was two blocks away dealing with a fire.

Henry had heard Chief Kat Campbell shout his name through the crowd of onlookers. For a moment, he had almost stopped and greeted her with the warmth and kindness she deserved. Instead, he ignored her, escaping the crowd unseen while the chief was occupied with some tall man she had just bumped into.

It's not that he didn't want to see Kat. He was genuinely looking forward to catching up and hearing how both she and James were doing. But tonight wasn't the right time. She was busy, and Henry was—well, he wasn't happy to be here.

He never thought he'd be back in Perry Hollow. He had

had no desire to return. There were too many bad memories of the last time he was here. The thread pulling through his skin. The scalpel at his throat. The fire and chaos and blood that followed. Moving to Italy had dulled the memories, but Henry was afraid seeing Kat would bring many of them back. That trip down memory lane, he decided, could wait until later.

When Henry finished unpacking, he looked at his watch, which was still set to Italian time. It was after eight A.M. there. Dario would definitely be awake. Which meant it was time to call home.

Henry's phone barely got out one ring before it was answered with a terse "*Pronto.*"

"*Sono Henry.*"

"Henry! How was your flight?"

Although Henry was fluent in Italian, Dario Giambusso insisted on speaking English with him. Henry suspected his editor was trying to show off. Or maybe his Italian was that bad, and Dario was tired of hearing him butcher his native tongue. Either way, whenever they spoke, English was the language of choice.

"The flight was"—Henry grasped for the right word—"long. But I'm here."

"Very good. Now you should relax. It's early there, no?"

Dario's voice was almost drowned out by a loud whirring noise. It was accompanied by the rhythmic slapping of bare feet on a hard surface. He was on his treadmill. Other than knowing English, a love of exercise was the only thing Henry and his editor had in common.

"It *is* early," Henry said. "But relaxation isn't on the agenda. I have a lot of background information to go through before I start contacting my sources."

"Don't run yourself ragged. You need sleep, too."

"I slept on the plane."

"Then maybe you can visit that lady friend of yours," Dario said, voice thick with innuendo. "Does she still live in town?"

He was talking about Deana, Henry's girlfriend before everything went to hell. Of course Dario knew about her. Most of the world did, just as they knew about what had happened to Henry. His story wasn't a secret. It was the reason, in fact, he had been sent to Perry Hollow instead of the reporter who usually covered this beat. Henry certainly didn't volunteer for the assignment. No, he had been handpicked by Dario, who thought Henry's history with the town was something he could exploit.

"Seeing Deana Swan isn't on my agenda," Henry said. "I just want to do my job and go home."

"That's very noble, Henry." The slapping noises got faster. Dario had just kicked up his speed. "But, in a way, you already are home."

Henry, no longer in the mood to talk, told his editor he'd check in as soon as he found something. Then with a quick *ciao*, he hung up.

Tossing the phone onto the bed, Henry retreated to the bathroom and stared in the mirror over the sink. His reflection contained so many flaws he didn't know where to look first. The large burn mark at his left temple had been there for so long that he barely even noticed it anymore. Same thing with the scar that ran from ear to chin, intersecting both of his lips in the process.

The others at his lips were more recent, and he still wasn't used to them. Not even after a year spent studying them in any mirror he could find. The plastic surgeons had managed to save what they could, but it was still clear something horrible had happened to him. His lips were now a series of unsightly bumps, populated with specks of white where the needle and thread had slipped through. When Henry ran his fingertips over them, it felt like he was trying to read Braille.

Tugging on his collar, Henry examined the right side of his neck. His skin was eggshell pale, even after months of living in Italy, and logic dictated that the scar there wouldn't be as noticeable because of it. But sometimes logic had no place where the human body was concerned, and the scar on his neck was the most visible one of all. It was a bright pink and wider than the others. Even when Henry wore a shirt and tie, it was still visible, a cruel reminder of his past peeking out of his collar.

"Welcome home, Henry," he muttered to his reflection. "Hopefully you'll leave in better shape than you did last time."

---

3 A.M.

"I don't know why anyone would want to hurt Connie. It's devastating. Absolutely devastating."

Emma Pulsifer used the sleeve of her nightgown to dab at her eyes. They were red and raw, the result of a crying jag that had lasted for the better part of an hour. Kat spent that time making calls to the appropriate authorities—county sheriff, prosecutor's office, state police—and then greeting the endless stream of cops and crime scene techs who arrived at the museum. Now she was back with Emma, who had calmed down enough to talk.

The two of them sat in a dim conference room next to the museum's back door. It was dry there and mostly free of the smoky residue left by the fire. Just down the hall, the small army of investigators got to work in the main gallery. Kat heard cautious footsteps on the charred floor and the low murmur of voices trying to piece everything together. Occasionally, the incandescent flash of a camera bounced down the hallway, causing Emma to flinch.

"Constance was a widow, right?" Kat asked.

"Just like me," Emma said. "There weren't any children."

"Did she have any other family that you know of? Any immediate next of kin you think we should contact?"

"Not that I know of. The historical society was her family. She devoted her life to it."

"Is there anyone in the historical society that didn't get along with Constance?" Kat asked. "Anyone who might want to do her harm?"

The suggestion seemed to horrify Emma, who dropped her jaw before answering, "Of course not. Everyone loved her. There were disagreements, naturally. But nothing that would result in murder."

She was mistaken there. Kat knew anything could result in murder. A grudge. An affair. A lie that spiraled out of control. Sometimes nothing prompted the killing. Sometimes people just snapped. The ominous warning scrawled on Constance's hand—THIS IS JUST THE FIRST—pointed in that direction. Kat didn't want to consider that possibility at the moment, so she asked, "What kind of disagreements are we talking about?"

"Well, this museum, for one," Emma said. "It's free to

the public, and some members disagreed with that. They thought we should charge admission. We're always short on funds, and the extra money would help. Connie disagreed. She said the town's history belonged to everyone. We were just the people who took care of it."

"And what did *you* think?"

"It didn't matter what I thought. Connie was the president. She had the final say."

Kat leaned back in her chair, crossing her arms. "How many members does the historical society have? I know there were you and Constance. Who else?"

"It was just the five of us. Father Ron is the secretary. Claude Dobson is the treasurer. And Mayor Hammond is the honorary member, as were all the mayors before him."

Kat had seen Father Ron and the mayor outside while the fire was still raging. As far as she knew, Claude Dobson, a retired high school history teacher, wasn't with them. She wasn't sure if that worked in his favor or not.

"When was the last time you saw Constance?"

"Tonight." Emma checked her watch, seeing they had entered a new day. "I mean, last night."

"What time was that?"

"A little before eight. I drove past the museum and saw the lights were still on. I popped in and found Connie still here, just like I thought."

"In the gallery?"

"In her office. It's across the hall."

Kat looked past Emma to the doorway behind her. An office sat on the other side of the hallway, its door closed. Someone had been smart enough to criss-cross it with police tape.

"I'm assuming she was alone," she said.

"It was just Connie at her desk, as usual."

"What did you two talk about?"

"Chitchat, mostly," Emma said. "I asked if she planned on going to the Chamber of Commerce fund-raiser later."

The fund-raiser was the premier social event of the year in Perry Hollow, which wasn't saying much. It probably looked like a rinky-dink affair to people from more metropolitan areas, but in a town where most wedding receptions were held in the Elks Lodge, the fund-raiser was a very big deal. Those who could afford it put on their best clothes, sipped cocktails, and gossiped the night away. Kat had been invited but politely declined the offer. She wasn't good at schmoozing, nor did she enjoy it. Besides, it had been movie night with James—part of her renewed push to spend more time with him. That night's selection was *Toy Story,* one of his favorites.

"Is the fund-raiser where you were headed when you passed the museum?"

Emma's nod turned into a flinch as another burst of flashbulbs shot down the hall. "It was. Connie told me she'd be there in a little while. But she never showed."

"Were any other members of the historical society there?"

"Yes," Emma said. "All of us."

"What time did it end?"

"I'm not sure. I left close to midnight. The others were still there."

The fire, Kat had learned, was first reported by Dave and Betty Freeman, who saw it from their bedroom window. The 911 call was made at 12:52. Whoever was still at the fund-raiser at that time was in the clear. Emma Pulsifer, however, wasn't one of them.

"Where was the fund-raiser held this year?"

"Maison D'Avignon," Emma said, referring to the French restaurant that had helped turn Perry Hollow from a crumbling mill town into something slightly more upscale. It was located on Main Street, five blocks up and four blocks over from the museum.

"And did you pass the museum on your way home?"

"I took a different route."

"Did you stop anywhere along the way? A place where someone else could verify your presence. A gas station, perhaps? Or maybe at the ATM outside Commonwealth Bank."

"No. I went straight home." Suspicion crept into Emma's voice. "And I don't see why any of this matters."

"I'm just trying to place your whereabouts when the fire started."

"I was in bed," Emma said, tugging absently on her pink nightgown. "I heard the sirens, looked out the window, and saw the flames. I didn't even know it was the museum that was on fire until I got closer."

Since Emma was also a widow, there was no one at home to back up her alibi. Kat had to take what she was saying at face value. She didn't want to, but for the time being, she had no choice.

"One last question before you can go," Kat said. "Why was Constance here so late on a Friday night?"

"Your guess is as good as mine," Emma said.

"Was she normally here at night?"

"In the past, no. But in the last few weeks or so, yes."

"Was she working on something?"

"Maybe."

Emma made no effort to elaborate, prompting Kat to say, "Either she was or she wasn't."

"She was. Possibly. On Thursday, she sent an e-mail to the rest of us in the historical society calling an emergency meeting."

"About what?"

"No one knows. But I have a feeling it had something to do with all the time she was spending here lately."

"And when did she want to have this meeting?"

"Tonight," Emma said. "She wanted to have it tonight."

Kat felt the yawn coming on as she guided Emma Pulsifer out of the museum via the back door. She managed to stifle it as she told Emma to expect more questions in the morning, both about Constance and about the museum itself. But once she was back inside the building, heading down the hall to the main gallery, the yawn erupted—jaw-stretching proof of just how tired she really was.

A sallow-faced man with gray hair standing in the middle of the gallery noticed—it was hard not to—and gave her a knowing smile. The man was Wallace Noble, the medical examiner, and Kat had known him since the days when her father was Perry Hollow's police chief.

"Long night, eh?" he said in a voice made raspy by forty years of smoking.

Kat replied with another, more modest yawn. "Yep. And I'm afraid this is just the beginning of a very long morning. This case looks like it'll keep me up for days."

"I thought you'd be used to it by now," Wallace said. "First the Grim Reaper killings. Then the Olmstead thing. You seem to get all the good crimes."

"I guess I'm just lucky," Kat said, although she knew the opposite was true. A lucky cop would be one who spent an entire career avoiding such cases. The only reason Kat felt fortunate was because she had somehow managed to survive them.

"This is far cleaner than those Reaper killings," Wallace said. "No amateur embalming here, thank God. Remember how he attacked his victims?"

Kat gave him a slight nod. As if she could ever forget. The Grim Reaper, one of the two most evil people she had ever encountered, liked to play games. He'd place a dead animal at the scene, distracting his victims long enough for him to sneak up on them. Then he'd render them unconscious with a handkerchief doused with chloroform. Then he'd kill them.

Slowly.

Painfully.

Henry Goll had been the only one to survive.

"Well, now there's this," Kat said.

Her gaze drifted around the gallery, which looked far different than when she first arrived with Dutch Jansen and Emma Pulsifer in tow. The darkness that had previously enveloped them was now banished by a few well-placed klieg lights powered by a generator outside. The blinding glare highlighted the destruction, from the fire-scarred walls to the floors already warping from water damage. Shards of glass were everywhere, glinting in the light.

Above Kat, a portion of the ceiling had been eaten away, revealing both the second and third floors. She remembered from her grade-school visits that on the second floor were rooms decorated just as they would have been during the town's founding. Above that, she assumed, was the attic, where Emma said the rest of the museum's collection was stored.

The devastation from the fire and the water damage that followed meant there was likely very little trace evidence to be found. Still, a few crime scene techs huddled around the crawl space where Constance had been discovered. Although her body was now lying beneath a white sheet on a wheeled gurney next to Wallace, Kat still pictured her slumped over that trunk, her wool skirt wet and clinging to the back of her legs. The techs, who were probably used to seeing far worse, worked in silence. One of them, wearing a baseball cap with a penlight duct-taped to the bill, dropped into the crawl space like a seasoned spelunker.

"I'm assuming the cause of death is blunt force trauma," Kat said.

"Probably," Wallace replied with a nod. "She was certainly hit hard with something heavy. A single blow to the back of the head. Cracked her skull right open."

"Any guess as to the time of death?"

"Fairly recent. The body was still warm, so I'm guessing no more than three hours ago."

Immediately, Kat started forming a timeline of events. If Wallace was correct, Constance had died between twelve-thirty and one A.M., around the same time the fire started. Kat assumed that whoever killed her dragged the body into the crawl space before starting the fire.

"What do you think the murder weapon was?" she asked.

Wallace gave a palms-up gesture of ignorance before opening his arms wide. "Take your pick. There were probably a hundred objects in here heavy enough to do that kind of damage. Bronze statues. Household items, which were heavier back in the day than they are now. Housewives back then must have had biceps the size of bowling balls."

"All the better to keep men like you in check," Kat said.

Wallace let out a low chuckle that quickly morphed into a smoker's cough and seemed to last a full minute. When he recovered, he said, "I'm off to do the autopsy now. I'll call you as soon as I find anything."

He started to wheel out Constance's body, pausing long enough to pull a cigarette from the pack in his shirt pocket and pop it between his lips.

"Don't worry," he said, the cigarette bobbing up and down. "I won't light it until I get outside. Not that it'll make much of a difference to this place."

Once Wallace was gone, Kat crossed to the other side of the gallery. She trod lightly, careful not to step on any of the debris that littered the charred floor. What she didn't see, oddly enough, were many evidence markers. The gallery contained exactly one, placed a few paces to the left of the museum's front door.

Two men knelt next to the yellow fold of plastic. One of them was a stranger. The other Kat knew very well.

"Lieutenant Vasquez," she said. "No offense, but I wish you weren't here."

Tony Vasquez was a detective with the Pennsylvania State Police's Bureau of Criminal Investigation. Neither the town nor the county had the manpower or expertise to handle crimes as big as homicide and arson, so the BCI was usually called to step in. As a result, Tony had worked on the Grim Reaper murders and the Charlie Olmstead disappearance. Now he was here once again.

"Frankly, I do, too."

"I'm assuming you're in charge."

"Yeah," Tony said. "Seeing how I know my way around the town by now, they figured I'd be a good point person."

"Well, you know the score," Kat told him. "You're in charge. I don't mind that you're in charge. And I'll do whatever I can to help."

Lieutenant Vasquez got to his feet. In addition to being a professional cop, Tony was also an amateur bodybuilder. Those biceps the size of bowling balls that Wallace mentioned? Tony had them. His sheer size never ceased to amaze Kat. He was so big that he looked out of scale with the rest of the gallery—like Alice after nibbling on the cake that made her grow.

"It's looking very likely that the fire hoses washed away all the evidence," he said. "No trace. No blood spatter. If there is any evidence, it's mixed in with this rubble. What did you find?"

Kat caught Tony up to speed on the events before and after she discovered Constance Bishop's body. She also detailed her interview with Emma Pulsifer and the whereabouts of the other members of the historical society when the fire broke out. Then it was time to talk about the thing she least wanted to talk about. The thing that indicated this was no ordinary murder.

"There was something written on Constance's hand."

"I know," Tony said. "I saw it."

"What do you make of it?"

"I'm not sure. It might be nothing."

"Or it could mean we have another Grim Reaper on our hands."

Kat couldn't get those five words out of her head. When

she closed her eyes, she still saw them, smudged and startling. THIS IS JUST THE FIRST.

Tony inhaled, his massive chest expanding and deflating. "Yes. That's a distinct possibility."

It wasn't what Kat wanted to hear. The answer silenced her for a moment as she pondered what it could mean for her and the town.

The man standing at Tony's side cleared his throat, forcing an introduction.

"Kat," the lieutenant said, "this is Larry Sheldon. He's an arson investigator with the state police."

Kat quickly sized up the newcomer while shaking his hand. He was younger than her, thirty if a day, and boyishly handsome. Wearing jeans, a button-down shirt, and a tie, he looked more like a math teacher than someone who'd be studying a crime scene at three-thirty in the morning. His wire-frame glasses, slipping off his nose, didn't help.

"You find anything interesting?" Kat asked.

"A lot that's interesting, actually," Larry said. "And before you ask, I'm ninety-nine percent sure that this fire was arson."

"How can you tell?"

"This is the point of origin." He turned to the patch of floor he and Tony had been examining. "Although a trail of accelerant at the wall caused the most damage."

Kat tapped him on the shoulder. "This is my first arson. You'll have to dumb it down for me."

"Oh, right. Sure." Larry paused to push his glasses higher on his nose. "The mark on the floor right here indicates that this is where the fire burned the hottest and brightest. That's the point of origin. The marking is typical of a fire in which an accelerant was used."

"Gasoline?" Kat said.

"Possibly. But my gut tells me it was kerosene."

Kat stared at the charred floor. "You can tell all that from a burn pattern?"

"No. I can tell from this."

Larry pointed to a twisted jumble of wood and metal lying nearby. The shards of glass surrounding it were different from the ones from the shattered display cases. These pieces were opaque, almost milky. It took a minute for Kat to realize it had all once been a kerosene lamp.

"Judging from the burn pattern, the accelerant wasn't poured onto the floor," Larry said. "It was thrown, if that makes any sense."

"Our guess is that someone smashed the lit lantern onto the floor," Tony added. "This building is old. The floor is untreated wood. The fire spread very fast to the walls, which are also wood. No drywall or Sheetrock here."

"Do you think whoever started the fire knew this?"

"Not necessarily," Larry said. "Truth be told, most arsonists don't even think about such things. They just want to watch something burn."

"Which brings me to my next question," Kat said. "What type of person would want to start the fire in the first place?"

"That depends on the arsonist's goal. More often than not, the fire is set for a specific reason. Sure, there are guys—and it's almost always a guy—who do it because they're messed up in the head."

"Pyromaniacs," Kat said.

Larry pointed at her like a game show host commending a contestant for guessing the correct answer. "Setting fires gives them a sense of power, of having control over a situation. But these cases are extremely rare. Whenever I investigate a fire, I assume there was something else at play. Collecting insurance money, for example. Or revenge."

"Or," Tony chimed in, "someone trying to destroy evidence after they just murdered someone."

"Maybe," Larry said. "But there's also the possibility that the fire, and not murder, was the ultimate goal here."

It was entirely possible that whoever set the fire had been caught in the act by Constance, who paid for the discovery with her life. But Kat didn't think so. All one needed to do was look at Constance's hand to debunk that theory. Still, she played along with Larry Sheldon.

"Say someone torched the museum just for the sake of torching it," she said. "How would we narrow down the suspects?"

"Have you interviewed the firefighters yet?" Larry asked.

"Not yet. Why?"

"Because those are your suspects. It's no big secret that pyromaniacs tend to gravitate toward careers that have to do with fire. So the first people you have to suspect are the ones who put out the fire in the first place."

If Dutch Jansen had been here, Kat had a feeling Larry wouldn't still be standing. He'd be sprawled on the floor, knocked out cold. Dutch was an old-school chief. He protected his own. And he wouldn't take well to someone like Larry Sheldon casting doubt on his squad, especially when the speculation was so far off base. Maybe what he was saying was true of fire departments in other towns, but not in Perry Hollow. Still, it didn't stop Kat from deciding to have Carl look into the records of all the town's volunteer firefighters. Just in case.

"Other than firefighters, what else should we be looking for?"

"People who were watching the blaze."

"Which was approximately half the town," Kat said.

"Did you notice anyone who seemed particularly fascinated by it?"

"Yes. Half the town."

"Was anyone taking pictures?" Larry was getting exasperated. "And if you say half the town was, then I'm just going to give up and go home."

Although it had only been a couple of hours earlier, it felt like a day had passed since the museum was engulfed. Kat remembered the atmosphere being quietly excited—like a crowd at a bonfire. But no one she saw had been taking photos of the blaze. She hadn't even seen a camera. "Not that I noticed."

"Was there anyone acting suspicious?" Larry said. "Anyone who looked even remotely out of place?"

One person immediately popped into Kat's head—the stranger with the blond ponytail and outdated clothes she had bumped into during the fire.

"Yes. A man," she said. "A stranger. He was the only person at the scene that I didn't recognize."

"Do you remember what he looked like?"

Kat certainly did. Tall. Vaguely foreign. Weird. "Think a sketch artist is in order?"

"It couldn't hurt," Tony said. "It might come in handy later if this guy really did have something to do with the fire."

Kat added talking to a sketch artist to her ever-growing schedule. It wasn't even four in the morning, and already her to-do list for the day was a mile long.

"Once the sketch is done, I'll compare it with photos of convicted arsonists recently released from jail," Larry added. "Maybe this guy was one of them."

Across the gallery, a small commotion rose from the crawl space. Kat heard excited chatter among the crime scene techs. One of them shouted for Tony.

"Lieutenant! You'll want to take a look at this."

Tony and Kat crossed the room as fast as they could. Not an easy task when the floor was unstable and covered with shattered glass. The investigator who had been in the crawl space was now sitting on the edge of it, his dangling legs disappearing into the darkness below.

"You're not going to believe this," he said.

He pointed a flashlight into the hole, brightening the space enough for them to see the trunk Constance had been slumped over. It was now open, revealing a burlap sack that filled most of its interior space. The mouth of the sack had been pulled wide open and lowered slightly to reveal its contents. At first, Kat thought the objects inside were pieces of old ivory. They had the same jaundiced coloring, the same dull sheen.

Then she saw the teeth.

And the eye sockets.

And finally, the smooth curve of what could only be a human skull.

4 A.M.

The sack lay on the floor, smelling of smoke, mildew, and damp earth. Everyone in the gallery stopped what they were doing to gather around it and watch the crime scene techs slowly remove its contents.

The skull came first, leaking chunks of dirt as it was placed on a plastic tarp spread across the floor. A hand was next, the fingers long and tapered. Then a foot, a femur, a rib cage broken into several pieces. Within ten minutes, the sack was empty and the full remains of a human being were scattered across the tarp.

"Why the hell," Kat said, blinking with disbelief, "was the museum keeping a skeleton under its floor?"

Tony Vasquez, standing beside her, shook his head. "Maybe it was part of their collection."

"In that condition?" Kat knelt next to the tarp, which in addition to the bones now held a sizable amount of dirt that had fallen off them. A few rocks and leaves were also among the debris, as was the dried and twisted form of a dead worm. "Certainly someone would have at least cleaned the bones. And I doubt they normally keep pieces of their collection in a burlap sack."

"But what else could it be?"

"I'm more interested in *who* it could be," Kat said. "Not to mention how it got here."

She thought of Oak Knoll Cemetery, the town's only

graveyard. Had a grave there been sitting empty for years, maybe even decades? It was a possibility—worse things had taken place in that cemetery—but she assumed no one from the historical society would resort to robbing graves. Then again, one of them might have resorted to murder. That made digging up a skeleton look like child's play.

"I've got a funny feeling about this," Tony said.

Kat shot him a look. "Like it's not a coincidence? Me, too."

Maybe it was all coincidental. Maybe the fire and Constance's murder and the words on her hand had nothing to do with a bag of bones under the museum floor. But they couldn't simply assume that it didn't. They needed to explore every possibility, especially since this—whatever the hell *this* was—was just the first.

"We need to find out where those bones came from," Kat said. "Which means we need to find out who they once belonged to. And in order to do that, we need to find out when and how he died."

"I know someone who can do that," Tony said.

"So do I. And I suspect we're both talking about the same person."

Kat stepped out the back door of the museum and into the autumn night. The air was chilly, with a slightly bitter sting that told her winter would soon be on its way. At least the cold woke her up a bit. She had no idea when she'd be able to sleep again—an incredibly depressing thought.

Cell phone in hand, she trudged to the rear of the property. A white picket fence about waist high separated it from the yard next door, its gate ajar and swinging lightly. Sensing her presence, a black cat stalking through the grass jumped onto the fence and perched there, staring at her with glinting green eyes. Seeing nothing of interest, it decamped to the neighbor's yard, leaving Kat alone again to dial her phone.

She shouldn't have felt bad about calling Nick Donnelly so early in the morning. He would have done the same if the circumstances had been reversed. Still, the panic that tinged his voice when he answered the phone made Kat feel slightly guilty.

"What's wrong?" Nick asked in that wide-awake way people speak when they are suddenly and soundly roused from sleep. "Is it James?"

"Relax," Kat said. "Nothing's wrong."

"But there's something going on in town, isn't there?"

Nick had helped Kat catch the Grim Reaper killer. In turn, she had helped him crack the Olmstead case when it brought him back to Perry Hollow. Kat was now hoping it was again her turn to get assistance.

"Yes," she said. "There's been a murder. And an arson. And a lot of stuff I can't even begin to comprehend right now."

"Looks like I've been away too long."

"You have."

Although he lived only forty-five minutes away in Philadelphia, almost two months had passed since she last saw Nick. And Kat missed him. Her son did, too. When you worked that closely with someone, their absence was more palpable when they were gone.

"So why are you calling—" Nick paused as he no doubt checked the clock on his nightstand. "Holy shit, Kat, it's four-thirty in the morning."

"I know," Kat said, her guilt now kicking in at full force. "I'm sorry."

"Couldn't it have waited until morning? Real morning. Not whatever the hell schedule you're on right now."

It couldn't, and Kat said as much. She quickly briefed Nick about the fire, the message on Constance's hand, the bones stashed under the floorboards.

"Damn," Nick said. "Have you called the state police?"

"Tony's here right now."

"Of course," Nick said. "So why are you calling me again?"

"Do you remember that forensic anthropologist who helped out with the Olmstead case?"

Nick cleared his throat. "Yes. Lucy Meade."

"Do you have her phone number?"

Kat assumed he did. She was pretty sure—but not certain—that the two of them had gone out on a date when the case was over. Maybe more. Nick had been oddly reticent on the subject.

"I do," Nick said, hesitating. "But—"

Kat thought she heard another voice, murmuring something she couldn't make out. A woman's voice. Nick whispered something back.

"Oh, my God. Is she *there*?"

"Yeah." Nick sighed, knowing he had a lot of explaining to do. "I'm just going to hand her the phone now."

Kat listened to the sounds of rustling sheets and a creaking bed. There was even a high-pitched giggle when Nick apparently dropped the phone. Finally, she heard the voice of Lucy Meade, forensic anthropologist and Nick's secret girlfriend.

"Hi, Kat," Lucy said. "I hear you have a skeleton on your hands."

"I do. I have no idea how old it is. Or where it came from. Or why it was in our town's history museum."

"And this has something to do with a murder?"

"Maybe. I don't really know."

But she sensed that the two were related. She had a creeping sensation—like an insect crawling up her neck—that Constance died because of those bones. It was why indentifying who they had belonged to was so important.

"Tell you what," Lucy said. "I'll be there as soon as I can. Let's meet up around six."

"That would be great. Thank you." Kat allowed herself a brief sigh of relief. This was one less thing she'd need to worry about. "I'll have the bones transferred to the morgue and meet you and Nick there."

Lucy chuckled. "Who said anything about Nick? I'm leaving him at home."

Kat ended the call, letting out a lengthy yawn as she shoved the phone back into her pocket. There was a lot to be done in the coming hours. Question the other members of the historical society. Look into the pasts of Perry Hollow's volunteer firefighters. Search Constance's office. Lieutenant Tony Vasquez would be handling most of it, but Kat wanted to help out as much as she could. Still, she wouldn't be of much use exhausted. And until she had to meet Lucy, she decided the best course of action would be to go home and get some sleep. It would only be for an hour, but that was better than nothing.

Rounding the building to the front lawn, she saw that things had finally quieted down on the street. The fire trucks were long gone. So was the crowd, which had been shooed away by Carl soon after Constance's body was found.

Now, only one person remained, an absurdly tall man watching Kat from the sidewalk. She recognized him instantly, just as she had during the fire. Only now she realized he hadn't been a figment of her imagination or a remnant from a slowly fading dream. Henry Goll really was back in town.

"So it is you."

"In the flesh," Henry said.

Kat quickened her pace across the lawn, urged on by his sudden appearance. Getting to know Henry had been the only good thing to come out of the Grim Reaper killings. At first, she hadn't known what to think of the tall, handsome man with the noticeable scars. He had been aloof. Quiet. Suspicious. Yet he eventually softened, opened up, began to trust her. By the time they had saved each other's lives, they were friends.

When he vanished soon after, Kat understood his reasons. But it didn't make her miss him any less.

"How did you know I was here?" she asked.

"I saw you during the fire," he admitted. "You were a bit preoccupied at the time, so I didn't say hello."

"Understood."

"But when I stepped outside and noticed that there was still police activity going on at the museum, I thought you'd be here."

"You thought correctly."

Kat had finally reached the sidewalk. She started to shake Henry's hand, changed her mind, and went in for a hug. She felt a little foolish as she wrapped her arms around his waist. Still, the hug was as long as it was tight.

"You shouldn't have left like that," she said. "You didn't even say good-bye."

Henry, stiffened to the point of paralysis by her embrace, cleared his throat. "I sent you a postcard."

"That's not a good-bye. That's an 'Oh, by the way, I skipped town.' I never thought I'd see you again."

"I'm sorry," Henry said. "It was wrong of me to vanish like that. And it's good to see you, too."

Kat took it to mean she should stop hugging him. But when she finally pulled away, she noticed that Henry Goll, the most stoic man she had ever known, was now smiling.

5 A.M.

He wasn't remotely tired, although he should have been exhausted. Sleeping on a plane isn't the same as sleeping in a bed, and his rest during the flight had been fitful at best. But it was 11 A.M. in Rome, and Henry was as wide awake in Perry Hollow as he would have been there. Jet lag was a bitch.

Kat Campbell, however, looked ready to sleep for days. When they climbed into their booth at the Perry Hollow Diner, the first thing she ordered was a pot of coffee. She then looked across the table at Henry and asked, in all seriousness, "What will you be drinking?"

Henry also ordered coffee, although a single cup and not the whole pot.

They were the sole customers at the diner, the only place in town that was open all night, so their java came quickly. Kat gulped hers down like a man stumbling parched from a desert. Henry sipped his, finding it disappointingly weak. Ten months in Italy had turned him into a coffee snob. If it wasn't espresso of the highest quality, his taste buds wanted nothing to do with it.

"How have you been?" Kat asked rapidly, fueled by the caffeine. "*Where* have you been? Tell me everything."

"But I want to know how you're doing," Henry said. "And James. And Nick."

"You first," Kat demanded.

He quickly brought her up to speed on all that had happened since they last saw each other. First was the recovery period, slow and painful. Then his decision to escape his past (again) and start a new life (again) in a place far away—this time Italy. Since he was already fluent in Italian, it didn't take him long to get a job at the country's largest daily newspaper. It was based in Rome, but he wrote almost exclusively about American issues.

"I'm like a foreign correspondent," he told Kat, "except I never leave."

He talked at length about life in Italy. The charming apartment where he could glimpse the top of the Colosseum from his bathroom window. The great food that forced him to double the length of his daily workouts. The amazing opera productions, including a performance of *La Traviata* at La Scala in Milan, which was the best thing he had ever seen and heard. The excellent wines, which got him through the frequent nights when what happened in Perry Hollow haunted his dreams.

As he spoke, he felt the heat of Kat's gaze on his face. She hadn't seen him since that horrible night in the Perry Mill. Henry had made sure of that. Now she was making up for lost time, studying him in an attempt to survey the damage. The attention to his scars would have annoyed him if it was coming from someone else. He let Kat look because he knew she cared.

"You can talk about it," Henry told her. "I don't pretend they're not there."

"It's actually not as bad as I thought it would be," Kat said. "You suffered a lot. And I assumed the damage would be worse."

"The doctors did what they could." Henry took a sip of his coffee. It was piping hot and came close to scalding his tongue. His lips, however, felt none of it. The scar tissue there desensitized everything. "The rest I have to live with."

Kat stared into her coffee cup, suddenly unable to look him in the eyes. "Henry, I'm sorry I didn't find you sooner. I'm sorry you had to go through all that."

Henry reached across the table and took her hands. They were soft and surprisingly delicate. He had expected someone as tough as Kat to have equally hardened hands.

"I refuse to listen to an apology from you," he said. "You helped save my life, and I will always be grateful for that. Besides, I had scars before all that happened." He pointed to the mark at his temple before moving down to the long line that sliced through his lips. "Or don't you remember these?"

"I just wish that I could have done something to spare you from getting more of them."

"I prefer scars to death," Henry said. "Besides, you have no idea how intriguing it makes me to the Italians."

That was probably the thing that surprised him most about living in Rome. Many women, and a good number of men, came on to him in bars, at work functions, on the street.

It helped that he kept himself in peak physical condition. But he had a feeling that the scars, which made him feel like a freak and an outsider in the United States, gave him an air of mystery to the Italians. In a country full of beautiful people, he stood out by being the opposite. During his first week in Rome, a woman had approached him in the Piazza di Spagna, asking if she could paint his portrait. Henry declined the offer.

"It sounds like you've created a good life there," Kat said. "But are you happy?"

She knew about Henry's past. The wife who died when she was nine months pregnant. The car accident that had given him his first round of scars. The torture he had been subjected to at the hands of the Grim Reaper. More than anyone else, Kat Campbell understood his pain.

"Yes, I'm happy," Henry answered.

He was lying but not by much. He wasn't *unhappy*. He was content to live in quiet solitude—that hadn't changed since his Perry Hollow days—and deep down he understood that's how it was meant to be. Both times he had grown to love someone, they had been taken away from him in very different ways. He now knew it was foolish to fall in love a third time, so he didn't even try.

But the funny thing about living in Rome was that he was never truly alone. The ancient city was always bustling, filled with tourists and locals alike, all pressing up against each other in the squares, on the buses, in the restaurants still thick with cigarette smoke. Henry enjoyed that feeling of being by himself yet simultaneously being a part of something bigger.

"Now another question," Kat said. "The big one. Why on earth are you back in Perry Hollow?"

"I'm on assignment."

"But you said you never leave."

"I don't," Henry said. "But something came up. A story. So my editor sent me here."

"What kind of story?"

"You ever hear of a man named Giuseppe Fanelli?"

Kat shook her head.

"He's an Italian businessman. Very rich. Worth billions. And very famous. He lives for publicity, good or bad. He's like the Donald Trump of Italy. With better hair, of course. A few days ago, we got word that he was tied up in something in the United States."

Kat gasped. "The mafia?"

"No," Henry said dryly. "But great job stereotyping an entire nation."

"If I ever get to Italy, I'll be sure to apologize."

"Fanelli's reputation is clean. He's a real estate developer. Over the summer, he formed a U.S. subsidiary of his European company. Fanelli Entertainment USA. It was registered in Philadelphia and created, we presume, for the express purpose of buying land and developing projects in America."

Kat straightened in her seat, suddenly—and seriously—interested. "What kind of projects are we talking about?"

"Megamalls. Skyscrapers. Soccer stadiums. Fanelli never buys any land unless he intends to build something huge there."

"So I'm assuming he bought some land close to here."

"He did," Henry said. "Closer than you think. As of two weeks ago, Giuseppe Fanelli is now the owner of one hundred acres of land in Perry Hollow, Pennsylvania."

Kat, who had been taking a sip of coffee as he spoke, swallowed hard at the news. "Where?"

"A site you and I know all too well."

He didn't need to give her another hint. Kat knew the town better than anyone. "The Perry Mill," she said.

Henry nodded solemnly. "It's the first piece of land he's purchased in the United States."

"What does he plan on building there?"

"We don't know," Henry said. "But I was sent here to find out."

Kat stayed quiet, staring once again into her now-empty coffee cup. It was a lot of information for her to take in. But Henry knew her sudden quiet had more to do with concern than comprehension. She was worried about what Giuseppe Fanelli intended to do in her town.

"It might be nothing," he said.

"But it's something," Kat replied. "You said yourself he only builds things that are huge. Now that he owns that land, God knows what he plans to put there."

"Just because he owns the land doesn't mean he can build whatever he wants."

Henry had worked for the town's newspaper once. Although his job had been writing obituaries, he was well versed in the workings of planning boards, zoning approvals, and building permits. Town officials had the ability to shoot down anything Fanelli proposed, a right Henry hoped they executed. Even if it was good for business, he wasn't sure Perry Hollow could handle the type of gargantuan projects Fanelli specialized in.

"How is Perry Hollow?" he asked. "Has it recovered since last year?"

Kat reached for the pot of coffee and poured herself another cup. "It's starting to. Business is picking up. Most residents are doing fine."

"And you and James?"

"We're getting there," Kat said with a sigh. "It's been a tough road."

Her son, one of the most charming boys Henry had ever met, had come face-to-face with the Grim Reaper, seeing things no child his age ever should. According to Kat, he was now seeing a therapist.

"I should probably see one myself," she said, "but I'm stubborn that way. It didn't help that there was more excitement a few months ago."

"Eric Olmstead and his brother," Henry said.

Kat seemed surprised, although not unpleasantly so. If anything, Henry sensed she was impressed that her tiny town had once again made international news. Although not as big as the Grim Reaper murders, the story of Eric Olmstead's quest to find the brother who had vanished decades before was enough to get the attention of his newspaper, if only for a day or so. Eric's mystery novels, after all, were just as popular in Italy as they were in the United States. And the case was so sensational that no editor could resist.

"I barely survived that one, too," Kat said.

"Maybe you have nine lives, like your name implies."

"I hope so. Because I have a feeling today is going to kill me."

They had yet to talk about the reason Kat was in the town's history museum at such an odd hour. Henry knew it wasn't just a fire keeping her up. Something else was going on. Something bad.

"Who was killed?"

Kat didn't even bother asking him how he knew. He was a reporter. Part of his job was to be observant. Certainly, she was aware that a mobile CSI lab parked in front of the museum would tip off even the worst journalist.

"Constance Bishop," Kat said. "President of the historical society. You ever come into contact with her during your time here?"

Henry hadn't. He hadn't been the most outgoing person when he lived in Perry Hollow. He hadn't come out of his shell until a serial killer started playing mind games with him.

"I know you'll catch whoever did it," he said.

"Once again, we have help. Don't be surprised if you see state troopers filling the streets while working on your article."

"Is Nick Donnelly one of them?"

Kat gave a terse shake of her head. It's what Henry had feared—Nick was no longer a cop. He had thought the state police would give him the benefit of the doubt. But some violations were too big to look past. Nick's, apparently, had been one of them.

"I hate to do this," Kat said, checking her watch and taking one last gulp of coffee, "but I need to run. I have to head out to the morgue."

"That," Henry said, "doesn't sound like fun."

"It won't be."

This time it was Kat who grasped his hands, squeezing them tight as she made him promise not to leave Perry Hollow again without saying good-bye. Henry swore he wouldn't. He would be working all day and was scheduled to leave the next morning. His last stop, he told her, would be to give her and James a proper farewell. The one he should have given them a year ago.

"I'm going to hold you to that," Kat said, placing some cash on the table and sliding out of the booth.

Before she left, Henry impulsively grabbed the sleeve of her uniform. The move startled not only Kat but himself as well. Usually, he was more composed than that. But there was one more bit of information he needed to know. Something that had been on his mind for a full year.

"Do you ever see Deana?" He had wanted to seem casual, to make it sound like an offhanded question, as if he had just thought of it. Instead, it came out strained and worried. "I'm curious about how she's doing."

"I haven't really seen her," Kat said. "She keeps a pretty low profile now. I know she's still in town. She got a job at the library after the funeral home closed. Other than that, I have no idea how she's doing. I'm sorry I can't tell you more."

Henry nodded his thanks before letting go of her sleeve. He remained in the booth as Kat wound her way around the old men and hungry night-shift workers trickling into the diner. Through the window overlooking the parking lot, he watched her get into her patrol car.

He didn't leave the diner until he was certain Kat had driven away. Henry didn't want her to see the slump-shouldered way he stepped into the gray gloom of dawn. He didn't want her to notice his sad expression as he faced east. And most of all, he didn't want Chief Campbell to see the direction he was headed in and realize his next destination.

6 A.M.

Kat drove to the county morgue accompanied only by the Crown Vic's radio and a sack of bones in the backseat. All the state troopers, Lieutenant Tony Vasquez included, stayed behind at the museum to work the homicide investigation. That meant Kat was alone on bone duty, an assignment that, while interesting, wasn't quite as vital as trying to identify a killer. She thought of it as desk duty—mere busywork to keep her from bothering the big boys.

She didn't mind. Much. Naturally, she wanted to be where the action was, but at least this way she could size up Nick's girlfriend without anyone else present.

On the way to the morgue, Kat swore she wouldn't make any snap judgments about Lucy Meade, pro or con. Nick was a grown man who could make his own decisions about who he wanted to date. Or sleep with. Or whatever he and Lucy were doing. Kat's main priority was to learn as much as possible about the skeleton found in the museum.

Still, she couldn't help keeping a mental checklist, especially when Lucy arrived right on time, pulling up to the morgue in a red Volkswagen Beetle. It was a vintage one, still in prime condition. That was definitely a mark in the plus column, with an extra point for punctuality.

When Lucy got out of the car, Kat was surprised by what she saw. Lucy looked to be a good ten years younger than Nick, with bright blue eyes and shoulder-length auburn hair that she tucked behind her ears before shaking Kat's hand. Petty jealousy usually dictated that youth and beauty went into Kat's minus column, but she stayed neutral this time. It was easy to see why Nick was attracted to her. Lucy was stunning.

"So you're the famous Kat Campbell," she said with a grin. "I'm so happy I finally get to meet you. Nick talks about you nonstop."

"All good things, I hope."

"All *great* things."

Flattery. Straight to the plus column every time.

"He even told me how you like your coffee." Lucy reached across the front seat of her Beetle, emerging with a giant thermos. "Black and strong, right?"

This was a tough one. Under any other circumstance, bringing coffee earned a place in the plus column. But Kat had practically a whole pot of java sloshing around in her stomach, and while the caffeine kept her mind alert, it wasn't sitting well with the rest of her body. Still, it was the thought that counted. Another plus.

Lucy must have seen the uncertain look on her face because she said, "You just had some, didn't you? Considering the hour, I should have known."

"No, it's fine," Kat said. "I just should have had some food with it, I think."

Lucy reached deep into the car again, this time returning with a flat box tied shut with some string. "Then it's a good thing I also brought doughnuts."

That was the moment Kat gave up trying to keep score. Lucy had passed with flying colors.

"So, these bones were found in the history museum?" she asked Kat once they entered the morgue.

"In a crawl space under the floorboards. They were in a trunk that a murder victim was found on top of."

"Any indication that the victim knew they were there?"

"Not that I know of," Kat said. "Our theory is that the body was put there by whoever killed her."

"So these bones might not have anything to do with the murder."

"Or they might be the key to solving it."

Kat took the bag of bones to the morgue's second autopsy suite, the first one being presently occupied by Wallace Noble and the body of Constance Bishop. Inside, she dumped the bones onto a stainless steel table in the center of the room.

Lucy grabbed a white lab coat and some latex gloves, putting them on before approaching the table. "Is this everything that was found in the trunk?"

"The whole shebang," Kat said.

"Well, right off the bat, I can tell that these are some old bones." Lucy started sliding them around the table, putting them in order from top to bottom. "I already see some bone rot."

"Do you think you'll be able to tell how old they are?"

"Possibly. Nothing exact, mind you. Maybe a ballpark figure."

"That's better than nothing."

Kat retreated to a corner of the autopsy suite and grabbed a doughnut, munching on it while she watched Lucy work. For her part, Lucy was all business as she studied the bones. She arranged them slowly and methodically, occasionally pausing to give one a closer inspection.

"These are pretty well preserved," she said, picking up a hand with fingers permanently splayed. She examined the back of the hand, then the palm, then the back again, swiveling it in a kind of morbid wave. "And while I can already tell this isn't a complete skeleton, there's a lot less scatter than I thought there'd be."

"Scatter?"

"A body left out in the open never stays in one piece for very long. Animals usually come along quickly, taking bones with them. A corpse left in a forest could be scattered for miles within two weeks."

Although she'd taken only two bites of her doughnut, Kat returned it to the box and closed the lid. Hearing about scattered bodies made her no longer hungry. "Since that didn't happen in this case, then it means the body was buried."

Lucy looked up from the table, a flash of approval in her blue eyes. "Nick told me you were a quick study."

"Thanks, but I had help," Kat said. "We found dirt with the bones."

"How did it smell?"

"Pardon?"

"The dirt. Did it smell fresh?"

"A little bit. Not as overpowering as a freshly plowed field, but close enough."

Holding the skull to her nose, Lucy sniffed deeply. "I see what you mean. That smell doesn't come from the dirt itself. It comes from microbes that are in the dirt, which die off and fade away."

"So this was all dug up very recently," Kat said.

"Within a day or two."

Kat couldn't help but be impressed. It was clear that Lucy Meade was whip smart. Another mark in the already cluttered plus column.

"You've told me more in five minutes than I could have found out in five hours," she said.

"Glad I could help," Lucy replied. "Now, if we're lucky, I'll also be able to find out how old the person was when she died and what killed her."

"*She?*" Kat emerged from the corner and edged close to the table. "How can you tell?"

Lucy pointed to a section of bones in the center of the table. They formed the shape of a wide heart, with a large hole in the center.

"The pelvis," she said. "It's bigger in women than in men, thanks to our childbearing capabilities. And if I was a betting woman, I'd go all-in on the fact that our Jane Doe here had at least one child of her own."

By that point, Lucy had finished arranging the bones on the table so that they were in the same order as the human body—skull on top, broken-off toes at the bottom. She pulled an iPhone from the front pocket of her jeans and started circling the table, taking pictures of the bones.

"If you don't mind, I'm going to send these to a colleague of mine in Harrisburg. He knows more about identifying the age of bones than I do."

"Would it be better if he saw one of them himself?" Kat asked.

"That would help." Lucy shoved the phone back into a front pocket of her jeans. "You want me to head over there?"

"Seriously?"

"Sure," Lucy said. "It's not that far of a drive. And with the equipment he has, we might be able to tell you with some accuracy how old these bones really are."

Kat didn't know whether to hug Lucy, jump for joy, or

both. Instead, she added a gigantic checkmark in her mental plus column.

"Take whatever bone you want," she said. "Any information you can get will be more than we know now."

Lucy's hands hovered over the table as she decided which bone to choose. Furrowing her brow and biting her lower lip, she resembled a kid in a candy store who was told she could buy only one item. Much like what a kid would do, she settled on the biggest one—the femur.

"Now this is interesting," she said, turning the bone over in her hands. "All of these were found in a trunk, right?"

"Technically, they were in a burlap sack inside the trunk."

"And there was no fire damage to either of them?"

"None," Kat said. "Why?"

Lucy lowered the femur so Kat could get a good look at it, pointing out charcoal-colored splotches on various parts of the bone.

"See those black areas? Those are burn marks."

"But that's impossible. The fire was clear on the other side of the room."

"I believe you," Lucy said. "Which means this wasn't the first time these bones have been in a fire. In fact, it's looking more likely that a fire is how this woman died."

Contrary to what Kat was expecting, every bit of information Lucy revealed only created new questions instead of answering old ones. The bones of someone's mother—an apparent fire victim dead for an unknown amount of time—had just been unearthed. They didn't know where the bones came from, nor did they know who they had once belonged to. And not even Lucy Meade would be able to tell Kat why on earth they had been hidden inside the museum.

* * *

Once Lucy and the femur had departed for Harrisburg, Kat went looking for Wallace Noble. Now that she knew a little about one person found in the museum, she wanted to get the scoop on the other, more recent set of remains. She found Wallace outside, smoking a cigarette in the morgue's parking lot.

"Postautopsy smoke?"

"It clears my head," Wallace said. "I try to think about anything other than what I was just looking at. Today, it's a young Sophia Loren."

"Nice. Unfortunately, I need to break your reverie."

Wallace dropped his cigarette and ground it out with his shoe. "Killjoy."

Instead of going back inside, he ambled to a nearby bench. One of those curved metal contraptions so popular in the eighties, it was both uncomfortable and unsightly—a fitting combination for a sitting area located next to the front door of a morgue. It was also freezing cold. Kat felt the chill through her uniform as soon as she sat down.

"The blow was on the right side of Constance's head," Wallace said. "From the location and the angle of the wound, I can tell she was hit by a right-handed male. A woman of average strength wouldn't be able to strike that hard. No offense."

Even though he was most likely right, Kat appreciated the coda. "None taken."

"Has a potential weapon been found?" Wallace asked.

"Not yet. You said yourself it could have been any number of items in the museum."

"Well, I can help you narrow it down. She was hit with the edge of something flat and heavy. It left a line of damage to the skull instead of a circle. So if you were thinking someone bashed her head in with a cannonball, you need to guess again."

A cannonball was exactly what Kat had been thinking. There were several in the museum—small ones the size of a grapefruit that someone strong enough could easily lift with one hand.

"There was no trace evidence found in the wound," Wallace continued. "No paint chips or fiber. Whatever she was hit with, it was undecorated metal. Judging from the impact, it was something heavier than your average stainless steel. I'm thinking lead. Or cast iron."

"Can you pinpoint the time of death?" Kat asked.

"When did the fire start?"

"Neighbors across the street reported it at 12:52."

"Then she died sometime between then and the time it was put out."

Kat's eyes widened. "Are you sure? The cause of death is blunt force trauma, right?"

"Actually, it isn't," Wallace said. "Turns out Constance died of smoke inhalation."

The only way Kat could have been more surprised would have been if Wallace had said drowning. She had seen the wound on Constance's head, complete with flecks of brain or bone or *something* that had come out of it. Constance Bishop must have been one tough woman to survive a blow like that. Adding to the shock was the fact that she might have still been alive as the firefighters were trying to put out the blaze.

"They could have saved her," she murmured. "If her body hadn't been dumped in that crawl space, then Dutch Jansen's boys would have seen her when they entered the museum."

"Technically, it wasn't murder," Wallace said.

"Close enough. Whoever set that fire killed her, so it's murder in my book. Especially after she was tossed into that hole in the floor."

"That's another thing. It's looking less likely that she was dumped there. I found fresh scrapes on both of her knees. There were similar ones on the inside of her forearms, not to mention a splinter near her elbow."

Another shock that Kat didn't see coming. "You're saying she crawled there by herself?"

Wallace nodded gravely. "If she had been dragged, the scrapes would have been slightly above her knees. The ones I found were below the knees, suggesting that her legs had been bent."

Kat processed the information, unsure what to make of it. If Constance had crawled across the floor at some point during the night, it could have been before the blow to the head—while trying to fight off her attacker, for instance. But the scrapes on her forearms made that seem less likely. A woman scurrying away from an attack would be on her hands and knees. The wounds on her arms suggested she pulled herself across the floor.

Kat tried to form a timeline of events, based on what little she knew. According to Emma Pulsifer, Constance was in the museum a little before eight. She might have left at some point during the night, but was back there after midnight. Maybe she had arranged to meet the person who struck her over the head. Or maybe the person's presence came as a complete surprise. Either way, Constance was left for dead on the floor as her attacker started the fire on the other side of the gallery.

Once the fire was burning and the assailant was gone, Constance headed to the crawl space. When Kat had entered the museum, the trapdoor in the floor had been closed. If Constance did climb into the crawl space herself, then she also closed the door after her. A tough task for an elderly woman with a devastating head wound. But it was possible. Anything was possible when you were fighting for your life. Still, that theory created one big question.

"Why would she go down there?"

"Maybe she thought it could be a refuge from the fire," Wallace said.

Again, it was possible but unlikely. "Why not just keep going down the hall? There's a back door there. That would have taken just as long as entering a hole in the floor."

"She probably wasn't thinking straight," Wallace said. "Remember, she was struck in the head very hard. It likely would have killed her if the smoke hadn't gotten to her first."

Kat thought back to the way she had found Constance slumped over the trunk with the bones in it. She had managed to get most of her body over it, almost as if she was trying to protect it.

"Maybe she knew exactly what she was doing," Kat said, thinking aloud. "She was hurt real bad. Probably in a lot of pain, not to mention surrounded by fire. Maybe she knew she was going to die and went into that crawl space for a reason."

"Which would be?"

"Trying to save the trunk that was down there. Or if she died, then making sure whoever found her body knew it existed."

"But why would she spend the final moments of her life doing that?" Wallace asked.

"Because Constance knew what was inside it," Kat said. "Other than the scrapes and the splinter, did you find anything else on her hands or arms? Any residue or dirt?"

Wallace dipped his fingers into the pocket of his pants and pulled out a cigarette. "I think I'm going to need a smoke for this."

"Why?"

"Because," he said, lighting up, "I found dirt under Constance's fingernails. Not the everyday grime we all have, but actual dirt. I'm talking fresh soil. She had definitely been doing some digging recently."

Kat turned to Wallace, stunned. "Constance is the one who dug up those bones?"

"It certainly seems like it."

"But I don't understand. This is getting weirder by the minute."

"And I haven't even gotten to the writing on her hand."

"It was a message from her killer," Kat said. "It has to be."

Wallace exhaled a long stream of smoke. "I have a theory about that. Let's say you were a right-handed killer and your victim was on the floor, lying on her back. Now, say you wrote a message on the victim's left hand. If you were standing at the victim's head—"

"The words would be upside-down," Kat said.

"Exactly. And that wasn't the case here. Which means that you, the killer, were standing in the other direction, by the victim's legs. Depending on your position, the words would likely appear either horizontally across the palm, beneath the fingers, or perpendicular to that, running beneath the thumb."

But that wasn't where the words on Constance's hand had been located. The message was written somewhere in between those two positions, appearing diagonally across her palm.

"What are you getting at?" Kat said.

"Here." Wallace pulled a pen from the pocket of his lab coat. "Write something on your left hand."

Grabbing the pen, Kat held up her left hand. She couldn't bring herself to write the same words that were on Constance's hand, so she simply scrawled a short and sweet MY NAME IS KAT.

"Now, look at the position on your palm," Wallace said.

Kat lifted her hand in front of her face. The words were in the exact same position they had been on Constance Bishop's palm.

"Are you sure?" Kat asked, not quite believing what she was seeing or hearing.

"Positive," Wallace replied. "The killer didn't write on Constance's hand. She—"

Kat broke in, finishing the sentence for him—"wrote that message herself."

---

7 A.M.

Kat sat in her Crown Vic, listening to the idle of the engine while trying to make sense of the situation. It was so strange that it bordered on the surreal. Yet the proof was there, and it pointed to one thing: the ominous message on Constance's hand hadn't been from the killer.

While Kat was relieved not to be facing another Grim

Reaper scenario, it still left too many questions for comfort. Why had Constance written on her hand? And what was she referring to? Was she predicting more murders? More fires? More bones? Running through all the possibilities gave Kat a headache.

When she called Lieutenant Tony Vasquez with the news, he seemed equally flummoxed but none too surprised.

"One of the CSI techs found a black Sharpie in the crawl space," he explained. "It was on the floor, right next to the trunk."

"Even more proof that the message was the work of Constance herself," Kat said. "You guys find anything else?"

"Nope," Tony replied, disappointment evident in his voice. "What about you?"

Kat briefed him on the state of the bones. Old. Female. Burned. Then she dropped the other bombshell that Wallace Noble had provided—not only had Constance known about the bones in the trunk, but she had been the one to dig them up.

"Why would she do something like that?" Tony asked.

"Beats me," Kat said, "but I imagine it had something to do with the historical society meeting she had planned for tonight."

And that was only a guess. Kat had no clue why the bones would be important; nor did she have an inkling about where the digging took place. The first location that sprang to mind was Oak Knoll Cemetery. She assumed someone would have reported a gaping hole in the ground, but just to be on the safe side, she radioed Carl Bauersox as soon as she was done talking to Tony.

"I need you to check out Oak Knoll Cemetery," she told him.

"What am I looking for?" the deputy said.

"Disturbed graves. Signs of recent digging. Anything suspicious. I'll meet you back at the station in twenty minutes."

Once Carl signed off, Kat started the car and flicked on the stereo. The coffee from the diner had worn off, and a post-caffeine crash was coming on. She needed a great song to get her energy up. What she got was "Disco Inferno" by the Trammps. Not great, even for disco, but appropriate. So Kat cranked up the volume and sang along. By the time the song ended, she was in her driveway.

She checked her watch as she got out of the car and crossed the front yard. She couldn't stay long. Fifteen minutes tops. She just wanted to check on James and arrange for a different babysitter, if necessary. Finding child care on short notice was one of the toughest aspects of being a single mom.

Inside, she found her son awake and sitting on the living room couch. Scooby, his beagle, was curled up next to him. The TV was on, broadcasting one of those obnoxiously bright cartoons that were a staple of Saturday mornings. The animated creatures arguing with each other were easier to take with eight hours of sleep under her belt. Without it, they just seemed shrill and spastic.

"Hey, Little Bear," Kat said, tousling James's hair. "You're up early."

"I couldn't sleep." He yawned for added emphasis. "Not without you in the house."

Kat felt a familiar twinge of guilt in the pit of her stomach. It happened whenever she realized her job was affecting her son's home life. Making it worse was James's condition. Although he was more functional and self-reliant than many other children with Down syndrome, he still needed extra attention. When Kat couldn't provide it, he often got sullen as a result.

During the Olmstead case, for instance, James's behavior had reached new and frustrating levels. When he was born, a pediatrician who specialized in children with Down syndrome said they tended to wear their hearts on their sleeves. James had decided to wear his on his fists. The result was a suspension from school, a very long grounding, and a nagging worry that more behavioral problems waited just down the road.

"I'm sorry," she said. "But I had to go to work. Something bad happened."

She skipped over what exactly that bad thing was. She tried to shield James as best she could from the perils of her job. Still, she suspected he knew more than he let on. A mother could only have so many brushes with death before kids at school started to talk.

"I know," James said. "Lou told me."

Hearing her name, Louella van Sickle swept into the living room carrying breakfast on a tray. Professionally, she was the police station's dispatcher. Personally, she was James's surrogate grandmother, always willing to watch him when Kat was tied up with work. Lou was the person Kat had called at one in the morning when the museum fire broke out.

"Your couch is lumpy," she announced. "I didn't get a wink of sleep."

"That's funny," Kat replied. "Neither did I."

Lou set the tray on the coffee table. The meal she had prepared—scrambled eggs, bacon, and toast—gave Kat another guilt twinge. Most mornings, she just let James pour his own cold cereal.

"So how bad was the fire?"

Kat looked at James, who ate with his eyes glued to the TV, blindly guiding a forkful of eggs into his mouth. She gestured for Lou to join her in the kitchen.

"Listen," she said once James was out of earshot. "It's more than a fire. Constance Bishop was murdered in the museum last night."

Lou excelled at three things—gossip, offering unwarranted advice about Kat's personal life, and being totally unflappable. Yet the news of Constance's death turned her face a chalky white.

"Jesus," she said. "I thought this town was done with all that."

"Me, too."

"How are you holding up? Are you okay?"

"I'm fine," Kat said. "Just tired. And busy."

She briefly told Lou about the rest of her night. Fire. Corpse. Skeleton. She left out the fact that Henry Goll was back in town. That was information too juicy for Lou not to share.

"I need to head back to the museum soon," Kat finally said. "There's still a lot of stuff to do there. So I was wondering—"

"If I could watch James the rest of the day?"

Kat nodded slowly. She had asked this favor of Lou on dozens of occasions. She knew that one of these days, Louella van Sickle was going to tell her no. She hoped today wasn't that day.

"Of course I will," Lou replied. "Although Al will be disappointed. He wanted to drive up to the Sands in Bethlehem today. Said he was in the mood for some blackjack."

Lou's husband had been bitten by the blackjack bug as

soon as state law was changed to allow legalized gambling. He had plenty of places to choose from. Each year, it seemed, a new casino was popping up somewhere in Pennsylvania. From the way Lou talked, all Al van Sickle wanted to do on the weekends was head to the tables.

"I owe you one," Kat said, knowing full well she still owed Lou for previous babysitting favors. "I don't know how long I'll be. Hopefully just until the afternoon."

"I hope so, too, for your sake. You look like the walking dead."

"I probably smell like it, too." Kat sniffed her uniform, which was the same one she had worn the day before. It reeked of smoke. And sweat. And desperation, which, while technically odorless, was something Kat had smelled on suspects and first dates alike. "I'm going to take a quick shower. Go check on James."

"Aye, aye, captain. Any other orders?"

"He has a science project due on Monday," Kat said, hedging and hopeful. "You could help him with that?"

Lou shooed her out of the kitchen with a flap of her hands. "Now you're just pushing it."

Kat hurried upstairs. The shower—cold and quick—perked her up a bit. So did a clean uniform that didn't reek. Then it was back downstairs, where James and Lou had pushed aside their empty breakfast plates for a glass jar and a book of matches. The sight caused her to halt at the bottom of the stairs.

"What are you two doing?"

James didn't take his eyes off the jar. "My science project."

"We're learning about oxygen," Lou said, picking up the book of matches.

She lit one before tilting the jar, laying the match at the bottom.

"Now what do you think will happen once you put the lid on the jar?" she asked James.

"I don't know." James stared at the flame, a triangle of orange and yellow that danced just beyond the glass. "The jar will fill with smoke?"

"Put the lid on and find out."

James began to twist the lid onto the top of the jar. He didn't even make it a full rotation before the lit match blinked out.

"What happened?"

"You cut off the flow of oxygen," Lou said. "Fire needs air to burn. When it doesn't get it, it goes out."

Because he was eleven—and because he was a boy—James found this trick fascinating. Kat could see the astonished gleam in his eyes from across the room as he asked, "Can I try it again?"

"Not so fast." Kat at last moved from the stairs to the coffee table, where she pocketed the matchbook. "I think you should come up with a different science project."

"But, Mom—"

Kat cut him off with one of those sharp glances only attained through years of motherhood. "Educational or not, I don't like the idea of you playing with matches. Especially today. Now give me a good-bye hug. I need to go back to work."

After James gave her a halfhearted embrace and Lou assured her everything would be fine, Kat trudged back to her Crown Vic and headed to the police station. As usual, she took the long way, rolling down the streets to make sure things were mostly in order. They appeared to be, although it was still early. Once townsfolk woke up to the news that Constance Bishop was dead, Kat had a feeling Perry Hollow would be buzzing with activity. Tragedies did that to small towns.

She pulled into the police station parking lot at the same time Carl did. They got out of their cars simultaneously and walked to the station's front door.

"Oak Knoll Cemetery is all clear," Carl said. "No disturbed graves. Nothing suspicious. Just a bunch of souls now with the Lord."

That was both good and bad news. While Kat was pleased to hear that no one had defiled the graveyard, it meant Constance had found the skeleton somewhere else. Somewhere a lot harder to pinpoint.

"You feeling up for some overtime today?"

Carl, who was thirty but didn't look a day over fifteen, made up in eagerness what he lacked in skill. "I'm on this case for as long as you are, Chief."

"Good," Kat said, nodding her approval. "While I'm over at the museum, I want you to search our records and see if any of the town's firefighters have a rap sheet. Arson. Property destruction. Things like that."

Carl paused at the door, holding it halfway open. "*Every* firefighter?"

He was referring to Boyd Jansen, one of the most decent and dependable men Kat had the pleasure of knowing. There was little to no chance Dutch would ever torch a building. But Larry Sheldon was an expert on arson. If he said firefighters were the prime suspects, then there had to be a good reason for it.

"Yes," Kat said. "Even Dutch."

* * *

It took Henry an hour and a half to reach his destination. He could have made it there in thirty minutes, but he meandered—half out of trepidation, half out of curiosity. He hadn't roamed these streets in a year, and he wondered how much had changed. So as the sun rose higher over Perry Hollow, Henry traversed Main Street. He passed his old apartment over the used-book shop he had frequented almost daily. He paused in front of the vacant headquarters of the *Perry Hollow Gazette,* his workplace for five years. Other than the FOR RENT sign plastered on the front door, the place looked exactly the same.

When he veered off Main Street, his path took him directly past the burned-out history museum. Seeing its charred façade made him think of Valhalla from the *Ring* cycle and its spectacular destruction by flames. Although Wagner's epic was too bombastic for his taste, Henry at least respected the opera tetralogy's boldness. And as he moved farther up the street, he found himself humming the cycle's "Magic Fire" leitmotif.

The humming continued as he passed the Sleepy Hollow Inn. At that point, he could have stopped walking, stepped inside, and gone up to his room. Henry knew it's what he should have done. He had people to interview, an article to research, a job to do.

Yet he kept walking, moving through the town's still-empty streets. The few people he did come into contact with were strangers who stole glances at his scars before suddenly looking away. That was no surprise. Henry hadn't been very sociable during his time in Perry Hollow. He really only knew Kat.

And Deana Swan, of course. The first woman he had

been with since the death of his wife. The only other woman he had grown to love.

The woman whose home he now stood in front of.

If someone had asked Henry what he expected to get out of visiting Deana's house, he wouldn't have been able to answer. Closure, he supposed. Not that such a thing was possible. Henry believed that most people wore their pain for the rest of their lives. Like scars, only invisible.

He certainly didn't want to see Deana again, let alone talk to her. That would be too much to bear. Henry knew he wouldn't be able to exchange quick greetings and a few minutes of chitchat. What had happened to their relationship was too dramatic—even operatic—for something as mundane as small talk.

In truth, Henry just wanted to linger outside a place he had once known very well. He wanted to gaze up at the window of Deana's bedroom and get a glimpse of the lilac walls beyond it. He wanted to find out if any of the good memories created there still existed or if they had all been eclipsed by the bad ones.

So far, it was the latter. Standing ramrod straight on the sidewalk, Henry tried to summon up a bit of the love he had once felt or the happiness he had experienced. Instead, he felt nothing but anxiety. What if a neighbor spotted him and got suspicious? What if Deana did? That would be interesting, trying to explain why he was there.

His worry was short-lived.

And completely justified.

For while Henry was still looking up at the house's second floor, the door of the attached garage rose in silence. He didn't even notice it until a vehicle emerged—a green SUV backing down the driveway.

Seeing the vehicle, Henry made a run for it. He dashed across the driveway, trying to escape undetected. But the driver saw him, as evidenced by the twin flares of brake lights at the back of the SUV. Henry halted in the middle of the driveway, directly behind the vehicle. He raised both arms like a suspect in a cop show. Caught red-handed. The SUV's driver-side door opened and a familiar face turned to peer out at him.

It was Deana, looking exactly the way he remembered her. Pretty face, kind eyes, surprisingly sensual lips. Those features that Henry had found so disarming more than a year ago stopped him short once again.

They stared at each other, neither one speaking. Henry didn't know what to say. Deana, he assumed, felt the same way. Her eyes flashed a hundred different emotions. Surprise. Joy. Pain. Regret.

When she finally did speak, it was in a hoarse whisper Henry could barely hear over the steady purr of the idling SUV.

"Henry."

Not a question. Not an exclamation. Just a quiet and stunned declaration that, despite being gone from her life for the past year, he still existed.

That was more than Henry could muster. His mouth opened as words formed in the back of his throat. He felt them there, brushing his tonsils as they struggled to take shape. Instead of letting them gestate, Henry cut them off and bolted down the sidewalk.

Deana called after him, her voice catching up to him a half-block away. "Henry! Wait!"

But Henry had no choice. He certainly couldn't go back and face her—not after all that he had been through. Running away was his only option. And instead of slowing down once Deana's voice faded, Henry quickened his pace. He sprinted without slowing until he reached the Sleepy Hollow Inn, his heart pounding the entire way.

8 A.M.

Back at the museum, Kat found Tony Vasquez and a few of his men sifting through the debris in the gallery. All of them carted around stacks of paper the size of phone books. Occasionally, one of them would pause to riffle through the pages.

"We got the museum's inventory off Constance Bishop's computer," Tony announced. "Now we're trying to make sure everything is still here."

"You think something might be missing?"

"Possibly." Tony peered into one of the ruined display cases. Spotting a sepia-toned photograph of workers lined up in front of the old sawmill, he crossed it off his sizable list. "Right now, we can't rule out robbery as a motive. Whoever did this might have been in the process of stealing something when Constance barged in on him. He then struck her on the head and started the fire to cover his tracks."

"I don't think the museum has anything valuable enough to warrant theft," Kat said. "Or murder, for that matter."

"That's not what the records say," Tony said, running his

thumb along the stack of paper, fluttering the pages. "Included with the inventory is the estimated value of every item."

He pointed to a bronze bust of Irwin Perry that now lay overturned in the display case. "That, for example, is worth two thousand dollars. There's an Andrew Wyeth sketch in storage that's worth twenty. Added up, the museum's collection totaled more than five million bucks."

Five million dollars. Kat had no idea. She doubted most folks in town did. All this time, the museum had literally been a treasure trove.

But not anymore. After the fire, the majority of the museum's collection was, if not outright ruined, at least in much worse condition than the day before. No wonder Emma Pulsifer had been adamant about trying to save a few things. If Kat had known it was all worth that much, she would have rushed into the smoldering building herself.

"I hope they had a good insurance policy."

"I do, too," Tony said. "If only we could find it."

"It's not on Constance's computer?"

"It might be. They removed it from her office and took it to the lab to search the hard drive."

"Is anyone searching the office itself?"

"Actually," Tony said, "I thought that might be a good job for you. There's a shitload of papers in there that need to be sorted."

Kat exhaled a long, tired sigh. Desk duty again. This time for real.

"Don't worry," Tony added with a smirk that Kat didn't like one bit. "You'll have help."

She left the gallery and headed down the hallway. The

door to the office was ajar, the police tape dangling off the frame like leftover streamers from a birthday party. Kat steeled herself with a deep breath and stepped inside.

Constance's office was a case study in organized chaos. There wasn't a single square inch, it seemed, that wasn't covered with reference materials, files, or stacks of paper two feet high. One wall contained shelves that stretched from floor to ceiling, each one weighed down by more paper and more books. Various knickknacks sat between the stacks—wood carvings, brass candle holders, figurines forged out of lead.

The desk was equally chaotic, with teetering stacks of more books, more papers, more folders. They formed a makeshift barrier between the rest of the office and the desk chair. Kat imagined Constance spending hours behind that wall of paperwork, cut off from the rest of the world, fully immersed in the past that she loved more than the present.

But instead of Constance, the desk chair was now occupied by none other than Nick Donnelly.

"Good morning, Starshine," he said, peeking past a leaning tower of history books.

Kat took an involuntary step backward. "Nick, what are you doing here?"

"You didn't really think I'd stay away, did you?"

Nick looked as tired as she felt. Leaning back in the desk chair, he strived to seem bright-eyed and bushy-tailed, as Kat's mom used to say. Instead, he merely looked worn down. Kat suspected she had the same weary slump to her shoulders and the same dark circles hanging under her eyes.

"To be honest," she said, "I actually did."

"Really? With a fire, a murder, *and* a skeleton under the floor? You know me better than that."

Now that he put it that way, Kat was surprised he hadn't gotten there sooner. Before he was ousted from the state police, Nick had had Tony's current job. He had been a great detective, smart and tenacious. He still was—only now he wasn't on anyone's payroll. Yet trouble always seemed to follow him. Or else he followed trouble. Kat wasn't sure which one was correct.

"I do," she said. "But you can't be here. This place is a crime scene."

"Are you talking about the museum itself or the messiness of the office?"

"Both."

"Tony knows I'm here," Nick said. "He told me I could wait for you in here, as long as I didn't touch any evidence."

"And did you?"

Nick raised his hands. "Not without gloves."

Kat left the room, heading back to the gallery. Sitting by the entrance was a small box of latex gloves. She grabbed two pairs before returning to Constance's office.

"Here," she said, tossing a pair at Nick before snapping the remaining gloves over her own hands. "I know you desperately want to start rooting through those desk drawers."

"Actually," Nick said, "I was hoping for the bookshelves."

"Suit yourself."

Nick got to his feet with the help of his cane, gripping the handle, which was in the shape of a pit bull. Fitting, considering his personality. As he thumped his way to the bookshelves, Kat took his place at the desk. The moment she sat down, a tilting pile of folders finally toppled, sending their loose-leaf contents directly into her lap.

Most of it was reference material, detailing historical

tidbits about some of the items in the museum's collection. Other folders contained correspondence with similar museums throughout Pennsylvania. Sorting through them, she placed each folder in a pile on the floor until only two remained.

Kat opened the first folder. It held a single sheet of paper—a photocopy of a painting, most likely from a history book. It showed a woman pressed against a wooden pole, her arms bent behind her back and bound at the wrists. She was surrounded by flames, which consumed her feet and licked the hem of her dress. The expression on her face was a combination of pain, regret, and resignation.

The image was well wrought but disturbing. Just looking at it gave Kat a sense of unease that she couldn't quite shake, even after she tucked the photocopy back into the folder.

"So what do you think of Lucy?" Nick asked as he leaned against the bookshelf, thumbing through a volume of Pennsylvania history.

If he was trying to sound casual, it didn't work. Kat knew that was the real reason he had traveled all the way from Philadelphia to be here. Yes, a corpse in a museum was part of it, but he mostly wanted to know if she approved of his girlfriend.

"Well, she likes old bones," Kat said. "Which definitely explains why she's interested in you."

"Very funny."

"I like her. She was a big help this morning."

Kat opened the final folder in her pile. Inside was a map, crudely drawn and completely uninformative. It contained no place-names or landmarks. Just a series of thin lines forming what looked to be a shoreline surrounded by trees, which were designated by tiny triangles. Between a tree and the water, someone had drawn a question mark with a red pen. Apparently Constance had been interested in geography as well as history.

"Do you really like her?" Nick asked, still on the topic of his girlfriend. "Or are you just saying that?"

"Yes," Kat insisted. "I really do. She's smart. She's pretty. She's a good catch."

"She's also tough," Nick added. "I actually tried to tag along when she left this morning. She almost ran me over."

"Smart woman," Kat said. "Does she know you've already been hit by a car?"

Nick used his cane to tap his right knee. "Yeah. I think that's why she didn't actually go through with it."

Kat started searching the rest of the desk, finding only identical folders filled with identical papers, a few brochures from nearby historical sites, and a good deal of takeout menus from every Chinese food place in the county. Everything Kat examined joined the growing pile next to the chair. Within minutes, the stack on the floor was knee high and the desk was bare, except for Constance's office phone and a notepad next to it.

Nick had moved on to another shelf, tossing books aside and peeking into notebooks bursting with loose pages. "And how's your love life? Any prospects?"

He was referring to Eric Olmstead, the man who had hired him to find his long-lost brother six months ago. Kat and Eric had dated briefly in high school, and when he'd returned to Perry Hollow, for a few days the sparks of attraction between them made it feel like no time had passed. But Kat had her son to worry about. Eric had his family to deal with. The sparks soon died out, and within a month, Eric was back in Brooklyn working on his next book.

"None," Kat said. "It's just me and James and the dog."

"Don't you ever get lonely?"

"No." Kat grimaced at the falseness of her voice. She had always been lousy at concealing her emotions. "Now, can we change the subject?"

"Sure. Pick a topic."

"Henry's back in town."

Nick dropped the notebook he was holding. It burst open when it hit the floor, sending loose paper fluttering around his ankles.

"Henry Goll?" he asked as he awkwardly bent to clean up the mess.

"Yep."

"The obituary writer who was targeted by a serial killer Henry Goll?"

"The very one," Kat said. "He lives in Italy now. He's here working on a story."

"Must be one hell of a story." Nick was now sitting on the floor, shoving paper back into the notebook. "How's he doing?"

"Fine, I guess. I think he's sadder than he admits. And—"

Kat was going to say *lonely* but stopped short. That word had been bandied about the room enough this morning, even though it accurately described not only Henry but herself, as well. Instead, she grabbed the notepad on the desk and pulled it toward her. The paper was white, except for a quote printed in black at the top. *"Those who cannot remember the past are forced to relive it."*

The top page, while unmarked, was indented slightly by

thin lines of curved script that showed faint traces of what had been written on the page before it. It looked to be two short words, like someone's name. Kat brought the notepad close to her face, squinting to see if she could make out a few of the letters. But the indentations were too faint and the words pushed too close together.

"And what?"

Kat lowered the notepad, seeing that Nick was now on the other side of the desk, leaning expectantly on his cane.

"You started to say something about Henry but never finished your sentence."

"Busy," Kat said. "I think he's really busy."

She opened the top drawer of Constance's desk. It was filled with the usual office clutter of staples, paper clips, and pens with chewed caps. She grabbed a pencil, making sure it was sharpened.

Nick watched her with a look of unbridled confusion. "What are you doing?"

"Someone—I'm assuming Constance—wrote something on the sheet of paper before this one. Whatever it is might be able to shed some light on what Constance was up to."

She slid an angled edge of the pencil's tip across the top page of the notepad. It was an old trick she and her girlfriends had used in junior high. They'd write a note on a top sheet, throw it away, and pass the page below it, which could only be read after shading it in with pencil. It was used as a precaution in case a teacher confiscated it or, worse, it was intercepted by one of the boys they were writing about. And while it might not have been sophisticated, the trick worked then in third-period algebra and it worked now in Constance Bishop's office. When Kat was finished rubbing the pencil over the entire piece of paper, she saw a handwritten name stick out in white against the scrapes of charcoal gray.

brad ford

Kat didn't recognize the name. If it was someone in Perry Hollow, he was certainly off her radar. She thought once again of the strangely dressed man she had seen on the street during the fire. She didn't recognize him, either, which meant she was losing touch with the town or it was growing too fast for her to keep up. Not a good prospect either way.

"While you were playing Nancy Drew," Nick said, "I found something of actual value."

He placed a spreadsheet on the desk and slid it toward Kat. She scanned it, eyes immediately going bleary because of all the columns of numbers and rows of dates. Still, she could tell it was a copy of the historical society's finances. And money, it seemed, was tight. Covering the past two years, the numbers on the spreadsheet got lower with each passing month, eventually turning from black to red before getting progressively higher again. Most of the expenses were for recurring charges. Electric bills. Maintenance costs. Office supplies. But the spreadsheet was also dotted with other, more random amounts. A thousand dollars here. Four thousand dollars there. The week before, Kat noted, someone had withdrawn two hundred bucks.

"I knew the historical society was struggling," she said. "I just didn't think it was this bad. They're swimming in debt."

"It wouldn't surprise me if even some members didn't know about this," Nick added. "Figures like these are something an organization's leadership might want to keep secret."

"Clearly, Constance Bishop knew. And so did whoever put this together."

Kat scanned the spreadsheet again. In the top left corner was the name of the man who had prepared it, along with his title: *Claude Dobson, Treasurer, Perry Hollow Historical Society.*

"I think," she said, "that it's time we paid Mr. Dobson a little visit."

Fifteen minutes later, Kat found herself staring at a wall of rifles. There were more than a dozen of them, ranging in age from old to downright ancient. Wood polished and barrels gleaming, they looked like a museum display in the middle of Claude Dobson's living room.

"You've noticed my collection," he said, ignoring that there was no way Kat couldn't have noticed them.

"Yes. It's quite the display," said Tony Vasquez, who sat next to Kat on Mr. Dobson's sofa.

It was just the three of them in the living room, Nick having been ordered to wait in the car. Ex-cops could sort through desks. Interviewing suspects was a different matter.

Since he was in charge of the investigation, Kat let Tony do most of the talking. She was content to sit back and study Claude Dobson, who had been a history teacher at Perry Hollow High School when she was a student. Although he was much older now, his appearance was much the same as it was then. Same downturned mouth. Same shock of white hair. Same ruddy cheeks that led to rumors that he kept a flask in his desk. The only changes Kat could detect were his jowly chin and rheumy eyes.

"History is my hobby," Claude said. "But historical weapons are my passion."

"Just rifles?" Tony asked

"Heavens no. I have several knives, a Japanese sword, a hand grenade from the First World War."

"Do any of them still work?"

Claude shot the lieutenant an exasperated look that Kat remembered well from her days in his classroom. "Have you ever heard of a samurai sword that stopped working?"

"I meant the guns," Tony said. "And the hand grenade."

"I suppose they would, if I bothered to use them. Which I don't. They're simply objects of beauty to show off and admire. Then there's the historical value, of course. This country—every country, quite honestly—was built on the use of weapons like these. Many people forget that. Ah, but you're not here to talk about my collection. You want to ask me about Constance."

"That's correct," Tony said. "How well did you know her?"

"Oh, exceedingly well. We worked closely together for decades. The historical society is a small, insular organization. We knew each other inside and out."

"Did you like her?"

"I didn't dislike her," Claude replied. "We had our ups and downs. But you can say that about many people."

"Mr. Dobson," Kat said. Having been a student of his, she didn't even consider addressing him any other way. "Emma Pulsifer told me Constance and other members of the group didn't see eye to eye. Especially about finances. I can only assume she was referring to you."

Claude Dobson turned his attention from Tony to Kat herself. Despite the watery eyes, his gaze was still potent. For a split second, Kat felt like she had been caught cheating on her homework.

"I had you as a student, didn't I?"

"Yes, sir. In 1989."

"If I recall, you were a mediocre one. C-plus material."

"I don't remember," Kat said, even as her memory managed to dredge up the fact that she had received a B in his class.

"So tell me, Chief. How does it feel to accuse one of your old teachers of committing arson and murder?"

"We're not accusing you of anything," Tony said. "We're just asking a few questions."

Kat piped up. "How did you know it was arson and murder? The police haven't officially announced that yet."

"Lucky guess." The former teacher's thin lips formed a flattened smile. "Or maybe it was the simple fact that the museum caught fire at the same time Constance was found dead inside."

"Where were you last night when the fire broke out?" Tony asked.

"I was at the Chamber of Commerce fund-raiser," Claude said. "Several dozen people saw me there."

"The party was still going on at one in the morning?"

"It was wrapping up at that time."

"Half the town came out to see the fire," Kat said. "But I didn't see you there."

"That's because I didn't go. Emma Pulsifer had left an hour earlier. Father Ron, Mayor Hammond, and I were still there when we heard the fire trucks. The two of them headed off to see the fire. I walked home."

Kat leaned forward, studying her former teacher for signs

he was lying. A rapid blinking of the eyes, for instance, or a twitching at the mouth. She saw nothing. "Weren't you the least bit concerned that the museum was on fire?"

"I didn't know it was the museum until Emma called me very early this morning with the tragic news about Constance."

"Let's get back to Mrs. Bishop," Tony said. "She was apparently spending a lot of time in her office lately."

"Ah, yes," Claude replied. "Her secret project. She tried to hide the fact that she was working on something, but it was obvious. Only Emma seemed not to notice. No surprise there."

"Do you know what the project was about?" Tony asked.

Claude shook his head. "I don't. None of us did. But we were about to. I suppose Emma told you about the emergency meeting Constance had called for tonight."

"She did," Kat said.

"While our meetings were often less exciting than watching paint dry, I was looking forward to this one. I suspect Constance had found something very interesting. Now we might never find out what it was."

On the way there, Kat and Tony had debated about mentioning the skeleton under the floor to the other members of the historical society. They eventually decided not to. Because the bones were apparently unearthed only recently, it was likely that Constance had been acting alone. If she wasn't, then the hope was that her accomplice would slip up and mention it without prompting.

"What about the name Brad Ford?" Kat said. "You ever hear Constance mention him?"

"Brad Ford." Claude rolled the name around in his mouth, tasting it like an oenophile did wine. "I can't recall ever hearing the name. Was he a relative of hers? I thought she didn't have any family."

"We don't know who he is," Kat said. "I found the name in her office and thought it might be related to her secret project."

"Constance didn't like to share too many things with me, since we disagreed on most of them."

"What else did you two disagree about?" Tony asked. "Money? We found your financial reports in her office. We know the historical society was deep in debt."

Claude crossed his legs and folded his hands on his knees. It was a sight Kat knew well. During class Mr. Dobson would often assume that same pose as he sat on the corner of his desk. When he did, his students would ready their notebooks, knowing a torrent of information was about to be unleashed. That morning was no different.

"Constance was good-hearted but foolish," he said. "And I'm not just saying that because, given my background in teaching history, I should have been president. She had lofty goals and silly notions that people in this town actually give a shit about history. Having been the one to teach it to most of them, I can assure you they don't. If they did, the museum wouldn't have been flat broke."

"Emma said some of you wanted to charge admission to the museum," Kat said. "Were you one of them?"

"My, that Emma talks a lot," Claude said. "But to answer your question, yes. I'm the mean old man who dared suggest we actually make people pay to enter the museum. Constance, of course, disagreed. She said charging a fee cheapened our mission."

"If money was so tight, why didn't you sell some of the collection?" Tony asked. "It was worth millions."

Claude uncrossed his legs, sighed, crossed them in the other direction. "And that was part of the problem. Constance kept buying new items. Because the museum building itself is on the state registry of historic places, we get some cash from the government. And there were fund-raisers, of course. Raffles, things like that. But as soon as the money came in, it went out again. Constance would spend it almost instantly on some godforsaken antique she insisted that the museum just had to have."

"And I suppose," Kat said, "she wasn't too keen on selling anything."

"She hated that idea more than charging admission. So we were left with too many items to put on display and no money in our bank account."

"Sounds like the historical society was on the path to bankruptcy."

"It was," Claude said. "And had things stayed the same, I'm sure that would have been the end result."

Kat arched an eyebrow. "You're making Constance's death sound like it's a good thing."

Her former teacher stared her down. "I'm sad that Constance is dead. I truly am. But this fire most likely saved us."

"How so?" Tony asked.

"Isn't it obvious?" Claude said, shaking his head in a fit of teacherly exasperation. "Insurance money. Practically every item in that museum was insured. Because of this fire, the historical society stands to gain millions."

"Were there any other members who knew about the insurance policy?"

"We all did," Claude replied. "Every single one of us."

Kat's heart started to beat faster, an excited thumping deep in her chest. Claude Dobson might not have been able to give her and Tony much information about who attacked Constance and started the fire, but he did provide something equally as valuable—a motive.

9 A.M.

"Do you think one of them did it?" Kat asked Tony once they were back in his car.

Nick, who had spent the time waiting for them sprawled across the backseat in boredom, lifted his head. "Who did what?"

"Members of the historical society," Tony said.

"One of them might have killed Constance," Kat chimed in.

Tony started the car and slipped on a pair of aviator shades. With the sunglasses, black suit, and determined set of his jaw, he looked more like a Secret Service agent than a state police detective. A *big* Secret Service agent. Lieutenant Vasquez was so huge that Kat was surprised the car didn't tilt over on his side.

"The key word here is *might*," he said. "I'd immediately suspect one of those history geeks if they all hadn't been at that party when the fire broke out."

"One of them wasn't," Kat said. "Emma Pulsifer told me she left around midnight."

By this time Nick had sat up and was poking his head into the front seat like an impatient child on a car trip. "That would give her plenty of time to swing by the museum and try to start a fire. Maybe she thought Constance was gone. But when Constance caught her in the act, Emma had no choice but to knock her over the head."

"I don't think Emma is strong enough for that," Kat said. "Wallace Noble really thinks this was the work of a man. I do, too."

On their way out of Claude Dobson's house, Kat and Tony had formed a plan. They'd split up and question the other two members of the historical society—Burt Hammond and Father Ron—simultaneously. Only now Tony was rethinking that strategy. Kat could tell by the way he stroked his Dick Tracy chin, lost in thought.

"I think I should talk to this Emma Pulsifer myself," he said. "Kat, I assume you can handle the other two on your own."

Kat didn't dignify the comment with a response. Of course she could handle a mayor and a priest. She and Burt Hammond didn't get along, it was true, and she'd hadn't been to church—any church—in years. But questioning them would be easy enough. She had a bullshit detector that was swayed by neither bureaucracy nor God.

"What can I do?" Nick asked.

Tony shot him a glance in the rearview mirror. "Realize you're no longer a cop and go home."

"Hell will freeze over before that happens."

"Listen up," Tony said. "I got serious shit for letting you get involved with the Olmstead investigation."

"I'm the one who told you about the Olmstead case,"

Nick shot back. "And if I remember correctly, you're not the one who solved it, either."

Listening to their back and forth, Kat pinched the bridge of her nose. A headache was coming on. She got them when she was tired. And when two former colleagues argued in her ear.

"Enough," she said with a finality that silenced both men. "Tony, you talk to Emma. Nick and I will interview the others. Then we'll meet up in two hours to compare notes."

"Fine." Tony shook his head, letting it be known he still thought it was a bad idea. He then turned to face Nick. "You have to follow three rules. First, let Kat do the talking. Second, seriously, let Kat do the talking. Third, don't slow her down."

Kat wasn't sure about the first two, but the third rule went out the window as soon as Tony dropped them off in front of town hall. Nick struggled with the steps leading up to the front entrance, leaning heavily on his cane. Once inside, he insisted on taking the stairs to the mayor's office on the second floor.

"You know you don't have to be so stubborn around me," Kat said as she waited for him at the top. "We could have taken the elevator."

Nick was out of breath by the time he finally reached the second-floor landing, pushing his response in labored puffs. "Elevators. Are. For. Sissies."

"And for former cops who destroyed their knee while saving my life."

"You're welcome, by the way." He walked right past her, the thump of his cane echoing off the marble floor. "Now let's go see the mayor."

That turned out to be easier said than done. Mayor

Hammond's outer office, where his secretary normally sat, was vacant. So was his inner office, with its wide-windowed view of Main Street. Granted, it was a Saturday morning, but Burt kept his office open until noon on those days. It was something he prided himself on—going out of his way to be accessible to Perry Hollow residents, even on a weekend morning. Except, apparently, that morning.

Kat stepped into his empty office. It was exactly what you'd expect from a small-town mayor with big-time ambitions. A Pennsylvania state flag hung next to Old Glory. Plaques and commendations covered the walls. Since the mayor was single and childless, the photos on his desk weren't of family. Instead, there were pictures of him glad-handing semifamous people. Kat spotted one of the mayor with the governor. Another showed him smiling next to a running back for the Philadelphia Eagles. Beside that was one of him shaking hands with an attractive woman in a short skirt and high heels, whom Kat didn't recognize. Maybe a former Miss Pennsylvania. Or the star of a reality show. You could never tell with Burt Hammond.

"Are you looking for the mayor?"

Kat whirled around to see his secretary standing in the doorway. She held an arm out in front of her, a hanger dangling from a well-manicured finger. On the hanger was a pale blue shirt draped in clear plastic. Of course, Burt Hammond was the type of person who sent his secretary to pick up his dry cleaning.

"We are," Kat said. "Do you know where he is?"

"He's at the rec center. You know him and the Halloween festival."

The Halloween festival, planned for later that night, was one of the mayor's pet projects. It had once been Perry Hollow's biggest annual event. A parade down Main Street. Everyone in costume. An influx of visitors from across the state sipping hot apple cider. Then the Grim Reaper had struck during the middle of it and all hell had broken loose.

This year Burt had decided to scale it down, moving the festival to the ancient rec center two blocks from Main. Although Kat was sad to see the downsizing of an event she remembered fondly from her childhood, it made sense from a public-safety standpoint. Plus, after what happened the year before, she doubted too many out-of-towners would be flocking to Perry Hollow to take part.

So they left the mayor's office, intent on finding him at the rec center. In the hallway, Kat turned to Nick as he limped toward the stairs.

"Call me a sissy," she said, "but we're taking the elevator."

The Perry Hollow Athletic Center was a square and squat building that always reminded Kat of a giant concrete block dropped in the middle of town. Built in the forties when the mill was running at its peak, the rec center was a relic of more prosperous days, a reminder of when the town had money for public buildings with state-of-the-art amenities. Seventy years later, it was still in use, although it had lost its state-of-the-art designation sometime during the Eisenhower administration.

The inside of the rec center was just as old and run-down as the outside. Walking past walls painted institutional gray, Kat noticed about a dozen things that needed improvement. Every third bulb of the buzzing fluorescent lights seemed to be out. Missing tiles in the floor left more gaps than an old man's smile. The place was so empty and dim that Kat was relieved to enter the gymnasium, which was bustling with people and was in the process of being festooned with Halloween decorations. A little color went a long way, even if it was mostly orange and black.

The workers in the gym were a select group of put-together mothers who seemed to have endless time and energy. Kat, who secretly referred to the group as the PTA Mafia, was wary of all of them. They always appeared friendly, smiling and saying how proud they were that the town had a "woman police chief." But she often detected a note of superiority in their voices, and more than a little bit of pity. They assumed—incorrectly—that she would rather have a husband who earned six figures and a normal son that she could drive back and forth to soccer games. Well, she did have a normal son, who was pretty damn good at soccer. As for the husband, she had had one once. Looking at how that had turned out, Kat wasn't sure she wanted another.

As she stepped farther into the gymnasium, a few members of the PTA Mafia offered obligatory waves before turning their attention to Nick. He was like catnip to those ladies. Handsome and intense, he was all the more mysterious now that he used a cane. The rumor persisted around town that he and Kat were having a secret, torrid affair. Yet another reason the women in the room stared at her with disdain as they stuffed straw into half-finished scarecrows and wrangled costumes onto mannequins on loan from the town's dress shop. Quite simply, they were jealous.

Other than Nick, the only male in the gymnasium was

Burt Hammond, who stood in the middle of the basketball court, the center of attention. It was, Kat knew far too well, where he liked to be.

Luckily for Burt, his height—inches past six feet—made it easy for him to stand out in the crowd. So did the fact that his frequent trips to the tanning bed left his skin taut and bronzed, even in the middle of winter. Then there was his mole—a dime-sized spot on his chin that the mayor used to his advantage. When he walked down Main Street, it was with his chin jutted forward, so people could tell from a distance that it was he who was approaching.

Burt's real job was owner of a lawn-mower dealership on the outskirts of town. But his passion was politics. Mayor Hammond lived for shaking hands, kissing babies, and presiding over town council meetings. He also liked to boss people around, Kat included. Standing alone at center court, he barked orders to two soccer moms balancing on ladders while trying to hang a banner across the far wall.

"It's still crooked," Burt said. "A little to the left."

One of the soccer moms—nervous atop the ladder—made an adjustment.

"More, please."

Another adjustment, another shaky move by one of the moms.

"There," Burt said. "That's perfect. Thank you, ladies."

With the banner hung and the members of the PTA Mafia descending their ladders with relief, Kat stepped onto the basketball court. Burt frowned when he saw her. His typical greeting.

"I'm assuming this is about Constance," he said.

"It is."

"I thought so. It's a damn shame what happened. Losing the museum was hard enough. But losing someone like Constance, well, I'm not sure how we're going to recover, quite honestly."

Kat was surprised by Burt's sincerity. They had butted heads over budget issues so many times that she honestly thought he didn't have a sincere bone in his body. But just before she got too impressed, he added, "And the timing couldn't be worse. I've spent a whole year trying to convince people that Perry Hollow is a great place to come visit. Now this happens."

"We're doing everything we can," Kat told him. "The state police are involved. A lot of people are working hard to find out who did this."

"And you're here to ask me a few questions, right?"

"We are," Kat said, jumping right in. "How well did you know Constance? Were you two close?"

"We weren't friends, but we were friendly. We agreed with each other on most historical society business."

"Were you very involved with the historical society?"

The question came from Nick, who had slid next to the mayor before violating Tony's first two rules.

Burt took a moment to size up Nick the same way he had examined the banner on the wall—with critical disdain. "And who might you be?"

"Nick Donnelly," Kat said. "He's assisting in the investigation."

"I remember now," the mayor said, eyes drifting to Nick's cane. "You're that state police detective who was fired for assaulting a hospital worker."

"That's me." Nick kept a death grip on the handle of his cane, most likely to keep himself from beating Burt over the head with it. "Although the assault was justified."

"About Constance and the historical society," said Kat, eager to change the subject. "Were you an active member of the group? Emma Pulsifer said it was more ceremonial."

"She would say that." Burt sniffed. "Emma often enjoys belittling the contributions of others. I was as active a participant as everyone else."

Over his shoulder, Kat saw one of the soccer moms waving to get their attention from the sidelines. "I'm sorry," she said, "but you're going to have to clear the court."

The soccer mom was standing near the emergency exit, her hand hovering in front of a fat, red button stuck to the wall. When she pressed the button, the gym floor began to hum beneath their feet. Kat and the mayor hurried to the sidelines, knowing what was coming next. Nick, blithely unaware, remained at center court.

"You better hurry," Kat told him. "Unless you want to get wet."

Nick remained in place a moment, confusion scrunching his face. Then the floor opened up at center court, forming a crack that ran the width of the gym floor. Nick yelped as he limped to Kat's side, never taking his eyes off the widening fissure. When it had opened a couple of feet, he finally saw the crystal-blue water rippling directly beneath the gym floor.

"Is that a swimming pool?"

"It is," Kat said. "Just like that scene in *It's a Wonderful Life*."

In the movie, Jimmy Stewart and Donna Reed accidentally did the Charleston right into the pool when the gym floor above it retracted. Folks in Perry Hollow were more careful about it. Whenever the need arose to make the transition from floor to pool, everyone in the rec center knew it was coming. Usually, a lucky child was plucked from the pool or gym floor to make the switch. Kat remembered pressing that red button when she was a kid. She still got a vicarious thrill whenever James was given the honor.

Nick looked equally awed as he watched the gym floor slide away. "I didn't know these things still existed."

"They don't, really," Burt said. "This is the only one on the East Coast. Honestly, this place shouldn't be in use anymore, but we have no choice. For years, we've been trying to come up with ways to fund a new rec center. But the budget gods are always against us."

Kat kept her eyes on the receding basketball court. The pool beneath it had roughly the same dimensions. Fifty feet wide. Almost a hundred feet long. Because it was so old, there was no shallow end. It was eight feet deep the entire way. Not an ideal thing to have in the middle of a Halloween party.

"Why are you opening the pool now?"

"The floor's been malfunctioning," Burt said. "We're testing it to make sure it doesn't open up when there's a bunch of kids on it. And if it does, we want to see how much time we have to clear them away."

From what Kat could tell, time wasn't on their side. Within a minute, the basketball court was gone, replaced by the shimmering surface of the pool. Just as soon as it was fully open, the floor started to close again. When the basketball court had finished sliding into place, it was time for another test and the floor split apart once more.

As the floor continued to open and close, Kat went down the same list of questions that were asked of Claude Dobson. She received the same answers. Yes, Burt suspected that Constance was busy working on something that she planned to reveal that night. No, he had no idea what it was. No, he had never heard the name Brad Ford. And just like Claude, he failed to mention any skeletons, literal or figurative, hidden within the museum.

"I'm assuming you knew the historical society was experiencing money trouble," Kat said.

"I did," Burt replied. "In fact, Constance stopped by my office last week to ask if there was room in the budget to give the museum more money."

"And was there?"

"Of course not. The money just wasn't there. She was upset with me, naturally. She said that as a member of the historical society, I should do more to help it. But my hands were tied. I've had to turn down lots of requests for more money. Just the other day, I had to say no to Dutch Jansen when he asked if funds were available to hire some of the volunteer firefighters on a full-time basis. He got mad at me, too."

Kat could relate. She had been in more than a few budget fights with the mayor. After the Grim Reaper killings, she begged for more money to hire another officer. Burt had refused. It was still just her and Carl, and once again they had a murder on their hands.

"But I was told you agreed with Constance that the museum shouldn't charge admission," she said. "Didn't you think that would help ease the money crunch even just a little bit?"

There was a row of benches that ran the length of the

gymnasium. Normally the territory of prune-fingered swimmers and wannabe basketball stars, they were now home to boxes of Halloween decorations and a few stray pumpkins. Burt pushed some of them aside and took a seat.

"I understood that it would bring in some revenue, but not enough to make much of a difference," he said. "Plus, I thought it would send the wrong message to out-of-towners. It would have been like inviting someone into your home and then charging them five bucks for your hospitality. As it is, we're having a hard enough time attracting visitors."

Perry Hollow had struggled mightily after the mill closed. It only started to come back after a few small businesses took a chance and set up shop. Now it was known for its quaint and quirky downtown, encouraging tourists to take a detour during their Sunday drives. Business wasn't booming, but it was solid, which was enough for the people who lived there. Only now the tourists weren't coming as frequently or staying as long. The Grim Reaper murders were to blame, although in the weeks that followed them, Perry Hollow had seen an uptick in visitors. Mayhem lured in people as surely as sugar drew flies. But that moment had passed quickly, replaced by a quiet that unsettled residents who remembered the darkest days after the mill closing.

"What this town needs is to take things to the next level," Burt said. "Everyone knows it. It was all anyone was talking about last night."

"During the Chamber of Commerce fund-raiser?" Kat asked.

Burt nodded, prompting Nick to chime in with "Is that where you were when the fire broke out?"

"It was."

"Can someone else verify your presence?"

"Just ask anyone," Burt said. "I made a point of greeting everyone there."

Kat pictured the mayor working the room with an untouched drink in his hand. She was certain he patted everyone on the back and laughed too loudly at jokes that weren't very funny before moving on to the next person. If that was socializing in Perry Hollow, she was all too happy to remain an outcast.

"Was anyone there acting suspiciously?" Nick asked.

Burt puckered his lips as he pondered the question. "Suspicious? Not that I can recall. There were some people who had had a few too many, but that's normal at a function like that."

"Anyone in particular?" Kat said.

"Well, I probably shouldn't be sharing this." Burt had lowered his voice and was now glancing around the gymnasium to see if he'd be overheard. "But there was a firefighter who was hitting the open bar pretty hard. His name is Danny."

"Danny Batallas?"

"Yes, him," Burt said. "He made a bit of a scene during the event. What made it even more embarrassing is that he's a salesman at my dealership. Thank God only myself and a few others witnessed it."

Kat tried to recall if Danny had seemed intoxicated at the museum blaze. She hadn't noticed anything out of the ordinary, but that was almost an hour after the party had ended. Besides, he had just finished putting out a fire. A rush of adrenaline like that could sober anyone up.

"Are you certain he was drunk?" she asked.

Burt shrugged. "Well, I'm not positive. But it's the only explanation I can think of for what transpired."

"And what exactly happened?"

"At one point during the party, he cornered me," Burt said. "He demanded that we talk about his salary."

Kat tilted her head at him. "At your dealership?"

"No. As a firefighter. He wanted to be a full-time, paid firefighter, instead of a mere unpaid volunteer. He said there might come a time when the town needed a paid fire squad. He said, and this is an exact quote, 'What if someone decides to set this whole town on fire? Then what will you do?' I told him that the party was the wrong place to bring it up and that we could discuss it in my office at a later time."

"Did he agree?"

"Not really," Burt replied. "He simply walked to the bar and got another drink. That was the last time I saw him during the party. Someone must have driven him home because he was gone by midnight."

Kat exchanged a knowing glance with Nick. He was thinking what she was—that Danny Batallas now looked guilty as sin.

"Do you know where we could find Danny today?"

"He's scheduled to be at the dealership right now," Burt said. "I'd stop by there first if you need to talk to him."

"Thanks for the tip. We'll be sure to do that."

The gym floor had receded for the umpteenth time, revealing the pool in all its chlorinated glory.

"I hope it helps, although I'm sure Danny has nothing to do with this," Burt Hammond said as he stared at the glimmering water. "But you better catch whoever the hell did this very soon. This town can't take any more murders. Or fires, for that matter."

10 A.M.

Henry's eyes were killing him, thanks to an hour spent poring over documents about Giuseppe Fanelli. The pages were now scattered around the room. Some weighed down the poor excuse for a desk. Others sat in lopsided piles on the floor or spread across the bed. Henry had read them all. When he closed his eyes, he still saw them—lines of business-speak typed in crisp Italian floating across the back of his eyelids.

And despite all that time spent reading, he hadn't learned anything concrete about Fanelli and his latest venture, Fanelli Entertainment USA. He certainly didn't have a clue about what Giuseppe Fanelli planned to do in Perry Hollow.

It didn't help matters that his mind insisted on drifting back to Deana Swan. More than once, Henry found his thoughts veering off the page he was reading and into the recent past. He'd think of the surprised expression on Deana's face as she saw him at the end of the drive. He wondered about his appearance and if she noticed the new scars on his lips.

Most of all, Henry thought about how Deana looked. The past year had left her unchanged. She still had the same kind eyes, the same sweet smile that could turn naughty in an instant. But there was something different about her. Something invisible yet still palpable. Maybe it was sadness. Or maturity. Probably it was just the strange sensation of seeing her again after such a long time. Whatever it was, it was distracting

Henry from the sole reason he was back in Perry Hollow—his job.

Henry closed his eyes and pinched the bridge of his nose. "Get it together, Goll. You've got work to do."

And now that it was mid-morning in Perry Hollow, he needed to start doing it. That meant phone calls. Lots of them. Sitting on the edge of the creaky bed, he grabbed his phone and dialed the home of David Brandt, partner at Everhart and Brandt, the real estate firm that helped sell the one hundred acres of Perry Hollow to Giuseppe Fanelli. Mr. Brandt—who answered on the first ring, Henry noticed—didn't seem to mind being bothered on the weekend.

"Yes, I'm the one who sold the land to Mr. Fanelli," he said after the obligatory introductions and opening chitchat. "It was a very big get for our firm."

"Just to clarify, this is the parcel that used to be occupied by the Perry Mill, correct?"

"It is," David Brandt said. "If you have a map of the area—"

Henry actually did have a map, buried somewhere under the hundred other pieces of paper on the bed. He riffled through them as David Brandt continued.

"—you'll see that the lot begins right at the edge of Lake Squall. It fronts the water for ten acres. Then it goes away from shore for another ten acres, making it a hundred square acres."

By that point Henry had located the map and was using an index finger to trace a rectangle around the area David Brandt was talking about. It was a big chunk of land, and probably very expensive.

"How much did Mr. Fanelli pay for the land?"

"I can't disclose the sum," Mr. Brandt said. "But I will say it was more than what the land was worth."

Henry discarded the map and reached for his notebook and pen. He scrawled *pagato più*—paid more—before realizing he didn't need to take notes in Italian. Shaking off the mental jet lag, he asked, "Why would he do that?"

"I don't really know. Apparently, he just really wanted the land."

"Were there any other potential buyers?"

"The town, of course," David Brandt said. "They've been interested in it for years."

Henry paused, pen frozen over the notebook. "I thought Perry Hollow *was* the owner of the land."

"No, the land was still with the Perry family. The town wanted them to donate it, but the family refused. Then town officials tried to get them to lower the price. The family made an offer, but the town couldn't meet it."

At last, Henry lowered pen to paper. He wrote, *"Town wanted land."*

"Do you know what Mr. Fanelli intends to build there?"

"We never discussed that."

So much for getting more information. It appeared that Mr. Brandt knew even less than Henry did. Still, he pressed on, asking, "I'm assuming Mr. Fanelli contacted you about purchasing the land?"

"He did," Mr. Brandt said. "Actually, *he* didn't. One of his employees did. She said she was a vice president of Mr. Fanelli's U.S. company."

"Can I get her name?"

"Sure. It's Trapani. Lucia Trapani."

"And she's based in Philadelphia?" Henry asked.

"I believe so, yes."

Henry scribbled down the name and phone number David Brandt provided. "Do you know how Mr. Fanelli heard about the land being for sale?"

"You'd have to ask Ms. Trapani about that." Impatience had crept into Mr. Brandt's voice. Henry was asking too many questions. "Or Mr. Fanelli, if you can reach him."

Henry thanked David Brandt for his time and hung up. He then prepared to call Lucia Trapani, but a knock on the door interrupted him before he got the chance.

"Hello?" said a meek voice floating in the hallway. "Is anyone there?"

Henry opened the door and saw the short and stout woman who had been behind the check-in desk in the wee hours of the morning. Her name was Lottie Scott—she had mentioned it three times during the two-minute check-in process—and Henry assumed she was the proud owner of the Sleepy Hollow Inn. Which meant she was also the cook, the plumber, and, judging from the set of towels she was holding, the maid.

Lottie looked surprised to see him. "Oh, you're here."

"I am," Henry said. "Is there something you need?"

"No. I just came up to replace the towels and make the bed." Mrs. Scott peered past him to the document-strewn bed. "Oh. I've interrupted you."

Henry explained that he planned to spend the day in his room working and that he wished not to be disturbed. He even asked Lottie if there was a sign he could hang on the doorknob to prevent any other intrusions. Naturally, there wasn't. All Henry could do was repeat that he was working while he accepted the towels.

"Don't worry, Mr. Goll," Lottie assured him. "You won't hear a peep from me."

"Thank you," Henry said. "I appreciate it."

After Mrs. Scott departed, Henry tossed the towels onto a nearby chair and returned to his phone. Since it was a Saturday, he didn't expect to reach Lucia Trapani. At best, he planned to leave a voice mail and hoped she'd get back to him. So it was a surprise when the phone was answered by an officious secretary who told him, "Ms. Trapani is outrageously busy today."

"But it's a Saturday," Henry said.

"Not where I work," the secretary replied with undisguised bitterness.

"I only need five minutes of her time."

"That's like asking for the Easter bunny. Five free minutes simply don't exist."

"Then one minute," Henry said, trying to summon patience from a well that was quickly going dry. "Surely Ms. Trapani has a minute available to answer a few questions."

"Who are you again?" The secretary was starting to sound like a snobby maître d' who was refusing to let him enter a restaurant because he wasn't wearing a tie. "And what is this about?"

Henry stated, not for the first time, his name, his newspaper, and why he was calling. When he was finished, Lucia Trapani's secretary said, "I think we'd both be happier if you just called the PR department on Monday. *They* don't have to come in on the weekend."

"Take down my number," Henry said, giving up for the time being. "Tell your boss that if she gets the chance, I'd appreciate it if she could call me back and answer a few questions. Today."

A flurry of half-whispered voices hissed out of the receiver. The secretary was conferring with someone, her hand trying to muffle the phone. Henry could make out snippets of the conversation. *Who? What newspaper? And he's where?* That was followed by some ear-scraping rustling as someone else took control of the phone.

"This is Lucia Trapani."

Henry was taken aback, not just by the fact that she was talking to him but also because her English was impeccable. Judging by her name—and the man she worked for—he had assumed he'd need to conduct the interview in Italian.

"Ms. Trapani, thank you for—"

"You're welcome," she said, cutting to the chase. "You're calling about the Perry Hollow land, right?"

"I am."

"And you came all the way from Rome to report on this?"

"I did," Henry said. "It's a big story. And from what I can tell, no one in the Italian press but us knows about it."

"I see. You want to break the news. Unfortunately, I spoke to a reporter about it yesterday."

Hearing that made Henry want to throw his phone out the window. He had traveled all that way just to be scooped. "Was it an Italian paper?"

"No," Lucia said. "More local."

The Philadelphia Inquirer, probably, Henry thought. Or maybe Miss Trapani was bluffing just to avoid talking to him. If another paper had broken the news, Henry would have heard about it by now.

"That doesn't matter to the readers of my paper."

"Of course. But what if I told you there's no story to break?"

This time Henry knew she was bluffing. "If there wasn't a story, then all your filings would have made it clear what Fanelli Entertainment USA actually does. They also would have explained why he bought land in Pennsylvania and not, say, New York or California. Finally, they would have provided some idea of what Mr. Fanelli plans to build on the land, because you and I both know it's going to be something huge."

"You're correct in that regard. Giuseppe never does anything small."

"So," Henry said, "would you care to comment?"

"No," Lucia replied. "At least not right now. It might have sounded like an exaggeration, but I really don't have five minutes to spare today."

Henry slumped on the bed, deflated. He needed to get something that day. Otherwise, his editor would start to get impatient, and Dario never liked to be kept waiting. There was also the fact that someone else could break the story before him, which would make Dario livid that the paper had spent all that money on travel for nothing.

"Please," he said. "I'm desperate here. Like Tosca."

Lucia Trapani surprised Henry once again, this time by laughing. "An opera buff, I see."

"Very much so."

"Is *Tosca* your favorite Puccini?"

"It is," Henry said.

"It's a good one," Lucia replied. "Although I prefer *Madama Butterfly*. I suppose I'm girly and sentimental in that regard."

"It has its merits," Henry said. "I saw it again a few months ago in Rome. It's more mature than I thought."

"Listen." Lucia Trapani sighed, like she was already

regretting what she was about to say. "I can drive out to Perry Hollow tonight. I'll give you an exclusive sit-down interview and tell you everything I know."

"Isn't that far for you?"

"Call it a favor for a fellow opera buff," Lucia said. "Besides, I'm used to the drive. I was just there last night, in fact. And I have to drive out there tomorrow morning to monitor some site work. If I have to, I'll spend the night at that wretched bed-and-breakfast they've got there."

"When do you want to meet?"

"My schedule is packed until tonight, so it's going to have to be late. How does nine-thirty sound?"

Anytime would have sounded great to Henry, so he agreed on nine-thirty. They arranged to meet for drinks at Maison D'Avignon, Perry Hollow's fanciest restaurant. It was an expensive place, and a few cocktails there would probably blow through the meager food budget the newspaper had provided. Henry didn't care. He was simply happy for the chance to get some information about Fanelli's plans.

He was in such a good mood that he didn't even mind when Mrs. Scott inevitably knocked on his door five minutes after he ended the call with Lucia Trapani. In addition to being overworked, the poor thing was also senile. Otherwise she would have remembered that he had specifically asked not to be disturbed.

"Mrs. Scott," he said, opening the door. "More towels?"

Henry blinked. Hard.

Instead of the proprietor, he saw Deana Swan, standing with her hands folded nervously in front of her. Henry took a step backward, his good mood gone in an instant.

Deana noticed and attempted a smile. "Hi, Henry."

Stunned by her presence for the second time that morning, Henry's first instinct was to close the door. He couldn't face her. Not now. Not ever. But Deana was quick and blocked the door's progress with her foot.

"Please," she said, the door bouncing off her shoe. "This will only take a minute."

Henry wanted to keep pressing the door against her foot in the hope she'd pull it away and leave him in peace. But Deana sounded desperate. As desperate as Tosca, he noted. So he released the door, letting it drift open until there was nothing between them.

"I know you don't want to see me," Deana said. "I completely understand that. Even more, I respect it. But you just vanished. I know why you did it, and I came to terms with the fact that I was never going to see you again."

She was on the verge of crying, the welling tears catching the light and setting off her big, blue eyes.

"And then suddenly you're here again. I don't know why or for how long. But I knew that I couldn't let you leave again without telling you how deeply sorry I am about what happened to you. He hurt you so much, Henry. You almost died. And it tears me up inside that I was in some way a part of that. I will never forgive myself, and I understand if you can't find it in your heart to forgive me."

Henry remained silent, his conflicting emotions too unruly to be conveyed in mere words. He still thought about Deana often. His clumsy stakeout of her house made that embarrassingly clear. Yet he wasn't ready to forgive her.

Yes, he knew she wasn't the Grim Reaper, who had killed two people and died while trying to make Henry his third victim. But Deana had provided him with one of the tools used to torment him. It wasn't intentional on her part. At the time, she had no idea about the consequences of her actions. She was an unwilling accomplice, an innocent bystander. But Henry needed someone to blame. Now that the Grim Reaper was dead, Deana was the only person left.

"I know what happened to you and Chief Campbell in that mill," she continued. "People in town still talk about it. I know what happened, and I'm sorry."

She paused, letting the silence stretch between them, as taut and vibrating as plucked piano wire. Henry made no move to break it.

"I want to sit down and talk about all this," Deana eventually said. "I think it would help both of us. But not now. I need to get to work and it's obvious I surprised you as much as you surprised me this morning. But I have an hour break at two. You can come over and we'll talk."

She paused, waiting for him to respond. But Henry didn't. He couldn't even manage a shake of his head.

"You need time to think about it," Deana said, biting her lower lip expectantly. "And I know you don't want to. But please try. It's important."

She hesitated a moment, leaning in the direction of the stairwell just down the hall but keeping her eyes on Henry. No doubt she was hoping he'd agree and let her avoid the suspense of waiting. But the nod Henry gave her was one of dismissal, not affirmation, and Deana eventually drifted away from the door.

Henry didn't observe her progress down the hall.

Instead, he listened.

To the sob she tried to muffle as she hurried through the

hallway. To her footfalls, getting faster once she reached the stairs. To the creak of the inn's front door as she slipped outside.

Only when she was gone did Henry close the door to his room. He stumbled to the bed, collapsing on top of its blanket of papers. Although his body had insisted on running on Italian time all morning, a wave of exhaustion suddenly crashed over him.

His eyelids, as heavy as steel doors, slammed shut. His mind, having been given too much to process, simply closed down. Henry relished the dark void. He retreated into it, practically sprinting into sleep.

When sleeping, he didn't need to consider meeting the woman who almost helped usher in his demise. There were no decisions in sleep. Or commitments. Or pain.

In sleep, Henry wouldn't be aware that Deana Swan was still in love with him and that he had no idea how to deal with it.

11 A.M.

When they left the rec center, Kat and Nick were supposed to track down Father Ron and ask him the same questions posed to the other members of the historical society. Instead, they took a detour, driving out to Burt Hammond's lawn-mower dealership in search of Danny Batallas. After hearing what the mayor said about him, Kat intended to get Danny's side of the story. If something had been on the young firefighter's mind during the party, she wanted to know what it was. Especially considering the fact that he disappeared less than an hour before the museum fire began.

Yet when they reached the dealership on the outskirts of town—a ten-minute drive—they were told that Danny hadn't come to work that day.

Not late. Not out sick. Just a total no-show.

The manager told Kat that every attempt to call him went unanswered. Kat got the same result when she called him herself, prompting her to go one step further and drive to Danny's residence.

His apartment—a basement unit in a house in the bad part of town—appeared to be empty. No one answered when she knocked on the door. When she crawled through the grass on her stomach to peer into the ground-level windows, she saw no sign that anyone was home.

For the time being, Danny Batallas was missing in action and an hour had been wasted looking for him, a fact not lost on Kat as she reported the details back to Lieutenant Vasquez.

"And that's all we've got," she said. "Please tell me you've made more progress."

"I have," Tony replied. "Sort of. Emma Pulsifer's story matches the one she gave you. She freely admits she left the fund-raiser before everyone else and that no one came into contact with her between then and the fire."

Kat, who was steering her Crown Vic down Main Street, on the way to All Saints Parish, tilted her head to pin the phone between her ear and shoulder. "It's suspicious, I'll give you that much. But between you and me, she couldn't have done it. She doesn't look strong enough to lift a stick, let alone something heavy enough to do the kind of damage that Constance Bishop suffered."

"I agree," Tony said. "Which is why I stopped by Constance's house and talked to her neighbor. Nice old man. Could talk your ear off, if you let him."

"What did he say?"

"That Constance left her house in the middle of the night four times last week."

"How does he know that?"

"He blames insomnia," Tony said. "I say it's because he's a Peeping Tom. Either way, he said she normally left around midnight. And, get this, the first three times he saw her leave, she was carrying a metal detector. Then the night before last, the metal detector was gone, replaced with a simple shovel."

Kat already knew what Constance had been doing and why it required a shovel. How a metal detector played a role in all of this was still a mystery.

"I also talked to the computer guys," Tony said, making Kat realize all the more how little she and Nick had accomplished. "There was nothing on it that would incriminate anyone. It was mostly historical society business. E-mails. Paperwork. That sort of thing."

"I'm assuming there wasn't anything about Brad Ford."

"Nothing," Tony said. "But I have a few guys checking on it. If someone by that name set foot in Perry Hollow in the last six months, they'll find out about it. I also had some troopers check Constance's phone records, both home and cell phone. There was nothing out of the ordinary, other than a flurry of calls from Emma Pulsifer early this morning."

"It was during the fire. I saw her make half of them."

"Constance, however, made one phone call last night. To a business with a French-sounding name."

"Maison D'Avignon?"

"Yeah," Tony said. "Whatever that is."

"It's a restaurant."

"Doesn't this town have any Mexican restaurants? Those names I can pronounce. And I'd actually have a place to eat other than that poor excuse for a diner."

Kat interrupted him. "What time did Constance call?"

"A little before ten o'clock."

"That was during the Chamber of Commerce fund-raiser. I bet Constance was calling one of the guests."

"Well," Tony said, "that narrows it down to only about a hundred people."

Kat turned right onto a side road that ran past Oak Knoll Cemetery. Just beyond it, the bell tower of All Saints Parish rose into view.

"We've already talked to three of them," she said. "And now I'm about to make it four. We'll meet you back at the museum as soon as we can."

She ended the call before steering the Crown Vic to the front of the church. All Saints Parish, tall and imposing at the southern end of town, was considered the crown jewel of Perry Hollow architecture. Kat had once heard it described as the town's version of Notre-Dame. While minuscule compared to that famed house of worship, it was still impressive. A circular stained-glass window was situated above the front door, with a matching one at the back of the building. To the right, a bell tower rose eighty feet, providing a perfect view of the town. A few gargoyles guarded the corners of the vaulted roof, which was supported by the traditional buttresses.

"Here we are," Kat said. "Hope your soul is in order."

"Fat chance." Nick got out of the car and eyed the church with suspicion. "I haven't been in a church in years."

"Same here."

Kat led the way inside, their footsteps—and Nick's cane—echoing throughout the vast and empty space. Peering into the nave, she saw only rows of empty pews and a few candles flickering along the far wall. The area around the altar was also abandoned, populated only by a silent statue of the Virgin Mary.

"Hello?" Kat called. "Father Ron? Are you here?"

A voice responded, sounding tinny and distant. "Is that you, Chief?"

"The one and only. Where are you?"

"The bell tower. Can you come up?"

"Sure," Kat yelled back. "Just give me a minute."

The door to the tower, located to the right of the entrance foyer, was open, revealing a wooden staircase that twisted upward.

"I'm going to take a wild guess here," Nick said as he peered up the stairs, "and say there's no elevator."

"No, there's not," Kat said.

Nick turned around and, with a sigh, headed for the front door. "I'll be in the car."

That left Kat to brave the staircase on her own. The steps, narrow and too rickety for comfort, hadn't been built for daily use. A long rope hung from the church's bell, making it easily accessible on the first floor for those who had to ring it. The stairs were for repairmen and, judging from the sloshing noises coming from the top, handy priests who sometimes gave the bell a good scrubbing. As Kat ascended, she saw drops of soapy water fall like rain past her head. A thick rivulet of water clung to the rope, riding it down to ground level.

Kat was out of breath by the time she reached the top. She was exhausted, as well. The caffeine high from the coffee she had consumed earlier had worn off. Now she was running on fumes.

Surveying the top of the bell tower through tired eyes, she saw a square and tiny room with open windows in all four walls that offered a bird's-eye view of Perry Hollow. In the center of the room was the church's bell—a brass behemoth that rivaled the Liberty Bell in sheer size. It hung from a wooden support beam over a square hole in the floor, the rope attached to it dropping far below to the church's ground level. A thin railing that looked as solid as a bridge made of toothpicks ran around the hole's perimeter.

Father Ron, armed with a mop and bucket of water, greeted Kat with a benevolent nod. Still fit and handsome as he neared his seventh decade, he wore the standard short-sleeved black shirt and clergyman's collar. Below the waist, however, was anything but traditional. Instead of dress pants, he wore jeans torn at the knees and spattered with wet spots. On his feet were Converse sneakers, also damp.

"Hey there, Chief," he said. "I've got a feeling this isn't a social visit."

"I wish I could say I was here to help you clean the bell."

"And I wish you were here to inquire about Sunday Mass."

Kat didn't go to church, at All Saints or anywhere else for that matter. Father Ron knew this and accepted it, but he still liked to apply pressure now and again. Kat never took offense. She liked the priest, understanding that they basically had the same job—convincing people to be on their best behavior. The only difference was the tools they used. Father Ron had his Bible. Kat had her Glock.

"I didn't know church bells got this dirty," she said.

"I'm doing it for Constance. She loved this church. Not for its religious significance but for its history. So when she's buried, I want the bell to ring as loud and clear as possible." Father Ron lifted the mop and slapped it against the outside of the bell, scrubbing in a circular pattern. "Plus, it helps take my mind off the grief. At least, I hoped it would."

"The two of you were close?"

"Very. We didn't agree on many things, truth be told. Religion. Politics. All the things intertwined between the two. But we both loved history and knew that it's too important to be forgotten. We were kindred spirits in that regard."

He plunged the mop back into the bucket, leaned on the handle, and looked out one of the wide windows. Kat followed suit, seeing Perry Hollow spread out before them, as small and pretty as a village in a model railroad display. The window they were peering through faced northwest, giving them an overview of Main Street and everything to the left of it. It was a picture-perfect view. From that height, even the smoke-stained museum looked pristine.

"I was born and raised in Philadelphia," Father Ron said. "It's a nice place. Clearly a lot of history there. But I never knew what it felt like to belong to a town until I came here."

"Constance felt the same, I assume."

"This town meant the world to her. Its past, especially. She was voracious in her pursuit of learning its history, good and bad. And if you ask me, she was killed for it."

Kat tore her eyes away from the view and settled her gaze on the man next to her. "Why do you say that?"

"Constance was working on something," Father Ron said.

"A secret project," Kat said. "I heard. Any idea what it was?"

"I'm afraid not. We all had theories as to what she was working on. I straight-out asked her about it. She wouldn't tell me, but she gave me a hint."

"Which was?"

"That whatever she was researching happened before the mill had been built. Before the town even existed, really."

Kat thought of the deed that Emma Pulsifer had so desperately tried to save. It now sat with other pieces of evidence, in worse shape than ever. Before the museum fire, she had never stopped to consider that the land Perry Hollow sat upon had existed long before the town did.

"I don't know much about that time period," she said.

"Quite frankly, neither do I. What little I do know came from Constance."

Father Ron lifted the mop from the bucket again. While scrubbing the bell, he gave Kat an abridged history lesson.

"Before Irwin Perry arrived and built his mill, the area was mostly uninterrupted pine forests. There was a village—a few homes, a blacksmith, a tavern—so minuscule it didn't even have a proper name. No one knows how long the village was here before the mill was built. I think that's what Constance was trying to find out."

"But why do you think her research is what got her killed?"

"It's more of a hunch, really. I have nothing to back it up. But in the past few days Constance seemed suspicious, almost paranoid."

"Did she tell you what was troubling her?"

"In a way, she did, although not outright," Father Ron said. "Earlier in the week, I was in the museum doing custodial duty."

Kat raised her hand. "Custodial duty?"

"Members of the historical society take turns cleaning the exhibits," the priest said. "We certainly can't pay someone else to do it, and frankly, considering the value of some of the items there, we didn't trust anyone else."

"And all of you did this?" Kat asked.

Father Ron offered a chagrined smile. "It's a requirement of membership. We each try to come in one night a week and tidy things up. Emma Pulsifer is great at dusting. And you should see how Claude Dobson wields a vacuum cleaner."

"And you were cleaning when?"

"Four nights ago," Father Ron said. "It was around eight and Constance came out of her office. She asked me if I had been inside it recently."

Kat stopped him with yet another question. "She didn't keep her office locked?"

The priest shook his head. "She kept the door closed at all times but never locked. Anyone could enter if they wanted to. No one ever did, of course. That was considered Constance's private space. I hadn't gone inside, and I told her so."

"But she thought someone had been in there, right?"

"That's right," Father Ron said. "She told me that a book on her desk had been moved at some point in the past twenty-four hours."

Kat wondered how Constance could have even noticed that, considering the chaotic state of her office. What was one out-of-place object in a heaping pile of files, papers, and pamphlets? She assumed that Constance realized the book had been moved because it, unlike everything else on her desk, was important enough to keep track of.

"Did you happen to see this book?"

"I did, but only from a distance. Constance opened her office door to point out where the book had been sitting and its new location. I was too far away to see a title, and I was afraid to ask her what it was. She was surprisingly upset about it. Kept talking about how foolish she was to leave it out like that and how she really didn't want anyone else to see it. She seemed terrified that someone would find out what she was working on."

Kat had a different suggestion. "Perhaps she was just being secretive."

"Secrets," Father Ron said. "Perry Hollow has a lot of them, as you well know. No one talks about them. But we know they're there, just waiting to be dug up. I think Constance discovered something in that book of hers. Something someone wants to keep buried. And they killed her for it."

"I know what Constance found," Kat blurted out. "I don't know where and I don't know what it means. If I told you, can you keep quiet about it?"

Intrigued, Father Ron dropped the mop back into the bucket. It sent up a wave of soapy water that splashed Kat's pant legs. The priest didn't even notice.

"If it's something that sheds light on the history of the town," he said, "I'd feel obliged to tell the others."

"You can't. Not just yet. So unless you promise to keep this between us, I can't tell you."

"There's always the confessional. That would guarantee my silence."

He was joking. Maybe. With his sly smile and serious eyes, Kat couldn't tell. Either way, she briefly considered it. But going to the confessional meant descending the bell tower stairs, and she was still too tired from her climb up.

"Constance found a skeleton," she said. "A woman's skeleton, to be precise. We don't know how old it is or where it came from, but it was located in the museum when the fire broke out."

The mop, pressured by the extra weight a dumbfounded Father Ron was putting on it, slipped out from beneath him. It flopped out of the bucket and onto the floor, the mop head spraying water as Father Ron stumbled forward.

"A skeleton?"

"Yup. Dug up not too long before Constance was killed."

Father Ron knelt to pick up the mop, his legs shaking. Instead of standing back up, he took a seat on the floor. "Why would she do such a thing?"

"I don't know," Kat said, sitting down next to him. "There are a lot of things I don't know, like if this was part of her research and if it had anything to do with her death."

"It's just like I told you," Father Ron said. "Someone wanted to keep it buried."

That seemed to be the case, but Kat still couldn't understand why. It was an old skeleton, most likely from someone who lived in the village before Perry Hollow was founded.

She couldn't think of anything that would make its discovery so dangerous that someone would commit murder over it.

"Do you recall Constance mentioning anything—anything at all—about a skeleton?"

Father Ron shook his head.

"What about burial grounds other than Oak Knoll Cemetery?" Kat persisted. "The people who lived here before the mill was founded had to bury their dead somewhere."

"Nothing," Father Ron said. "Have you checked Constance's office?"

Kat climbed to her feet before helping the priest do the same. "I've looked through her papers and didn't see any mention of a graveyard."

"What about the book?"

"I found lots of books," Kat said. "But nothing that looked important. Then again, I might have missed it. Most of what I saw is stuff only Constance would understand."

"Like what?"

"Random documents. Loose papers. Names of people no one knows. You ever hear her talk about someone named Brad Ford?"

Father Ron told her no. Just like all the others.

"I also found some financial papers," Kat said. "Those I could understand. Did you know the historical society was deep in the red?"

"I did," he said. "I'm ashamed to admit that I've spent quite a few hours praying about it."

"Why is that something to be ashamed of?"

Father Ron lifted his eyes to the heavens. "Because I suspect He has more important things to concern Himself with."

He dropped the mop back into the bucket and headed

toward the staircase, letting Kat go first. She took the steps slowly, making sure to grip the rough handrail the entire way down. That stairwell was not the kind of place where you wanted to lose your balance.

"When was the last time you saw Constance?"

"The night I was cleaning the museum. But I spoke to her on the phone last night."

"Before the Chamber of Commerce fund-raiser?"

"Yes," Father Ron said. "Sometime around seven. She told me she'd try to be there but that she had a lot of work to do. I assumed it was the kind of work she couldn't talk about and said no more. I also assumed she wouldn't be going to the party, so it didn't surprise me when she didn't show up."

They had reached the bottom of the stairs. Kat looked for Nick in the sanctuary, but it was empty. Peering out the open church door, she saw him sitting in the passenger seat of her Crown Vic, his face frozen in boredom.

"Was there anything that happened at the fund-raiser that did surprise you?"

"Other than the fact that people were surprised to see a priest drinking a glass of wine?"

"Besides that," Kat said. "Did you see anyone acting suspicious? I was told one of the town's volunteer firefighters got a little drunk."

"I didn't see that. The only thing I remember being unusual was that the fire alarm went off."

"Are you talking about the fire trucks on the way to the museum?"

Father Ron shook his head. "No. The fire alarm went off inside the restaurant. It was a false alarm, but they still had to clear the place out."

Kat felt a renewed sense of energy buzz through her body. This was something new. Something that both Claude Dobson and Burt Hammond had failed to mention.

"What time was this?"

"Shortly before the museum fire. About fifteen minutes or so. A lot of us were still outside when the fire trucks went by. Because the restaurant was emptied out, the area around it was a madhouse. People spilling out into the street. Groups getting separated. It was pretty chaotic."

And, Kat thought, a pretty convenient way for someone to slip out of the party unnoticed and make a surprise visit to Constance Bishop inside the history museum.

Maison D'Avignon looked like it had been plucked off the streets of Paris and placed in the center of Main Street. Café tables flanked the front door, which was painted a vibrant red. Boxes in the windows overflowed with flowers—daffodils and tulips in the spring, geraniums in the summer, robust mums at the moment—and ivy crawled up the walls. Atop the mansard roof was a weather vane in the shape of a snail, a nod to the escargots the restaurant served.

Kat didn't give the restaurant even a cursory glance as she stood on the sidewalk in front of it, talking into her cell phone.

"Are you ready?"

"Yes," Nick said. "My watch is set."

He was currently in front of the history museum, ready to time Kat's progress from one location to the other. The restaurant manager had confirmed Father Ron's statement about the fire alarm. It had gone off at the tail end of the fund-raiser.

At twelve-forty, to be precise. The fire at the museum was called in twelve minutes later. Kat's goal was to see if someone could conceivably pull the fire alarm, walk to the museum, conk Constance Bishop over the head, start the fire, and then meet up with others in that amount of time. Deep down, she doubted it.

"Okay," she said. "I'm going in three. Two. One."

Kat started off, going at the same pace as a speed walker. She knew running would be the fastest way to get there, but also the most conspicuous. A passerby would be less likely to notice someone speed walking up the street than sprinting. Especially if that person was dressed up for a formal function.

The shortest route to the museum was to walk five blocks north on Main Street before cutting left and going four more blocks. After one block's distance, she checked in with Nick.

"How's my time?"

"One minute."

When she had traversed another block, Nick, like clockwork, said, "Two minutes."

A block a minute. Definitely not fast enough. Kat increased her speed, noticing a few strange looks from people walking in the opposite direction. She slowed down again, crossing the three-block mark five seconds before Nick called out the time.

"Three minutes."

The key was to make good time on the approach to the museum. The way back was made easier, thanks to the fact that by then the streets had been filled with people emptied out of the restaurant by the fire alarm. *Rather chaotic* was how Father Ron had termed it. Especially once the sirens of the fire trucks alerted them to the real fire. Someone could have left the museum at twelve-fifty and met others halfway without looking too suspicious.

Kat finished the fourth block and started on the fifth. She was halfway over it when she realized Nick hadn't called out the time.

"How am I doing?"

There was no answer.

"Nick?" she said. "Are you there?"

Still no answer. She glanced at her phone to see if they had been disconnected. It happened often in a town as remote as Perry Hollow. But the call was still going on. Kat could see the seconds ticking away.

Something was wrong.

"Nick. Please answer me."

She walked faster, unconcerned that her quickening gait would look out of place to others. She was jogging by the time she rounded the corner and veered off Main Street. Up ahead, the smoke-scarred roof of the museum popped into view four blocks away.

When she was three blocks away, she caught sight of Nick, as well. He stood in front of the museum, phone clenched in a hand that dangled by his side. Instead of looking at his watch, he was studying something farther up the street.

Kat squinted, looking past Nick and seeing what had caught his attention. It was the Sleepy Hollow Inn, situated just down the street from the museum. Smoke rolled out its open door and flames danced just beyond the first-floor windows.

"Not again," Kat murmured. "Please, not again."

The words on Constance Bishop's hand zapped into her head. THIS IS JUST THE FIRST.

She hurried up the street, flying past Nick, hoping against hope that her eyes were deceiving her. But she knew they weren't. It was happening again. The Sleepy Hollow Inn was on fire, and in the queasy pit of her stomach, Kat knew it wasn't an accident.

NOON

The smell roused Henry from his slumber. An acrid odor, it suddenly seemed to be everywhere. When he inhaled, it stung the insides of his nostrils. Still held in sleep's grip, he couldn't immediately place it. It was sharp. Bitter. Intense. Like he was standing too close to a campfire.

Smoke.

That's what he was smelling. A lot of smoke. Somewhere very close by.

He sat up and opened his eyes. The sting of the smoke made him close them again immediately. It was closer than he had first thought. It was inside the Sleepy Hollow Inn. Inside his room.

A fire.

The last remnants of sleep vanished from Henry's brain as he pieced the situation together. The inn was on fire and he was still inside, stuck on the third floor.

He jumped out of bed, wide awake now, his body a

sparking jumble of hot-wired nerves. He needed to get out. Of the room. Of the hotel. And he needed to do it now.

But first he had to assess the situation. How close was the blaze? What was his best escape route? Most important, how much time did he have left?

Squinting through half-opened eyelids, Henry saw that a fair amount of smoke had infiltrated his room. It curled under the door before rising to the ceiling, where it collected in thick billows that rolled back down toward him. Its presence made him cough—deep, chest-rattling heaves that sucked the breath right out of him.

He stumbled to the door, reaching blindly for the handle. It was hot to the touch but not so warm that he couldn't twist it open. Then it was into the hallway, where the smoke was as gray and impenetrable as an English fog. Henry pulled the collar of his T-shirt over his nose and mouth before moving down the hall, desperately searching for an exit.

There wasn't one. Henry realized that as soon as he reached the stairs. The smoke was worse down there, rising through the narrow stairwell like it was being funneled through a chimney. Leaning over the banister and peering into the gloom, he could make out the searing orange glow of flames.

The fire danced across the first floor, a wall of flame where the front door should have been, officially blocking his most obvious escape route. It was now aiming for the second floor. Flames crawled up the walls and climbed the staircase, slithering up it step by terrifying step.

Henry had no choice but to retreat. He hurried down the hallway, the heat of the flames below reaching out to him and making beads of sweat pop onto his skin. Back in his room, he closed the door and looked around, desperately trying to plan his next move.

The towels Lottie Scott had delivered earlier sat on a chair near the door. Henry grabbed one and stuffed it under the door, trying to block more smoke from entering the room. Next, he ran to the room's only window. Opening it would clear out the remainder of the smoke and buy him some time.

It wouldn't budge, not even after Henry yanked on it with all the strength he could summon. The window was locked. Or it had been sealed shut. Or it was too weathered and warped to move. Whatever the cause, it didn't matter to Henry. He just needed to get it open.

He returned to the chair, lifting it by the seat back and charging toward the window. The chair's legs smashed through the glass, letting in desperately needed air. Henry felt it immediately. Cool and fresh—a balm for his smoke-scarred lungs.

Gulping it down in deep breaths, he continued to push the chair through the window, breaking away all the shards of glass that clung to the window frame. He gave the chair one last shove before letting go, watching it sail out the window and disappear from view.

Leaning on the windowsill, Henry pushed his entire upper body out the window. His room was located in the rear of the building, overlooking a small courtyard that was mostly dirt. The ground was about twenty-five feet below. Maybe more. It was hard to tell from that height. Making matters worse was the fact that his room had the bad luck to be situated over a set of concrete steps that led to the inn's basement. Not only did they add more distance between him and solid ground, but they also provided a hard and potentially deadly surface on which to land if he was forced to jump. The chair hadn't survived the fall too well. It was now in pieces—mere splinters of wood scattered on the steps and surrounding sidewalk.

A jump would be risky.

Not that Henry had much of a choice. The fire had reached the third floor. He could hear it consuming the floor and walls just beyond the door. A horrible crackling sound, it made him want to cover his ears.

The smoke, too, had increased. The towel under the door had managed to block a lot of it, but smoke still seeped in. Henry saw wisps of smoke insinuate themselves into the room and twist their way toward the ceiling.

He turned his attention to the window again. He heard sirens, somewhere distant but getting closer. Fire trucks. The fact that they were on their way offered no relief. Surely they'd be at the front of the building. He was at the back. No one would know he was still inside.

He looked down, seeing that smoke was pouring out of the basement door. The fire was there, too. Sharp licks of flame shot out of the door, stretching as far as they could reach before retreating. Yet another reason why he couldn't jump. He'd literally be leaping out of the frying pan and into the fire.

An earsplitting creak rose from just beyond the door. It quickly became an equally loud groan, followed by a crashing sound that made Henry's heart race even more.

The floor in the hall had given way.

The building was crumbling around him.

Henry eased himself onto the windowsill, legs dangling inside the room, upper body outside of it. Gripping the window frame for support, he leaned backward and looked up. The roof began several feet above him. There was about five inches of overhang from which rain gutters hung. If he stretched, there was a good possibility that he could reach it and pull himself onto the roof.

Again, it wasn't an ideal situation. Henry had no idea what he'd do once he was on the roof. But he had no choice. Not with more smoke seeping into the room. Not with another horrible crashing sound coming from just outside his door.

Henry lifted his right leg, bending it at the knee until the bottom of his shoe was touching the windowsill. He did the same with the left. Then he started to rise slowly, gripping the window frame the entire time.

Soon his head was past the window, moving beyond it. Then his shoulders. He could no longer see what was going on inside the room, but he could certainly hear it. More crackling. More creaks. More noises of a building falling to pieces all around him.

He wasn't sure, but he thought he heard the door to the room bending from the pressure. The sound was ominous—a deep groan of wood being stretched to the breaking point. Accompanying it was a series of pops as the door started to splinter from within. Soon it would burst open, letting the flames and smoke flood the room.

Henry was fully standing now, balanced on the windowsill. Looking up, he saw the overhang of the roof, just within arm's reach. He stretched out a hand, his fingertips scraping along a shingle before slipping off.

The sudden movement threw off his balance, and for a terrifying second Henry thought he was going to tumble from the window ledge. He grabbed the rainspout that hung from the roof, bending it as he tried to regain his composure.

Below him, the room was quickly filling with smoke. It

puffed out the open window in gray tendrils that twisted around his body. It was hotter down there, too. Henry could feel the heat from the fire on his legs and feet.

He reached for the roof again, the palm of his hand pressing into the stubble of the shingles. This time, his fingers stayed. Now his right hand was on the roof. His left still gripped the edge of the window.

It was now or never.

Henry took a deep breath as he let go of the window frame. He raised his left hand above his head, reaching for the roof. He touched it, slipped, touched it again. Now he was stretched over the open window like a shade that had been pulled tight—both hands on the roof, both feet on the windowsill.

A loud crash echoed through the room. The door. Finally giving way and sending a blast of hot air rushing toward him. Henry pulled himself upward, legs now dangling, as a tide of fire and smoke rolled past him out the window.

Grunting from the exertion, his arms burning as hard as the fire below him, Henry kept pulling until his head and shoulders were above the edge of the roof. With one last push, he propelled himself higher, leaning forward until his chest was flat against the shingles. With legs kicking and arms clawing, he scrambled fully onto the pitched roof.

He had made it.

He was, at least for a minute or two, out of harm's way.

Just like the night before, the street was a rush of activity. The fire trucks had screeched to a halt in front of the Sleepy Hollow Inn. The sidewalk across the street teemed with onlookers. Oblivious drivers turning onto the road were blocked by

Carl Bauersox on one side and Tony Vasquez on the other. The motorists tried to backtrack, doing awkward three-point turns in the middle of the street while dodging more cars that turned on to it. Standing amid the chaos, staring at the fire in rapt disbelief, was Kat Campbell.

Watching the flames dance behind the hotel's windows, Kat could only think about the words of warning scrawled on Constance's hand. Had she known there'd be another fire? Is this why she'd written them? Kat doubted she'd ever know for sure, but it was something to consider. Especially now that the Sleepy Hollow Inn was ablaze, its owner a numb figure standing alone in the middle of the street.

"It's gone," Lottie Scott cried to no one and everyone. "All gone."

Kat joined her, wrapping an arm around her shoulders. But it was cold comfort. Lottie's pride and joy—and Perry Hollow's only hotel—was a goner, no matter how fast the fire squad put the blaze out.

As they worked to douse the flames, Kat tried to count their ranks, seeing if Danny Batallas was among them. But they were moving so fast, and the scene was so chaotic, that she couldn't keep track. She found herself counting the same firefighter twice or mistaking one for another. The only person she recognized without a doubt was Dutch Jansen, who led the charge as they unleashed water onto the burning hotel.

Remembering what Larry Sheldon had told her, Kat also kept an eye on the steadily growing crowd. Once again, she recognized a lot of them. Dave and Betty Freeman, no doubt rattled by two fires on their street in less than twelve hours, held hands and exchanged worried looks. The four remaining members of the historical society stood side by side, watching flames consume yet another Perry Hollow landmark.

Scanning the throng, Kat caught a flash of blond hair in the middle of the crowd. It vanished behind a cluster of onlookers, only to reappear a moment later farther down the street, away from the crowd.

Kat left Lottie's side and pushed into the crowd, again losing sight of the man. She only found him once she was also beyond the wall of bystanders. She couldn't make out a face—the person was, strangely enough, looking away from the fire—but she could tell that the blond hair belonged to a man. It was pulled into a ponytail and trickled down his neck to a black-collared trench coat.

"Stop right there!"

Although she could have been shouting at anyone, the man in the ponytail knew she was talking to him.

"You in the ponytail! Stop walking and stay where you are!"

The man started to run, his trench coat flapping behind him. Kat gave chase, trying hard to keep up with the stranger. But he was taller and he was faster. The man seemed to realize this as he glanced back to see her receding figure. A smile crossed his face—a smug one that would have infuriated Kat had she not seen Nick Donnelly standing a few feet up the street. When the man reached him, Nick thrust his cane into the street.

The stranger, caught by surprise, tripped over it. He fell to the asphalt, arms thrust forward, trench coat billowing over him.

Nick pressed the tip of his cane in the center of the man's back. "The chief told you to stop."

Kat caught up to them and flipped the man over. He was wearing the same clothes as the night before—white shirt, black pants, weird buckled shoes. But as he sat up, his coal-black eyes were wide with fear.

"What the hell are you doing?" he yelped, looking first at Kat, then Nick. "What did I do?"

"You didn't stop when she told you to," Nick said.

"That's not a crime."

"It is when I'm the police chief," Kat said, angrily tapping her badge. "Now I need to see some ID."

"What? Are you kidding me?"

Kat knelt until she was eye level with the stranger. "Do you see my face? Does it look like I'm kidding?"

The man had scraped his hands during the fall. He looked down at his palms, which were speckled with dirt and blood. Wincing, he reached into his coat and pulled out a wallet. He opened it and held it out so Kat could see the driver's license inside.

According to the license, the man's name was Connor Hawthorne. He was twenty-seven and hailed from Salem, Massachusetts. Yet none of that explained what he was doing in Perry Hollow.

"Here for a visit?" Kat asked.

"Work, actually."

"And what kind of work is that?"

"I don't have to answer that." Connor Hawthorne climbed to his feet, trying to wipe dirt from his trench coat but smearing it with blood instead. "I'm an American citizen. I have rights, you know."

"You do," Kat said. "But as police chief of this town, I have the right to question people I find suspicious. So let's just save both of us a whole lot of trouble and tell me what kind of work brought you to Perry Hollow."

Connor tilted his head and smiled. It was the same smug grin he had given earlier, only now it made Kat more unnerved than infuriated. Everything about Mr. Hawthorne was slightly unsettling, from the razor-sharp cheekbones to his too dark eyes.

"I'm a witch," he said.

Nick let out an incredulous laugh. "Don't you mean warlock?"

"There's no such thing as a warlock," Connor said, his voice a strange brew of defensiveness and annoyance. "Besides, men can be witches. It's not gender-specific."

"Thanks for the lesson," Kat replied. "What does it have to do with my town?"

"Unless you're going to arrest me, I don't have to say another word."

Patience wasn't Kat's strong suit, especially when she could tell the mysterious Mr. Hawthorne was hiding something. Yet he was right. He didn't have to tell them anything, even if she did arrest him. Which she couldn't do.

"I have no grounds to arrest you. At least not because you're a witch."

"I know," Connor said. "Isn't freedom of religion a bitch?"

And so was the fact that Kat couldn't slap cuffs on him simply for being an asshole. But she didn't have a choice. She was obliged to let him go.

"Mr. Hawthorne, I don't trust you. And I'm going to keep an eye on you. So whatever brought you here, you better stay on your best behavior. Do I make myself clear?"

Connor wasn't allowed to answer. A scream—short and

startled—echoed up the street, cutting him off. It was followed by a collective gasp rising from the crowd. Kat, too far away to see what was happening, took a few steps forward, straining to get a better view. After a few more shuffles down the street, she saw what the crowd was looking at.

It was a man. Staggering along the roof of the Sleepy Hollow Inn. Vanishing and reappearing in the wafting smoke.

"Oh, my God," Kat said. "It's Henry."

The roof was hot, close to scorching. Henry felt it through the soles of his shoes, which were slowly melting. They stuck to the shingles—also melting—and caused him to stumble awkwardly. But that was the least of his problems. Now that he was on the roof, Henry had no idea where to go next.

Standing in the center of the roof, he looked to neighboring structures, seeing if one of them was close enough for him to leap to safety. The nearest one, a residence by the looks of it, was at least ten yards away. Definitely not within jumping distance.

He backtracked, heading up the pitched roof until he was at the very top. There was more support there, which would come in handy if the roof started to cave in. Judging from the increasing heat and the roar of the flames inside the hotel, that would be sooner rather than later.

His perch gave him a view of the opposite side of the street, where it looked like most of Perry Hollow had gathered. Some stared up in openmouthed shock. Others couldn't bear to look. A small group formed a circle of joined hands, their heads bowed.

They were praying, Henry realized. Praying for him.

He recognized two of the people standing in the crowd—

Kat Campbell and Nick Donnelly. They were shouting something he couldn't hear, gesturing wildly in ways he couldn't understand. Kat was especially emphatic, waving her arms toward the right side of the roof.

Following her flailing arms, Henry saw the top of a ladder rise into view. A second later, a firefighter appeared, clinging to the top rungs.

"Come on!" he shouted. "Hurry!"

Henry bolted across the roof, trying hard not to lose his balance, trying even harder not to notice the sounds of collapsing wood getting louder from within the hotel. He willfully ignored the smoke that seemed to rise between the shingles like vapor from a steam grate. All he noticed was the ladder. If he reached it, he'd be safe.

Having made it across the roof, he now had to descend its slope. It was a tricky proposition. The angle was steep, and his increasingly gummy shoes made it even harder to navigate. Henry's first instinct was to sit down and slide toward the ladder. He dismissed the thought quickly. If the heat radiating off the roof was turning his shoes to liquid, imagine what it would do to his pants. No, he needed to descend on foot.

Henry started down the roof, walking with his legs widened, arms extended for balance.

The firefighter on the ladder frantically waved for him to move faster. "We don't have much time, man!"

Henry tried to pick up the pace. He was halfway down the side of the roof, slipping a little but remaining upright. The firefighter began to descend the ladder, making room for him to climb on.

"Just get to the ladder," Henry muttered under his breath. "Be fast. Don't fall. Just get—"

He stopped talking, listening instead to another ominous sound coming from inside the hotel. It was one he hadn't heard before—a sizzling noise, underscored by a sharp whistle that reminded him of a tea kettle at full boil.

The shingles at his feet seemed to melt away, replaced by licks of orange as the fire officially broke through the roof. Thriving on this new patch of oxygen, the flames leaped high, consuming even more of the roof's surface.

Henry fell backward, landing hard, the shingles iron-hot through the fabric of his pants. The hole in front of him widened and large chunks of the roof disappeared into the fiery depths.

Desperate to get away, Henry crab-crawled backward, scurrying once again up the roof. The fire followed his path, eating through the areas he had just escaped, making him move even faster. It seemed like the flames were intent on grabbing him, punching through the roof in a desperate attempt to drag him kicking and screaming back into the hotel.

Henry managed to evade each grasp, pushing himself higher and higher. He soon found himself back at the roof's peak and almost tumbling down the other side. But he caught himself—barely—and sat for a second, mind spinning.

He needed to get off the roof. Immediately. And now that the ladder was no longer an option, he was left with only one choice.

He had to jump.

Henry didn't want to. There was probably forty feet between the roof and the ground. It was enough to hurt him badly. Enough to kill him. But at least he had a chance of surviving the fall. Remaining on top of the Sleepy Hollow Inn would only lead to one result.

To his right, the fire continued to chomp across the roof. To his left, another hole opened up, spewing flames. He couldn't wait any longer. He had to jump and he had to do it now.

Hopping to his feet, Henry allowed a split-second glance at the street below. The prayer circle was still in full swing. In fact, it looked like it had grown.

Good. He was going to need all the help he could get.

Exhaling one last, terrified breath, Henry started to run down the roof. His mind, no doubt coping with the prospect of imminent death, shot off in strange tangents. He thought of the Ring Cycle again and Valhalla burning. The only production he had seen—at the Met, during college—had used shreds of fluttering orange silk to represent the flames. Skipping amid real fire now, he realized how realistic they had been.

His thoughts jumped to Gia, his wife, dead going on six years now. He flashed back to the accident that killed her. The same one that caused his first round of scars. Then his son entered his thoughts. His unborn son. The child snatched away from him before he could leave the womb.

His thoughts leaped again. To Deana, of course. And how good she smelled when he held her in bed. How soft she felt in his arms. Then, oddly, to Kat. Her smile at the diner that morning. Her awkwardness the first time they met.

Henry was jerked back to the present when a new hole opened up in the roof, right beneath him. Only momentum allowed him to clear it, his legs seemingly skimming on the air. Then he fell forward onto his stomach. The force of the impact knocked most of the air out of his lungs. The undiluted terror he felt evaporated the rest.

Yet he still moved, sliding downward on his stomach, hands out in front of him, the lip of the roof getting closer.

Henry twisted his body when he reached the edge, aiming to hit the ground feet first. His legs went over the side first, the roof vanishing out from under them. Gravity immediately took over, tugging him downward, the edge of the roof sliding past his crotch, his stomach, his chest.

He clawed at the shingles, refusing to completely surrender to gravity even as the remainder of his body cleared the roof. Henry's fingers, now bloody and burned, scraped along their last patch of shingles before bumping against the rainspout.

Then, faster than he wanted to and more terrified than he thought he'd be, Henry Goll slid off the roof.

Kat couldn't bear to look. Not anymore. Not after Dutch Jansen and his ladder were pushed away by the mounting flames. It was bad enough seeing Henry stumble helplessly across the roof, trapped and terrified. But she couldn't bring herself to watch him jump from it, or worse, plummet into the flames. So she squeezed her eyes shut and turned her head for good measure, waiting for the reaction of the crowd to tell her what had happened.

She heard a collective gasp, followed by a surge of motion. Nick grabbed her arm and shook it until her eyes opened.

"He didn't fall," he yelped. "The son of a bitch is still hanging on!"

Kat reluctantly turned her head, seeing that Henry was now dangling from the rain gutter attached to the lip of the roof. His body, suddenly halted, swung forward, bringing him perilously close to the hotel's fiery exterior wall. He turned his face away from the flames as, above him, the rainspout sank under his weight.

Kat knew he couldn't stay that way. The walls were

unstable. The flames and smoke were everywhere. He needed to let go eventually. And she would be there to help break his fall.

"We can catch him," she said, now dragging Nick toward the burning hotel. "It's not too late to help him."

Others joined her, surging forward. On the edge of her vision, she saw Carl Bauersox step into the fray. Tony Vasquez did the same, running right beside her. Soon there were about a dozen of them scrambling past the fire trucks. Dutch Jansen, back on the ground, tried to get them to stop, shouting that the fire was too strong and the building too unstable. They ignored the order, giving him no choice but to join the circle forming below Henry.

Kat shouted up at him. "Let go! We've got you!"

Henry didn't hesitate. One quick glance at the ground was all he needed to convince him to let go.

He fell faster than Kat thought he would, a straight drop to the group beneath him. There was a flurry of movement—hands reaching upward, kicking legs, bodies tumbling like pins in a bowling alley. Kat felt the heel of a shoe, Henry's presumably, glance off her shoulder before knocking into Tony's chest. They fell forward, pulled into the scrum, piled on top of one another.

When it was all over, Henry was on solid ground. A little worse for wear, maybe, but mostly unscathed. When he stood, the crowd watching from the other side of the street let out a cheer. His rescuers patted him on the back before shaking hands and congratulating themselves on their success. They lifted Henry onto their shoulders, not stopping when he began to protest.

Dutch Jansen shooed them away, pushing them out of range of the fire until only Kat, Nick, and Tony remained.

"You've got to move, folks," Dutch told them. "Give us room to put out this goddamn fire."

Tony helped Kat to her feet. She tried to do the same for Nick, who was flat on the ground, wincing in pain. It was his knee, she knew. He had hurt it during Henry's rescue.

"You okay?" she asked, offering him a hand.

Nick grunted as he pulled himself into a kneeling position. "I've been better."

Kat slid a shoulder under one of Nick's arms and lifted him into a standing position. Tony joined in, supporting Nick's other side. Together, the three of them began to shuffle away from the hotel.

They made it two steps before Dutch Jansen was upon them again, shouting. "Get out of here, Kat! It's too dangerous!"

Behind them, the fire raged. Kat felt its heat on her back, as intense as it was deadly. Sneaking a glance back at the hotel, she saw that the roof was completely engulfed by flames leaping high into the air. Dutch was right. It *was* too dangerous.

"Nick," she said, "you need to move faster, okay? Can you do that?"

If he responded, she didn't hear it. All she heard was the roar of fire and the sound of breaking timber.

The inn's roof was about to collapse.

It emitted a loud, drawn-out crack—like a tree just before it topples. Then the roof caved in, crashing into what remained of the third floor of the hotel before continuing on to the second. The fall continued as the combined weight of the roof and the third floor smashed through the inn's second level and then the first.

The whole thing—level after level of burning building—came to a stop in the basement. The impact sent up a wave of flames that burst outward, hurtling toward them. The rush of hot air that followed shoved them forward, almost lifting them off their feet. Kat hit the ground again, no longer able to see, no longer hearing her screams.

She rolled onto her back, squinting against the orange brightness of the blaze, seeing that with the roof and floors gone, there was nothing left to support the exterior walls. The one closest to them leaned forward, set loose from the rest of the hotel. Flames danced along its surface.

The wall tilted even more, creaking and crackling. Then it fell forward.

"Kat! Look out!"

It was Nick. Just behind her. Shoving her forward. Kat rolled along the ground, feeling the sidewalk beneath her. Then she hit the curb, bouncing into the gravel-dusted street.

She came to a stop facing the fire at a sideways view. The ground was now vertical. The falling wall horizontal. Disoriented and confused, she saw that Nick had also pushed Tony, who was rolling the same way she had.

Now it was only him, caught in the shadow of the fiery wall. He looked her way, wide-eyed and frightened. His expression changed, just for a second, when he saw that she was out of harm's way. It was, Kat realized, a look of relief passing across Nick Donnelly's face.

Then the wall crashed down on top of him and Kat could no longer see him at all.

1 P.M.

Kat forced herself to stop crying long enough to make a phone call, although there were plenty of tears left to be shed. She felt them pressing at the corners of her eyes, waiting to be released. But she had to be composed. Just for a few minutes. Sitting on a bench outside the hospital, she sniffed once and wiped her cheeks. Then she dialed her phone.

Lucy Meade answered a few rings later, her voice friendly and unsuspecting.

"Hey, Kat," she said. "I was just about to call you. I've got big news. My friend took a look at the femur. He agrees it had been in a fire. Even more, he got an age. According to him, the owner of those bones died more than three hundred years ago."

Kat stayed silent, not quite sure what she should say and how she should sound. Lucy noticed the lack of response and said, "Kat? You still there?"

"Lucy." Her voice was a tremulous croak. "I'm calling about Nick. Something terrible has happened."

"What do you mean?"

She tried to explain everything as best she could. Nick's surprise arrival in Perry Hollow. Him helping with the case. The fire at the bed-and-breakfast. But when it came time to break the really bad news, she found she couldn't. The words just wouldn't come.

"Kat," Lucy said, "what happened to Nick?"

"The wall—" Kat tried and failed to choke back a sob. "It collapsed on top of him."

Lucy's shock was palpable, even over the phone. Kat heard a sharp intake of air, followed by a worried "Is he okay? Tell me he'll be okay."

He'll be okay. Those were the words Kat so desperately wanted to say. But it would have been a lie. She had no idea if Nick would be okay. That could only be answered by the doctors currently trying to save his life.

"He's in surgery now," she said. "He's hurt really bad."

Kat didn't know with certainty all the things that were wrong. She was only aware of what the paramedics had uttered on the way to the hospital. Broken bones. Trauma to the head. Second-degree burns. Internal bleeding. Sitting numb and motionless in the back of the ambulance, she realized that the paramedics were surprised Nick was still alive.

"Is he going to survive?" Lucy asked. "Be straight with me, Kat."

"I don't know. I honestly don't know."

Lucy said she'd be there as fast as she could. Kat told her she'd call immediately if anything changed. Then the call was over, and not a moment too soon. Just as Kat was saying good-bye, the tears started to flow again.

This time, she knew, there would be no stopping them.

Weeping openly, she returned to the hospital's emergency room and took a seat next to Henry Goll. There were bandages on his fingers—the gutter he hung from had cut them badly—and a mean-looking scrape on his chin. Kat could only imagine what they looked like to the others in the waiting room. Probably like a pair of chimney sweeps—faces blackened with ash, holes the size of dimes burned into their clothes.

The stench of smoke rising off them was so strong that no one even tried to sit near them. They had a whole corner to themselves. Perfect, Kat thought, for inconsolable crying.

"Sorry for being such a wreck," she told Henry. "In the past year, Nick and I have grown very close."

Henry gave her a surprised glance. "You two aren't—"

Kat stopped him before he could go any further. "God, no. That would be like sleeping with my brother. If I had a brother."

Sitting in the sterile waiting room, tears forming clean streaks down her soot-smeared cheeks, Kat realized that Nick was the closest she'd get to having a sibling. That made the thought of losing him all the more terrifying.

"I just don't know what I'll do without him."

Henry put an arm over her shoulder, a gesture Kat found as surprising as she did comforting.

"Nick will be okay," he said. "If I remember correctly, he's as stubborn as they come."

He was right about that. Kat had never known the true meaning of the word *determination* until she met Nick Donnelly. He was fueled by an inner fire most people didn't possess. It's what had driven him to become a cop and, when that abruptly ended, a private detective. It's why he had come to Perry Hollow, even though the death of Constance Bishop had nothing to do with him. And it's what had allowed him to save Kat's life, not once but twice.

"Yes," she said, trying to sound convinced. "He's definitely going to pull through."

Yet when she saw a doctor enter the waiting room and look in their direction, she braced for the worst. She gripped Henry's hand as he approached, knowing the first words out of his mouth were going to be that Nick hadn't made it. She stared at the floor, not wanting to see the pained regret in his eyes as he came to a stop in front of her.

"Chief Campbell?"

Kat refused to respond, forcing Henry to do it.

"How can we help you?"

He sounded so strong. So calm. Even after his own brush with death that afternoon. Kat was grateful for his presence, and wondered what kind of wreck she'd be if Henry hadn't been there.

"We've just got Lieutenant Vasquez situated in his room," the doctor said. "He'd like to talk with the chief."

Not a word about Nick. Considering the circumstances, Kat took that to be a positive sign and loosened her white-knuckled grip on Henry.

"I guess I'll go talk to him," she said.

Her legs felt rubbery as she moved out of the emergency wing and into the general hospital. Part of it was nerves—her whole body felt numb and jittery at the same time. The rest was exhaustion, both physical and mental. She felt so tired that she was surprised she could even walk at all.

But walk she did, down hallway after hallway painted the starkest shade of white Kat had ever seen. Not for the first time, she wondered why hospital décor was so mind-numbing. People *needed* something to look at during their dark hours there. Something to focus on other than their pain. Instead, she had more white walls sliding past on her way to the reception desk.

The nurse stationed there gave her directions to a room on the second floor where Tony Vasquez would be spending the night. Although he'd managed to avoid the collapsing wall, Tony still hadn't escaped unscathed. The rubble had caught up to him as he was trying to tumble away. The result was a few broken bones and even more bruises. Still, he was lucky. He had been a few seconds away from being in the same condition as Nick.

Entering his room, Kat found him in bed, propped up by a stack of pillows. His left leg was in a cast. His right arm was in a sling. A bandage on his forehead slowly seeped red.

"Any word on Nick yet?" he asked.

Kat shook her head. "Still waiting. How are you?"

"Fan-fucking-tastic."

"I guess you're going to be here a while."

"At least a day or two," Tony said. "Which is why I just called Gloria."

He was referring to Gloria Ambrose, who ran the state police's Bureau of Criminal Investigation. That made her Tony's boss. And Nick's, once upon a time.

"Is she coming to Perry Hollow?"

"Sort of," Tony said. "She's in Hawaii right now."

"Hawaii?"

"Even state police bigwigs need to go on vacation. She's going to try to catch the next flight out here. Even then, she still won't arrive until tomorrow morning."

Kat began to get dizzy from confusion. "Why are you telling me all this?"

"Because," Tony said, "it's pretty obvious that I can't do much work from a hospital bed. And until Gloria gets here, we need someone to lead the investigation."

"And that would be me?"

Tony paused to sit up higher, wincing the entire time. Kat saw a paper cup on the table next to his bed. Sitting within it, like a pair of robin's eggs at the bottom of a nest, were two blue pills. Painkillers that he refused to take for fear it would slow his thoughts.

"Gloria thinks you'll manage just fine," he said. "I do, too."

Honestly, Kat had forgotten all about the investigation during the chaos of the fire. It was jarring how quickly priorities could change. One minute she was concerned about a homicidal arsonist on the loose. The next, she was praying that her best friend would survive the hour. Now Tony wanted her to once again focus on catching a killer.

But she couldn't. Not with Nick's life hanging in the balance. She needed to be at the hospital when he was out of surgery. She needed to see him and hold his hand and tell him that everything would be okay.

"I'll give you the names of the key people," Tony said. "They're close to finishing the inventory of the museum. I have another—"

"Tony, stop." Kat stood by his bed with her arms crossed. She shook her head like a stubborn child, refusing to hear any more. "I can't just take over your investigation. There's got to be someone from the state police who can do it."

"Not one who knows the town inside and out like you do," Tony said.

"They can manage without me for one day."

"And that might be one day too late."

Kat felt the frustration building up inside her. It caused her shoulders to tighten. A slight twinge of pain flared at her lower back.

"You don't get it, do you? The investigation is no longer my main priority. Nick is. And I need to be here for him."

Tony narrowed his eyes and thrust his jaw forward. He

could look mean when he wanted to, and he did that afternoon, even stuck in a hospital bed and gasping with pain. "You know the fire at that hotel was not a coincidence. Someone set it on purpose. Just like at the museum. And he's probably picking the next place to torch this very minute. So if you want to be here for Nick, then get out there and catch whoever the hell is doing this. He would want you to."

Kat had no doubt about that. And if the roles were reversed and she was the one clinging to life, she knew Nick wouldn't stop looking for the person who had caused it.

"But what if Nick . . ."

She let her voice trail off, unable to say the word blaring like a siren in her brain. *Dies*. What if Nick dies and she misses being able to say her final good-byes?

"He won't," Tony said, also preferring that the word remained unspoken. "So put that thought out of your head right now."

Through the open door, she heard footsteps bouncing through the hallway. Someone was running. Right to Tony's room, from the sound of it. Kat's entire body clenched up, once again preparing for bad news. Turning to the door, she saw Henry skid into view.

"Nick's out of surgery," he announced. "The doctor wants to talk to Kat."

It was freezing in the hospital's intensive care unit—the kind of artificial chill that seemed to seep directly into your veins. Standing in the middle of it, talking to Nick's doctor, Kat had to hug herself to keep warm. What the doctor was telling her didn't help matters. Hearing it alone would have made her blood turn cold.

"Your friend is in very bad shape. He sustained multiple injuries, most of them life-threatening."

"What kind of injuries?"

Kat knew the doctor slightly. His name was Samil Patel and his son was a classmate of James. Yet knowing him didn't make hearing the news any easier. There was little emotion in Dr. Patel's voice, no attempt to soften the blow.

"The worst of them is a cerebral contusion. Mr. Donnelly managed to avoid a skull fracture, which is good. But the contusion could result in brain hemorrhaging, so we have to monitor it very closely."

He went on, listing all the ways in which Nick had been hurt. Fractured ribs. A broken collarbone. Damaged organs. ("Internal bleeding is still a possibility," Dr. Patel added.) Kat pretended to listen patiently, when in reality she tried not to hear a single word. She didn't want to know how much Nick was suffering. That only made the situation worse.

"Doc," she said, "just tell me if you think he's going to survive."

Dr. Patel shrugged, an uncertain rise and fall of the shoulders that offered Kat little hope.

"I'd put his chances of survival at fifty percent," he said. "The next twenty-four hours are going to be crucial. I'm most concerned about the head trauma. Mr. Donnelly is in a coma at the moment."

Kat's legs buckled. For a brief moment, she was sure she was going to pass out. But she recovered, planting both feet on the floor and saying, "How long do you think it will last?"

"I don't know," Dr. Patel replied. "Maybe a few hours. Maybe a few days. Maybe forever."

Forever. The word immediately lodged in her brain, refusing to budge.

"We're monitoring his brain functions," the doctor said. "The fact that there's anything to monitor at all is a good sign. It means he'll probably make it. But if parts of his brain stop working properly in the next few hours—which could happen—then your friend's condition will only get worse."

From her vantage point in the ICU hallway, Kat could see the inside of Nick's room. If she craned her neck a bit, she could even make out the foot of the bed. Nick himself, however, remained frustratingly out of view. She pictured him as a vegetable, growing old in a hospital bed. Never moving. His skin wrinkling and turning yellow with age. A Rip Van Winkle beard sprouting on his chin, growing whiter and longer with each passing year.

"Can I see him?" she asked.

"I'm afraid not. It's usually customary to wait at least two hours after surgery until a visitor can see a patient. Even then, the visitor should be a family member."

Kat looked up at Dr. Samil Patel, eyes brimming with tears. Their sons knew each other. They played together at recess. She hoped this bond, however inconsequential, would make him take pity on her.

"Please," she said. "I'm the only family he's got."

The doctor must have seen something in her eyes beyond mere tears. Determination, maybe. Or pure fear that she'd never see Nick again. Whatever it was, he relented.

"It'll have to be quick," he said. "No more than a minute or two."

Dr. Patel led her to a nearby sink and made Kat wash her

hands. Then he ushered her to Nick's door. Apprehension made her pause at the threshold. She was fully aware that it might be the last time she ever saw him. A minute or two to say good-bye just didn't seem right.

Steeling herself with a deep breath, Kat stepped inside.

Nick lay unconscious in the room's only bed, a blanket pulled up to his waist. He looked so small, so fragile. His entire head was covered by a helmet of bandages, wisps of hair peeking out from under it. His hands had been placed on his stomach, one on top of the other. Kat didn't like the position. It made him resemble a corpse just waiting for the coffin.

Although the room he had been placed in was quite large, the sheer amount of hospital equipment crammed into it made it look much smaller. Nick was attached to all of it. Kat noticed a heart rate monitor, its beeping green line spiking across the screen. On the other side of the bed was an EEG machine, monitoring his brain activity in dozens of thin white lines that undulated against a black background. A breathing tube had been inserted into his nose. Another tube ran from the crook of his right arm to an IV stand next to the bed.

"Nick." Kat didn't know if he could hear her. Even if he couldn't, she continued talking anyway. Some things needed to be spoken. "I hope this isn't the last time I see you. But if it is, I want to thank you for saving my life again today. I know you'd shrug it off like you always do, but I still wouldn't be on this earth if it wasn't for you. So I thank you. James thanks you."

Her thoughts drifted briefly to her son, playing at home with Lou, hopefully oblivious to the drama going on in the rest of the town. James adored Nick, and Kat knew he'd be worried when he found out something bad had happened.

She also knew he'd insist on coming to the hospital for a visit. And she vowed to make sure it happened eventually.

But first, she needed to fulfill a promise to Nick. One she said aloud among the beeps and pulses that filled his hospital room.

"I'm going to find the person responsible for this. I swear I will, Nick. And when I do, I'm going to make him pay."

Standing in the open doorway, Dr. Patel cleared his throat. "I'm afraid time's up," he said.

Kat quickly reached out and clasped Nick's hand. Just like the rest of the ICU, his skin was ice-cold. She held on to his hand for a few seconds, trying to will some of her warmth into it. Then she let go and allowed herself to be led from the room.

Exiting the ICU, Kat felt more tired than she had in years. She had gone without sleep before, most notably when James was young and she was a single mom trying to keep food on the table. But she was much older now, and the sleep deprivation, coupled with the stress of the day, threatened to break her.

Her movements were sudden and strange—weird lurchings that probably made her look drunk as she walked the hospital's halls. Her eyes were getting bleary. Kat noticed a white fuzziness encroaching on the edges of her vision. She tried not to yawn, for fear it would set off a nonstop chain of them that would last for hours.

She needed sleep. At least a few hours of it. But sleep wasn't on the agenda. Not for a while, anyway. Not until she found whoever was going around torching buildings in Perry Hollow.

Before returning to Tony's room and agreeing to take over the investigation until a replacement could arrive, Kat took a detour to the nearby ladies' room. She made a beeline toward the sink, where she splashed cold water on her face. It was bracing but not enough to wake her up.

Kat needed more.

She turned the water on full blast, making sure it was as cold as possible. She waited, thrumming her fingers on the countertop and examining herself in the mirror. Her reflection, with its bloodshot eyes and blotchy skin, horrified her. Dark circles, as swollen and purple as a bruise, hung beneath her eyes. And the less she looked at her greasy hair, the better.

Kat averted her gaze, staring down at the sink instead. Water had filled it to the halfway point. Enough for what she had in mind.

She leaned over the basin.

She counted to three.

Then, taking a deep breath, Kat plunged her head into the water.

---

2 P.M.

Henry stood completely still, letting the hot spray of the shower rush over him. It felt good having the water rinse away all the grime and soot he had accumulated that afternoon. The dirt ran off his body in dark streaks, exposing patches of slick, rosy flesh. The cleaner he got, the lighter he felt.

He reached for the shampoo and sniffed. It smelled too

perfumy, like something he would have found in the Sleepy Hollow Inn. Still, beggars couldn't be choosers, and he was most definitely a beggar in the house of Kat Campbell. Since she'd been kind enough to offer the use of her shower, he wasn't going to turn up his nose at the shampoo just because he didn't like the scent.

Lathering up his hair, Henry thought about all the other things he'd have to borrow from Kat. Everything he had brought with him to the United States had been destroyed in the fire. His clothes. His wallet and passport. Even his phone, which meant his editor couldn't get in touch with him. He imagined Dario Giambusso frantically calling and wondering why he wasn't picking up.

Not that Henry would be able to tell him much. The flames had also consumed his notes on the Fanelli article, leaving him with nothing to show for his work. The only thing Henry had going for him was his meeting with Lucia Trapani later that night. He hoped that would at least appease Dario. If he ever got the chance to talk to him between now and then.

Henry stuck his head under the stream of the shower and rinsed off his hair. Watching the soapy water swirl around his feet before spiraling down the drain, he thought about the other woman he was scheduled to meet that day.

It was two o'clock, the time Deana Swan wanted him to come over. Henry hadn't decided whether he would go or not when the fire at the bed-and-breakfast and its aftermath made the choice for him. Yet he couldn't help but wonder if Deana was still waiting for him, sitting in the breakfast nook of her quaint little kitchen. That was where he had usually found her, no matter the time of day. In the evenings, when he'd come over after work. In the early hours of the morning, after he had spent the night. As he stepped out of the shower, Henry realized that it would have been nice to see Deana that way one more time.

But it was too late for that now. By the time he got there—and he still wasn't sure he wanted to go—she'd be gone. Deana wasn't one for patience. He remembered that from their time together. One rainy Sunday afternoon he had tried to introduce her to opera, playing a recording of *Parsifal*. She had lasted all of five minutes before begging him to switch to something else.

Once he toweled off, Henry got dressed in new clothes Kat purchased for him on the way back from the hospital. The store—a tiny men's shop on Main Street—had a limited selection in his size. The jeans, although the right length, were sized for someone with far more gut than he possessed. When he belted them, the waistband bunched awkwardly around his hips. His shirt wasn't much better. The fit was fine, but Henry didn't think red and black flannel was really his style.

Exiting the bathroom, Henry heard voices coming from below. He descended the stairs into Kat's living room, which opened up into an adjacent dining room. Beyond that was the kitchen, now filled with state troopers. They stood shoulder to shoulder—there wasn't enough room to sit down—eating sandwiches from the Perry Hollow Diner and washing them down with coffee gulped from chipped mugs.

Henry couldn't see Kat. Barely an inch over five feet, she was blocked by the taller cops. But he could hear her voice, rising from an area near the kitchen sink.

"I know we're all exhausted," she was saying. "It's been

a long day already and we've got a lot of work under our belt. But we need to do more. Now, we need to focus."

Inside the kitchen, a few of the troopers had shifted position. In the sliver of space between them, Henry could see Kat leaning against the kitchen sink with a man who looked so young he was almost boyish. She introduced him as Larry Sheldon and let him have the floor.

"I'm afraid we have a serial arsonist on our hands," he announced. "We don't know why he's targeting this town and we don't know if he plans to torch anything else. But my educated guess is that there's a reason behind his actions and that, yes, he has other targets in mind."

One of the troopers in the back, a short woman with blond hair, raised her hand. Henry admired the determined way she stood on her tiptoes and stretched her arm in an effort to be seen behind her taller colleagues. He imagined Kat had done the same thing when she was a young cop just starting out.

"So the fire at the bed-and-breakfast has been officially ruled an arson?"

Larry Sheldon nodded. "It was started in the basement with the use of an accelerant, most likely gasoline. The inn's owner said that she seldom locked the basement door, saying she didn't think anyone would have any reason to go down there. Well, someone did, and another fire happened. Now, I'm not saying we could have stopped it, but we definitely didn't see it coming."

"We were all focused on the fire at the museum," Kat added. "We all thought it solely had something to do with Constance Bishop."

The younger version of Kat again raised her hand. "So Constance Bishop's death isn't related to the fires?"

"We're not sure," Larry said. "It might be that Constance was unlucky enough to be in the museum when the arsonist tried to set fire to it."

"But is there a connection between the museum and the bed-and-breakfast?"

Kat fielded that question. "Not that I'm aware of. The museum was owned and operated by the historical society. The Sleepy Hollow Inn was owned by Lottie Scott, who has no affiliation with them. Other than being on the same street, there's no connection."

"That being said," Larry added, "we have nothing to suggest the arsonist is picking buildings at random. Most serial arsonists choose their targets for a reason. I doubt the guy we're looking for is much different."

"Are you sure it's a he?" This, surprisingly, came not from the female trooper but from the man standing next to her.

"Yes," Larry said. "Fewer than eighteen percent of arsons in the United States are committed by women. And of those, many are one-shot deals perpetrated by women trying to escape abusive relationships or scorned women with serious mental-health problems getting revenge. Few women set buildings on fire just for the hell of it."

"Then there's the medical examiner's report," Kat said. "From the size and depth of the wound to Constance's skull, he concluded that she was attacked by a man."

One of the troopers raised his voice. "Are there any persons of interest?"

"Yes. This guy."

Kat held up a police sketch of a narrow-cheeked man

with dark, deep-set eyes. His hair, rendered on paper in sweeping strokes of the artist's pen, hung in a ponytail. She handed photocopies of the sketch to the nearest trooper, who passed them around.

"His name is Connor Hawthorne," Kat said. "Caucasian male. Age twenty-seven. Hometown is Salem, Massachusetts. We have nothing that directly links him to the fires other than the fact that I saw him at the scene of both. I bumped into him at the museum fire last night and chased him down at the hotel fire this afternoon. He slipped away after I saw a friend on top of the Sleepy Hollow Inn's roof. We need to track him down, find out what he's doing here, and find out where he was when both fires started."

The troopers all studied the sketch, committing the image to memory. One of them asked, "Is there anything else we should know about this guy?"

"Yeah," Kat said. "He claims to be a witch."

"Did he start the fires with a magic spell?"

The group started to laugh, but Kat shut them down with a raised hand and a mean-looking stare.

"This isn't a joke," she said. "This is my town. People I know and love have been badly hurt, even killed. If Connor Hawthorne is the man behind it, I want him caught. Now get out there and do it."

With that, the meeting was over. The troopers filed out of the house, using both the front and back doors. A few of them gave Henry odd glances as they passed. Perhaps they recognized him from his escapades atop the Sleepy Hollow Inn. More likely, they noticed his scars. Henry had forgotten how rude American stares were. He much preferred the Italian way.

When all of the troopers were gone, Henry caught up to Kat, who stood alone in the kitchen. She gripped the counter, taking deep, chest-raising breaths. Nerves, Henry knew. Used to her two-person police force, she had been intimidated taking charge of a room full of troopers.

"You did great," he said. "Very forceful."

Kat thanked him with a nod. "I was impersonating Nick."

"I could tell."

A mug left behind by one of the troopers sat on the counter within arm's reach. Kat grabbed it and checked to see if there was still coffee inside. Seeing that there was, she downed it.

"You must be exhausted."

"There isn't even a word to describe how tired I feel," Kat said. "But instead of sleeping, I need to talk to the couple who lives across the street from the museum. I'm hoping they saw something last night that can point us in the right direction."

"What about James? Do you need someone to look after him?"

Kat didn't slow down, moving directly into the living room. "He's with Lou. They went to buy flowers for Nick and Tony and bring them to the hospital. I thought it would be a good way to get them out of the house before all the cops arrived."

Henry caught up with her as she was opening the front door. He slipped around her, blocking her exit. He could tell when someone was heading for a crash. Working in a newsroom, he had seen it plenty of times. He had been on the receiving end of several, and he knew that once someone hit the wall, it would be a while before they could get back up again.

"You need to slow down, Kat. I know you don't want to, but you *need* to."

"I don't have time to slow down," Kat said, trying to sidestep past him.

"Then you need to pace yourself. Going full throttle won't get you where you need to go."

Kat huffed, the annoyed exhalation rustling the curl of hair that hung over her eyes. "I'm just trying to do the best I can. And right now, that means finding out everything I can about who might be starting these fires."

Henry let her pass but followed her down the sidewalk to the Crown Vic in the driveway. Kat tried to lock the passenger-side door, but he got to it first and flung it open. When she climbed behind the wheel, Henry slid inside, too.

"Henry." A second huff, more agitated than the first. They had been through this before, a year earlier. "You can't tag along."

"And you can't do this by yourself."

"I'm not trying. You saw all those guys in the kitchen. Until tomorrow morning, I'm their boss."

Henry wasn't talking about the investigation. He was talking about the sleepless marathon Kat was attempting to run. "You need someone to watch your back. I'm going to be the guy who does it."

"Listen," Kat said. "I know you want to help. But you don't live here anymore. These fires don't concern you."

"Really? It didn't feel that way when I was clinging to a rain gutter after escaping my burning hotel room."

Even though Kat let out a third huff, Henry knew she was relenting. Starting the patrol car, she said, "Fine. But fasten your seat belt. Your day just got a lot more interesting."

There were dozens of couples in Perry Hollow just like Dave and Betty Freeman. Kat saw them all over the place. Married so long they started to look alike—hair the same shade of gray, identical toothy smiles, tortoiseshell glasses they probably mixed up more often than not. Kat, whose own marriage had lasted less than a year, felt a twinge of envy. She'd never get the chance to share a bed with the same person for fifty years, like the Freemans had done. Nor would she ever have someone by her side, finishing her sentences, like the Freemans did that afternoon.

"We're on edge right now," Dave Freeman said. "Two fires in one day on our street, it's—"

"Terrifying." Betty had taken over. "Completely terrifying. We don't know what's causing them."

"Or who's causing them."

"That's right," Betty said. "Who's causing them. All we know is that something—"

"Weird. Very weird."

"—is going on."

The pair sat side by side on their floral sofa, staring at Kat with eyes made all the more wide and innocent by the thick lenses of their glasses. They were waiting to be reassured, she knew. Hoping that she'd tell them their fears were unfounded.

Kat tried her best. "There's nothing to worry about. The state police are assisting in the investigation, and we're chasing down every lead."

"That's all well and good," Mr. Freeman said, "but what

are you doing to prevent more fires? I want to know that our house won't be next."

"There are troopers everywhere. They're keeping a close watch on every part of the town. They'll make sure there won't be another arson."

The Freemans weren't buying it, and Kat couldn't blame them. Even as she was talking, she realized how falsely optimistic her words sounded. If an arsonist roaming the town wanted to set something on fire, chances were pretty good that he'd find a way to do it.

The couple turned to Henry Goll, who sat uncomfortably on an antique high-backed chair built for someone half his size. "Are you with the state police?" Betty asked.

"No, ma'am." Henry shot Kat a desperate glance, begging for her assistance. "I'm—"

"He's a reporter," she said, opting for the truth. "He was inside the Sleepy Hollow Inn when the fire broke out. Now he's using that experience to help with the investigation, which is what I'd like both of you to do, as well."

"Help how?" Dave Freeman this time, sounding both apprehensive and excited about the prospect of aiding the police. "You mean like a neighborhood watch?"

"We already have that," his wife said. "Don't you remember? I was the first to volunteer."

"Because you like to spy on the neighbors."

"It's not spying," Betty insisted. "It's—"

"Being watchful." Her husband rolled his eyes. "I know. You use that excuse all the time."

Kat pictured Betty Freeman spending most evenings ducking behind the curtains of their living room window, watching the activity outside. Craning her neck, she looked past them to the picture window situated just behind the sofa. It provided a head-on view of the history museum across the street.

"Were you being watchful last night?" Kat asked.

"No," Betty said.

"Yes," her husband replied.

Kat looked back and forth between them. "Which is it?"

Mrs. Freeman chose her words very carefully. "I might have looked outside once or twice last night. You know, just to keep an eye on the neighborhood."

She cast her eyes downward, ashamed of her admission. Kat, on the other hand, was positively elated. Betty Freeman could be a world-class voyeur and she wouldn't care. Just as long as she was able to glean some information out of it.

"And did you see anything strange last night?" Kat asked.

"At the museum or on the street in general?"

"Both."

Dave Freeman sighed. "Get ready for an earful."

His wife slapped his knee. Dave chuckled. The gesture made Kat suddenly, irrationally jealous. These two people were lucky to have each other, and despite their bickering, they knew it.

"Well," Betty Freeman said, "it was pretty quiet all night. I did see a light on at the museum for most of the evening. I figured Mrs. Bishop was there burning the midnight oil. And then Mrs. Pulsifer stopped by. I saw her walk right into the museum."

"When was this?"

"About eight o'clock," Betty said.

This was in line with what Emma Pulsifer had told Kat

right after the fire. She had checked in on Constance before departing for the fund-raiser at Maison D'Avignon.

"Other than that, did you see anything out of the ordinary?"

"Anyone suspicious," Henry added. "Or did you hear anything."

"As a matter of fact, I did," Betty said. "We were watching TV and I heard something strange outside. Dave heard it, too."

"I did," her husband confirmed. "It sounded like clicking."

"*Clicking?* Where on earth did you come up with that?" Mrs. Freeman turned to Kat. "It was a tapping noise. Not a clicking."

Dave shrugged. "I heard what I heard."

On the coffee table in front of them was a half-finished crossword puzzle. A retractable pen sat on top of it. Betty Freeman picked it up and started to push it open and closed.

"*That's* clicking," she told Dave. "The noise sounded like this."

Using the tip of the pen, she tapped the coffee table in a quick, steady rhythm.

"Is that the same speed as the tapping you heard?" Kat asked.

"More or less, although it was lower pitched."

"And what time was this?"

"About nine, I think."

That was practically four hours before the fire broke out at the museum. No matter what caused the tapping—or clicking—sound, Kat was doubtful it had anything to do with the blaze.

"And there was nothing else after that?" she asked.

The Freemans answered that no, they witnessed nothing else out of the ordinary until the glow of the flames at the museum woke them up eight minutes before one. Kat thanked them for their time and told them to call her if they thought of anything else.

"We're sorry we couldn't tell you more," Dave Freeman said. "Please, just catch this guy, it's—"

"Scary right now," his wife added. "The whole town is just—"

"Terrified."

Kat assured them she would. Then she and Henry left the house, stepping outside into a bright autumn afternoon. The sky was a deep cerulean blue, and the trees in the Freemans' yard were ablaze with color. The air was mostly warm, cut ever so slightly by a hint of chill. It was a perfect day—the kind that made Kat want to skip work and take a long stroll through the woods. But such a sojourn was out of the question, as her ringing cell phone rudely reminded her. Thinking it might be news about Nick, she answered it in record time.

"Chief Campbell here."

"Chief? This is Trooper Randall Stroup."

Kat let out an audible sigh. The call wasn't about Nick. She supposed that, in his case, no news was good news. "How can I help you?"

"I'm here at the museum," the deep-voiced state trooper said. "We just finished up the inventory of the historical society's collection."

"I'm right across the street. I can literally be there in a minute."

"That'll be great. It'll be easier to explain in person."

Kat was already halfway across the street, the museum growing closer with each step. "And why is that?"

"Because," the trooper said, "I'm not sure you're going to like what you hear."

3 P.M.

Randall Stroup was a big guy. Huge, in fact. He dwarfed even Henry, which, considering Henry was six five and more than two hundred pounds of solid muscle, was no small feat. Just being in his presence made Henry stand up straight and puff out his chest. He couldn't help it. And Randall absolutely towered over Chief Campbell, looking capable of flattening her to the floor using only the palm of his hand.

"What do they feed you boys in the state police?" Kat asked him. "Do they put growth hormones in your food? Stock the vending machines only with protein shakes?"

Trooper Stroup, without even cracking a smile, stated the obvious. "We work out."

"Yeah. I can see that."

The three of them were in the meeting room at the rear of the museum, standing at a table covered with papers and photographs stacked in tidy piles. According to Stroup, the pages listed every item in the Perry Hollow Historical Society's collection. The pictures were Polaroids of the entire collection, taken by Constance Bishop for insurance purposes.

"We went through all of it," the trooper said. "Since so

much was damaged in the fire, it took a while to figure out what was what. Anything we were unsure of, we called Emma Pulsifer and she verified it for us."

Henry moved down the length of the table, scanning some of the photos that topped the piles. He was more than a little impressed. Granted, he didn't have the eye of an appraiser, but some of the items in the museum looked to be extremely valuable. He regretted never stopping by to take a look around when he'd had the chance.

"Was there anything missing?" Kat asked.

"A couple of things, actually. The first is this."

Randall Stroup handed her a Polaroid. Looking over her shoulder, Henry saw that it was a picture of an antique iron. Made of cast iron, its triangular shape was more pronounced than modern ones. The handle, also cast iron, rose from the base in an elegant curve and was accented with a rod of wood in the center.

"Apparently, it was part of an exhibit on household chores in the eighteenth century," Randall said. "We searched the whole place and didn't find anything like it. Nor is there any paperwork or mention of it being loaned out to another museum."

Kat studied the photograph, her finger tracing the iron's back edge. "Gentlemen, I think we've found our murder weapon."

"An iron?" Henry said.

That elicited a nod from Kat. "The damage found on Constance Bishop's skull was in a straight line. Like she had been hit with the edge of something heavy."

She grabbed a nearby chair and asked Trooper Stroup to sit in it. Once he did, she mimed picking up an iron, fingers curled around the invisible handle.

"The culprit grabbed the iron from the exhibit. Just like this." Kat stood behind the trooper, using him as her unwitting victim. Raising her hand, she said, "The iron was raised, flat side facing up."

She brought her hand down, pretending to strike Randall in the head.

"One heavy blow was all it took to knock Constance to the ground. Thinking she was dead, he then started the fire. Then he took the iron with him, although I'm not sure why."

"That's easy," Henry said. "He knew the fire would destroy any evidence left behind. But cast iron doesn't burn."

Kat tapped her temple. "Now you're thinking like a cop."

Henry wasn't sure that was a good thing, although he knew it was bound to happen sooner or later. Lord knows he had spent enough time with them.

"But that's not the most interesting thing missing from the museum," Randall said. "There's this."

He whipped out another Polaroid, laying it on the table so they both could see it. The photo showed a cylinder made of heavy paper that had once been red but was now brown with age. A thin wire poked from one end of the cylinder and lettering ran along its side, too faded to read. Not that Henry needed it to know what the object was. It was pretty clear that they were looking at a stick of dynamite.

"Let me guess," Kat said. "This is the part I'm not going to like."

Trooper Stroup gave a single, swift nod. "Bingo."

"What would a museum be doing with dynamite?" Henry asked.

Kat, the only Perry Hollow native in the room, provided the answer. "It was in their exhibit about the early days of the town. I remember seeing it in grade school. We had a whole lesson on the history of logging."

"Call me crazy," Henry said, "but I thought logging involved saws."

"The dynamite was used after the trees were cut down. There'd be acres of nothing but tree stumps. Pulling them out of the ground took too much time and manpower. It was easier to just blow them up. It was called stump blasting."

"Well," Randall said, "that dynamite is now unaccounted for."

He didn't express what they were all thinking—that the dynamite could now be in the hands of an arsonist. The idea alone sent a shivery jolt of fear zipping around Henry's body. Kat felt one, too. He knew it by the way her face suddenly paled. Not by much, of course. Just enough that he could tell she was now more scared than when they first walked into the museum.

"I assume there's nothing else that's missing," she said. "Unless you want to tell me that the museum also had a few hand grenades lying around."

"They had one." Randall produced a snapshot of a World War II–era grenade sitting against a plain white backdrop. "We found it in a storage room upstairs, so that's been accounted for."

"Thank God for small favors," Kat said.

"But," the trooper continued, "we found something that *didn't* belong in the museum."

He retreated to a corner of the room, where a cardboard box sat on a folding chair. When he brought the box back to the table, Henry saw that it contained a single item—a hardcover book. The title was *Witchcraft in America*. The author was someone named Connor Hawthorne.

"Isn't that the—"

"Guy we're looking for?" Kat said. "Yes, it is. And he's apparently not only a witch but a writer as well."

"We found it on the second floor," Randall said. "Under a bed in one of the rooms on display. Whoever it belonged to, they went out of their way to hide it."

"It belonged to Constance," Kat replied. "I guess she hid it after someone started snooping around her office."

"But it's just a book," Henry said.

He took it out of the box and flipped it over. On the back was a photograph of an intense young man with shoulder-length blond hair and sharp features. It looked uncannily like the police sketch that had been passed out to the state troopers. Most of the front cover was taken up by an illustration of a woman about to be burned at the stake. The flames were up to her ankles, ready to consume the rest of her.

"I've seen that picture before," Kat said. "Constance had a copy of it on her desk."

A narrow ribbon of purple silk had been placed near the back of the book. Henry opened it to that spot, seeing several pages brightened with green highlighter. He set the book on thc table and pressed it flat. Kat moved in quickly, practically squeezing herself between Henry and the table in order to scan the book. She nudged him with a sharp poke of her elbow, trying to force him to edge to the side. Instead, Henry put one of his arms around her shoulders, pulling her against him until they were both centered in front of the book. With his hand resting on Kat's shoulder, they began to read.

* * *

Kat was so weary that she had trouble focusing on the page. She was fine when she was moving and talking. The adrenaline kept her going in that regard. But if she rested, even for a mere second, her exhaustion quickly bubbled to the surface, threatening to pull her under. Her mind got hazy and her eyes grew weak. Staring at the book, all she saw were blurry words running into each other until they formed unreadable streaks across the page.

She closed her eyes and slapped her cheeks. The light sting of the blows did the trick, and when she opened her eyes again, the first sentence on the page was crystal clear.

And chilling.

"*Witches are everywhere,*" it read. "*They always have been and always will be. One could be living next door and you wouldn't know it.*"

Kat suspected Connor Hawthorne, a self-proclaimed witch himself, had meant the passage to be benign and reassuring. *You have nothing to fear,* he seemed to be saying. *We're just like you.* Yet an ominous undercurrent lurked just beneath his words. There was something frightening about the prospect of having a witch for a neighbor. The fact that you might not even know it made it even more disturbing.

Yet Kat read on, half eager and half afraid to find out more.

> *While it's true most witch trials during the late seventeenth century took place in Massachusetts, others occurred throughout the colonies at roughly the same time period. Many of these recorded incidents have been overshadowed by the infamous witch tri-*

als of Salem in 1692. Many more are lost to history. Then there are those that we know happened but have very little documentation about. The trial of Rebecca Bradford is one of them.

Kat inhaled sharply, enough for Henry to lift his heavy hand from her shoulder and say, "You okay?"

"I know that name. Constance had jotted it down at her desk."

Only Kat had read it as a man's first and last names. Turning the page of Connor Hawthorne's book, she now understood that she had been badly mistaken.

The only mention of Rebecca Bradford I have found is located in the journal of William Daniel Paul, a judge who presided over several witch trials in the late seventeenth century. It was found in the attic of a home in Boston in 1964 and now resides in the archives of the Boston Public Library. In addition to offering great insight into the paranoia of the times, he goes into great detail about some of the cases he was involved in.

In a passage dated June 29, 1692, William Paul mentions being summoned to the Pennsylvania colony to oversee the case of a young mother accused of witchcraft in an unnamed village. That woman was named Rebecca Bradford.

Her situation was similar to many women accused of witchcraft during that time period. Her husband had succumbed to pneumonia the previous winter, leaving her the single parent of a young son. She lived in a cramped cabin with her husband's four sisters, all of them struggling to make ends meet by farming the land and treating the sick with herbs from their humble garden. The allegations of witchcraft began after she had healed a child who was on her deathbed. The child's condition improved so dramatically that many, including her parents, suspected some unnatural forces had been at play.

I can't say with any certainty that Rebecca Bradford was a witch. The judge doesn't go into very much detail about her alleged crime or her actions. But he does make mention of an amulet Rebecca wore that had been filled with a mixture of horehound, an herb often used to protect against evil forces, and calendula, which was rumored to help bring about a favorable verdict if carried with you into court. The appropriate use of herbs in her amulet leads me to believe that Rebecca was indeed a witch.

Despite this damning evidence, which would have resulted in a guilty verdict in a place like Salem, William Daniel Paul dismissed Rebecca's case immediately. He admitted in his journal that he personally believed Rebecca to be guilty of practicing witchcraft. But since Pennsylvania had been founded on the promise of religious freedom, he did not feel it was his right to try Rebecca Bradford for her beliefs. She walked away a free woman.

He makes one more mention of the case in an entry dated a few months later. Without mentioning

Rebecca by name, he describes receiving news about a case he had presided over in June. He says a young woman accused of witchcraft and her next of kin had died in a fire. The only survivor was the woman's son, who was sent to live with a relative in Philadelphia. The judge, who had convicted quite a few witches in his day, expresses no sadness or remorse about the woman's death—the rest of the entry details, in quite elaborate fashion, everything he had consumed for dinner that evening.

That was the end of the highlighted passage. Kat read on for a sentence or two but saw that the author had moved on to the sad story of another woman killed by ignorance and man's inhumanity to man. The only other item of interest was a notation made in the margin, presumably by Constance Bishop's hand.

"Perry Hollow?"

"What would make Constance think that such a thing happened here?"

"Well, it did mention Pennsylvania," Henry said.

"I know, but this could have occurred anywhere."

She backed away from the table and slipped past Henry, who lifted his hand from the open book. It sprang free, the pages fluttering of their own accord. The sudden movement dislodged a piece of paper that had been stuck in the middle of the book. A corner of it now poked out from the pages.

Using his thumb and forefinger, Henry slowly slid the paper out of the book. "It's an envelope."

He shoved the book aside and laid the envelope on the table. Flicking it open, he peered inside before sliding it toward

Kat so she, too, could have a peek. Inside were a few folded pieces of paper so old they had to be parchment. Time had darkened them to a sickly yellow that reminded Kat of dried mustard.

Henry had already started to burrow two fingers into the envelope, but Kat grabbed his hand. "Gloves," she said. "This is still evidence."

Randall Stroup, who had stood by patiently as they read, was one step ahead of her, holding out a pair of rubber gloves. Kat put them on before carefully reaching into the envelope. When she pinched a corner of the parchment, it instantly crumbled into tiny flecks that slipped around inside of the envelope.

"Shit."

Grimacing, she tried again, this time using only the pad of an index finger to try and coax the documents free. It seemed to work, so she continued the gentle slide until the parchment was a brittle rectangle sitting on the table's surface.

"Now the hard part," Kat said. "We need to open them up."

She waited until Henry, too, snapped on a pair of rubber gloves. Then she had him press lightly on the bottom of the pages while she attempted to unfold the top half. Kat held her breath as she slowly lifted the pages. Although they made a discouraging crackling sound at the crease—not unlike a candy wrapper being ripped open—she continued. Along the sides, more chips of paper broke free and dusted the tabletop.

It occurred to Kat that she should stop and let an expert open the pages. Someone with a steadier hand. Someone trained to delicately pry the secrets from ancient documents such as this one. But then she glimpsed the handwritten date at the top of the first page.

"10 November, 1692."

She finished cracking the pages open, much faster than she should have and leaving the tabletop littered with dark yellow flecks that resembled gold dust. Kat blew them away before laying the documents flat on the table.

There were three pages in total, each one bearing identical creases where they had been folded. Kat leaned in close to the first page, squinting for good measure. Directly below the date was an introduction: *"Dearest brother."*

"It's a letter," she said.

Henry was beside her again, so near that Kat could feel the warmth of his breath when he spoke. "What does it say?"

"I have no idea."

Again, Kat could barely read it. This time, though, it was because the handwriting had faded so much it was barely visible. Large brown spots, from either water or mildew, dotted the pages, blocking out whole sentences. What she could make out was a cramped script that packed both the front and back of each page. There were twice as many lines as a normal letter, scrawled so close together they practically formed a solid block of text. Words that Kat recognized seemed foreign and unfamiliar. The letter *f* where an *s* should have been. Random capitalizations. Some common words had too many letters. Others had too few. It might as well have been written in another language.

"I'm dying to know what this says," she said. "There has to be a reason Constance hid it inside this book."

"This should help," said Randall Stroup as he thumbed

through the copy of *Witchcraft in America*. Several typewritten pages had been tucked into the back. The trooper scanned the first one quickly. "It looks like Constance Bishop tried to decipher it."

He passed the pages to Kat, who saw it was another letter. The date on this one was October 23, a mere week ago. And it was addressed to Connor Hawthorne.

Mr. Hawthorne,

This is in regard to the letter I told you about in our last correspondence. Because of its age and delicacy, it would be unwise to put it through the rigors of photocopying, scanning, or any other such modern nonsense. Instead, I have tried to transcribe it to the best of my weak abilities. I'll admit, it was more of a struggle than I first thought it would be. Time has damaged the pages themselves, making some words completely illegible. In the transcript, those areas are indicated by the note "indecipherable."

The second problem was the words themselves. It's amazing how much the English language has changed in a short three hundred years. I've taken the liberty of smoothing over some of the more archaic passages, settling for something easily understandable. (I shall leave the true translation for the experts, if it should ever come to that. I sincerely hope it does.) I think what follows is a mostly accurate reproduction of the text of the letter. Some of the words may be different, but I think the tone shines through. I'm very curious to find out if you, as I do, think we have cracked a small, but not insignificant, historical mystery.

Warmest regards,
Constance Bishop

Kat set the introductory page aside. "I have a feeling this letter is a copy."

"You think Constance mailed the original?" Henry asked.

"Yup. That's why Connor came to Perry Hollow. He and Constance were working together."

Kat turned her attention to the translated letter. Like the original, it contained the date, followed by the two-word salutation: *"Dearest brother."*

> *You are no doubt surprised to be receiving this letter, having not yet forgotten our quarrel the last time we spoke. I am a foolish man, brother, and my words those many months ago haunt me still. It was not my intention to mock your calling so viciously. I fear that I am the cause of great distress in your life. If that be the truth, then I offer humble apologies. This land needs men of God to lead its multitude of sinners to righteousness. You shall do great things on your chosen path and save the souls of scores of men. It is my devout hope that my own soul may be among them. I seek your prayers, my dear brother, for I am a broken, horrid man.*
>
> [Indecipherable] *from Philadelphia. How long I shall remain here, I do not know. I arrived quite suddenly, without planning my next course of action. You see, my dearest brother, I have run away.*

For the past six months, I have been living in a small village a few days' journey outside of the city. There wasn't much there, really. Just a cluster of houses, a blacksmith, and a few farms, all surrounded by hills coated with pine forests. The place is so small and haphazardly organized that the village settlers have yet to come to a consensus regarding its proper name.

Chief among the villagers is a man who made a great sum of money in his youth trading furs. In his later years, he settled here to farm the land and start a family. Weeks earlier, he journeyed to Philadelphia, inquiring about a tutor for his two children, a son and a daughter. An acquaintance of mine told him I was seeking employment and gave him my credentials. The man called on me and persuaded me to return to his village as his family's new instructor.

I did not take to my new employer, a rather crude man of dubious morality. Nor did I enjoy schooling his son, aged ten, who is already quite like his father, demanding and cruel. But the daughter, aged eleven, is a handsome girl of good humor and keen [Indecipherable]

[Indecipherable] *within weeks of my arrival, illness overtook the girl. Her condition grew so grave that many in the household, myself included, feared she would not survive. Because there is no physician in the village and summoning one from Philadelphia would have taken days, her father brought in a young widow named Rebecca who resided in a ramshackle cottage outside the village, beside a lovely lake. She lived there with her young son and several of her husband's sisters. Wild women, they were. Big-boned and unruly, with dirty faces and unkempt hair. Rebecca was the only beautiful one among them, which made her stand out, in my opinion. Many men in the village—and jealous women as well—took note of her beauty.*

Rebecca and her sisters got by harvesting flowers and herbs in their garden. As such, she had acquired a reputation for being knowledgeable about unusual and potent plants. There were whispers that her gift arose only after the passing of her husband and that she acquired them through dark forces. Yet my master, a desperate man not content with God's plan for his daughter, brought this woman to his household. She spent several days there, attending to the sickly child and spooning foul-odored broth between her lips.

On more than one occasion, I overhead the master of the house conferring with the woman in darkened corners. On the second day of her stay, I entered the basement to retrieve a sack of flour for the elderly cook. Surprise overtook me when I discovered my employer and the woman alone together beneath the stairs. My master had placed one of his rough hands on the woman's arms, which she swatted away with visible force. When I inquired if all was well, I was told [Indecipherable]

Later that evening, the admonishment of my master echoing in my dreams, I was awakened by the sound of voices in the garden, which my bedroom window overlooked. I saw my master and the woman standing in the shadows. A struggle appeared to be taking place. My master was close to her, pushing against her and forcing his lips upon hers. It was clear to me that Rebecca was not encouraging his advances and that I needed to intervene. Yet before I could leave the window, she lashed out, striking my employer across the cheek with an open hand. My master held her wrist, admonishing her with surly harsh words that I could not hear. He departed quickly after that, leaving Rebecca alone to weep in the shadows.

In the morning, the girl's condition improved miraculously. Her recovery was so swift and sudden it left even her parents in much disbelief. Others in the village crowded the household to see the child's progress for themselves. Swiftly, there were murmurs about the woman who had nursed her back to health. No sickly youth could recover with such haste, some proclaimed. Others suggested the nursemaid had somehow enlisted the aid of dark magic to save the child's life. Soon the accusations became repeated as though they were fact. The village in its entirety was convinced this woman who claimed to walk with the Lord was secretly the Devil's mistress.

Within days, an official query was demanded by my employer, who claimed the woman had practiced witchcraft on his innocent and ailing daughter. A trial was ordered and a judge was summoned. He dismissed the allegations outright, not for lack of evidence but by citing the very laws upon which the colony was founded.

Rebecca and her kin kept to themselves after that. No one saw her in the village; nor did anyone venture out to their lonely residence in the woods to trade or purchase her herbs. I suppose, brother, there wasn't much to trade with. The weather had seen to that.

It was a cruel summer, you see. It was as if Heaven and Hell had exchanged places, with the infernal heat of the underworld bearing down on us from above. Crops withered and died within days. Animals became mere piles of bones and fur before they, too, succumbed. A few villagers went mad from the heat, begging for relief, even though there was none to be had. One man, who [Indecipherable]

After several months of these unbearable conditions, some in the village began to whisper that it was the work of Rebecca and her sisters. They had cursed the village, some said, as revenge for accusing her of witchcraft. Soon the whispers got louder until everyone in the village was discussing it outright. Soon, it appeared to me that everyone was convinced that the heat and drought were not the work of our Lord but of one woman and her wretched kin.

My employer took it upon himself to travel to the home of the women. He returned with tales so horrifying that [Indecipherable] *ripped off their clothing next to the lake and danced naked in the moonlight, chanting foreign words to the sky and cursing his very name. Outraged and frightened, the men of the village cursed the judge who came to the village and did nothing* [Indecipherable] *vowed that justice would prevail.*

In the dead of night, they summoned every able-bodied male and marched to the woman's cottage to confront her. The widow, wearing only her nightclothes, was roused from her sleep [Indecipherable] *took the son back to the village, where he would be tended to by the womenfolk. As the men pulled Rebecca from her house, her sisters tried to fight them off, to no avail. The door was pulled shut and barricaded, preventing them from leaving. Outside, Rebecca was thrust onto her knees and told to admit that she was doing the Devil's work. One of the men gathered there demanded that she prove her loyalty to the Lord by saying a prayer. If she refused, they warned, they would burn down her house with her sisters still inside. All the cursed woman needed to do was say a prayer, but she refused, claiming she was a follower of the rules of nature, as dictated by our Creator.*

[Indecipherable] *set fire to the nearby house, which was still occupied by Rebecca's sisters. The women screamed as the flames grew. I have never known such terrified cries, dear brother. I hear them still, resounding in my nightmares—an endless echo that cannot be silenced. As the house burned, the screams died away one by one, until there was nothing but silence as the dwelling was only smoke and ash.*

While the fire raged, my employer dragged Rebecca to a thin birch tree. He pressed her writhing body against it while throwing a loop of rope at me. He then ordered me, as his humble servant, to bind her wrists behind her back. The difficulty was great. She struggled so, thrashing and biting with all the force of a deranged animal. My hands trembled while I fashioned the knots that held her in place. I was frightened, brother, not only of her power but of the prospect that what was transpiring was somehow against the will of the Lord.

Others scoured the forest floor for sticks for kindling, which were placed at the pitiful woman's feet and set ablaze. Rebecca stayed mostly quiet through her ordeal, even as she watched the fate of her sisters and the flames engulfed her legs. She spoke only when the pain became too much to bear.

"Curse you!" she screamed to those of us still assembled there. "May the fires of Hell rise up to consume this place."

A good many of my compatriots interpreted her words as final proof that she danced with dark spirits. They were pleased to be rid of her and felt none of the creeping guilt that tortures me now. How I wish I could be similarly certain of my actions. Yet, dear brother, my doubts linger. It is my [Indecipherable]

[Indecipherable] *put their remains into cloth sacks and buried them next to the smoldering house.*

Rebecca's bones were kept separate and deposited into a sack that had only the day before carried oats for my master's horses. The sack was placed in a wooden box lined with lead by the blacksmith. There was great fear among some of the men that without the lead, her evil spirit could escape her burying place and further torment the village. We buried her remains next to the lake. She lies there now, inside a lead-lined box instead of a proper casket.

It is my darkest fear, dear brother, that I have assisted in the execution of five innocent women. The only strength I can summon comes from knowing that Rebecca's young son was spared the piteous view of his mother's demise. The boy was shunted off to a distant relative in Philadelphia. Before his departure, the villagers informed him of his mother's passing, filling him with tales of how there was a terrible fire that consumed his entire family. It was scandalous how good Christian folk could cast untruths with such ease and cunning. These lies, I fear, will come back to haunt them one day. As for myself, dearest, dearest brother, I left the wretched village within the week. My hope is to find Rebecca's son and confess our sins to him. Once I do, perhaps I will be rid of the heaviness my actions have created in my heart. You shall receive word from me again soon, brother. Until that time, I beseech you, pray for my soul.

When she was finished reading the letter, Kat remained silent. What could she say in the face of such brutality? The fact that five innocent women—one a mother, no less—had been killed in such a cruel manner made her sick to her stomach. She felt even worse knowing it all had happened in her town. Yes, she was well aware that the events occurred before Perry Hollow ever really existed. But the land was the same. Folks in her town walked the same ground those ignorant villagers had walked. And that land, she now knew, was stained with blood.

"Well," she finally said, "it looks like Constance found Rebecca Bradford."

"We can't be certain those bones in the museum belonged to the woman in that letter," Henry said. "It could have been anywhere in Pennsylvania. You said so yourself."

"The bones had been burned, Henry. Before last night. Years before."

Three hundred years, in fact. That's what Lucy Meade had told her just before she learned the bad news about Nick. Then there was the fact that Constance Bishop had been seen leaving her house with a metal detector. When she had first heard about it, Kat thought it strange that she would use such a device to search for bones. Now it all made sense, considering poor Rebecca Bradford's lead-lined resting place.

"Those bones are what's left of Rebecca," Kat said. "And Constance found them."

She assumed that Constance had also tried but failed to uncover the remains of the rest of the Bradford clan. They were still out there, waiting to be found. And Constance certainly wanted them to be. It was why, as she was dying, she had written that message on her hand. That once cryptic phrase that now made complete, dreadful sense.

THIS IS JUST THE FIRST.

Constance hadn't meant murders. Or fires. She had meant skeletons, buried somewhere beneath Perry Hollow.

Kat left the conference room and charged down the hallway, propelled by a newfound sense of energy. Henry followed, remaining close behind her as she pushed through the museum's back door. The small patch of yard behind the building looked different in the daylight. Far prettier than Kat had realized. A cluster of light blue asters sat beside the wooden fence at the rear of the property. The gate was still ajar, creaking gently back and forth among the blooms. Next to the fence, a sprawling sycamore rained yellow leaves onto a bench beneath it.

The only thing keeping the spot from looking picture-perfect were the two state troopers standing close to the museum. Their backs were turned to the yard as they studied a patch of the exterior wall next to the door. One of them was the female trooper who hadn't hesitated to speak up in Kat's kitchen an hour earlier. Seeing Kat, she spoke up again, calling out, "Chief, you might want to take a look at this."

"What did you find?"

"Vandalism," the trooper said. "We missed it during the night. Only noticed it this morning when the sun came up."

The troopers parted, giving Kat an unobstructed view of the wall. The vandalism, rendered in black spray paint that scarred the whitewashed siding, consisted of a series of connected lines surrounded by a circle. The lines formed a rough five-pointed star, just like the ones children draw in their first bursts of artistic creativity. Each point touched the circle, as if straining to break free of its borders.

"Is it just me," Henry said, "or is this day getting weirder as it goes along?"

Kat had no choice but to agree. There were fires and corpses and skeletons hidden beneath the floor. And now, just when she thought it couldn't get any stranger, she found herself staring at a spray-painted pentagram on the wall of the place where all this trouble started.

Just below the pentagram was a small brass plaque embedded into the wall. The sign proclaimed that the museum had been designated a state historic landmark. Perry Hollow was so old that such plaques weren't uncommon. Kat saw them here and there, yet rarely paid attention to them. The fact that a pentagram had been painted next to one finally got her attention.

"Do you remember seeing one of these at the bed-and-breakfast?" she asked Henry.

"I hope you're asking about the plaque," he said with a wry lift of his brow.

"I am."

"I didn't notice. Why?"

Kat hurried around the side of the museum, picking up speed as she crossed the wide lawn and leaving Henry far behind her. She burst into a jog once she hit the street, not slowing until she reached what was left of the Sleepy Hollow Inn.

That block was closed to both cars and pedestrians, thanks to the rubble that had spilled into the street when the hotel collapsed. Kat ducked beneath the police tape stretched from tree to tree around the scene and surveyed the damage.

Debris was everywhere—a jumbled pile of wood, bricks, and shattered glass. Shingles from the roof littered the street, and tufts of blackened insulation rolled like tumbleweed across the lawn. Kat moved cautiously, stepping around the rubble until she reached a small set of concrete steps. It was the hotel's front stoop, one of the few things still standing. At the top, instead of a front door, was a view of the smoldering pit that had once been the Sleepy Hollow Inn.

Standing on the stoop, Kat leaned over the edge and scanned the debris. She saw charred pieces of paper, smashed plates, and still more shingles. Lying on the other side of the stoop was a portion of the fallen wall, its siding warped from the heat. It now resembled melted candle wax that had been cooled back to a solid form. But on that piece of wall, partially obscured by the half-melted siding, was a brass plaque similar to the one located at the museum.

"Why did you run off like that?" Henry, finally catching up to her, stopped on the other side of the police tape. "I'm supposed to be helping you, remember?"

"Sorry. I had to look for something."

"Did you find it?"

"I did," Kat said, eyes still fixed on the tiny plaque. "And I think I also figured out the reason behind the fires."

---

4 P.M.

"He's trying to get revenge."

Lieutenant Tony Vasquez, still confined to a hospital bed, lifted himself as far as his broken bones would allow. "Who is?"

"Connor Hawthorne," Kat said. "He's trying to get revenge on Perry Hollow for something that happened hundreds of years ago."

She paced in front of Tony's bed as she recounted everything she had learned that afternoon. The antique iron. The missing stick of dynamite. The book and letter that told the strange, sad story of Rebecca Bradford and her sisters. Then there was the pentagram, which symbolized that something far more evil than mere arson was taking place.

"He knows that there was a massacre on the land where Perry Hollow now sits," she said. "So he's targeting the oldest buildings. The museum was on the state registry of historic places. So was the Sleepy Hollow Inn. This is his way of making the town pay for its sins."

She thought of Rebecca's last words as recorded in that crumbling letter. *"May the fires of Hell rise up to consume this place."* It had taken more than three hundred years, but now her final wish was coming true.

"It's a good theory," Tony said, "but why would he kill Constance Bishop, as well?"

"Maybe she caught him in the act of setting the museum on fire," Kat replied, thinking aloud. "Maybe he was just using her to dig up as much information as she could. Or maybe it's just another piece of his vendetta. There's no better way to get revenge on a town's history than by killing its chief historian."

"How many other places in town are registered historic landmarks?"

"I don't know," Kat said. "But I've got someone checking right now."

That someone was Louella van Sickle, who had had the unfortunate luck to be leaving the hospital with James just as Kat and Henry were arriving. Kat ordered her to head to the library and look up all the other buildings in town that had earned landmark status. As for James, he was still at the hospital, sitting in the waiting area with Henry.

"Once you get that list, post a trooper at every door," Tony said. "If you can, I'd shut them down entirely. Are you sure this Hawthorne guy is the man behind all this?"

Before that afternoon, Kat hadn't been sure. But now, in her mind, Connor was the only suspect. Constance's letter had certainly made it sound like Connor was the only other person who knew about Rebecca Bradford. There was a certain logic to the thought that one witch would try to avenge another. The pentagram they found only sealed the deal. Once he had spray-painted the museum wall, Connor might as well have stamped his forehead with the word GUILTY.

Yet she couldn't be content to end the investigation there and go on a manhunt for someone who might not still be in town. She needed to consider other possibilities, like the fact that someone else might have known Rebecca's story.

"Rebecca had a son," Kat said. "He was sent to live with relatives after she was killed."

"You think the arsonist could be a descendant somehow?"

"Weirder things have happened." Kat resumed pacing. It felt good to be thinking and moving at the same time. It kept her alert, making her temporarily forget she hadn't had a wink of sleep in sixteen hours. "Maybe one of Rebecca's distant relatives moved back to Perry Hollow after learning what had happened to her."

"Is there anyone in town named Bradford?"

Kat shook her head quickly. Perry Hollow was a small, close-knit community. If there was a Bradford in their midst, she'd know of him. That left someone whose name had been changed, most likely through marriage.

"Is there an easy way to check statewide birth records?"

"There's a way," Tony said, "but it's far from easy. The state's Department of Health has a database of all birth certificates."

"I think we should search for Bradfords. If anyone currently in Perry Hollow had a parent or grandparent with that last name, I want to know about it."

"Just so you know, that could take hours."

"I understand," Kat said.

She also knew they didn't have the luxury of time. There could be another fire—or worse, an explosion—within the hour. But she couldn't leave any investigative avenue unexplored, so she told Tony to make a few calls. It's what Nick would have done.

Tony stretched for the bedside phone but fell short, thanks to the sling enveloping his injured right arm. Kat brought it to the bed and dropped it in his lap.

"Give them my cell phone number and tell them to call me if they get any hits," she said.

"Will do." The lieutenant gave her a salute before dialing. "Oh, and Kat, I know this is the last thing you want to hear, but you're pretty damn good at this."

Although Kat appreciated the compliment, Tony was right. On a day when her best friend was in a coma, half her town had the potential to go up in flames, and she was so tired she could fall asleep in the middle of a hospital hallway, it was indeed the last thing she wanted to hear.

Kat's son sat next to Henry, flipping through an ancient copy of *Highlights for Children*. The magazine didn't seem to interest him. James turned the pages with impatience, hoping for something more interesting just around the corner. Eventually, he gave up, dropping the magazine onto the coffee table in front of him.

"I don't like it here," he declared.

Henry didn't, either. Hospital waiting rooms always made him feel uncomfortable, and he had spent too much time in this one already. Like James, he just wanted to leave.

"Where would you like to be?"

"Home," James said.

"We can't go home without your mother."

James let out a sigh that was both annoyed and annoying. "But it's boring here."

"True," Henry said. "So let's get out of here and go for a walk."

James, who had been slouched in his chair, perked up at the idea of leaving the building. "Where?"

"Outside. Just until your mom comes back."

"Can I get some candy, too?"

"Sure," Henry said. "Whatever you want."

They left the waiting room and proceeded to a vending machine down the hall, where James used the spare change from Henry's pocket to purchase a pack of licorice. Then it was through the automatic doors and into the clear, autumn air.

"I remember you, you know," James said as they followed the sidewalk to a tree-dotted area next to the hospital. There were a few picnic tables there, occupied by weary-looking nurses on their dinner breaks and hospital visitors trying to chain-smoke their worries away.

"You do?"

The boy gave him a single, certain nod. "You saved my life."

"I wouldn't go that far."

"That's what my mom says. She says you're a hero."

"Well," Henry said, "she did the same for me. So I think we're even."

James held out a piece of licorice. "Do you want some?"

"Sure."

Henry took the candy, gnawing on it as he and James wound their way through the mostly bare trees. Their leaves, victims of the changing seasons, covered the ground, and James cut through them in long, sliding strides. There was no sign of the troubled boy that Kat had alluded to during their catch-up session early that morning, which relieved Henry. James had witnessed a lot, and it worried Henry that the trauma would make the boy hardened before his time. But that afternoon, he was as carefree as a child his age should be. Giggling. Kicking up leaves. A joyful glint in his eyes as they fluttered back down to the ground.

The boy's exuberance made Henry think of his own son, gone before he had ever arrived. He wondered what it would be like to be the father of a young boy. It probably felt a lot like that afternoon of shared candy and aimless walking.

For a time, he actually thought fatherhood would happen. During those heady, final days of his wife's pregnancy, Henry had mistakenly believed his life was blessed. He was handsome and successful. His wife was gorgeous, fiercely intelligent, and ferociously funny. Their unborn son would arrive happy and healthy.

But it wasn't meant to be.

Something—be it God, or fate, or some other higher power he couldn't begin to grasp—had a different plan for him. So the crash happened, killing his wife instantly. Their child, mere minutes from entering the world, was taken with her. And Henry was left broken, physically and emotionally.

Then came the second stage of his life. Perry Hollow, Pennsylvania. The place he had retreated to in order to escape his past. But then Kat and James Campbell entered his life. So did Deana Swan. He learned to open up. To live again. To love again. Then it was all snatched away once more.

It had taken years for Henry to make peace with what had happened to his wife and son. He suspected it would take an equal amount of time to come to terms with what had happened to him in Perry Hollow. Yet time healed. Henry knew that from experience. A year ago, it hurt too much to even be near a boy like James. But now, he could go for a walk with him and not feel overwhelmed with pain. Now, when James stretched out his small hand, Henry could reach out and hold it.

"I think we should head back," he said. "Your mom might be waiting for us."

"Do we have to?"

"I'm afraid so, sport."

"Are you going to go away after that?"

The question, so innocently invasive, stopped Henry cold. James halted, too, standing in an ankle-high pile of leaves.

"I have to," Henry said. "I don't live here anymore."

"Can we come visit you?"

"Maybe. But it's pretty far away."

"How far?"

"Really far," Henry said. "On the other side of the world."

"I'll miss you." James dropped Henry's hand and moved

in for an impulsive hug. He tried to wrap his short, little-boy arms around Henry's waist, only making it halfway. Just like his mother's awkward embrace that morning.

"What's that for?" Henry asked.

"To thank you."

"For the candy?"

James shook his head. "For being my hero."

Before leaving the hospital, Kat swung by the ICU to check on Nick. Creeping into his room, she saw that Lucy Meade had returned from Harrisburg. She sat by Nick's bed, balancing a portable CD player on her lap. A Beatles song lightly trickled out of it. "Blackbird." An oldie but a goodie.

"How's he doing?"

"Still unresponsive," Lucy said. "I was hoping the music might cause a reaction."

Although only a few hours had passed since Kat last saw her, Lucy looked like a completely different person. The vivacious young woman who had impressed her with her wit and knowledge was gone. In her place was a person burdened by worry.

"I don't understand why he was even here," she said. "He wanted to come along, but I told him he couldn't. It's stupid, but I thought you and I would actually be able to bond without him around."

"He came because he wanted to help," Kat replied. "He hides it well, but it kills him that he's no longer a cop. So he tries to live vicariously through those of us who still are."

"That's what drew me to him." Lucy reached for one of his hands, caressing it lightly. "He was so intense, it was almost scary. Yet there was a gentleness there, too, just below the surface. Like there was a reason he needed to seek justice so badly."

Kat knew what that reason was. She supposed Lucy did, too. Nick Donnelly's entire life was defined by his sister's murder when he was ten. And although her killer had gone unpunished, Nick was hell-bent on making sure no other criminals would get a free pass. It's what led him to dig up cases that were four decades old or show up uninvited to current crime scenes. He wanted justice. For everyone.

Both of them gazed down at Nick's ghostly pale face, trying to collectively will him back to consciousness. Although his body twitched slightly, Kat knew it was just a muscle spasm. His eyes remained closed. His arms stayed limp. The menagerie of machines he was hooked up to continued their dull and steady beats.

"I'm not sure what to do here." Lucy had started to cry, the tears streaking her cheeks. "Part of me wants to just cut and run, you know? To tell him good-bye and not ever come back. But another part of me needs to stay. Because I'm pretty sure I love him, Kat. And now I don't know what to do about it."

The CD player changed songs. "Yesterday." Another goodie, but sad, too. As it played, Lucy's quiet sobs drifted in and out of the music.

"He'll pull through this," Kat said. "And when he does, you'll be able to tell him how you feel. I suspect he'll be pleased to hear it."

Lucy wiped her eyes, ashamed to be so emotional in front of someone who was practically a stranger. "What if he doesn't? I don't know what I'll do without him."

Kat had said the exact same thing three hours earlier,

when she needed comforting. Now the situation had changed. Now she was forced to be the comforter. Putting an arm around Lucy's shoulders, she said, "We can't think like that. We need to focus on Nick and helping him get better any way we know how. The music, for example. It helps. I know it does."

A bit of hope peeked through Lucy's voice. "You think so? At first, I wasn't going to do it. I thought it might be too stupid."

"It's not stupid at all," Kat said. "And it's the Beatles. They're Nick's favorite."

"I know."

The song on the CD player changed again. This time it was "In My Life," Kat's personal favorite, although it made her cry every time she heard it. This time, for Lucy's sake, she held back the tears.

"I need to get back to work," she said.

"Is there any progress in the investigation?"

"We have a motive," Kat said. "And a suspect. Now all we need to do is find him."

Lucy's face, once so soft with grief and fear, suddenly hardened.

"You will." She looked again at Nick, tears filling her eyes once more. "And when you do, don't go easy on him."

Kat was quiet on the drive back from the hospital. Checking in on Nick had left her too sad to talk much; plus, she was absolutely spent from the day's events. Henry, too, stayed silent, seemingly lost in his own thoughts. The only sound in the car came from the backseat, where James had emptied his pack of licorice and was now crumpling the wrapper.

"Where are we going?" he asked.

"To the police station. Lou has to watch you some more."

"More? Can't we go home?"

James's voice, Kat noticed, was *this close* to becoming a whine. He didn't like spending so much time in the care of a babysitter, even one as familiar as Lou van Sickle. It made him irritable and restless, as evidenced by the way he slid around in the backseat.

Kat tried to tamp down the guilt that always flared when James felt neglected. She was under a lot of pressure at the moment. Until tomorrow, she was in charge of not just Carl and Lou but of a whole score of state troopers. James, of course, couldn't grasp that.

"I told you," she said. "I have to work extra hard today."

James, staring anxiously out the window, repeated what she had told him earlier. "Because there's a bad man out there."

"That's right. A very bad man."

"But what about trick-or-treating?"

That was a very good question, and one Kat hadn't thought of. It was Halloween, after all. There'd be hundreds of kids roaming the sidewalks in an hour or so, not to mention packing a gymnasium by eight that night. And with an arsonist still at large, that was too much of a public safety risk for Kat to take.

"I think that'll have to wait a day," she told James as she reached for the patrol car's radio.

"What do you mean?"

Kat dodged the question as she spoke into the radio. "Lou? You there?"

Lou van Sickle's voice crackled back. "Affirmative."

"I need a big favor."

"In addition to the one I just finished?"

"Yes. And this one's even bigger."

The radio's static couldn't hide the disgruntled sigh that followed. "You know, Al still wants to hit the blackjack tables later."

"This will only take a minute," Kat said. "I just need to get the word out that trick-or-treating has been canceled."

She eyed the rearview mirror, noticing the pale look of dread spreading over James's face. Again, she felt like the worst mother in the world. She had just called off trick-or-treating, which to a kid was tantamount to shooting Santa Claus.

"Are you serious?" Lou asked.

"Deadly."

"What about the Halloween party?"

"I don't know," Kat said. "Maybe it will be okay if we get enough adults to chaperone and put some state troopers on patrol outside the rec center."

By that time, they had reached the heart of town. Kat steered clear of Main Street in an attempt to avoid the late-afternoon traffic that always accumulated there. Instead, she turned right, heading down a side street that would take them to the police station.

"Funny you should mention that," Lou said. "Besides the museum and the bed-and-breakfast, the town has three other buildings on the historic landmark list. The rec center is one of them."

"What are the others?"

"The library and All Saints Parish."

The list made sense to Kat. All three buildings were notable in some way, from the rec center's retractable gym floor to the bell tower at All Saints. Plus, there was the fact that they had greater importance than, say, the flower shop on Main

Street. The loss of even just one of the buildings would reverberate through town. An arsonist with a chip on his shoulder could rationally target any of them.

Or, worse, all of them.

Kat mentally processed what she knew about each location, assessing which building might be in the most imminent danger. The church was probably deserted, making it the least likely location for casualties to occur. That left the library and the rec center as the places that could still have people in them. If they did, Kat needed to get them out of there immediately.

"Is Carl still there?" she asked Lou.

"Yep. Where should I send him?"

"The library," Kat said. "Tell them to close early, just in case."

"Where will you be?"

Through the windshield, Kat saw the gray roof of the Perry Hollow Athletic Center break over the horizon. She thought about the Halloween festival slated to take place there. Burning it down would indeed send a message to the town.

"I'm going to check out the rec center," she said. "Hopefully, no one will still be there."

"Does that mean the Halloween festival is canceled, too?" Lou asked.

Kat glanced back at James again, who looked to be on the verge of tears. It was going to take him a long time to forgive her for this.

"Yes," she said. "Halloween in Perry Hollow is officially canceled."

Signing off, she brought the Crown Vic to a stop a block from the rec center. She then turned to James, who looked more worried than disappointed. He sensed her steadily mounting fear.

"Mom, what's going on?"

"Henry and I need to check on something really quick," Kat said.

"Is the bad man in there?"

Kat didn't have an answer. In all likelihood, the rec center was safe and sound. But there was also a chance that a witch with a massive grudge was inside, getting ready to light a stolen stick of dynamite, so she avoided the question altogether.

"Just stay in the car with the doors locked. Do not open them for anyone but Henry or me. Understand?"

James's nod, quick and nervous, sent yet another wave of guilt crashing over her. It was hard being the child of a police chief. Kat knew that from experience. Her father had once been Perry Hollow's chief, and she distinctly remembered watching him head off to work each morning worried that he might never come back. It required a measure of bravery she had been too young to handle. Now she was asking the same of James and hated herself for it.

"Does Henry have to go?" James asked, voice rising with trepidation. "I want him to stay."

Kat would have preferred that herself. But she had no idea what awaited her inside the rec center. She needed the extra set of eyes Henry provided. His sheer size didn't hurt, either.

Turning around, Kat reached into the backseat and grasped her son's hand. "There's nothing to worry about, Little Bear. We'll be back in a minute. I promise."

She and Henry got out of the car and slowly made their

way across the wide expanse of grass leading to the rec center. When they got close to the building, Kat scanned the nearby parking lot. It was empty. Apparently the preparations for the Halloween festival were finished and everyone had gone home. At least they had that going for them.

The rec center's front door was locked. Another good sign. Kat pressed herself against the glass door, trying to see if any lights were still on inside. The only brightness was the reddish glow of an exit sign on the wall near the door.

The place, it seemed, was empty.

"Let's make one trip around the building," Kat said. "I won't be satisfied until I check every door."

They trudged around the side of the building, encountering an emergency exit that was securely locked. Then it was on to the back of the rec center, where a set of double doors led directly into the gymnasium.

One of them was damaged.

Kat took a step backward, eyeing the door. The handle had been broken off, presumably by something heavy. Like an antique iron, maybe. What remained of the handle lay on the ground in bits of stainless steel. A small rock sat on the ground between the door and its frame, keeping it ajar. Although it was possible that someone was still inside, the rock pointed to another scenario—that someone had recently left and possibly planned on coming back.

Looking to Henry, Kat pressed an index finger to her lips. Then she slid her Glock out of its holster. She wanted desperately to run back to the Crown Vic and call for backup, but the clock was ticking. Connor Hawthorne had an agenda. He also had dynamite. Sooner or later, he was going to use it.

Kat didn't want to give him the opportunity during her minute-long trip back to the car.

She beckoned Henry to lean in close and whispered in his ear. "I'm going in first. Do not enter until I give the all clear. If something happens to me, run like hell back to the car and get James as far away as possible."

She held his gaze, making sure he understood her instructions. Henry nodded once. He was on board.

He stepped aside, holding the door open for her. Kat passed the Glock from one hand to the other, taking a moment to flex the fingers of each. Then, with one last glance at Henry, she pushed into the building.

---

5 P.M.

The only light inside the gymnasium came from the open door—a slash of brightness that narrowed to a sliver before vanishing completely. Kat avoided it, stepping instead into the darkness beside it, like a prowler skirting the glow of a lit window.

Once inside the gym, she stood motionless for a moment, straining to detect the presence of someone else inside. A sound. A movement. She sensed nothing but a vast and empty stillness.

Not having any idea where the gym's light switch was located, she again had to rely on her flashlight to guide her. With her Glock gripped in her other hand, she trotted to the locker rooms on the opposite end of the gym. A quick search of both of them turned up empty. After that, she peered into the hallway that led to the front of the rec center. It, too, looked deserted. Whoever had broken into the place was now apparently gone.

Returning to the gym, Kat let her gaze roam the entire room. By that time her eyes had adjusted to the darkness, and she saw that more progress had been made for the Halloween festival. Decorations were everywhere, from hay bales in the corners to scarecrows in the bleachers. Black and orange bunting swooped from the rafters, colliding with sheets that had been turned into makeshift ghosts and strung up with fishing line.

Dotting the gym were a handful of mannequins that had been dressed in costumes and posed elaborately. A figure in tattered clothes and wearing a Frankenstein mask had its arms stretched menacingly, like it was going to lurch forward at any moment. Nearby was a mummy, dripping from head to toe with toilet paper, and a vampire that was blessedly more *Dracula* than *Twilight*.

The only figure that gave her pause was a witch standing at a remove from the others. Although it had been given the stereotypical costume—black dress, pointy hat, scraggly broom—Kat thought of Rebecca Bradford as soon as she saw it. Had she really been a witch? Connor Hawthorne certainly thought so, but seeing as how he was now trying to burn down half of the town, Kat took his opinion with a grain of salt. She preferred to think of Rebecca as a strong-willed woman just trying to provide for her son. They were very much alike in that regard, and it made Kat shudder to think what might have happened to her and James if they had been around in 1692.

Turning away from the witch figure, Kat looked to the swimming pool, which was still uncovered in the middle of the gym. The water, crystal clear earlier that morning, now looked like swill. Dark, oily globs floated on the surface and brownish clouds spread through the water just below it. If the goal was to turn the pool into something resembling a witch's cauldron, Burt Hammond and his team had succeeded admirably.

The sharp smell of petroleum rose off the water, so noxious that Kat wanted to take a step backward. Instead, she covered her nose and knelt at the pool's edge. When she dipped a finger into the water, ooze dripped off it like molasses.

It was motor oil. The swimming pool had been turned into an oil slick.

Kat tried to peer deeper into the water. Through the slime, she saw the faint outline of something resting on the bottom, something she couldn't quite make out.

"Is it clear?"

Henry Goll's voice, echoing through the gym, startled her. Kat turned to the door, seeing him standing at the threshold, looking around apprehensively.

"The gym, yes," she said. "The pool, no."

Henry joined her by the water. "What the hell happened in here? It looks like a swamp."

"It wasn't like this a few hours ago. My only guess is that someone is trying to clog the inner workings of the pool."

"Why?"

Kat, watching her reflection in the grungy water, saw her shoulders lift and fall in a shrug. "To destroy it, I guess."

"That's better than fire," Henry said. "And there's something on the bottom?"

"Yup."

She turned her attention back to the pool. Again, the smell of motor oil overwhelmed her, but she held steady, taking short, shallow breaths through her mouth as she pointed her flashlight at the water. The dark globs swirling on the surface occasionally parted, offering brief glimpses of the thing on the pool's bottom. It was dark. Long. Human-shaped.

"Jesus. There's a body down there."

"Are you sure?" Henry asked.

"Not yet. But I will be soon."

Kat removed her holster and duty belt, letting them both drop to the floor. Next to go were her shoes, which she kicked off and slid toward her holster. She then shed the top of her uniform, leaving her T-shirt on for modesty's sake.

Henry blinked at her, confused. "You're not going in there, are you?"

"Someone has to."

Kat whirled her index finger, indicating to Henry to avert his gaze. Then she slipped off her trousers and pulled off her socks. She felt awkward stripping down in front of Henry, even in the gym's dimness, but it was better than getting her entire uniform soaked.

Not that Henry was looking anyway. He was too busy unbuttoning his flannel shirt.

"You're not going in alone," he said. "God knows what could be down there."

He removed his shirt, revealing a trim and well-muscled physique. Kat had always known Henry was strong. Other than the scars on his face, his body was the first thing she had noticed about him when they met. Which, she suspected, was the point. Women did it all the time. A killer body often drew strangers' eyes away from a flawed face.

And Henry's body was certainly impressive. Kat, who mostly kept her eyes on the murky pool, couldn't help but steal a few glances as he sat down on a nearby bench to take off his shoes and slide out of his jeans. When he stood again, Kat saw that he was wearing only a pair of tight black briefs.

Henry caught her staring and blushed accordingly. "I live in Italy now. They don't sell tighty whities there."

"I'm not judging," Kat said. "Especially because you're about to see the world's ugliest bra."

She pulled off her T-shirt, revealing a bra that had once been white but was now faded to a dull gray. Between that and her very old, very utilitarian panties, she suspected she looked like the world's worst underwear model.

But Henry wasn't looking at her bra. He stared instead at the two circular scars that marred her upper chest, right near her heart. That's where she had been shot by the Grim Reaper a year earlier. Her life had been saved by the Kevlar vest she was wearing at the time, but the bullets still had left their mark.

"Are those from last year?" Henry asked.

Kat nodded. "Turns out we both have scars."

Their eyes locked—two kindred spirits who both knew what it was like to live with daily reminders of how close they had come to death. Their silent communion made Kat feel more exposed than she had when taking off her trousers.

"I guess we should dive in," she said, breaking the eye contact to turn toward the pool. "So to speak."

She sat on the edge of the pool and swung her legs into

the water. It was cold and greasy, the surface coated by a thin slime. Beads of the oil floating on the water stuck to her skin. Submerging herself in this swill wasn't going to be pretty.

Henry joined her at the pool's edge. "Are you sure you want to do this?"

"I *know* I don't want to do this," Kat said. "But I'd be a terrible police chief if there was a corpse down there and I didn't try to identify it."

"Then here goes nothing."

Henry slipped into the water first, submerged up to his neck. The slime clung to him, too, smearing across his shoulders and sliding off his chin. Kat followed, the chill of the water making her gasp. It was a cold slap to her lower back that instantly erased all tiredness she had been feeling.

Treading water, she tried not to get as slimed as Henry had. It was impossible. The oil was everywhere. She felt it attach to her skin immediately, like hundreds of tiny hands trying to clamber onto her for rescue.

Or else drag her under.

Bobbing with her head out of the water, Kat took several deep breaths. Calisthenics of sorts for her lungs. Then she counted to three and slid beneath the surface.

The water was cloudy—like swimming through a thick fog. Brown and brackish, it reminded Kat of the Atlantic Ocean. It stung like saltwater, too, so much so that she was forced to close her eyes. Pushing deeper, she could feel the presence of Henry swimming beside her. She reached out, blindly groping for his hand. When she at last felt it, she gripped it tightly. She felt more comfortable knowing he was right there with her.

Even though she couldn't see it, Kat sensed when the bottom was near. It was the same way she could tell she was approaching a wall when walking with her eyes closed. The force of their movements seemed to bounce off the pool's bottom and radiate back toward them. But there was another energy at work there, too. A rush of pressure suddenly being unleashed. The water vibrated with it.

Her eyes still squeezed shut, Kat thrust her free hand forward. Her fingertips scraped the bottom, which was hard and slightly grainy. Concrete. The sign of a very old swimming pool.

She let go of Henry, using both hands to feel around the area directly in front of her. Henry was doing the same thing. Occasionally, one of his hands would bump her shoulder, or their legs would get briefly snagged together. After one such entanglement, Kat found herself spinning away from him. She struck something with her shoulder.

The body at the pool's bottom.

Only it wasn't a body. It was smooth. And cold, absorbing the water's chill.

It was, she realized, metal.

Kat smoothed her palm over its surface. It was a cylinder of some sort. Like a bucket, but with a rounded top. Opening her eyes, she saw flashes of red through the cloudy water. Squinting, she could make out several words painted in yellow on the cylinder's surface. One of them stood out through the murky water.

Gasoline.

Her jaw dropped in shock. A bad, bad move. Fetid water poured into her mouth. Kat pushed it back out, removing more air from her lungs in the process. She twisted in the depths, a tightness forming in her chest as she searched for Henry.

Instead, she saw another gasoline container. Its cap had

been removed, letting a cloudy trail of gas puff into the water and rise like smoke to the surface. She spotted another one behind it. And another one just beyond that. All of them in a six-foot row, belching out their contents and making the pool even more cloudy, more dangerous.

Someone swooped up behind her. A pair of hands grabbed her waist, making her let out another useless underwater yelp. She twisted in their grip, seeing that it was Henry, eyes wide open and flooded with worry. He wrapped an arm around her waist and started to swim, pushing them upward in forceful kicks.

"Gas," he said once they broke the surface. "The pool is filled with gasoline."

Kat, out of breath, responded in gasping half sentences. "I—know. I saw—it."

Henry began to spin in the water, searching for the nearest ladder. He saw it on the other side of the pool.

"We have to get—"

Kat raised a finger to quiet him. She had heard something. Coming from just beyond the door. She wasn't sure, but it sounded like footsteps.

"Someone is coming," she whispered.

A figure appeared in the doorway. It was silhouetted by the setting sun, preventing Kat from making out any details other than that it seemed to be a man. Not that she had much time to look. When the figure took a step deeper into the rec center, Henry tugged on her arm, pulling her to the side of the pool.

Paddling lightly in the greasy water, they pressed their backs against the pool wall closest to the door, where their sudden visitor was least likely to spot them. Henry turned to Kat and mouthed one word. *Arsonist.*

Kat had been thinking the same thing. Whoever it was had left for a brief time, returning to finish what he had started. What that unfinished business was, Kat had no idea. All she knew is that they were completely helpless. Their clothes—and her Glock—were on the other side of the gym, scattered on one of the benches beside the pool. If they were discovered, the intruder would certainly get to it before she could. She prayed that wouldn't happen.

Holding her breath, she listened as the man took several more steps into the gym. He was close to the pool now. Heart-poundingly close. When she heard another step, she slipped beneath the pool's surface. Henry did the same.

They were barely under before a shadow fell over that end of the water. The figure was now poolside.

Looking upward, straining to see through the swill floating all around them, Kat spotted the darkened figure kneel next to the pool. Panic filled her brain.

He saw us, she thought. *He knows we're here.*

Yet the figure didn't act like he had noticed them. Instead, he reached into his pocket, pulled something out and held it to the water.

Kat simultaneously struggled to remain underwater while straining to identify the man and figure out what he was holding. The water was so cloudy—brown puffs everywhere, blobs of oil obscuring the surface—that it was almost impossible to see. It wasn't until the man touched the object to the water's surface that she realized what it was.

A cigarette lighter.

Henry saw it, too, and propelled himself to the surface. Kat followed suit, her head bursting out of the water.

"Stop!" she yelled.

She couldn't see the figure. There was water in her eyes and oil on her face. All she could make out was his gloved hand, low to the water, thumb spinning off the lighter as a tiny flame sprung to life.

The fire was instantaneous—a wall of flame leaping off the water's surface and zipping toward them in a lightning-quick *whoosh*.

Kat's survival instincts immediately kicked in. Already lowering herself back down in the water, she took a frantic gulp of air. Then she was under, the flames rolling overhead, inches away from her face. The fire was white as it sizzled on the water's surface, turning first light blue and then blazing orange. Even fully submerged, Kat felt its heat. The pool's surface seemed to be boiling. The searing hot bubbles thrashed around her, threatening to pull her closer to the flames.

A hand locked around her wrist. Henry again, yanking her deeper. Transfixed by the blaze overhead, Kat let herself be pulled. The water got slightly cooler the deeper they went. Darker, too, as the murky water clouded the color of the flames. Yet Kat could still see them—that blinding white changing to orange—even as she landed on the pool's bottom.

Henry had both arms around her waist, air bubbling from his nose and mouth as he tried to weigh them down. They were next to the pool ladder, and he latched on to the bottom rung, arm looped around it to keep them from floating upward.

A thought occurred to Kat as they lay at the bottom of the pool. Now that they were submerged, there was no way to get out until the fire died away.

The realization set off sirens of panic inside her brain. She wondered how long the fire would burn. It couldn't be long. Despite the several dozen gallons of gas in the water and an unknown amount of oil on the surface, there was nothing for the flames to latch on to. It would go out within seconds. It had to.

But then Kat thought of her gas stove at home. Fire didn't need a solid surface to burn. All it needed was something to consume. With this in mind, she looked to the identical red containers in the pool's center, each one spewing out more fuel for the fire. The blaze on the surface, she realized with mounting fear, could last a while.

She tried to estimate how long they had been underwater. Five seconds? Ten? When she realized she didn't know, she worried about how long she could hold her breath without passing out. She recalled reading somewhere that it was five minutes. Or maybe that was how long until you died. She couldn't be sure.

While she was thinking, a tightness had once again formed in her chest. This time it stayed, a pressure pushing against her rib cage, making it feel like her whole chest was going to explode.

She wanted air.

She needed it.

One of Henry's arms ratcheted tighter around her waist, making Kat realize she had been struggling in his grip. Her legs kicked. Her hands clawed at the water, trying to paddle desperately higher even though she knew that was the last thing she should be doing. Her thirst for oxygen was so great that she was risking death to get it.

She tried to fight her way out of Henry's grip, elbowing

his chest and kicking backward. But he was stronger than she was, a fact made clear when he flipped her around to face him. Holding her gaze, he shook his head. He removed a hand from her writhing body and placed a finger to his lips.

Kat got the message. She needed to relax. To not struggle. To save the oxygen she had left.

Closing her eyes, she settled against Henry's chest. As he hugged her tight, she went limp and tried to ignore the pressure expanding in her chest, to forget that she had been underwater for at least two minutes. Probably more.

She thought of James, waiting for them alone in the car. She hoped the figure, who surely had fled after starting the fire, didn't spot him outside. She hoped that James kept the doors locked, just as she had instructed. Above all, she hoped, with the desperate love that only a mother could have, that if she died in that pool, James wouldn't be the one to find her.

Those grim thoughts quickly faded, replaced by a deep nothingness. She was on the verge of passing out. The lightness in her brain was a sure sign of it. So was the floating sensation she suddenly felt.

Opening her eyes one last time, she saw that she really was drifting higher, no longer bound by Henry's arms.

He had let her go.

She grabbed the ladder, halting her ascent. She forced her body down one rung, then another, trying to ignore the panicked voice in her head screaming that she should be climbing up, not down. But Kat pressed onward, grabbing another rung and lowering herself until she was close to Henry's face.

His eyes were closed and his head was tilted limply to the side. He was on the verge of losing consciousness.

Kat flicked her gaze upward, where the fire was still raging, still as white hot as it had ever been. Turning back to Henry, she smacked his cheeks, trying to rouse him. He didn't respond. Not knowing what else to do, she put her mouth over his, trying to push what little air she had left from her lungs into his.

Henry's eyes snapped open. They danced with surprise when he realized that he had almost passed out. He seemed even more shocked that Kat's lips were pressed against his own. Yet he didn't back away from her. Instead, he pushed forward in what could only be interpreted as a kiss.

Kat kissed him back, not fully understanding what was happening or why. But deep down, she knew. They were going to die in the cloudy depths of that pool, ironically drowning in a fire. With less than a minute to live, they didn't want to die alone.

So they clutched each other, bodies pressed together as they traded empty-breathed kisses. The pressure that had once been in Kat's chest was now spread throughout her entire body. All thoughts melted from her brain. Now she was thriving only on feelings. Terror. Desire. Despair. They all merged together in a roiling ball of emotion as she closed her eyes and prepared to let consciousness slip away.

Above them, the muffled roar of the fire seemed to mutate into a loud hum. Kat became vaguely aware of a large shadow sliding over them. Death, she thought, descending upon her like a massive black hand.

But Henry noticed it, too. Breaking off their kiss, he looked up, watching the shadow continue its journey overhead. On the other side of the pool, Kat spotted a second shadow, hovering toward the first.

It was the gym floor, sliding back into place. The steady

movement of both ends cut off the flames. Kat could see the fire getting smaller, weaker. Then the two sides of the gym floor met, slamming together with a resounding thud that snuffed out the blaze.

Although plunged into darkness, Kat and Henry swam as fast as their exhausted bodies would allow. They broke through the surface, discovering about six inches of air between the water and the underside of the gym floor. They breathed it in, swallowing it down in deep, happy gulps. Then they pounded on the barrier overhead, signaling it was safe to open up again.

Within seconds, the gym floor cracked open, shining a sliver of light across the slime-slicked water. As the light expanded, Kat and Henry dog-paddled toward it, the brightness illuminating their faces. Henry's face had turned crimson from lack of oxygen and was slick with the black ooze of the pool. Kat imagined she looked the same way—as gasping and red-faced as a baby emerging from the womb.

When the hole above them got large enough, Henry reached up and grabbed an edge. He hoisted himself onto the still-retracting floor before turning to pull Kat up, as well. Too spent to walk, they slid across the floor, moving to a part of the gymnasium that was solid and immovable.

The gym itself was choked with thick, black smoke that was slow to dissipate. It hung in the stagnant air, swirling lazily like stubborn storm clouds. But through the haze, Kat could see a rectangle of late-day sunlight from the door that led outside. Standing next to it, hand resting on the red button that controlled the gym floor, was James.

"I'm sorry I didn't stay in the car," he said.

6 P.M.

The ambulance, brought to the scene as a precaution, remained parked outside the rec center. Kat sat on a stretcher in the back, wrapped in a wool blanket and tightly hugging her son. Although her uniform was back on, high and dry but reeking of smoke, she kept the blanket, if only to shield James from the oil that had dried onto her hair and skin.

Sitting with them was Larry Sheldon, who detailed what had been found inside the rec center gym. The gasoline containers, which could be purchased at practically every hardware store in the state, had been wiped free of fingerprints. The water from the pool erased any trace evidence they might have contained. About a dozen two-quart bottles of motor oil were found in the rec center's Dumpster, also minus any fingerprints. The brand of oil was Champion Agriline, intended for tractors and, once again, easily available at hardware stores.

In short, they had nothing.

Larry knelt in front of James, taking the boy's hands in his. "The man you saw running out of the rec center—"

"The bad man," James said.

Larry smiled. "Yes, the bad man. Are you sure you didn't see his face? Not even a tiny bit?"

They had been through this once before. While waiting in the Crown Vic, James had spotted a figure fleeing the scene of the fire, but it was only for a second. The man had been running along the side of the building, and by the time James noticed him, he was already disappearing around the corner. Once James saw smoke pouring out of the door, he realized something was wrong and left the car against Kat's orders.

For that, Kat couldn't have been more proud. She gave James a squeeze, making him wriggle in her grip. She could tell he didn't like being coddled this way, especially in front of a stranger, but she refused to let him go.

"I didn't see anything," James answered. "Just his clothes."

Larry looked to Kat hopefully. "And you?"

"Same thing," she said. "All I caught was a hand, which doesn't matter because he was wearing gloves. I'm assuming Henry told you the same thing."

"He did," Larry replied. "Unfortunately."

"So we still have nothing."

"That's about right. I don't understand this guy. I mean, why set fire to a swimming pool, of all things? Why not the building itself? It makes no sense."

It did to Kat. She understood the arsonist's intentions perfectly.

"Because the building is worthless," she said. "That pool, however, is historic. Not to mention irreplaceable. He's trying to do the most damage."

Outside, a crowd had gathered. They streamed past the open door of the ambulance on their way to the arsonist's latest target. This time, at least, the town had been lucky. Other than smoke damage and a very messy swimming pool, Perry Hollow's rec center remained mostly unscathed.

One of the people arriving at the scene was Lou van Sickle, who climbed into the ambulance. She carried a plastic bag that bulged at the sides. Clean clothes for Kat.

"Here you go," she said. "By the way, word on the street is that you and Henry Goll decided to go skinny-dipping. Got so hot it set the pool on fire."

Kat laughed in spite of herself. "That's not quite how it went."

But it was close enough. Kat's face reddened as she thought about what she and Henry had done in the pool before James saved them. It meant nothing, of course. They had both been terrified and desperate, unable to express their emotions in words. Now that they had survived, she didn't want to talk about it. Not with Lou and certainly not with Henry. Kat was grateful that he had been ushered to his own ambulance, where he was no doubt being examined by paramedics just as she had been. It spared them from having to see each other, if only for a little bit.

When Lou handed her the bag of clothes, Kat opened it and sniffed. They smelled gloriously free of smoke. She couldn't wait to put them on.

"Now I think it's time to take our hero out to dinner," Lou said, taking James's hand. "How does the Perry Hollow Diner sound? You deserve a milk shake for your good deed."

Kat, keeping hold of her son, whispered in his ear, "I'm so proud of you, Little Bear. Go and have fun with Lou."

"You're not coming with us?"

The look James gave her—apprehensive and disappointed—split her heart in two. He knew he had come close to losing her that afternoon. Now he didn't want to let her out of his sight.

"I still have work to do," Kat told him. "The bad man is still out there and I need to find him."

She gave him one final squeeze, as tight as her tired arms could muster, and watched him be reluctantly led away by Lou. Larry Sheldon also departed, saying he'd be inside the rec center if she needed him.

Alone in the back of the ambulance, Kat collapsed backward onto the stretcher. Exhaustion numbed every part of her body. She needed sleep. She craved it so badly it hurt. But she couldn't sleep. Not yet. A fact that made her want to cry.

And that's exactly what she did. Lying on her back, she let the tears flow. The warm drops slipped over her temples and into her already damp hair as sobs racked her body. In that moment, she didn't care about the fires or Constance Bishop or those poor women murdered long ago. She only cared about what they were doing to her body, her brain, her sanity. She was on the cusp of giving up. Of just curling into a ball and sleeping until Gloria Ambrose swooped in and took over. It would be so easy to just shut her tear-reddened eyes and let sleep overwhelm her.

But then she thought of James and how close he had been to becoming motherless. She thought of Constance, slumped over that trunk, head bashed in. And she thought of Rebecca Bradford and her cluster of sisters—innocent women who died, horribly, for no reason.

She had to keep going, no matter how exhausted she was. For their sake.

So Kat forced herself to sit up. She smacked her face twice, once on each cheek. When that didn't work, she reached under her arm, pinching a bit of skin just below her armpit. It hurt. A lot. But the pain jolted her awake. She did it again, this time with the other arm. It did the trick. She was ready to get going again.

Quickly, she changed into her uniform before stepping out of the ambulance. The crowd, she saw, was still milling about the rec center. A large group stood near the door, talking among themselves and trying to peer into the smoky building.

Standing away from them was Mayor Burt Hammond. He stared at the building in disbelief, his hands on his head. The town had been dealt another blow, and the mayor looked to be physically feeling its effects. If a light breeze had knocked him over, Kat wouldn't have been surprised.

She approached him slowly. "I'm sorry about the Halloween Festival. I know you worked really hard."

"Forget the festival," Burt said. "I'm worried about the town. Three fires in one day. All of them vital pieces of Perry Hollow's history. What the hell is going on?"

"We have a motive. We have a suspect. Everyone is looking for him. If he's still around, we'll find him."

"Of course he's still around." Burt jerked his head in the direction of the rec center. "Otherwise, *that* wouldn't have happened."

Kat couldn't believe the change in the mayor's voice. It was tinged with accusation, like he was blaming her for what was happening.

"We're doing everything we can," she said.

"Well, you need to do more," Burt snapped. "People are scared, Kat. I hear them talking. Everyone's worried their house might be the next thing to go up in flames. There's even talk of forming a militia."

"Wait—forming a *what*?"

"You heard me," Burt said. "Mob rule. People on the streets with guns."

Kat wanted to cover her ears. She knew the town was scared. She just didn't know it was this bad. She pictured crowds of people marching down Main Street, hunting rifles at the ready. It's probably how the men of the village had approached Rebecca Bradford's homestead.

"That's a bad idea," she said. "Really bad."

"That's what it'll come to, unless you stop it."

Beyond Burt, a patrol car just like her own pulled up to the curb, Deputy Carl Bauersox behind the wheel. He spotted her as soon as he got out of the car and beckoned with a wave of his hand. Finally, a reason to escape the mayor's wrath.

"I understand, Burt," Kat said as calmly as she could. "And I promise you that I'll catch this guy. I just need a little more time."

The mayor couldn't resist one parting shot. "We're all out of time, Chief."

He turned and started to trudge toward the rec center. Kat went in the opposite direction, heading to Carl's patrol car.

"Is it true you were skinny-dipping with Henry Goll?" the deputy asked once she reached him.

"If I say yes, will you tell me there's a break in the case?"

"Potentially," Carl said. "I finished looking into the backgrounds of all the volunteer firefighters. It was hard because some of them didn't grow up here and I had to call other departments to look through their records, too."

Kat nodded while gesturing for Carl to speed things up.

"Anyway," he said, now talking faster, "the last of them just got back to me. Dutch Jansen is all clear, just like I knew he would be. Most of the other squad members check out, too. Some of them have a few misdemeanors. Traffic tickets. Bar fights. That sort of thing."

"Carl." Kat grabbed the deputy's shoulders in frustration. "Just tell me what you found."

"One of them was arrested for arson when he was a teenager," he said. "Quite a few times. He set his family's shed on fire. Then a neighbor's garage. Finally, an abandoned house a few blocks away. Burned the whole thing to the ground and spent a few months in juvie because of it."

Kat already knew who he was talking about. It was the same person who had been acting strangely during the Chamber of Commerce fund-raiser the night before. The same guy who hadn't bothered to show up to work that morning.

"Chief," Carl said, even though he didn't need to. "It's Danny Batallas."

Henry woke up gasping. He had fallen asleep in the back of the ambulance, dreaming that he was still underwater and unable to take in air. And even though he was now awake, he continued to feel damp and breathless, almost as if he was still submerged.

He sat up and wiped his brow. His face was slick with sweat. That explained the damp part. Looking around, he saw that the ambulance doors had been closed for privacy, creating a sterile darkness. The two windows offered little additional light. Just twin squares of brightness that faded with each passing moment. Outside, dusk was falling.

Behind him, the voice of a woman broke through the darkness. "You were having a bad dream."

The presence of someone else in the ambulance didn't startle Henry. Even in sleep, he must have known he was not alone.

"Kat?" he said.

"No."

Henry rolled over on the stretcher that had been his temporary bed. He got on his hands and knees before flipping into a sitting position. Now he could finally see the other person in the ambulance.

"How are you feeling?" Deana Swan asked.

"I've been better."

"You look okay. A little tired. That's why I let you sleep."

She offered him a half-smile. Her eyes, bright even in the dim ambulance, contained a sad weariness. "You stood me up today. I honestly thought you'd come."

"I'm sorry." Henry mopped his brow again. It was stifling in there. "Things happened."

"The fire at the Sleepy Hollow Inn," Deana said. "I know. I heard all about it. And then when I got word that you were in the fire at the rec center, I knew I had to see you, even if you didn't want to see me."

Henry wished it was that simple, but his feelings for Deana were a writhing mass of conflicting emotions. He wanted to see her and avoid her in equal measure. Being alone with her again, he felt the urge to both embrace her and run away. Instead, he stayed where he was, motionless.

"It's good to see you, Henry," Deana said. "I'm not sure I told you that."

"Why are you here, Deana?"

"I just want an hour of your time. That's all. After that, you don't ever have to see me again if you don't want to. I'll completely understand."

Henry couldn't summon the will to resist. Considering that he had almost died twice that day, spending sixty minutes with Deana Swan wasn't the worst thing in the world. Besides, it felt good to be alone with her again, talking soft and close the way they used to. It was just like old times.

Almost.

"Fine," Henry said. "Let's talk."

Deana's face brightened, making her look as pretty as the day Henry first saw her. "I have a better idea," she said. "Let's go for a walk."

Henry threw open the ambulance doors, startling an EMT drinking coffee right outside. He apologized and thanked him for giving him a chance to rest before helping Deana hop to the ground. Side by side, they crossed in front of the rec center—now lit up with klieg lights and crawling with crime scene techs. Once on the sidewalk, Deana steered them to the right. Henry didn't need to ask where they were going. He knew she was guiding him to her house. Once again, he didn't resist.

Neither of them spoke as they walked. There was so much to say that they didn't have the first clue where to begin. Henry wanted to tell Deana that he had thought of her often during the past year. Dreamed of her even, in nighttime reveries so vivid he could have sworn she had been lying next to him. But he knew that might give her a false sense of hope, make her think there was a chance they could go back to the way things were a year ago. That, Henry told himself, wasn't going to happen. It couldn't. So he remained silent.

As they navigated the streets of Perry Hollow, it dawned on Henry that the town was too quiet for a Saturday night. While the town was never what you'd call bustling, there was usually some activity taking place there. Teenagers looking for trouble. Adults looking for ways to forget theirs. Bursts of laughter from front porches or open windows.

That evening, there was nothing. The few people they did pass looked watchful and worried, eyeing Henry's scars with suspicious, sidelong glances. He easily ignored them. Back in Perry Hollow for less than a day, he was again accustomed to the way people in town stared.

"I hear you're helping Chief Campbell with all the fires going on," Deana said, her voice full of forced cheer. "I bet that's exciting."

"I'm not really helping," Henry replied. "More like looking out for her."

And making out with her inside a fiery swimming pool. It was still too soon to be able to wrap his head around that particular development. All he knew is that it would certainly make for some awkwardness once he saw her again.

"I was real sad to hear about what happened to Constance Bishop," Deana said. "She was a nice woman."

A couple in their fifties, holding hands and laughing like people half their age, grew suddenly stone-faced as they passed. Deana, shrinking from their glares, began to talk faster.

"I saw her a lot at the library. She was always researching something. Always made a point to say hello when she saw me."

"How do you like working at the library?" Henry asked.

Deana shrugged. "It's all right. Truth is, I needed the job. Things were tight after the funeral home closed. A lot of people wouldn't hire me because of, well, you know. But I have a friend, Doreen, who works at the library. She's the one who got me the job."

A woman approached. A jogger. Reflective tape was stuck to the sleeves of her sweatshirt, catching the glare of a streetlight flickering to life as she passed. Seeing them, she did a double take.

That was the moment Henry realized that people weren't staring at him. They were looking at Deana Swan. Judging her. Hating her. For the first time, he thought about how difficult living in Perry Hollow must be for her now. He wondered if she had any friends besides this Doreen, a person she had never mentioned during the months they were dating. He remembered what Kat had told him early that morning in the diner, that no one saw very much of Deana. He imagined her hidden deep inside her house, stepping outside only to go to work and back again. Just like he used to do.

They were at her house now. Deana walked a little faster, visibly nervous as she led Henry up the driveway, across the front walk, to the door. Before following her inside, he touched her shoulders, bringing her to a stop.

"I need to know," he said, "if you're happy. Because if you're not, then get far away from here. Just run away and forget your past. I've done it twice now."

Deana touched a finger to his temple. Gazing at his face, she traced his scar all the way past his mouth.

"It's not that easy, Henry. Besides, I'm the happiest I've ever been."

She opened the front door and they stepped inside. The place looked just as Henry had remembered it. Comforting. Like being enveloped by a warm hug. In the living room, a plump woman with bleached blond hair sat on the couch, flipping through a copy of *People*. She stood when she saw Henry.

"Thanks, Doreen," Deana told her. "I owe you one."

Doreen gave her a sisterly jab in the ribs with her elbow before nodding a silent hello to Henry. Then she was out the door, closing it behind her.

Deana moved deeper into the house, disappearing up the stairs. "I'll just be a minute," she called down. "Make yourself at home."

Henry remained standing, back to the door, craning his neck to see if he could spot Deana moving around the upstairs landing. He had no idea why she had brought him here, other than to maybe show him off to Doreen. He grew uncomfortable. The last time he was inside her home, they had made love, intense and passionate, in her bedroom. Was Deana there now? Waiting for him to come up in hopes of a repeat?

He felt the urge to leave. It would have been easy. He was two feet from the front door. All he needed to do was slip out. Then he'd never have to see Deana again. Never need to worry about her feelings and expectations.

But then he heard footsteps on the landing as Deana descended the stairs. She moved slowly, with caution. When she reached the halfway point, Henry saw her shoes. Then her legs. Then he saw the baby she held in her arms, asleep, wrapped in a blanket as white and puffy as a cloud in summer.

"Henry," Deana said, "this is your son."

7 P.M.

Night had fully descended by the time they reached the house where Danny Batallas lived. For that, Kat was thankful. It would make their job if not easier, then at least less visible. The fewer people who saw their approach, the better.

She parked her Crown Vic on the street. Carl did the same. The state trooper they had brought along—good old Randall Stroup—parked his vehicle on the opposite side of the street. The three of them then conferred outside Kat's car.

"Danny lives in the basement apartment," she told them. "There was no sign of him this morning, but that doesn't mean he's not there now. And while he's shown no signs of being dangerous in the past, again, it doesn't mean he's not."

All three of them had put on their Kevlar before leaving. Kat hoped it wouldn't be necessary, but it was better to be safe than sorry.

The house—a ramshackle two-story dwelling with peeled siding—looked to be unoccupied. All the windows were dark, although a porch light flickered intermittently. The place was surrounded by a chain-link fence, a sun-faded sign on the unlocked gate warned them to beware of their dog.

Kat opened it anyway, the gate groaning as they pushed through it. It was the only noise on an otherwise silent block. Kat led the way as they crept across the yard. She kept low to the ground, scanning the dark corners of the property. A light popped on in the house next door, revealing a motionless silhouette watching them through the window. They had been spotted.

The three of them pressed on, quickly reaching the house. Kat stuck close to it, her shoulder brushing the siding as she rounded the corner into the backyard. Along the way, she glanced down at the basement windows located near her ankles. Like the rest of the house, they were also dark. If Danny Batallas was home, he sure didn't want anyone to know it.

The door to the basement unit was located in the back, next to the garage. Just like that morning, it was locked. This time, though, Kat didn't bother to knock.

"Stand back," she whispered to the others. "I'm going to kick the door in."

Randall Stroup put a hand on her shoulder. "I can do it, if you'd like."

"No need," Kat said. "I'm actually pretty good at this."

Leaning back, she raised her right leg and smashed her boot against the door, just above the knob. The door frame splintered instantly. When Kat kicked it again, the door broke free and flew open.

"Now!" she yelled. "Go!"

Randall rushed through the door, pounding down the steps into the basement. Carl followed, with Kat close behind. On her way through the door, she flicked on the overhead light, illuminating the drab and dirty stairwell. The area around the bottom of the stairs brightened. It was Randall, also turning on the lights.

Guns raised, the three of them spread out through the apartment. The place was designed like a series of attached train cars, with one narrow room leading directly into the next. At the bottom of the stairs was the kitchen, all stained linoleum and fluorescent lighting. A tiny table with one short leg propped up by a phone book sat near the door. A dead plant hung beside one of the rectangular windows.

A closet door sat next to the fridge. Randall flung it open and looked inside.

"Kitchen is clear," he said.

Kat pushed into the next room, which was a living room of sorts. Decorated like a den from the seventies, it had shag carpeting and faux-wood paneling. Candy wrappers and potato chip bags littered the coffee table. An end table contained an ashtray with a half-smoked cigarette poking out of it.

"Living room is clear," she yelled before moving on to the adjoining bathroom. There wasn't much to it. A toilet. A sink. A shower. Kat opened the door to the linen closet, seeing only towels and washcloths tossed haphazardly on its shelves.

"Bathroom is also clear."

The final room was the bedroom. Kat hit the light switch before moving inside. The room was small and sparsely furnished. Other than an unmade bed, it contained a nightstand cluttered with a lamp, clock radio, and several copies of *Penthouse*. A weight bench and dumbbells sat in the corner, next to a rickety desk crammed with a computer and printer. There was no door on the bedroom closet, giving Kat an easy view of Danny's jeans, T-shirts, and clothes for work.

"Bedroom is clear," she said.

She stared at the empty bed. Something black and shiny peeked out from beneath the tangled sheets.

A cell phone.

Kat grabbed it. Scrolling through its touch-screen menu, she found the log of calls, both incoming and outgoing. Danny had made several calls during the past few days, all to places with helpful labels. Work. Firehouse. Mike's Pizza. Someone he had anointed Sex Fiend.

There were fewer incoming calls, many from the same places he had dialed. Kat saw that a half-dozen from his workplace had come in earlier that morning in the directory of missed calls. According to the phone, Danny had yet to listen to the accompanying messages.

In the directory of received calls, however, was one that Danny had answered shortly after seven that morning. No number was listed with it. Whoever called him had used a block on the caller ID.

"Chief." Carl's voice rose from the living room. "I think I found something."

Kat dropped the phone back onto the bed and returned to the living room, where Carl and Randall stood over the coffee table. The wrappers and chip bags had been cleared, revealing a small stack of paper. Kat riffled through it, alarm growing with each passing page. Maybe Connor Hawthorne wasn't their man after all.

She turned to Randall Stroup. "Get on the radio and try to get someone from motor vehicles. I want to know the make, model, and license plate number of whatever Danny Batallas is driving. Then put out an APB and round up all the troopers not guarding one of the historical buildings."

She moved on to Carl. "Head to Main Street and ask around if anyone has seen Danny all day. You know where to go."

"The diner, Big Joe's, and the Sawmill," the deputy said, nodding. "Where are you going to be?"

"Talking to Dutch Jansen. I want to find out everything he knows about Danny Batallas."

His name was Adam.

That's the first thing Henry learned about his son.

He was delivered by C-section on a rainy day in June. Because she wanted to keep it a secret, Deana had had it done at a hospital in a neighboring county. Other than her coworker, few people in Perry Hollow even knew she had a child. She told Henry she wanted to keep it that way, at least until the town's collective memory faded.

"I don't want people to look at him the way they do me," she said softly, while cradling the baby. "I don't want him to grow up thinking he's different."

"Is he healthy?" Henry asked. "No problems?"

"He's as healthy as can be." Adam was awake now, wriggling in Deana's arms. She kissed the tip of his nose. "Would you like to hold him?"

Henry hadn't even considered it. He was still in shock, a lump of numbness on the living room sofa. He wasn't sure his arms, as stable as jelly, were capable of holding a baby. Still, he found himself nodding. Yes, he wanted to hold his son. More than anything.

Deana lifted Adam and placed him in Henry's arms. All numbness vanished as soon as he felt the weight of his son in his hands. It was replaced by a newfound strength, an overwhelming urge to do everything he could to protect this child.

"Support the head," Deana said, guiding his hands. "There you go."

Henry gazed down at the boy. Adam had blue eyes, like his mother, and blond hair that was already starting to curl. But the rest of his facial features clearly came from Henry. Same nose. Same strong chin. Same smile. Looking at his son, Henry saw his own reflection.

"I can't believe I'm a father," he said. "I'm still amazed."

Only that seemed like too weak a word to describe how he was feeling. *Overwhelmed* was more like it. Or *stupefied*. Or *gobsmacked*. He could have recited an entire thesaurus and still not gotten to the root of how he felt.

He was a father. Of a healthy baby boy. It's what he'd always wanted. It's what he would have had, too, if not for a snowy night, an overturned truck, and a car accident that destroyed life as he knew it. Now that it was a reality, it felt as if the past six years had been a test of his patience, the longest labor in history. Fate had provided him with the child he had always desired. It just had taken a lot longer than he expected.

Henry thought of Gia. He couldn't help it. All these years later, he still missed her. And he knew she'd be happy that he had helped create life after all, that something good had come from his miserable existence.

He began to weep, gentle tears that contained both joy and regret. One of them slid from his cheek onto Adam's. The tiny splash made the baby wrinkle his nose. Henry smiled and wiped it away with his index finger.

"Why didn't you tell me?"

"I wanted to," Deana said. "But I didn't know how. I didn't even know where you were."

Henry felt a slow burn of shame as Deana told him about her attempts to find him. Google searches that led her to Web sites written in Italian. Phone directories in other countries. She said she had even considered hiring Nick Donnelly to try to find him, but she feared he would then tell Kat. It was a risk she couldn't take.

"So I gave up," she said. "By disappearing entirely, you made it clear you didn't want to be found. And I had come to terms with the fact that Adam would never know his father. But it still felt wrong. I felt guilty that—"

Deana's voice cracked, caught on a wave of emotion. She swallowed hard, trying to suppress it, but the tears came anyway.

"I felt terrible that after all you had been through, you'd never get the chance to know that you were a dad."

But now Henry knew. Now he was able to hold his child. Now his son—his son! He still couldn't wrap his head around it—would grow up knowing who he was. Henry was going to make sure of that.

"I'll support him," he said. "Any way I can. You won't have to raise this child alone. I'll be there, too."

"But how, Henry?" Deana asked. "You live in Italy now. That's half a world away."

"I don't know. I'll think of something."

He had to move back to the United States, that much was certain. Maybe try to get a reporting job somewhere nearby. If that didn't work, then he'd try his hand at something else. He didn't know what, nor did he know where.

All Henry knew as he cradled Adam in his arms was that his life had unexpectedly changed yet again.

"I was surprised to get your call. With all these fires going on, I think we both have better things to do than hang out here."

Dutch Jansen looked around the lounge of Maison

D'Avignon, rolling his eyes at the mahogany bartop decorated with tea lights and the bottles of wine hanging from wrought-iron racks.

"I bet you prefer the Sawmill," Kat said, referring to the bar on the southern end of Main Street. Its scratched booths, squeaky barstools, and no-nonsense drinks seemed more Dutch's speed.

"Yeah," Dutch said. "I stick out like a sore thumb here."

He was dressed in scuffed jeans and a sweat-stained T-shirt. And although the bar was practically empty, he shifted uncomfortably whenever someone better dressed walked by. Kat knew that would be the case, which is why she chose this place as their meeting spot. She didn't want to confront Dutch on his home turf. She wanted to keep him off balance and vulnerable.

"You see Danny Batallas at all today?" she asked, sipping from a cup of coffee the size of her head.

Dutch took a swig of beer before answering. "Nope."

"How much do you know about him?"

"He's been on the squad a year or so," Dutch said. "Good kid. Knows his stuff. Never reckless. Some of the newer guys tend to get reckless. They want to be a hero so bad that they end up doing some pretty stupid shit."

"Like starting fires?"

Dutch, pint of beer in hand, contemplated Kat over the rim of the glass. "You might want to start watching what you say, Chief."

His defensiveness was understandable. Kat would have been the same way if he had said something disparaging about Carl or Lou. But Dutch didn't know what Kat knew. He hadn't seen what she'd seen in Danny's apartment.

"Before he came to Perry Hollow," she said, "Danny

lived in Scranton. In his early teens, he was arrested. Several times. Those arrests were for starting fires."

Dutch slammed his beer on the table, livid. "You did a background check on him?"

"On all of the firefighters," Kat said. "Including you. Now, I know you're—"

"Pissed off? Damn right I am. While my boys and I were out there putting our lives on the line for this town, you were looking for skeletons in our closets. I thought you were better than that, Kat."

"And I thought you were smart enough to do your own background checks when letting someone join the fire department."

Dutch looked away, knowing she was right. "We're a volunteer squad. My guys get squat for all the work they do. Kind of makes it hard to recruit people, don't you think? So when a kid like Danny walks into the firehouse and says he wants to sign up, I'm not going to tell him no. Besides, what he did as a teenager is no concern of mine. We all do stupid shit at that age. God knows I did."

He took a long sip of his beer, swallowing hard. He had nothing left to say.

That meant it was time for Kat to reach for the shopping bag at her feet. Inside was the stack of papers found at Danny's place. She picked up the pages and wordlessly slid them across the bar toward Dutch Jansen.

"What are these?"

"We found these in Danny's apartment."

The fire chief grew mad again, almost instantly. "You searched his place?"

"Just look at them."

Dutch picked up the stack and riffled through the pages. Kat watched him closely, gauging his reaction. She assumed it was the same way she had looked upon seeing the diagrams, the step-by-step instructions, the tips for buying dangerous items without looking suspicious. She noticed Dutch's eyes widen when he got to the picture of a Coke bottle with a piece of cloth stuffed into the neck and secured with tape.

"Jesus," he muttered. "A Molotov cocktail?"

"It gets worse," Kat warned.

Dutch flipped to the next page. That one, Kat knew, contained a variation on the Molotov cocktail, only this time the bottle was replaced by a propane tank. The directions referred to it as a fire bomb. When Dutch groaned, Kat knew he had reached the last page. It was a photograph printed from the Internet, showing a block of C-4 stuck to a stripped-down digital clock with duct tape and placed on top of two bags of fertilizer.

"He's learning how to make bombs," Kat said. "And I need to know why. Did you notice him acting strangely the past couple of days? Like he was upset about something?"

"I did," Dutch said. "And he was upset."

"About what?"

"A lot, actually. He was sick of working as a lawn-mower salesman and getting paid on commission. You can imagine how the demand for lawn mowers declines once fall rolls around. He was worried about money. Couldn't understand why I was the only squad member to pull in a salary. Kept complaining about tightwad local governments not caring about their towns."

"Sounds like he had a lot on his mind," Kat said.

"He's just a hotheaded kid spouting off about shit,"

Dutch replied. "It's not like he'd actually go out and do anything about it."

"Looks to me like he already has. So if you have any idea where he is, tell me now."

Dutch, who looked like he was about to puke, shook his head. "Other than his apartment, I have no idea."

"Would any of the other firefighters know?"

"Maybe," he said. "I'll ask around."

He stood, faltering slightly, as if burdened by a two-ton weight. Kat could relate. It's how she had felt all day.

"I'm sorry, Dutch," she said. "I wish it was someone else, too."

Dutch's gaze slid to the pages on the bar. Even though the picture of the fertilizer bomb was on top and in full view, he said, "It is someone else. Danny had nothing to do with this. I'm sure of it."

He left the bar without saying another word. Kat gathered up the pages and dropped them back in the bag. She waited a minute or two, not wanting to go back outside into a town that was slowly but surely descending into chaos. Every muscle in her body was sore. Every joint ached. She wanted Gloria Ambrose to come to Perry Hollow and take this entire mess off her hands. She wanted Nick to wake up and tell her that he was perfectly fine. And she wanted sleep. More than anything, she wanted to collapse into bed and sleep for twenty-four hours straight.

Instead, she gulped down the rest of her coffee, its heat stinging the back of her throat. Then it was out of the restaurant and into the uncertain night.

Main Street was mostly deserted, as she knew it would be. Folks in Perry Hollow weren't stupid. They knew enough to stay indoors when there was a madman on the loose. By now, they had more than enough experience in that regard.

The only person Kat saw was a tall man with blond hair slinking up the sidewalk a few yards ahead of her. He stopped when he spotted her, frozen in surprise. Kat paused, too, awaiting his next move. They stared at each other a moment, like a predator and his prey just before the kill.

Then, without warning, Connor Hawthorne started to run.

8 P.M.

"Connor, stop!"

He didn't, of course. Instead, he darted into a narrow alley that ran alongside the restaurant. Kat followed, sprinting as fast as her tired and aching legs would allow. Deep in the alleyway, they passed a back entrance to Maison D'Avignon and skirted by a row of trash cans. Connor knocked one of the lids onto the ground as he passed. Kat hopped over it and kept on running.

They emerged behind the restaurant, feet crunching over a gravel parking lot, before racing into another, smaller alley. Kat's shoulders brushed the damp concrete walls as she kept pace with Connor. Then they burst out of the alley and sprinted across the side street located just beyond it.

A house sat on the other side of the road. Rather than following the sidewalk, Connor ran up the driveway, around the house, and into the backyard.

It was dark back there. Darker than the alleyway, which contained at least a little bit of light from the street. The yard, on the other hand, was pitch-black, making it hard to keep sight of Connor and his black trench coat. Kat only managed by quickening her pace and focusing on his hair, which glowed faintly in the pale moonlight.

By now they had reached another backyard. This one had a swimming pool, which Connor almost ran right into. He caught himself and spent a few steps balanced like a tightrope walker on its edge. When he recovered, he swerved around it, heading into the yard of the house next door.

All of the yards on that street were separated by rows of hedges taller than Kat herself. When Connor vanished through one, she did, too, the branches smacking her face and clawing at her hands. By the time she emerged, Connor was on the other side of the yard, pushing through the next hedge.

Kat ran faster, sprinting over a back patio and tripping the motion sensor on the lights. Then it was through another hedge, into another yard. A dog was in that one. A German shepherd, chained next to his doghouse. It lunged at both Connor and Kat, chain taut, teeth bared.

They ignored him, diving through yet another hedge, where the tail of Connor's coat got caught on one of the branches. Kat, right behind him now, saw him get jerked to a stop. Reaching out, she grabbed the coat, yanking it backward.

Connor continued to surge forward, arms spinning in an attempt to gain momentum. The move worked, making Kat lose her grip on the coat. She heard the tear of fabric as it also broke free of the branch. Then Connor was off again, running across the lawn. It was bordered by a patch of woods that he dove into without hesitation.

When Kat reached the trees, she saw that he had increased the distance between them. He was a good ten yards ahead of her, dodging around trees and ducking beneath branches. Kat did the same, managing to gain back some ground. When they burst from the woods, she was now only about five yards behind.

The trees gave way to another yard, with yet another one after that. Instead of a hedgerow, they were separated by a low wall of shrubs.

Connor hurdled over it.

Kat stormed through it.

Up ahead was a white picket fence that stood about waist high. Connor once again tried to hurdle it. A big mistake on his part. While his first leg cleared the top, the foot of his other leg caught the fence and sent him tumbling over.

Making his move even more stupid was the fact that the fence had a gate. Kat pushed through it and found Connor on the other side, struggling to get to his feet. She drew her Glock and leveled it at him.

"Do you want to stop like a good boy?" she asked. "Or do I have to shoot you?"

Connor raised his hands in surrender. "I didn't do anything wrong."

He looked past her, chest deflating faster than a flat tire. Kat craned her neck, trying to get a glimpse of what he was looking at. To her surprise, she saw the back of the museum. Connor Hawthorne had inadvertently led her there in a matter of minutes. And on the back wall, staring at them like a giant eye, was the pentagram he had painted there.

* * *

They were inside the museum, sitting at the conference table still covered with pictures of its inventory. Connor, cuffed and uncomfortable, was seated at one end. Kat sat across from him, staring him down.

"Why did you run when you saw me?"

"For the same reason you chased me," Connor said. "You think I'm the one starting those fires."

"And are you?"

He shook his head. "That would go against everything I believe in."

"Then why are you here?"

Connor leaned back in his seat. When he tried to cross his arms, the cuffs stopped him, chain crunching. Instead, he rested his hands in his lap.

"I'm not saying anything else without my lawyer present."

"And what's his name?" Kat said sarcastically. "Severus Snape?"

Connor gave her a blank look. "Who?"

"Never mind."

Kat sized up the man sitting across from her. His ponytail had come loose during the pursuit, and his straight blond hair now hung like curtains that framed the deliberately blank window of his face. Although he was undeniably tall and strong, the drooping locks made him look frail and more feminine.

"We can wait for a lawyer and waste a ton of time I don't have," Kat said. "Or you can just tell me why you're in Perry Hollow. After all, you said you've done nothing wrong."

Connor hesitated, thinking it over. Finally, he said, "I came here to see Constance Bishop."

"And why did you do that?"

"Because she asked me to."

"Why?" Kat asked. "Were the two of you friends?"

"Let's just say we both shared a common interest."

Kat nodded. "Rebecca Bradford."

"So you know all about that?" Connor asked with a sly smile.

"Not everything. Care to fill in some of the details?"

To her surprise, Connor did. He talked about stumbling upon Rebecca's story while doing research for his book. He mentioned being surprised to discover the incident, given that the persecution of witches was more of a New England phenomenon. And he talked about how, a year after the book's publication, he received a letter from a historian in Pennsylvania saying she thought she knew where Rebecca's death and burial had taken place.

"That was the first time I heard from Constance," he said. "She mentioned finding a letter in a bunch of old documents in her history museum. She thought it might be an account of the Bradford family fire and that the incident could have occurred in her town. I replied, saying I was eager to see it. Constance wrote me back, including a rough translation of the letter."

"And did you think, like Constance did, that the letter was referring to Rebecca Bradford?"

"I did," Connor said. "I became convinced that Rebecca and her family had been executed right here in your quaint little town."

"When did she ask you to come to Perry Hollow?"

"Yesterday," Connor answered. "I received a phone call

early in the morning. To my surprise, it was Constance. She told me she had found Rebecca's remains."

"Did she say where?"

Connor shook his head. "She only asked me to get here as soon as I could. She said she wanted to show me before it was too late."

Kat sat up, suddenly intrigued. "Too late for what?"

"Before someone tried to bury her again."

He told Kat that he had driven to Perry Hollow from Salem, reaching town a little after eleven Friday night. Constance told him she'd be waiting for him at the museum, so that's where he went. When he arrived, he found her standing in the middle of the gallery, a sack at her feet. The skeleton was inside.

"So she showed you the remains of a woman executed for witchcraft," Kat said. "How did that make you feel?"

"Are you asking me if I was angry?" Connor replied.

"Yes. Were you?"

"Of course. If Rebecca Bradford really was a witch, then she was killed for practicing something that's completely harmless. If she wasn't, then she was killed for no reason at all. So were the other women in her family. In my mind, five innocent women died. Considering that, yes, it made me extremely angry."

"Angry enough to want to get revenge on the town where it happened?"

Connor, remaining cool in the face of the accusation, asked, "Do you consider yourself to be a Christian?"

Kat nodded, although she was more of a nonpracticing, take-everything-the-Bible-says-with-a-grain-of-salt one.

"So you're familiar with the Ten Commandments then."

"I am," Kat said. "'Thou shall not kill' is a big one around these parts."

"Witches have something similar to that. Our main commandment is 'Do what you will, but harm none, for what you do comes back thrice.'"

"Sounds simple enough," Kat replied. "What about the casting-spells part? Doesn't that harm people?"

Connor sighed, his expression wavering between utter disdain and genuine sympathy that she could be so uninformed.

"You don't know anything about witchcraft, do you?"

"I don't." Kat really didn't mind that fact. She considered it to be on the same level as Scientology or the idiots who followed the Reverend Moon. It was a cult. Nothing more. "Is that the same thing as being a Wiccan?"

"It is," Connor said. "Wiccan actually means 'wise one.' And those of us who are practicing witches believe in harmony with nature and all its living things. We don't dance naked under a full moon. We don't turn people into toads. And we certainly don't worship the devil."

"Then why did you paint a satanic symbol on the side of the museum?"

"The pentagram?" Connor said. "That's not satanic."

"It sure as hell looks that way."

"It's Wiccan," Connor explained. "The five points represent the cycle of life. The top point represents a higher power. The other points represent the four elements—earth, air, water, and fire. All of them are balanced within the circle, the same way there is balance within each person. That balance also makes it a symbol of protection against evil."

Kat listened carefully, trying to understand. "So you

spray-painted the pentagram in an effort to protect the museum?"

"Yes," Connor said. "With Constance's permission. She even provided me with the paint."

"Constance was worried about the museum?"

"Yes. And her own safety as well."

Kat remembered her conversation with Father Ron. He had mentioned that Constance had seemed paranoid and frightened in the past few days. Maybe she had had good reason to be. Or maybe Connor was simply lying.

"She was nervous," he told Kat. "Visibly shaking. Always looking to the door, as if someone might burst in at any moment. When I asked her what was wrong, she said that someone else knew about her search for Rebecca Bradford. Someone who didn't want the incident to become public knowledge."

"Did she mention any names?"

She had not. According to Connor, Constance had simply told him that she had received word earlier the same night that someone knew about Rebecca and Constance's research.

"She was worried about something bad happening to the museum or to herself," he said. "So when I left the museum around midnight, I painted the pentagram on the wall. Quite honestly, it doesn't do much good. But I figured it might help, it being close to Samhain."

Kat was getting a headache. "Wait. Sam *what*?"

"Samhain. It's the Wiccan New Year. It takes place on the last day of October. It's the time of year when the veil between the spirit world is the thinnest, letting us get closer to our ancestors and calling upon them to stand with us in the new year."

"Halloween, in other words."

"Not really," Connor said, "although modern Halloween has co-opted many of its traditions. Samhain is actually Celtic. It marks the transition between the lighter half of the year and the darker half. Centuries ago, they used to celebrate it with bonfires. They thought the flames were cleansing."

Kat's heart stopped when she heard that. Whoever was starting the fires around Perry Hollow had picked an ironic time to do it. Unless he knew all about Samhain and its meaning. Instead of punishing the town for its sins, Kat wondered if the arsonist was actually trying to cleanse it.

"Why were you still in town when the fire was started at the museum?" she asked Connor. "I bumped into you on the street."

"I remember. I stayed because I didn't want to leave the town unprotected. Once I saw the museum was on fire and then heard that Constance had been found dead inside, I knew that she was right. Someone really is trying to stop people from learning about Rebecca Bradford."

"Which again begs the question why you ran away from the police instead of stopping and telling us all you knew."

It was pretty much the same question she had asked fifteen minutes ago. The conversation had come full circle, back to the very beginning. If it was in the shape of a pentagram, Kat's point on the star would have represented impatience.

"I'm not stupid," Connor said. "I knew I was a suspect. But while you were protecting the town, I thought I could help out in my own special way."

"More pentagrams?"

Connor wasn't amused. Which was fine by Kat. She hadn't intended it to be amusing.

"No," he said. "With this."

He reached into his coat pocket. It was hard with the handcuffs, but he managed to snag something between his index and middle fingers. As he lifted his hands to the table, Kat saw a small Ziploc bag squeezed between them. Inside the bag were dried stems, leaves, and the brown, brittle buds of what had once been a flower.

"What is that?"

"Wolfsbane," Connor said. "Some people, myself included, use it for protection from those who wish to do us harm. Hang it over a doorway and it will repel evildoers. I've spent the day placing it all over town, including over the doorway of your police station."

He paused expectantly, much to Kat's annoyance. Did he want her to thank him? She was miffed that he had been right outside the station and no one managed to see, let alone catch, him in the act.

"That was real nice of you," she said dryly. "I would have preferred it if you had just stepped inside and told us everything you knew. Then maybe I would have believed you. But that running thing you keep doing? It makes me think you've got something to hide."

"I regret running."

Kat rolled her eyes. Of course he would say that *now*.

"But I didn't know who to trust. Remember, Constance didn't tell me who might be trying to cover up the history of Rebecca Bradford. She only said that someone was."

Kat studied his face, searching for signs that he was lying. Connor knew it, too, and kept his features completely still. His eyes locked onto hers, unblinking. When Kat looked away, the corners of Connor's mouth slid upward in a smug half-smile.

"You're still wondering if you can trust me, I can tell," he said. "I think I know a way to convince you."

"How?"

"Before I left the museum last night, Constance gave me something to look after. Insurance, I suppose. In case something happened to her and the history of Rebecca Bradford was once again lost."

Connor again shoved a hand in his pocket, fishing around for something inside. "I can't reach it. You're going to have to take these cuffs off."

Kat didn't even blink. "Not a chance."

"Then you'll have to reach into my pocket and get it yourself."

From the smile still plastered on his face, Kat assumed Connor didn't think she'd do it. So she called his bluff. Getting up, she walked behind his chair and said, "Right pocket or left?"

"Left," he said.

"Put your hands on the table, palms flat against it."

Once he did, Kat got in close, her chest pressing against the back of his chair.

"If you do something stupid, like, I don't know, try to attack me and run away again, I will hunt you down and make sure you spend a long time in jail. With such a pretty mouth, I think you'll be real popular there."

She patted Connor on the shoulder, making sure he understood loud and clear. Then she reached deep into his left pocket, fingers searching for whatever was in there. Kat had no idea. Eye of newt, maybe. Or more wolfsbane. Turns out it was just a single sheet of paper, folded twice. Opening it, she saw that one side had been covered with pencil-thin lines.

"It's a map," Connor said.

"I know. I've already seen it."

A copy of it had been inside one of the folders on Constance Bishop's desk. Kat recognized the crudely drawn shoreline and triangular trees. But instead of bearing the same red question mark she had seen on Constance's map, this one had a big, bold X. Just below it was written a location, scrawled in equally large print.

THE MILL.

---

9 P.M.

Kat shouldn't have been driving alone, not on this unlit stretch of Old Mill Road. Her exhaustion had roared back as soon as she got in the car. She had been fine in the museum, the spark of confronting a suspect keeping her wide awake. But now Connor Hawthorne was in the care of Carl Bauersox and Kat was all alone struggling to keep her eyes open. Dry from overuse, they blurred her surroundings, making the road a series of hazy gray curves she struggled to follow.

Her brain was hazy, too. More than once she zoned out, lulled by the hum of the car's engine and the streaking road in her headlights. It almost made her miss her turn. She snapped out of it at the last possible second, jerking the wheel to the left and veering off Old Mill Road.

The Crown Vic bounced onto what had once been a dirt access road but was now a rut-studded bare patch in the grass. Lake Squall sat to her left, shimmering in the moonlight. To her right was a patch of woods thinned by autumn. And just up ahead was the former site of the Perry Mill.

For decades, the mill had crowded the southern end of Lake Squall—a rambling cluster of outbuildings and maintenance sheds, loading docks and railroad tracks. When the mill closed, a lot of the smaller structures were left to crumble and rot. Then the main building burned down, leaving no piece of the enterprise still standing. It had all been cleared out in the past year. Now the land was a vast expanse of grass and gravel.

Not having the time—or the energy—to search the hundred-acre plot on foot, Kat let the car roll over the landscape. She gently guided the steering wheel back and forth, making the headlights sweep over scrub brush and weeds tall enough to lash the car's front bumper.

She braked when the headlights caught a massive rectangle of blackened earth. A grave, of sorts, marking the spot where the mill's main building had been located. That was the site of the first blaze to destroy a piece of Perry Hollow history. One year and three fires later, Kat hoped there wouldn't be any more.

She moved on, driving close to the edge of the woods. A few deer had ventured out of it to nibble on the grass. They snapped to attention when the Crown Vic approached, their eyes glowing white in the headlights. As the car got closer, they fled into the woods, white tails bouncing.

At the end of the property, Kat steered the patrol car in a wide left turn and headed back toward Old Mill Road. This time she stayed near the lake, where it was still and quiet. The water, as smooth as a mirror, reflected the moon. There was barely a breeze, and what little wind did exist passed silently through freshly bare trees. Other than the weeds slapping against the car, the only sounds Kat heard were the muffled rush of the occasional car driving on Old Mill Road and the hoot of an owl hidden somewhere in the woods.

Rolling on, Kat started to get bored by her search. And frustrated. And more than a little annoyed that she had thought there'd be something to discover on this vacant stretch of land. She put pressure on the gas pedal, no longer rolling through the weeds but actually driving. She couldn't wait to get back into town, where she was really needed. This was just a dumb idea, a mistake that she could only chalk up to being very, very tired.

She was halfway across the property when she spotted a deer taking a drink from the lake. Startled, the deer sprang away from the water and toward her car. It ran alongside her a moment, bounding through the grass in that frightened, reckless way that deer were known for. When it leaped in front of the Crown Vic, Kat swerved to avoid hitting it.

The deer darted right. Kat careened left, the grass, weeds, and distant trees a blur in the sweep of the headlights. Also in the glow was a patch of darkness. Rumbling closer, Kat saw that it was a hole. A sizable one.

She veered right this time, the headlights once more passing over the hole. It was wide—several feet, at least—and deep enough to mess up her night even more if she was to hit it. As she slammed on the brakes, the Crown Vic skidded, on the verge of spinning right over the edge. But the tires finally gripped the earth and tugged the car to a stop.

Kat sat completely still, breath heavy, heart pounding. The sound was matched by the rogue deer, still running, passing the car. It reached the hole, leaped over it, then continued running, vanishing in the darkness.

When it was gone, Kat climbed out of the car and retrieved an extra-large flashlight from the trunk. Then it was on to the edge of the hole, the beam of the flashlight aimed into its depths.

At least six feet deep, it had been dug by hand. The sides were uneven and dotted with shovel marks. The end across from her sloped roughly upward, making an easier way out for the person who had done the digging. Kat noticed shoeprints in the dirt going in both directions. Pieces of rotted wood were scattered at the bottom.

Rounding the hole, she descended the banked side. She slipped at the halfway point, sliding the rest of the way on her behind. At the bottom, she bumped against something solid and cold. Something that definitely wasn't old wood.

Clearing away the dirt with her hands, she found a chunk of something that resembled coal. Only it was far too large to be a piece of coal. Heavier, too. Kat could barely lift it.

When she dropped the chunk of rock, it clattered against another piece that was sunk deeper into the ground. Kat noticed other pieces as well, jutting from the wall of the hole and jaggedly poking out of the pieces of wood. She reached out to the block she had tried to lift and rapped it with her fist.

It was lead. Kat realized it as soon as her knuckles knocked against it. She also knew why there were chunks of it sitting at the bottom of a hole, just as she understood who had dug the hole in the first place.

The digger was Constance Bishop, who had ventured out here several nights in a row, first with a metal detector, then with a shovel. The chunks of lead and the disintegrating wood were the last remaining pieces of the coffin that she had unearthed.

And the land—the site of the mill that not only gave Perry Hollow its name but also its reason for being—was the final resting place of a woman named Rebecca Bradford.

Henry slipped through the front door of Maison D'Avignon at nine thirty-one. Not too bad, seeing how he had still been at Deana's only five minutes earlier. The evening had gone by cruelly fast, the hours seeming to zip by in a matter of seconds. Yet there were moments—watching Adam sleep, for example, or feeling his surprisingly strong fist grip his index finger—when time seemed to stop, expand, stretch until forever. A minute felt like a lifetime.

He wondered if parenthood was really just a series of time shifts. Watching your child sleep for five minutes could seem like an entire day. Then years could pass in the blink of an eye. Henry imagined every parent in the world trying to adjust to the various speeds, wishing life would go at a single slow, steady pace. He had been a father for no more than two hours, and already it left him reeling.

He had been cradling Adam again when he realized it was close to nine-thirty. That's when he was scheduled to interview Lucia Trapani about Fanelli USA. He didn't like the thought of leaving his son. He loathed it, in fact. But he needed to meet her, if only to try to reschedule the interview for another time. The fire at his hotel had left him without a number to call and cancel. Standing her up would guarantee he'd never get the story. And that was something he still needed to do.

Yes, he planned to give Dario his two weeks' notice as soon as he got back to Rome. And yes, he could have shrugged off the story and never contacted his editor again. But for the time being, he was still being paid to find out about what big project Giuseppe Fanelli had planned for the United States. If he did, then Dario would certainly provide him with a glowing recommendation when Henry moved back to Pennsylvania to be with his son.

Deana drove Henry to the restaurant. Because Doreen was long gone, they had to take Adam, as well. The mad rush of diaper bags and stubborn car seats gave Henry another glimpse of being a parent. If pressed to describe how it felt in a single word, he would have said *frenzied*.

But now he was at the fanciest restaurant in Perry Hollow, without a wallet and with a fresh sheen of sweat on his forehead. Standing by the front door, he took a moment to compose himself, checking his reflection in the mirror that hung behind the maître d's stand.

That confirmed it. He looked like shit.

The rush to get there had left him panting, his cheeks rosy from stress. His hair, combed only by his fingers, jutted out at weird angles. He was certain bits of oil from that fire trap of a swimming pool were still nestled among his locks.

Turning away from the mirror, he pulled his shirt to his nose and sniffed. He smelled bad, too. The jeans and flannel shirt had survived the rec center fire intact, but now they reeked of smoke and gasoline, with just a hint of chlorine for good measure.

Still, he had no choice but to step farther into the restaurant, making a right into the darkly elegant bar. There were exactly two people inside. One was the bartender. The other was a woman perched on a bar stool, scrolling through messages on her BlackBerry.

In her mid-forties, she was attractive, with olive skin and

auburn hair. She was dressed in a black suit, an emerald blouse peeking out from under her jacket. On her feet were heels so high and elaborate that they looked more like torture devices than footwear. Henry had spent enough time in Rome to know that the shoes were Italian and that the woman had to be Lucia Trapani.

Glancing up from her phone, she caught his reflection in the mirror behind the bar. "From the way you're looking at me," she said, "you're either a lumberjack trying to pick me up or that reporter who bugged me for the interview."

"I'm the reporter," Henry said, taking the stool next to her.

Lucia stared at the ice in her glass. "I thought so. What are you drinking?"

"Whatever you're having, I guess."

"Two bourbons," Lucia told the bartender before turning to Henry. "So, Mr. Goll, what's so urgent that you made me drive to a town that seems to be on fire all the time?"

He must have looked surprised by her knowledge because she added, "They were talking about it on the Philadelphia news stations. Even if they weren't, I would have known. Part of my job is to keep tabs on what's happening in Perry Hollow."

Their drinks arrived. Lucia swirled the amber liquid around the glass before taking a sip. Henry merely gulped his. After the day he had had, he needed a good belt of something.

"A fan of small towns, are you?"

Lucia grimaced. "Hardly. I keep track to make sure I didn't fuck up royally."

"You're the one who picked Perry Hollow?"

"It wasn't Fanelli, that's for damn sure," Lucia said. "He

has no grasp of United States geography. He just wanted land for his first American venture. He didn't care where it was. That was my job, to find the perfect place. I looked for proximity to major cities, reasonable land prices, low tax bases. Perry Hollow had everything we needed, not to mention a freshly cleared patch of lakefront property. Plus, it was in Pennsylvania, which is important with this kind of thing."

Henry's notebooks had been turned to ash during the fire at the Sleepy Hollow Inn, and he hadn't thought to stop at some point during the day and get more. With nothing to write on—or with—he begged a pen from the bartender and began taking notes on cocktail napkins.

"Is everything okay?" Lucia stared at him with bemused concern. "I have to say, you look frazzled."

"It's been a long day," Henry said. "Back to Mr. Fanelli's project, what does being in Pennsylvania have to do with it?"

"The laws, of course. While more and more states are allowing it, we wanted a place that had been at it but not too long. We didn't want to go someplace where competition was already entrenched. So New Jersey was out. Louisiana was out. We didn't even think about Nevada."

Henry stopped writing. He gave Lucia a quizzical look while scratching his head with the end of his pen. "What exactly does Mr. Fanelli plan on building here?"

Lucia Trapani laughed—a throaty, incredulous laugh that Henry had only heard before in the movies.

"You honestly don't know?" she said. "He's entering the United States gaming industry. Fanelli Entertainment USA is going to build a casino in Perry Hollow."

Henry, a pale man to begin with, was certain the news made his face a whole lot whiter. He knew from the way he got cold in an instant, like all the warm blood had just left his body. It wasn't surprise from learning about the casino project that did it. It was the fact that building a casino in Perry Hollow was about the worst idea he had ever heard. The town's roads weren't built for that kind of traffic. The burning of the Sleepy Hollow Inn meant the town had exactly zero hotels.

Then there was Kat and her practically nonexistent police force. Henry knew without a doubt that she and Carl Bauersox were good cops, but they'd be overwhelmed by having a casino dropped into their midst.

Years earlier, about three lives ago, he had gone to Atlantic City for fun and Las Vegas for work. He liked both places well enough. He'd even consider going back someday. But the glitziest hotels and brightest neon couldn't quite hide the seedier parts of both cities. Pawnshops and gambling addicts. Prostitutes and junkies. Where casinos went, they were sure to follow. Picturing all of that in tiny, sleepy Perry Hollow broke his heart.

"Is it a done deal?" he asked. "Has it been approved by town officials?"

"Almost. We still need to introduce it before the planning board next month."

"It's going to be a tough sell. People in this town like things the way they are. They won't want it approved."

"Considering the state Perry Hollow is in at the moment," Lucia said, "I don't think they'll have a choice. Besides, we're working on a great pitch. You should see the concept art for the hotel. It puts the Bellagio to shame. Mr. Fanelli doesn't believe in moderation. He goes big."

Her BlackBerry started to vibrate, buzzing its way down

the bar toward her hand. She glanced at it before sighing. "Speaking of the devil. That man never sleeps. It's probably why he's so fucking rich."

Excusing herself, she slipped off the stool and headed deeper into the empty restaurant, hips swaying. Her heels clicked on the hardwood floor, quickly and steadily. It sounded like somebody trying to tap out a rhythm on a typewriter. Henry echoed the sound with the tip of his borrowed pen, rapping it against the bar.

It took at least five taps to make him realize he had heard that sound once before that day.

10 P.M.

Kat was yawning so hard she thought she'd never stop. Her hands felt numb on the Crown Vic's wheel, barely steering. Despite discovering Rebecca Bradford's grave, she was still more tired than she had been all day. No more adrenaline rush to keep her going. She was running on fumes.

When her cell phone rang, she answered it quickly, in mid-yawn.

"Hey, Chief." It was Carl, sounding just as tired as she did. "Randall Stroup got a hit on Danny Batallas's vehicle. He drives a black Ford pickup. Want the license plate number?"

"Text it to me," Kat said. She was too busy driving to write it down and she knew she'd never remember it. Her brain was mush.

"Righto, Chief."

Kat ended the call and turned down Main Street. It was mostly empty, populated by a few stragglers rushing home. It reminded her of how the town had looked in the days after the mill closed. Barren. Deserted. A ghost town haunted by the few people who had decided to stick it out.

Her phone buzzed, alerting her that Carl had sent the text. She tapped the touchscreen, revealing the message that Danny had a vanity plate. FYRMAN. Either he took his job too seriously or he enjoyed it far too much. Knowing what she had found in his apartment, Kat assumed it was the latter.

The phone rang again while she was still eyeing the text. She answered it, even though the number was one she didn't recognize.

"Kat?" It was Henry, his voice a rushed whisper. "I know what Dave and Betty Freeman heard."

Kat was confused, unshakable exhaustion clouding her brain. "What?"

"The clicking they heard outside last night," Henry said. "It was a woman. Walking in high heels. And she's here."

"Where are you?"

"Maison D'Avignon. At the bar."

Kat, still steering down Main Street, glanced out the window and saw the striped awning and red door of Perry Hollow's finest restaurant. She slammed on the brakes.

"I'm right outside," she said. "I'll be there in a minute."

She was there in two, plopping down on the stool next to Henry and ordering a tall glass of water from the bartender. No more coffee for her, no matter how many hours she stayed awake. Sipping her drink, she followed Henry's gaze to a well-dressed woman standing between the bar and the equally empty restaurant. She was on her phone, talking rapidly in what Kat could only assume was Italian. The woman wasn't a native of Perry Hollow, that much was certain. Even the wealthiest folks in town didn't dress like that.

"Who is she?"

Henry told her everything. The woman's name. The fact that she worked for Giuseppe Fanelli. By the time he got to the part about their plans to build a casino alongside Lake Squall, Kat started to feel nauseated. Perry Hollow wasn't equipped to handle something as big and unpredictable as a casino. If it was built, it would be the end of the town as she knew it.

Across the room, the woman ended the call. She quickly made her way back to the bar, heels clicking sharply on the floor. The sound stopped when she saw Kat's uniform.

"I have a feeling I've just been hoodwinked." She turned to Henry. "Was this whole interview a setup?"

"Lucia Trapani," Henry said, "meet Chief Kat Campbell."

Kat offered her hand, but Lucia refused to shake it. Instead, she slid onto the bar stool far more elegantly than Kat had done and ordered another drink.

"If you're here to ask me about the fires," she said, taking a moment to size up Kat before dismissing her, "then start now. My time is valuable."

"Were you in town last night?" Kat asked.

Henry answered the question for her. "She was. When I spoke to her on the phone this morning, she said she had driven in last night."

"You have a good memory." While the tone of Lucia's voice was polite, her expression was anything but. She stared daggers at them, making Kat feel lucky that looks couldn't kill. The glare on Lucia Trapani's face seemed lethal enough.

"What brought you to Perry Hollow?"

"Business. I attended the fund-raiser held by your local Chamber of Commerce."

"Who invited you?"

"No one," Lucia replied. "I crashed it."

During the whole exchange, Henry had been hunched over the bar, scribbling notes on a seemingly endless series of cocktail napkins. Glancing up from them, he asked, "How did you find out about it?"

"Through someone at the realty firm who sold Mr. Fanelli the land. David Brandt is his name. He plays golf with the mayor. Said it might be a good way to introduce myself to some of the other business owners here."

Kat assumed Lucia Trapani had made a very good impression, at least to the men in the room. She was undeniably beautiful, with just a hint of maturity that made her seem attainable. The women, however, probably hated her. Women such as Lucia excelled at making other women feel inferior.

"What time did you arrive at the fund-raiser?" she asked.

"Around ten," Lucia said, taking another sip of bourbon.

"So you went to the history museum *before* the fund-raiser?"

Lucia stopped mid-sip. Lowering her glass, she looked at Kat with a combination of admiration and annoyance. *At last,* her expression seemed to say, *a formidable opponent.*

"How did you know?"

"Your heels," Kat told her. "The neighbors across the street from the museum heard them around nine last night. Next time you're thinking about sneaking around town, it might be a good idea to wear flats."

"I wasn't sneaking," Lucia said.

"Then what were you doing?" It was Henry this time, giving Kat a break from asking all the questions.

"Stopping by the museum, of course."

"Wasn't it closed?" Kat said, taking over again.

"I had an appointment of sorts."

"With Constance Bishop?"

"That's correct. We had some business to discuss."

"Such as?"

"Such as why the bitch was trying to blackmail Mr. Fanelli."

It wasn't the answer Kat had been expecting. She recoiled in surprise, knocking over her glass of water in the process. Liquid rushed over the bar and landed on her lap. She reached for a napkin, but it was stolen by Henry before she could grab it.

His notes. Of course.

"That doesn't sound like something Constance would do," Kat said, off the bar stool and trying to flick away the water seeping into her trousers. "Are you sure she was blackmailing you?"

"She denied it," Lucia said. "She swore up and down that wasn't her intention. But I didn't buy it. She knew exactly what she was doing."

"This is about Rebecca Bradford, isn't it?"

Once again, Lucia gave her that impressed-but-pissed-off look. "Yes. It recently came to my attention that an event of some historical merit happened on the land Mr. Fanelli purchased."

Kat, resigned to spending the rest of the conversation wet, returned to the stool. "How did you find out?"

"Because someone sent me this." Lucia reached for a leather satchel on the floor that had been tilted against her stool. She pulled out a book, handing it to Kat. It was a copy of *Witchcraft in America*, Connor Hawthorne's book. "It was mailed to my office two days ago. No return address. No way to track it. Just the book and that paper."

Kat turned the book in her hands. It was a new copy, shiny and clean. A slip of paper had been inserted into one of the later chapters, drawing attention to the passage about Judge William Daniel Paul. Typed across the paper was a terse note: *"The witch's name is Rebecca Bradford. She and four other women were brutally murdered on your land and buried there. Meet me Friday at the Perry Hollow Historical Society. Midnight. Bring money."*

"And you think Constance sent this to you?"

"Of course," Lucia said. "It's not that unusual. You know, president of a struggling historical society maybe trying to get some cash. It's happened before and it will surely happen again."

"So you went to the museum and confronted her?"

"I did. But not at midnight. The element of surprise is one of a businesswoman's best secret weapons."

"You went early," Kat said. "At nine. Was Constance there?"

"She was. I told her that I knew all about Rebecca Bradford, and I expressed my concern about the situation."

Concern. That was an understatement. The company Lucia worked for was planning to build a casino on the same site where a massacre had occurred. Kat didn't know too much about business, but she assumed something like that didn't make for good PR. And if the land was declared a historic spot—which it very well could be, considering what had happened there—Giuseppe Fanelli's first project in America wouldn't even see the light of day.

"So," Lucia continued, "I made Mrs. Bishop an offer to keep quiet about it."

"A bribe?"

Lucia sighed. "Mr. Fanelli doesn't offer bribes. He offers philanthropic donations."

"How much was this donation?" Kat used air quotes when saying it. Even though she hated it when others used them, the situation called for it.

"A million dollars."

Once again, Kat was stunned. If Fanelli was willing to offer a million bucks in hush money, imagine how big—and profitable—he expected the casino to be.

"Did she accept it?"

Lucia shook her head slowly, as if she still couldn't believe it twenty-four hours after the fact. "Constance said that while the historical society needed the money, she couldn't accept it if it meant rewriting local history."

Constance Bishop had turned down a cool million because taking it wasn't the right thing to do, a fact that made Kat's heart swell with both pride and sorrow. There were few people she could think of who would have rejected such money. Certainly no other members of the historical society. Kat imagined that Claude Dobson or Emma Pulsifer would have grabbed the money without a second thought. Burt Hammond would have given her a pen to write the check.

"Did it make you angry that she turned down your offer?"

Lucia gave her a smile that looked as lethal as her glare. "I'm assuming that's a veiled way of asking me if I killed her."

Kat knew Lucia couldn't have hit Constance over the head or started the fire at that time. It was far too early. But she definitely could have come back later in the night, especially once the fire alarm cleared the restaurant. Instead of taking Main Street, Lucia could have slipped through the backyards to the museum, just as Kat and Connor had done earlier. It took two minutes total.

"It's simply a question."

"I wasn't pleased, of course," Lucia said. "But I respected her decision. It didn't change the fact that the casino would be built. All it really did was save the company a million dollars. But I did wonder why she had sent me a copy of the book. I mean, why else send it if not for blackmail purposes? When I asked her, she acted surprised."

Again, Henry looked up from his notes long enough to ask a question. "So she denied sending it?"

"That's right," Lucia said. "She said she hadn't told anyone about what happened on that land. That's when I showed her the book and note I got in the mail. When Constance saw it, she demanded to know who had sent it. She said it wasn't a well-known book. Actually, she seemed shocked that I had a copy."

As well she should have been, Kat thought. Constance Bishop had tried to keep her research under wraps. Sneaking out in the night. Hiding everything she knew from everyone but Connor Hawthorne. That's why she had been so unnerved by Lucia's presence. She had just learned that someone else knew what she was researching.

"When we spoke earlier today," Henry told Lucia, "you mentioned talking to a reporter about the land here in Perry Hollow."

Lucia nodded at the memory. "Yesterday, yes. I tried to brush him off, but he was as persistent as you."

"So it was a man?" Henry said.

"Yes. Why?"

Although this was all news to Kat, she understood where Henry was going with his questions. "Did he give a name?"

"He didn't," Lucia said. "He just said he was a reporter and wanted to know what Mr. Fanelli planned on building here. He said he worked for the local newspaper. Since I knew it was going to get out one way or another, I told him it was a casino. He thanked me and hung up."

"Then you weren't talking to a reporter," Henry said, shaking his head at the thought of a professional journalist not asking a few follow-up questions. "I'd be fired if I did something like that."

"We know this man didn't give you a name," Kat said. "But did he mention a newspaper?"

"He did. It was this town's paper. The Perry Hollow something or other."

"The *Perry Hollow Gazette*," Henry said, naming his former employer.

Lucia snapped her fingers. "That's it. I remember being surprised because I had never heard of it before."

That's because it no longer existed. The *Perry Hollow Gazette* had been defunct for a year. Its last issue, still sitting in a locked honor box outside its old building, featured a story about the Grim Reaper killings—a constant reminder that bad things had taken place in town. Every time Kat walked past it, she felt like kicking the box in, stealing the remaining papers and torching them.

"Was I duped?" Lucia said, looking like she could use another stiff drink.

"You were," Kat told her. "Someone was only posing as a reporter. Possibly the same person who's starting these fires."

It wasn't hard to piece together. Someone else knew about Rebecca Bradford. He also knew Fanelli was going to build on the land where she had been buried. He'd sent a copy of the book to Lucia before calling to get the scoop on what was being built.

Yet more questions remained, the big one being who would do such a thing, followed closely by the matter of why. If it was Danny Batallas starting these fires, what on earth did it have to do with Rebecca Bradford? Kat also wondered how he would have found out about her in the first place, especially since Constance had insisted on being so secretive.

"When you and Constance discussed the book, did she mention how *she* had found a copy?" Kat asked. "If it's an obscure book, how did she learn about it?"

She assumed Constance had purchased the copy that was discovered in the museum. But it still didn't explain how she had learned about the book in the first place. It wasn't as if she had started researching the Bradford case before reading it. Nor was it likely that Connor had sent her a copy. He didn't know the incident mentioned in his book had taken place in Perry Hollow until Constance told him about it.

"Actually, she talked about that," Lucia said. "She said she stumbled upon it a few months ago."

Kat leaned forward, waiting expectantly. Henry, she noticed, was also at rapt attention, his pen poised over a fresh cocktail napkin.

"Where?" he asked.

"The library, of course," Lucia said. "This town does have a library, right?"

Henry sat in the passenger seat of Chief Campbell's patrol car, gripping the edges of his seat as the vehicle veered around a corner on their way off Main Street. Five minutes had passed since they left Lucia Trapani at the restaurant. Not a lot of time, but enough to get a good grasp on what was happening.

"Someone sure wants to stop that casino from being built."

"You mean other than me?" Kat said. "Once they hear about it, I suspect a lot of people in town won't like the idea."

"Enough to set half of Perry Hollow on fire to prevent it from happening?"

It was the only explanation for the fires sprouting up all over town. Someone else knew about both Rebecca Bradford and the casino. The book, Henry assumed, was sent to Lucia Trapani as a way of derailing the project. When that didn't work, the person decided to start torching things in an attempt to scare them off.

"You don't think someone was simply trying to squeeze money out of Fanelli to keep quiet?" Kat asked.

"Maybe," Henry said. "But if that was the case, why start the fires? For that matter, why kill Constance Bishop?"

"I'm still not sure she was the main target." Kat jerked on the steering wheel again. "It's possible she stumbled upon whoever is doing this while they were starting the fire at the museum. Collateral damage, so to speak."

"Do you think it was a member of the historical society?"

"I'm not ruling anyone out," Kat said. "Not even Connor Hawthorne."

"And where is Mr. Hawthorne?"

"In the capable hands of Carl Bauersox."

Kat made another turn, barreling into the driveway in front of Deana Swan's house. She brought the Crown Vic to a halt, remaining inside as Henry unbuckled his seat belt. This was now his job.

He exhaled before getting out of the car and cutting across the lawn. He rang the doorbell. It was loud, just as he remembered it. Hearing it clang deep inside the house, his first thought was *I hope it doesn't wake the baby*. But when the front door opened, Henry saw that little Adam was already awake. Deana was holding him, a bottle in hand and a towel tossed over her shoulder.

"Hey," she said, genuinely happy to see him. "I was wondering what time you'd be back. How'd the interview go?"

She looked past Henry, seeing Kat's patrol car in the driveway. Anxiety flooded her face.

"What's going on? Has there been another fire?"

"Not yet," Henry said. "But I need a favor."

Deana kept her eyes on the patrol car. "What?"

"We need you to open the library for us."

11 P.M.

They made an odd group, the four of them, crammed into Kat's patrol car. She and Henry rode up front. Deana Swan was in the back with the baby. Glancing in the rearview mirror, Kat saw her huddled over the infant's portable car seat, making sure everything was secure.

No one had bothered to tell Kat what Deana was doing with a baby. There wasn't enough time for explanations. Not that Kat required one. Yet another thing she and Henry needed to talk about once this was all over.

Since there was a baby on board, Kat drove slowly, winding the Crown Vic down side streets on the way to the library. The slow pace gave her time to scan the houses along the street and the people who lived in them. The homes were all decorated for Halloween. Lit jack-o'-lanterns flickered on front porches, and ghoulish displays filled yards. Kat spotted scarecrows, fake cobwebs, strands of lights blinking orange and purple. And on nearly every front porch, sitting in stillness among the festive décor, were people with hunting rifles cradled in their arms.

Kat wasn't surprised by the sight of the guns. Perry Hollow was a hunting town, after all. Most households had guns. What startled her was the fact that Burt Hammond had been right. Folks in town, spooked by all the fires, had armed themselves, prepared to take matters into their own hands.

Now they crowded their porches, waiting and watching.

Watching the street. Watching their neighbors. Watching for any sign that someone was going to come and try to set their house on fire. Many of them stared blankly at the Crown Vic as it rolled by. They had already decided that Kat, Carl, and the state police weren't doing enough to protect them.

Kat didn't care what they thought. She was doing the best job possible under extremely difficult conditions. She just prayed that no one did anything stupid. She had her hands full already. She didn't need an accidental shooting to complicate matters.

When she turned onto Main Street, Deana Swan spoke up from the backseat. "What are you two looking for again? A book?"

"Not quite," Kat said. "We know the book. We want to find out who might have taken it out recently."

"Why?"

"Because whoever has been starting these fires might have found that book in the library."

Kat knew it was a long shot. There was no guarantee whoever sent a copy to Lucia Trapani had actually checked it out of the library. Still, they at least needed to look.

The library was located on a corner of Main Street, right across from Town Hall. Parking in front of it, Kat saw a lone state trooper guarding the door. It was the same female trooper she'd noticed in her kitchen and outside the museum. The one who reminded her of her younger self.

While Henry and Deana argued over who would stay with the baby, Kat approached the trooper.

"What's your name?"

The trooper answered quickly. "Hicks, Chief. Tracy Hicks."

"Well, Trooper Hicks, you've been doing a good job today. But I need you to keep it up. We're going to be inside the library for a few minutes. If you see or hear anything, even if you think it's only your imagination, you run inside and get me, okay?"

Trooper Hicks saluted her. "Yes, Chief."

By that time, both Deana and Henry had exited the Crown Vic. Henry carried the baby, leaving Deana's hands free to unlock the library's tall double doors. Kat stood beside her, listening to the jangle of keys as she looked up and down the street.

"Got it," Deana said, pushing the door open. She stepped inside, followed by Henry and the baby.

"Remember," Kat told Trooper Hicks. "Don't hesitate to come running."

She looked up as she passed through the doorway, noticing something green hanging just above it. Wolfsbane. A gift, she supposed, from Connor Hawthorne.

She hoped it would help.

Henry tried to keep a tight grip on Adam's carrier. It was a bulky thing—a bean-shaped contraption made of hard gray plastic that kept banging against his legs as he walked. The carrier was also surprisingly heavy. It doubled Adam's weight, making Henry's arms burn from exertion. Like many a father before him, he assumed there had to be an easier way to transport a child.

"How do you manage this all on your own?" he asked Deana. "This thing weighs a ton."

Deana, carrying a much lighter diaper bag, flexed a sizable bicep.

"It's a good workout," she said. "I might be stronger than you now."

She was definitely more stubborn. Henry hadn't wanted to bring the baby along at all, suggesting at first that Deana just hand Kat the keys to the library. But she insisted on doing it herself. He had also wanted to wait in the car with the baby, but Deana wouldn't hear of it. It was understandable, of course. He had only known about his son for a few hours. Naturally, Deana wasn't prepared to leave Henry alone with him. Although she'd have to eventually. Henry would insist on it. He only wished that time was now, especially since they were moving deeper into the darkened building.

Just inside the door, Deana flicked a switch and fluorescent lights buzzed into brightness overhead. It didn't make Henry feel any better. There was something creepy about an empty library. It was unnervingly quiet, with too many places for someone to hide. Now that he had a child to protect, Henry imagined danger everywhere.

The building itself, another reminder of Perry Hollow's more prosperous days, was large and complicated. In order to get to the circulation desk, you had to traverse a long hallway with tiled floors. Doors on either side opened up into various reading rooms, still pitch-black inside as the three of them passed.

The hallway deposited visitors into the heart of the library—a massive octagonal room with the circulation desk, as wide and imposing as a judge's bench, in the center. Fanning outward from the front desk, like spokes on a wheel, were wooden bookshelves that stretched from floor to ceiling.

There were two ways to reach the bookshelves. The most common route was directly around the front desk, under the watchful eye of whatever librarian was on duty. The other way was via a small passage that ran the circumference of the room. This made it easy to slip in and out of the stacks without anyone noticing. Naturally, it was the route Henry had used when he frequented the library.

Deana hit another switch when they entered the room, adding more light. Yet, Henry noted, it wasn't enough to clear the shadows from deep inside the stacks. Nor did it illuminate the circular passage around them.

"There's a computer at the circulation desk," Deana said. "Information about all of our books is stored in a database. If someone checked it out, I'll be able to see it."

She slipped behind the desk and dropped the diaper bag on top of it. Then she moved to the library's computer and tapped a few keys. "The system is shut down at the end of each day. I'm rebooting it now."

"How long will that take?" Henry asked.

"A few minutes."

A noise erupted from somewhere deep within the building. It was an unidentifiable bang, like a door being slammed shut or an open window hitting the sill. Instinctively, Henry lifted Adam's carrier to his chest. Kat, he noticed, dropped a hand to her holster.

"Would there be anyone else here at this hour?" she asked Deana. "Like a janitor or maintenance worker?"

Deana shook her head. "Not that I know of."

"What about other doors? Is there another way in?"

"There's an emergency exit, but it's always locked."

"That doesn't mean someone can't get in," Henry said. The bashed and broken door at the rec center was proof of that.

He looked at Kat, who still had her hand resting near

her Glock. She was nervous, which made him nervous. Finally, she said, "Where's the door? I'm going to check it out."

The library's emergency exit was at the rear of the building. To access it, Kat had to cut through the stacks, enter a dank and darkened hallway, and descend a short flight of concrete steps. The door was closed when she reached it, although that didn't mean much. Kat herself had closed the library's front door after they entered.

Unlike those tall, wooden sentinels, this door was metal and opened by a push bar that ran the width of it. Kat pressed the bar and nudged the door open, instantly tripping an alarm.

The noise—an earsplitting honk that rivaled a car alarm in sheer annoyance—blasted through the entire library. It didn't shut off until Kat pulled the door closed again, shaken by the sudden assault of noise. If someone had been inside the building, he didn't leave that way. They would have heard it.

"False alarm," she shouted up the steps behind her. "That was just me. You'll hear it again in a minute when I go outside."

She looked to her right, where the concrete steps continued beyond the door into what appeared to be the library's basement. It was pitch-black down there. The kind of dark that could swallow you whole if you were foolish enough to venture into it. Reaching for the flashlight on her duty belt, Kat descended the stairs anyway.

The flashlight brightened things but not by much. From what Kat could see, the space was filled with relics of another era. She spotted card catalogs pressed up against microfilm machines. Wooden desks on uneven legs had either been stacked against the wall or were loaded down with electric typewriters.

She crept past them carefully, aiming the flashlight into

every inky corner and darkened crevice. All she saw were tangles of cobwebs and drops of water falling from the pipes that ran along the ceiling. Nobody crouched behind a broken bookcase. No one lurking in the shadows. Just an unoccupied basement that Kat couldn't wait to leave.

Backing out of the cellar, she climbed the steps once more to the emergency exit. This time, she gave advance warning of her actions.

"I'm about to go outside again," she yelled.

When she pushed on the door, it once again set off eardrum-bursting blasts from the alarm. She exited quickly, turning around and shoving the door closed as fast as she could. Through the door, she heard the alarm shut off.

Instantly, she heard another noise, this time from outside. It was a swoosh of metal on leather, followed by a click. The sound of a Glock being readied for shooting.

"Don't move!"

Kat froze. "Is that you, Hicks?"

The voice behind her sounded quizzical. Kat swore she could hear Trooper Hicks squinting in the darkness. "Chief?"

"It's me," Kat said, at last turning around.

"I heard the alarm," Trooper Hicks said. "I came running. Just like you told me to."

"That's good," Kat replied. "But it's just me."

She checked their dim surroundings, unable to make out much. They were in an alleyway behind the building—that much she could see. On the other side of the alley was the back wall of a hardware store. To her left was more wall and the zigzag of a fire escape. The only way out was to the right, where a narrow side street led back to the brightness of Main.

While Hicks continued to scan the alley, Kat examined

the door's exterior. It appeared to be intact. No sign of tampering. Definitely no indication that someone had smashed it with an antique iron. When she tried the handle—a regular knob on this side instead of the bar—it wouldn't budge.

She was now locked out.

"Smooth move, Campbell," she muttered. "Real smooth."

"Locked yourself out, Chief?"

"Yep," Kat said, sighing.

It would have been easier for her to pound on the door until Henry or Deana heard her and opened it again. But that would have prompted the alarm again, and frankly, they had all heard it too many times in the last five minutes. So they chose to trudge out of the alley, down the side street, and onto Main.

The street, when they reached it, was free of traffic, just as Kat hoped it would be. Her Crown Vic, parked at the curb, was the only car she saw. Still, she glanced up and down the sidewalk, checking if anyone else was around. She saw no one, which led her to look closer, seeking out possible hiding places. The shadow of a neighboring building or a darkened doorway. There was nothing.

"Looks quiet," Hicks said.

Kat nodded in the affirmative. "Good."

She turned and faced the library, a gasp catching in her throat.

The library's front door—the one she was certain she had closed behind her—was once again open.

As far as Henry could tell, Adam was a heavy sleeper. The baby slept his way through both the ride to the library and being carried inside the building. Not even the alarm from the emergency exit, triggered by Kat, woke him up, a feat that amazed Henry. But just when he thought his son was able to sleep through anything, Deana called out from behind the circulation desk.

"The system is up."

The sound of his mother's voice—sharp and excited—set off Adam, who began to wail immediately. The pitiful sound made Henry set the carrier on a nearby table and lean over it in an attempt to shush him. Adam, all writhing legs and swatting hands, opened his eyes and started to cry harder.

Henry's first instinct was to just take the baby, carrier and all, back to Kat's patrol car. He didn't have a good feeling about being in that library, especially after Kat left. But now that the system was up, they couldn't leave without at least looking to see if someone other than Constance Bishop had checked the book out of the library. It was the only thing that kept him there, even as Adam's crying grew louder.

"I don't know what to do," Henry told Deana. "Are there any tricks to make him stop crying?"

"Give him your finger," Deana said. "He likes having something to latch on to."

Henry pushed his extended index finger into the carrier, letting Adam grasp it with all five of his tiny ones. The baby grew quiet, his wails dying into a mere whimper.

"That's it," Henry whispered. "Daddy is here. There's nothing to cry about."

Behind him, Deana started tapping on the computer's keyboard. "What's the name of the book?"

"*Witchcraft in America.*"

"Who's the author?"

"Hawthorne. Connor Hawthorne."

Deana resumed her tapping, entering the information. When she clicked the mouse, the computer made a slight beep.

"Found it. There's one copy in circulation."

Henry's eyes were still on Adam, watching intently as he fell back to sleep. He could see the baby drift deeper into slumber, each part of his body succumbing one by one. His legs grew still. His head tilted to the left. The last thing to go was his right hand, which slipped away from Henry's finger before dropping to his side.

Certain that Adam was sound asleep, Henry crept away from the carrier. "Who last took it out?"

"It doesn't say," Deana said. "I'll have to scan the actual book to find that out. Let me check the stacks."

She stepped away from the desk, moving toward one of the towering bookshelves behind it. Henry remained where he was, trying to keep an eye on both Deana, moving deeper into the stacks, and Adam. He didn't want either of them to leave his sight. At least not until Kat returned. Yet Deana was already beyond his field of vision, heading toward the end of the row.

"Did you find the book yet?"

Deana's voice echoed through the canyon of shelves. "Not yet. It's nonfiction, right?"

"Yes."

"I don't see it," Deana said. "I'm right at the spot where it should be located, but it's not there."

Henry looked away from the stacks—it was pointless, really, since he could no longer see Deana—and back to the table. Adam was motionless inside the carrier, still fast asleep. The baby's presence tugged at Henry, making him edge away from the circulation desk to be closer by just a few inches.

Behind him, he heard Deana riffling through shelved books. Eventually, she said, "Got it! It was on the wrong shelf. I'll have to tease Doreen about her stacking skills tomorrow."

She emerged from the stacks cradling a book against her chest. One glance at the cover—a painting of a woman being burned at the stake—told Henry that she had indeed found the right book.

Deana approached the circulation desk. "Now, let's see who had this out last."

When she scanned the book, the computer beeped—a brief burst of noise in the otherwise silent library.

"Huh," Deana said.

"What does that mean?"

"It means I don't recognize this name."

She scanned the book again, setting off another beep from the computer. A second later, another, different noise shot into the library. Footsteps. Fast ones that were loud enough to make Henry and Deana both look to the front of the room. Even Adam reacted, squirming awake and letting out another frightened wail. Just beneath it, a noise within a noise, were the footsteps, getting louder.

They belonged to Kat Campbell and the state trooper stationed outside. Both women burst into the room, guns drawn.

"You need to get out of here," Kat said. "Right now."

Henry and Deana both did the opposite. They froze.

"What's going on?" Henry asked.

"Someone else is in the building," Kat said.

Deana gasped. "The arsonist?"

"I'm not sure. But I don't want you in here when I find out."

Henry heard more footsteps. Different ones. Faster and louder than the previous ones. They erupted from the passageway that circled the stacks, echoing off the bookshelves, making it hard to pinpoint their location. They seemed to be nowhere and everywhere all at once.

Then they vanished, just as suddenly as they had arrived. Replacing them was an earsplitting siren that filled the library.

The emergency exit's alarm.

"The back door!" Kat shouted, nudging the trooper forward before following after her.

The two cops sprinted toward the closest row of shelves, disappearing through them on their way toward the back door. Deana edged away from the desk, standing at the threshold of the stacks. Henry remained where he was, not sure what to do or where to go. The alarm stopped briefly, signaling the exit was now closed again. Which meant the arsonist was outside. Which meant they should stay inside. Then it started up again, telling Henry that either Kat had left the building or that the arsonist had again entered.

He looked left to Adam squirming and shrieking in his carrier. Then he looked right, to Deana, who had turned to watch Kat's swift retreat.

"We need a plan," he said. "Any ideas?"

Deana didn't move. Standing rigidly between the two bookshelves, she seemed focused on something farther down the row.

"Henry," she said with terrifying urgency, "take the baby."

Henry had returned to the circulation desk, using it to push himself higher until he could see past Deana to what she was staring at. It was a bright glow located a few yards from her feet, shooting off white-hot sparks. At first, Henry thought it was a Fourth of July sparkler, burning itself out on the floor.

Before he could even ask himself why it was there, he realized that it wasn't a sparkler.

It was a stick of dynamite.

And there was no way Deana was going to get around that desk before it went off.

"Go, Henry!" she shouted. "Now!"

Henry pushed off the desk and ran as fast as he could to the baby. He didn't stop as he grabbed the carrier by its handle, scooping it off the table as he continued toward the front hallway. The carrier swung back and forth, the motion making Adam cry even more. Henry ignored it. He had to.

On his way through the door, he allowed himself one last look at Deana. It was brief. A fraction of a second. Just long enough to see her leaping over the desk, following him out of the library.

"I'm right behind you!" she yelled. "Keep Adam safe!"

Henry faced forward again, plunging into the library's front hallway. His thoughts evaporated as his mind sharpened, taking in only what he needed to. He didn't hear the sound of his shoes pounding the hallway tile. Nor did he feel the carrier secure in his clenched hand. He was only focused on the door ahead of him.

It was open.

Waiting for him.

Just a few feet away.

Behind him, the dynamite exploded.

Henry didn't hear it. His entire system—brain, ears, nerves—wasn't wired to take in something so unearthly loud.

They shut down immediately, leaving him deaf to the sound of the explosion obliterating everything behind him.

Instead, he felt it.

The force of the blast shoved him forward, an invisible army of hands propelling him down the hall as his surroundings crumbled around him. The floor seemed to fall away. The walls turned to dust. The ceiling, broken into chunks, rained down on him.

Then Henry was out the door, still being pushed. He flew down the front steps so fast his feet barely touched them.

Once on the sidewalk, he fell forward, having just enough time to clutch the carrier to his chest. Adam was inside. Still writhing. Still shrieking.

Henry felt him press against his stomach as he continued to tumble.

Off the sidewalk.

Into the street.

Past Kat's car, its horn blaring.

As soon as he stopped tumbling, Henry started dragging himself toward the car. The carrier was below him, scraping on the asphalt. He no longer heard Adam. He no longer heard anything. His ears were ringing—an insistent buzz that he just wanted to end.

He was at Kat's car now, forcing himself to sit up. He propped himself against the passenger-side door, unconcerned about his own possible injuries, and pulled the carrier away from his body. Adam was inside, face crimson from crying. But he was moving. Which was good. And he wasn't bleeding. Also good.

Henry removed Adam from the carrier, checking even

closer for signs of injury. Convinced that his son was unharmed, he clutched the baby to his chest and turned around. He peered over the hood of the car, squinting against the dust pouring out of the library's front door, trying to spot Deana emerging through the haze.

She wasn't there.

MIDNIGHT

Kat pried herself off the street, face-first, the skin on her cheek sticking slightly to the asphalt. That was from the blood that smeared her face. Her knee was also bleeding. She felt it—moist and throbbing. Cool air rushed through her torn pants, stinging the wound.

She and Hicks had just sprinted out of the alley behind the library when it exploded. The blast—sudden and deafening—threw them into the middle of the side street that led to Main. She remained there, still not believing what had just happened while simultaneously thanking her lucky stars she hadn't been closer to the library itself when it did. Large chunks of stone and concrete surrounded her. Smaller ones trickled out of her hair. All around her, loose pages of scorched books fluttered to the ground like dying butterflies.

Flat on her stomach, she managed to move her arms. Similar to the rest of her body, they were numb and sluggish—like quickly drying cement. Still, she pushed herself onto her knees, the wounded one throbbing even more. Then she climbed to her feet.

Trooper Hicks was already up, trying to find her balance on unsteady legs. She looked as battered as Kat felt. Uniform torn. Scrapes picking through the gaps in the fabric. Twin drips of blood leaked from the corners of her mouth, making her look like a vampire after a fresh kill.

"You hurt, Hicks?" Kat asked.

The trooper didn't reply. She was too busy staring wide-eyed at the large hole that dominated the wall of the library. It looked like a plane had smashed through it, Kat thought. For all she knew, that's what could have happened. It had certainly sounded like a plane crash. A chunk of the building's roof was also gone, providing an escape route for the dust and smoke swirling inside.

Kat knew of only one thing that could have caused such destruction.

The dynamite taken from the museum had finally been used.

Then another thought shot into her head—Henry had still been inside the library.

And Deana.

And the baby she was certain both had parented.

Kat ran toward Main Street. Her legs resisted, especially the left one. But she forced them to move, picking up speed as she rounded the front of the library. There was less damage there than in the back. The walls, although cracked, were still intact. Dust coated the street, pushed through the front doors. Her Crown Vic, parked in front of them, had been turned an ashen gray. Jostled by the blast, its horn blared steadily, like a monotone siren.

And standing beside it was Henry, the baby against his chest.

"Thank God," Kat said, repeating it over and over as she limped toward them. "Thank God. Thank God. Thank God."

Henry, neither seeing nor hearing her, stumbled toward the library. "Deana!" he shouted. "Say something if you can hear me!"

Kat grabbed his arm, shaking him to attention. "She didn't make it out?"

"No." Henry pulled away from her. He was growing agitated, worry making his movements jerky and rough. "She said she'd be right behind me."

He moved closer to the library, dust raining down on him. In his arms, the baby was crying. Loud, terrified wails that eclipsed the sound of the Crown Vic's horn.

"I have to find her," Henry said. "I have to help her. She could still be alive."

Kat looked to the library's gaping doors. Dust still swirled around inside, haunting the interior like restless ghosts. It was clear Henry wanted to rush inside. Only the baby prevented him from doing so. Kat knew she'd have to go in. And soon, if there was any hope of finding Deana alive.

Turning from the library, she surveyed Main Street. The blast had roused most of the town, and the first bystanders were appearing, shuffling zombielike into the streets. Kat recognized many of them, their faces growing ashen from both shock and dust. Lucia Trapani stood just outside Maison D'Avignon, teetering unsteadily on her heels. Claude Dobson, out of his suit and into a pair of pajamas, stopped in the dead center of the street, arms limp at his sides.

"Call an ambulance!" Kat barked. "Now!"

Behind Claude, sprinting to the scene from the police

station, were two welcome faces—Carl Bauersox and Randall Stroup.

Kat waved them over. "There's someone still in there. Help me find her."

She didn't wait for a response. They'd either follow her into the library or they wouldn't. But Kat was going in, no matter what.

Yet both men trailed her up the library's front steps and through the door. Inside, visibility was zero, thanks to the dust, and breathing was hard. Kat fumbled for her flashlight with one hand and covered her nose and mouth with the other. Breathing through the spaces between her fingers, she started off down the hallway.

The floor had mostly been turned to rubble, making it difficult to walk. Kat moved slowly, occasionally swinging the flashlight to the walls and ceiling to make sure they, too, weren't on the verge of crumbling. They seemed stable enough. Kat hoped they stayed that way.

She called over her shoulder to the two men behind her. "Keep an eye out, guys. She could be anywhere."

They kept going, Kat in front, constantly sweeping the flashlight. Back and forth. Up and down. Wall to wall. Floor to ceiling. When they reached the hall's halfway point, the beam of light caught something in its glow—a flash of white on the floor. Kat held the light steady, inching forward to get a better view.

What she saw was a hand.

A tilt of the flashlight revealed the arm the hand was attached to and a bit of shoulder. Another tilt illuminated the bloody and blackened face of Deana Swan.

"I see her!"

Kat surged forward, tripping over debris, until she was kneeling next to Deana. She grabbed her hand and felt for a pulse. One existed, although it was faint—the product of a heart on the verge of giving up.

"Deana, it's Chief Campbell. I'm going to get you out of this."

Deana didn't open her eyes. Kat wasn't even sure if she could. There was a large gash over the right one, oozing blood. More blood trickled from a wound on her forehead and flowed freely from both nostrils.

But she could speak, and a single word escaped her dust-coated lips.

"Adam."

"He's safe," Kat told her. "Henry has him."

Carl and Randall had caught up to them and were now on either side of Deana, sweeping rubble away from her body. From the open door, Kat heard the wail of an ambulance. Help was on its way.

"We're going to get you out of here in a minute," Kat said. "You'll be fine."

Deana coughed. A clot of blood came with it, sticking to her bottom lip. She then moaned slightly before trying to speak again.

Kat put a finger to her lips. "Don't talk. Just stay still."

Deana persisted, each word riding out on a rattling gasp. "The. Book."

The ambulance had at last arrived. Kat heard it screech to a halt just beyond the door.

"We'll talk about that later."

Deana attempted to shake her head. Kat, fearing movement would make her condition worse, pressed a hand to her forehead to keep her still.

"Ronald. Bradford."

"Is that a friend?" Kat asked, confused. "Do you want us to contact him?"

Another cough from Deana. Another horrifying surge of blood. It bubbled out of the corner of her mouth as she continued to speak.

"The book," she whispered. "He had the book."

A trio of paramedics stormed into the library, shooing Carl and Randall out of the way first. Kat kept hold of Deana for as long as she could, hoping her touch would provide some small bit of comfort, praying that it wouldn't be the last time they spoke to each other. But when a paramedic pried her away, Kat had no choice but to leave.

"Ronald Bradford," she said, stumbling toward the door. "I don't know who that is."

But deep down, Kat did. Only that wasn't the name she knew him by. And as she left the library, crossing the threshold from one area of chaos to another, Kat knew exactly where to find him.

It was shock.

It had to be.

That was the only explanation Henry could come up with for what he was going through. His body was numb from head to foot, creating the disturbing sensation that he didn't exist at all. He couldn't feel anything. Not the thrumming of his heart or the baby in his hands. Every two seconds he looked down just to make sure that Adam was still in his grasp and that he hadn't dropped him without realizing it.

When people touched him—Kat, Carl Bauersox, a concerned paramedic—it took Henry a moment to realize they were doing it.

With the sense of touch momentarily gone, Henry's other senses were aflame with alertness. He smelled everything. The smoke. The cordite. The mildewed scent of old books pushed into the street. His eyes seemed to pick up every dust particle, every chunk of rubble, every smear of blood. When the paramedics emerged from the library carrying Deana on a stretcher, the blood was so bright that Henry had to look away.

This sensory overload continued as he and Adam were led to the back of an ambulance with Deana. Each sound was as loud as a trumpet's blare. The ambulance was so sterile that Henry could taste the disinfectant.

Still, he was physically numb, even when the ambulance started rocketing toward the hospital and the paramedics shoved him out of the way. It was like an out-of-body experience, with him floating over the action, witnessing everything but feeling nothing.

It was the same emotionally. He should have been feeling everything, deeply and forcefully. Fear should have pumped from his heart and coursed through his veins. Relief should have been present, too—a deep, blessed thankfulness that he and his son were, for the most part, unharmed. But there was nothing.

Henry assumed this was his mind's way of processing all that had happened. He had almost been killed. So had the son he barely knew.

Then there was the devastating but undeniable fact that Deana was dying. Henry could tell that from the way she looked. From the frantic attempts of the paramedics to stabilize her. From the words they used, which blasted into his brain. Severe trauma. Crushed chest. Weakened pulse.

All he could do was sit there and watch them try to save Deana's life, knowing deep down that it was a losing battle. She was strong but not superhuman. Her body was failing, and everyone in the ambulance knew it. Even Adam seemed to sense something horrible was happening. He let out a series of heartbreaking wails that filled the ambulance.

"Hush, my love," Henry said.

When that didn't work, he tried Italian, whispering it to Adam.

"Silenzio, il mio amore. Silenzio."

It didn't help. Adam kept crying with a ferociousness Henry had never seen before. The wails ricocheted off the interior walls of the ambulance, eclipsing the noise of the sirens outside and the frantic sounds of the paramedics inside.

Henry began to worry that Adam really had been hurt during the blast. Something internal that he couldn't have noticed. He was so small, after all. So fragile. Of course he wouldn't have escaped injury when everyone else was hurt. But Adam's movements were normal. So was his appearance. Even the crying, though agonizingly loud, was a sign of normalcy.

Then it dawned on Henry that Adam might be experiencing what he was going through. Shock. Numbness. Feeling everything so much that he felt nothing at all.

Adam knows what's happening, he thought. *He understands that his world is about to change.*

Then Henry heard a voice, barely audible through the crying.

It was Deana's voice.

Speaking her son's name.

"Adam."

The word emerged in a weak whisper that faded as soon as it reached the air. But it was enough to summon Henry to Deana's side. He nudged one of the paramedics out of the way, knowing the man wouldn't push back. It was too late to save her. The paramedics knew it. Henry did, too.

And from the way she unfolded her hands at her sides, Henry could tell that Deana also knew it. He didn't know how much pain she was in. Not much, he hoped. Ideally, none.

Still, he lifted Adam until the baby's tiny hand was in hers. Deana closed her fingers over it, holding the hand as if it was the most priceless object in the world. Henry wanted to believe that she was imparting some final bit of maternal instruction to their child. He imagined her wisdom and advice silently moving from her hand into Adam's, telling him things that he needed to understand.

That she would no longer be there to take care of him.

That Henry was now going to be the person charged with his care and that Adam needed to be patient with him.

That she didn't want to leave this way and wished that she could be around to watch him grow.

That she loved him with all her heart.

Henry believed all of this because, after a few seconds, Adam's crying vanished. He simply let Henry hold him while his mother clasped his hand. And in that new and blessed silence, the short, sad life of Deana Swan came to an end.

"Don't you even think about going there alone."

"That's exactly what I'm doing."

"No, Kat. I forbid it."

"You're the one who put me in charge, Lieutenant. If you're having second thoughts, then I'll gladly stop what I'm doing."

Holding her cell phone close to her ear, Kat heard Tony Vasquez's lowered voice. "You and I both know that's a lie, Chief."

She had called to tell him about everything that had happened that evening. He deserved to know what was going on and, she thought sadly, to receive a warning that more people would be joining him at the hospital. She also wanted his advice on what to do next, although that didn't mean she was prepared to follow it.

"I'd be more comfortable if you weren't alone," Tony said, aiming for a more reasonable tone. "Take Carl with you. Or one of the troopers. God knows there's enough of them in town to help out."

But they were all busy, and Kat told him as much. There was crowd control at the library to contend with, solved by using gentle giant Randall Stroup to stem the growing stream of onlookers. Carl Bauersox was sent back to the station to check on Connor Hawthorne and field incoming calls. Every other law enforcement officer brought into town for the day was told to get back on the streets to look for Danny Batallas.

Kat was also on the streets of Perry Hollow, but heading toward a different location. Her Crown Vic had been rendered useless after the explosion, leaving her to make the journey on foot. She didn't tell Tony that, but judging from her exhausted huffing, he probably already knew.

"I'll be fine," she said. "He knows me. He trusts me. He's not going to do something stupid."

The man in question was Father Ron, also known as

Ronald Bradford. He was the last person to check Connor's book out of the library. He knew more than he had let on, and Kat was determined to find out how much.

"Just because he's a priest doesn't mean he can't be violent when cornered," Tony said. "People do a lot of irrational shit when they're scared."

"And," Kat countered, "they also do irrational shit when they see a SWAT team burst through the door. I don't want to scare him. Hopefully, he'll surrender without incident."

Up ahead, the bell tower of All Saints Parish came into view—a dark and silent sentinel in the sky. There was no turning back now.

"Tony, I'm almost there. I'll call you soon. I promise."

"Kat, I'm warning you—"

She ended the call and shoved her cell phone deep into her jacket. Then she limped the final few blocks toward the church. Her body protested, as she knew it would. Her aching joints creaked with displeasure, and her heart beat erratically in her chest. But Kat pressed on, feeling lucky she could even jog at all. She realized she would collapse at some point. Probably soon. But she knew it wouldn't be right then. It couldn't be.

Father Ron lived in a modest rectory that sat behind All Saints Parish. When Kat reached it, she saw that the house, tidy and trim, was dark. So was the church. And in that darkness, Kat sensed that she wasn't alone. She felt a nearby presence, as if someone, somewhere, was watching her every move.

She stopped in the street, studying her surroundings. The only light came from the moon, which shone through the oak trees that lined the curb, casting gnarled shadows onto the ground.

Behind her, a twig snapped.

Kat whirled around, seeing something lurch out of the darkness. It was a person, looking like nothing more than a shadow as he emerged into the street.

Kat drew her Glock and aimed it at the shadow's chest.

"Stop right there! Hands up!"

Two slender silhouettes rose above the figure's head. Arms being raised.

"Chief Campbell, it's me." Although it was shot through with fear, Kat recognized the voice.

"Father Ron?"

A noticeable gulp. "Yes."

"Step into the light. Let me see you."

The figure moved closer and the shadows melted away, revealing the face of Father Ron. He was wearing a dark sweatsuit, his Converse sneakers on his feet. He stared at the blood on her cheeks, confused.

"What's going on? What happened to you?"

Kat tried to keep the Glock trained on Father Ron's chest, but even that was difficult. Her arms felt like they had ten-pound weights tied to them. "Why didn't you tell me your last name was Bradford?"

"You never asked. Chief, you don't look good. Maybe I should take you to the hospital."

"When I mentioned the name Bradford today, you could have told me it was your last name. Why didn't you?"

"That's not the name you said. You said Brad Ford. Chief, why are you doing this?"

Kat could have given him a dozen different reasons. Because his last name was Bradford. Because he knew all about the tragic end of another person with that name. Because it supported her theory that someone—most likely a descendant—was trying to punish the town for what had happened there. The answer she gave, however, was shorter.

"Because you lied to me. You told me you didn't see the book Constance had in her office. The one she was so worried about. But you did, and then you checked it out of the library to read it for yourself."

"Yes, I lied," Father Ron said. "I admit it. When Constance was talking about the book, I saw the name and the cover. The next day I went to the library and found a copy. But it wasn't anything sinister. I just wanted to know what she was researching."

"And how did you feel when you found out?"

"I was surprised," Father Ron admitted. "But I knew right away it was merely a coincidence."

"Did it make you mad?" Kat asked. "I'd be mad."

A shifting cloud of emotion passed over the priest's face. First was surprise, followed by confusion and shock. The final one was disbelief, as he realized what he was being accused of.

"Chief, you don't think I started all those fires, do you?"

Kat didn't know what to think anymore. All she knew was that a man who may or may not have been related to Rebecca Bradford was standing right in front of her. He knew the history, he knew what Constance Bishop was working on, and he was lurking outside as the town was literally exploding around him.

"What are you doing out at this hour?" she asked.

"I was asleep," Father Ron said. "A loud noise outside woke me up."

"That was the library."

The priest furrowed his brow. "The arsonist struck that, too? Was anyone hurt?"

"Yes," Kat said, thinking of how Deana Swan had looked amid the rubble. "Badly."

"When did this happen?"

"Forty-five minutes ago."

"Then that's not the noise I heard," Father Ron said. "This was a few minutes ago. I'm not sure, but I thought it came from the bell tower."

As Kat half turned to face the church, she remembered the list of the town's historic sites. The museum had been one. So had the Sleepy Hollow Inn, the rec center, and the library. The last building on that list—and the only one not damaged—was All Saints Parish.

"The church," Kat said, heart suddenly galloping. "It's the only one left."

At last, Father Ron lowered his hands. "You don't think—"

"The arsonist is going to strike the church?" Kat said. "Damn right I do."

"Then we have to stop him."

Kat didn't agree. *She* had to stop him. Father Ron had to stay behind. She wasn't going to let him follow her into a darkened building, no matter how much she needed backup. She didn't trust him. She couldn't trust anyone.

"I can't let you go in there with me," she said.

"All due respect, Chief, but that's my church. The only way you can keep me out is to handcuff me to my porch."

Kat reached for her cuffs. "If that's how it's going to be, put your hands behind your back and turn around."

"You can't be serious."

"We're wasting precious time here," Kat said. "It's either this or I shoot you in the leg."

Father Ron chose the handcuffs, thrusting out one of his arms for her to slap the cuffs around.

"Forgive me, Father."

"You're already forgiven," he said, as Kat guided him to his porch and clicked the other end of the handcuffs to the railing. "I'll be praying for you."

Kat gave an appreciative nod. "Thanks. I think I'm going to need it."

She then headed for the church, hoping her body would feel a burst of adrenaline. When it didn't arrive, she came to the realization that there was no more adrenaline left. She would have to search that church through sheer force of will.

Reaching the front of All Saints Parish, Kat saw that a single vehicle had been parked outside. It was a pickup truck, as black as the night sky overhead. Kat approached it with caution, moving in wide, nervous strides. She held the Glock in one hand. The other was at her hip, finding the handle of her flashlight. When she reached the pickup, she aimed the flashlight's beam into the cab.

It was empty.

The driver's seat was bare. The passenger seat contained only a crumpled pack of cigarettes. Kat moved to the back of the pickup, checking the bed. It, too, was empty, although she saw a splash of liquid inside. Gasoline. She could smell it.

She backed up to get a good look at the license plate. It said FYRMAN. Just as she suspected.

Kat faced the church. From the front, it looked just as dark and empty as it had from outside the rectory. The only thing out of place was the front door. Just like at the library, it was wide open.

Steeling herself with a deep breath, Kat moved to the entrance as fast as her exhausted body would allow. She paused at the threshold, saying a little prayer herself. Then, after whispering a quick "Amen," Kat stepped into All Saints Parish, not knowing if she would ever leave.

The numbness left Henry as soon as they reached the hospital. There, amid the fluorescent brightness and nervous energy of the emergency room, he began to feel things again. Adam in his arms. The floor beneath his unsteady feet. Pain dotting his whole body.

And grief. Henry felt that more than anything else. It was a startling flow of emotion that filled his body and caused him to collapse into the nearest chair.

Deana was dead.

Their child would grow up with no memory of her.

And Henry had again lost someone he had once loved.

A pair of nurses approached, saying they needed to examine Adam. Henry ignored them, hoping his silence would send them away. But they were an insistent pair. One grabbed onto Henry's shoulders while the other tried to pry Adam from his arms. The baby screamed in response, kicking so forcefully that the nurse almost dropped him.

"We're fine," Henry snapped as he grabbed Adam and held him against his chest. "*He's* fine."

The pair backed away and let Henry leave the emergency room. He found himself in an empty hallway, where he paced with frustration. Adam continued to cry, although the kicking had stopped. It wasn't until Henry offered a finger to latch on to that the crying subsided altogether.

"It's all right, little guy," Henry whispered. "I'm here. Your daddy will always be here."

And his mother wouldn't be, a realization that left tears stinging the edges of Henry's eyes. He thought about Deana and the raw deal that she had been given. Life couldn't have been easy for her. She had suffered more than her share of grief, loneliness, and shame. Yes, she had made a terrible mistake a year earlier. And yes, Henry had suffered because of it. But he knew, deep down, that's all it was. A mistake. He had forgiven her as soon as he laid eyes on Adam.

He also knew that Deana hadn't deserved to die the way she had. She hadn't deserved to die at all. The sheer unfairness of her death filled him with an emotion that went beyond grief, beyond anger. It was rage he was feeling. Pure and undiluted.

Making it burn even more was guilt. Deana wouldn't have been anywhere near that library if it hadn't been for him. She had insisted on coming along, but the journey was all Henry's idea. He could have stopped her from coming. He could have insisted she stay home. But he hadn't, and it was his fault that she was now dead.

The grief, Henry knew, would fade with time. So might the anger. But the guilt would stay with him forever unless he did something about it.

He set off down the hallway, finding a stairwell at the end of it. Making sure not to jostle Adam, he climbed to the second floor, twisting into one hallway and then another. Soon he was outside a hospital room. One he had visited earlier that afternoon. Without pausing, he pushed inside.

Despite the hour, Tony Vasquez was awake and sitting

up. Someone else occupied a chair next to the bed. A woman with sad eyes and a downturned mouth. He assumed it was Lucy, the girlfriend of Nick Donnelly that Kat had talked about. Both of them contemplated Henry's sudden presence, too fretful and exhausted to be surprised.

"You're Henry, right?" Tony said.

Henry didn't answer the question. "Have you talked to Kat?"

"A few minutes ago."

"Where is she?"

"The Catholic church in town. Why?"

Again, Henry didn't provide an answer. Instead, he held out Adam. "Can I trust you with my son? I'm going to help Kat catch the man who killed his mother."

1 A.M.

Kat saw the body as soon as she reached the top of the bell tower. It was a man, on his side and facing away from her. Yet one quick glance told her who it was. She could tell because she had been looking for him all day. Because his truck was parked outside.

Now Danny Batallas was dead, lying in a pool of blood that looked sickeningly bright in the beam of her flashlight. When Kat aimed the light toward the back of his head, she saw a deep gash and shattered bone.

Just like Constance Bishop.

The antique iron that had struck them both lay on the

floor next to Danny's feet. Kat rushed to his side and felt for a pulse. There wasn't one.

"Who did this to you?" she whispered. "And why—"

Her voice faded once she saw the propane tank in the corner. It looked so out of place that she was surprised she hadn't noticed it sooner, even with a dead body nearby. The tank's cap was gone, and the handkerchief stuffed inside it did nothing to halt the smell of leaking propane. The scent made Kat more light-headed than she already was. It didn't knock her down, but it was enough to force her to look away.

That's when she saw the other tank.

It, too, was in a corner. And stuffed with a rag. And definitely out of place in that dark and quiet tower.

Quickly, Kat stood, leaning left to look beyond the enormous bell that hung in the middle of the room. She then leaned right, checking the other side of the tower. Each movement brought a glimpse of another propane tank.

Four tanks. All stuffed with handkerchiefs that served as makeshift fuses. Kat had found pictures of ones just like them in Danny Batallas's apartment. They were called fire bombs, she remembered. And they were made to do one thing—explode.

She knew she needed to get out of the bell tower, even as a dozen questions raced through her brain. They bounced into her head, one after the other, as she edged around the bell on her way toward the door. Why had Danny been up here? Had he brought the propane tanks? If so, why was he now dead?

But the answer to the last one was clear.

Danny was dead because he hadn't been alone.

Not now.

Not all day.

Someone had helped him start the fires. Someone who

then killed him once the elements were in place to destroy the town's last remaining historical landmark. Someone who was still inside the church. Kat felt his presence—a silent hum of energy in the darkness.

She spun around and faced the door. He was there. Waiting at the top of the steps. She heard his breathing, sensed the hammering of his heart.

"I know you're there," Kat said, training her Glock at the darkened doorway. "You might as well show yourself."

Movement came from the top of the steps. The shadows separated slightly, revealing the silhouette of a man standing in the doorway. Kat aimed the flashlight in the same direction as her gun, the frantic beam at first catching only bits and pieces of the man. A hand. A shoulder. An ear.

She steadied the light, pointing it squarely at his face. The harsh glow revealed a man she recognized. A man she had seen several times that day.

"I can explain," Burt Hammond said, squinting in the glare. "Just hear me out."

He carried a plastic bucket filled with liquid that sloshed around inside it. Kat hoped it was water, but she knew better. Water didn't smell like that. Water didn't tickle the inside of her nose. It didn't make her eyes sting.

The bucket was filled with gasoline. She recognized the odor from a thousand trips to the gas station.

Kat tightened her grip on the Glock. "Hands up. Right now."

Burt dropped the bucket, gasoline splashing over its side. Two pale palms rose in the darkened doorway. The flashlight glinted off his sweat-slicked face. His eyes, twitching and fearful, pleaded with her.

"It doesn't have to end this way," he said. "Please. Just listen to me."

"We'll talk at the station. You can tell me how you knew about the casino."

"I can tell you now." Burt's voice was a mixture of terror and eagerness. He wanted to talk. To explain himself. To maybe even bring Kat around to his way of thinking. "A friend of mine told me about it. David Brandt. He works in real estate. We were playing golf last week and he mentioned that he had sold the old Perry Mill tract to a billionaire in Italy. I pieced together the rest."

"And Rebecca Bradford? You're the one who saw the book on Constance's desk. You're the one who sent it to Lucia Trapani."

Burt nodded nervously.

"When Constance called that stupid meeting for tonight, I knew that's what she was going to talk about."

"So you killed her before she got the chance."

"I did it for the historical society," Burt said. "We had so much debt, Kat. We were drowning in it. I knew that this could be the thing that saved us. If Constance stayed quiet about what happened on that land, then we might get some money. A win-win situation for everyone."

But, Kat knew, his plan had backfired. Lucia had arrived early, meeting Constance instead. When their meeting was over, Constance had called Burt during the fund-raiser at Maison D'Avignon. He's the one who'd pulled the fire alarm there, using it as an opportunity to sneak away unnoticed and run through the neighboring backyards to the museum. Depending on his pace, it would only have taken him a few minutes.

Burt kept talking, spilling out a desperate torrent of words. "I was going to try to reason with Constance. But she was not a reasonable woman, Kat. She was angry. More angry than I'd ever seen her. She kept yelling that I had betrayed her. That I had betrayed this town. She pushed me, too. Shoved me right into one of the exhibits. She told me that she was going to reveal all the terrible things that had happened on that land. And I couldn't let her do that. There was too much at stake. So when Constance turned around, I grabbed the first thing I could get my hands on."

"An iron," Kat said.

"Yes."

"You hit her with it."

Another "Yes" from Burt, this time more ashamed. "I just wanted to stop her. I didn't mean to kill her."

"But you did. At least, you thought you did. And to cover it up, you grabbed a kerosene lamp, smashed it to the floor, and set the museum on fire."

"I didn't want to, but I had to. Evidence was everywhere. My fingerprints were everywhere."

Then, Kat knew, he'd rushed back to Maison D'Avignon, getting there just as the fire trucks sped past on their way to the museum.

"What about the other fires? Why did you set them?"

Kat didn't bother asking Burt *if* he had set them. She already knew that. The shame burning his cheeks told her so.

"Last night, watching the museum burn, it hit me that maybe the fire was the best thing that could happen to the museum. Yes, I knew we'd lose some things. Some very precious things. But it was heavily insured. It would be rebuilt. It would come back better than ever. I knew it would. And watching those flames dance, I also knew that the town, the whole town, could do the same thing."

"But you're trying to destroy it."

Burt laughed—an ironic, crazed chuckle. When she heard it, a dagger of fear jabbed Kat in the gut.

"Destroy it? Don't you see, Kat? I'm saving it."

"From what?"

"Itself."

"There's nothing wrong with Perry Hollow. It's recovered since the mill closed."

"But it's sinking again," Burt hissed. "You see it, Kat. I know you do. Fewer visitors. A couple of shops closing here and there. And the town will continue to decline unless someone makes a drastic change."

"Burning down a few old buildings isn't going to do that."

Burt nodded again. Trying to placate her. Trying to pander. "You're right. But a casino will. Funded by the one of the world's richest men. That will change the town completely. Like a phoenix rising from the ashes, the town can be reborn. But first it has to be approved, and you and I both know that's a tough sell. Or it would have been. But not now."

Kat understood now. She understood completely. Burt knew the casino plan would have many detractors, who'd fight it tooth and nail. So his goal was to hurt the town, to cripple it so badly that even those against a casino would have no choice but to approve it for the money its construction would bring to Perry Hollow.

Burt continued, babbling madly. "Imagine how quickly it'll be approved now that we need the resources to rebuild the hotel and rec center. The library. The church."

That last word shoved the dagger of fear deeper into Kat's body. It was clear that Burt wasn't finished yet. That there was still one more building to go. He needed to do what he had tried to do at the museum—erase his sins with the cleansing power of fire.

"Did Danny help you start the fires?" Kat asked. "Or was he just a convenient scapegoat?"

"He threatened me last night. He really said those things about burning down the town. He was capable of it. I knew that when I hired him."

Burt had done a background check. Of course. Kat felt like an idiot for not realizing it. He had known all along about the arson in Danny's past.

"So you called him around seven this morning. I saw it on his phone."

"I told him he was a suspect in the museum fire," Burt said. "I assured him that I knew he was innocent, but that he needed to lie low for the day. I told him to get out of town. Not to come in to work. Not to answer his phone. But before he left, I suggested he do a computer search of ways to start fires, maybe print out a few things, to see if he could come up with any ideas about who might be doing it."

And, Kat knew, to leave a trail of incriminating information in his wake. Burt was smart enough to know that someone needed to take the blame for these fires. Who better than a young firefighter with a few arsons under his belt?

"Why did he believe you?"

"Because I was his boss," Burt said. "In more ways than one. As mayor, I could make him a full-time, paid firefighter. Not that he needed much convincing. He was very willing to help out. So eager."

"You told him to meet you here, didn't you? At a little before one."

"Yes," Burt said. "I told him I was trying to clear his name."

And when the firefighter arrived, Burt and his weapon of choice were waiting for him. Poor, naïve Danny Batallas. He fell for every lie that had been fed to him. Now he was dead. The fact that another life had been lost in her town, under her watch, made Kat burn with anger.

"And all of this was for Perry Hollow?" she said. "The fires. The deaths. None of it had anything to do with you and your career?"

Burt pursed his lips, pretending that he had never thought about it before. "Yes, this will change things for me, too. Cement my reputation. Maybe take me from being a lawnmower salesman and mayor to something bigger."

"Like the state legislature," Kat suggested. "Or the governor's office."

She was certain that's what had been going through Burt's mind when he started fire after fire. And it gave Kat even more reason to despise him.

"There was a baby in that library," she said. "And his mother, who is most likely dead by now."

Her anger had reached full boil and was spreading from her chest to all points of her body. Her heartbeat pounded inside her head. Her index finger twitched on the Glock's trigger, aching to squeeze it.

"Her blood is on your hands, Burt. So is Danny's. So is Constance's."

"It wasn't supposed to be like this, Chief. I swear. I was just going to start a fire in the library's basement. But when I got inside, I heard voices. I didn't know what to do. I got scared."

So he blew the place up, almost killing them all. He was no better than the bastards who had killed Rebecca Bradford and her family, and it took all the willpower Kat possessed not to shoot him dead on the spot. He certainly deserved it. But she was better than that. Better than *him*.

"The ironic thing, Burt, is that Constance located Rebecca Bradford's remains. Her skeleton is in police custody. More people know about her. Lots more. They know what happened on that land. All those deaths. And I have a feeling that at this very moment, Mr. Fanelli is looking for a new place to build your precious casino."

"You're lying."

"I'm not," Kat said. "I saw the bones. I saw Rebecca's grave and we'll find the others. The secret's out, and everything you did today—all that death and waste—was for nothing."

"I don't believe you."

But he did. He believed every word. Kat could tell by the way his fearful eyes glinted in the flashlight's glow. He resembled an animal, wild and afraid, caught in a hunter's spotlight. And he acted the same way a terrified animal would.

He pounced.

He lunged toward her without warning—a beast bursting out of the shadows. Kat raised her Glock and fired off one unsteady shot. It missed, clearing his shoulder and allowing him to shove her toward the massive church bell behind her. The railing around the bell broke apart easily, splintering against her legs. Chunks of wood fell through the hole in the floor beneath the bell, dropping to the tower's ground floor.

Burt continued to push until she was against the bell itself, which rocked from the force of the collision. It rang once—a deep, vibrating tone that filled the tower.

The bell soon rocked in the other direction, now pushing Kat forward. She tried to fire her Glock again, but Burt grabbed her wrist and thrust it upward, her arm jerked over her head. Her knuckles banged against the bell, pain shooting through her hand, her fingers opening against their will.

The Glock slipped away, knocking against the bell before falling.

Past the bell.

Through the hole in the floor.

All the way down to the bottom of the tower.

The bell shifted again, rocking backward this time, moving away from Kat and leaving nothing to support her. Her arms whirled frantically, trying to keep her balance, trying to keep herself from falling through the gaping hole. Kat glanced down, seeing the rope dangling from the bell, tracing its path eight stories to the ground.

She was going to fall. She knew it. Felt it in every panicked bone of her body.

But then the bell rocked forward again, reconnecting with her back, pushing her toward Burt Hammond. Kat swung the flashlight, slamming it against Burt's skull. The flashlight ricocheted off his head, its beam streaking the ceiling.

She tried again, but Burt blocked the blow with an upraised arm. He pressed his free hand against her face. Pushing backward. Smashing her nose. Reducing her vision to blurry slits between his fingers. Then he shoved. Hard.

The back of Kat's head slammed into the bell. Her mind went black. So did her vision. They were eclipsed by an explosion of pain. Kat's legs buckled and her arms dropped to her sides. She was vaguely aware of the flashlight slipping from her fingers, just as the Glock had done.

Meanwhile, Burt's hand still pressed against her face. He shoved her head into the bell a second time. Another detonation of pain. Another dulling of the senses.

Kat's legs collapsed beneath her, pitching her forward. Burt backed away and let her drop. She fell hard. Face-first. Her chest taking the brunt of the blow and knocking most of the air out of her lungs.

Then Burt was upon her again, flipping her onto her back with the ease of someone handling a rag doll. That's what Kat felt like. An inanimate object. Hollow. With neither a brain nor bones. When Burt leaped on top of her, it dislodged what little breath she had left.

He sat on her chest, his weight pressing against her ribs, pinning her to the floor. His legs clamped around her, locking her arms in place. Kat's kicks, weak and futile, did nothing to dislodge him.

"I don't want to do this, Kat," he said. "I don't. But it's too late now."

His hand crept into her field of vision. It was clenched into a fist, except for the thumb, which pointed upward. In the center of the fist was a simple cigarette lighter. With one click, a flame appeared.

"You'll die a hero," Burt said. "I'll make sure of that. When they find you and Danny, they'll know that he started the fires and that you died trying to stop him."

He moved the lighter toward her. The flame danced just inches from Kat's face. Coming closer. And closer.

"We'll mourn you, Kat. I promise. You'll be remembered."

Kat shut her eyes. She couldn't watch anymore. Couldn't

see the moment of contact. Instead, for the second time that day, she pictured James. If this was how she was going to die, she wanted her last thought to be of her son. Not of fear. Or fire. Or pain.

Memories flooded her brain. The positive pregnancy test that at the time was the last thing she wanted. His crimson face as he emerged, wailing, from her womb. Him as a baby, a toddler, the boy he was now, the man he'd eventually become.

Kat was still picturing James when she felt the fire. It was on her left shoulder—an instant and intense heat that made her eyes snap open. Looking down, she saw the flames rising off her uniform, eating away at the fabric, biting into her flesh with white-hot teeth. The pain was unbearable. The sight was worse.

The fire grew with terrifying speed. It quickly spread down her sleeve and roared toward her collar. Every inch of progress created more agonizing pain.

Kat wanted to close her eyes again, but she saw that Burt had moved the lighter to her right shoulder.

Another click.

Another sudden leap of flame.

In a second it would be pressed against her uniform, creating another fire. A few seconds after that, she'd be engulfed. A scream formed in Kat's throat, begging to be released. She swallowed it down, summoning words instead.

"Stop," she grunted. "I won't tell. I swear."

Burt halted, wondering if he should believe her.

"You're right," Kat said. "This will save the town. I know it will."

Burt moved his thumb away from the lighter. The flame vanished.

The fire at Kat's shoulder, however, continued to burn.

Getting larger.

Burning hotter.

Searing her skin so badly that tears leaked from her eyes.

Burt shifted with doubt. Not much but enough to give Kat room to move. She lifted her shoulder slightly. Close enough for the flames consuming her uniform to leap to the sleeve of Burt's shirt. It ignited quickly, the cuff flaring like a candle's wick.

Seeing the flames, Burt rolled off her, trying to pat the fire out with his hands. Kat, arms now free, did the same, desperately slapping an open palm against her shoulder. When that didn't work, she tore at the uniform, ripping it open and yanking it from her body. Once it was off, she rolled on top of it, smothering the remaining flames.

Kat then moved toward the door, dragging herself across the floor. Her shoulder, raw and throbbing, still felt like it was on fire, slowing her progress.

Burt, realizing he had been fooled, rushed toward her. He had grabbed the iron next to Danny and was holding it aloft, arm trembling from the weight, a snarl on his face. It was how he must have looked right before killing Constance. And Danny. Now it was Kat's turn, and even if she beat him to the door, he'd surely overtake her at the top of the stairs.

Crawling even faster, Kat spotted the bucket a few inches away. She stretched for it, her fingers curled around the lip of the bucket. She yanked it toward her, gasoline splashing her hands.

Burt was upon her now. Standing over her.

Kat got a hand under the bucket.

She lifted it.

She tossed.

The gasoline rained down on Burt in a full-on assault that soaked his face, his hair, his clothes. He stumbled backward in shock, the iron dropping from his grip. Kat also fell back, gasping with fear and exhaustion. She dropped the bucket.

"Try using that lighter now," she said.

Burt sat down, sopping wet. Gasoline dripped from his body and spread across the floor. It pooled beneath him and rolled toward all four corners of the bell tower.

"It's over, Burt," Kat said. "Give up."

But Burt had no intention of doing that. Kat could tell by the way he looked to the shadowy corners and saw the propane tanks sitting in each one of them.

"I'm sorry," he said. "I can't."

He was still holding the lighter. It poked out of his clenched fist, now as deadly and explosive as the stick of dynamite he had used earlier.

"Burt, stop!" Kat froze in the doorway, too scared to move. "It's not worth it."

But Burt Hammond had already made up his mind. All fear had left his eyes. In its place was the dim light of defeat. Life as he knew it was over. His grand plan wouldn't happen. He'd be tried for three murders and four arsons. He would die in jail.

To Kat, he looked like someone who knew he was doomed. Someone who thought it would be easier if he just ended his life right then and there, taking her with him.

She started inching backward through the door, toward the tower's stairs. It didn't matter how close she got. If Burt lit himself on fire, she wouldn't make it out alive. The entire bell tower would explode in seconds.

"Please, Burt," she begged. "Don't do this."

Burt closed his eyes. "I'm sorry, Kat. Forgive me."

He lifted a trembling thumb to the top of the lighter. He pressed down, ready to spin it to life.

A gunshot cut him off.

The single report blasted through the bell tower. Kat recognized the sound. She'd know it anywhere. It was a Glock.

Her Glock.

In an instant, Burt was flat-backed on the floor, a bullet hole the size of a dime in the middle of his forehead. The lighter sat beside him. Kat slid across the floor toward it, brushing it aside, pushing it straight into the chasm beneath the church bell, where it could do no more damage.

She then looked to the doorway, seeing Henry Goll emerge from the darkness of the stairwell. In his hands was the Glock she had dropped.

"Are you okay?" he asked.

"I think so."

Kat didn't know for sure. Her shoulder hurt like hell, and her head still throbbed. That, coupled with exhaustion and the fact that she had almost died for the second time that day, left her brain feeling like cotton candy. But she could sit up, which was good. Standing, however, might be more of a problem.

"How's Deana?" she asked, trying to push herself off the floor.

The brief shake of Henry's head told her everything she needed to know. Deana was gone, and the news caused Kat to drop back to the floor.

"I'm so sorry, Henry," she said. "I truly am."

Wordlessly, Henry stepped into the bell tower. He spent a

brief moment surveying the scene—two corpses, propane tanks and all—before helping Kat to her feet. She couldn't stand on her own, relying on Henry for support. It was a role reversal from their night in the burning mill a year earlier. Then, Kat had done the heavy lifting.

As they started the long descent down the stairs, the sirens of approaching emergency vehicles rose outside. The state police, arriving at last. Only that didn't make any sense.

Kat turned to Henry. "How did you get here?"

"A new friend."

She realized who he was talking about when they emerged from the church. Parked outside was a red Volkswagen Beetle. Standing next to it was Lucy Meade.

"Thank God you're okay," she said, crushing Kat with a hug so enthusiastic that it made everything hurt even more. Kat, though, didn't mind.

"I was so worried," Lucy continued. "Are you hurt?"

"Yes, but I'll live."

"We need to get you to the hospital."

Kat waved away the suggestion, burned shoulder be damned. First, she needed to find Father Ron, remove the handcuffs, and say a few thousand Hail Marys. Then she needed to go home, hug her son, and take a long, hot shower. After that maybe, just maybe, she could finally get some sleep.

"No," Lucy insisted. "We have to go to the hospital. Tony just called. Nick is awake."

2 A.M.

The hospital.

Again.

Kat had spent more time there in the past twenty-four hours than was good for her. This time, however, she wanted to be there. She needed to be.

Creeping into Nick's room—thanks to Dr. Patel, bending the rules once more—she saw that he was indeed awake. His eyes, wide open and vibrant, latched on to hers immediately. Kat practically ran to his bedside and scooped one of his hands into both of hers.

"You look like shit," Nick said.

"I could say the same thing about you."

Actually, Kat couldn't tell which one of them looked worse. Nick's head was still wound with bandages, and his skin had the chalky pallor of a corpse. But her appearance was no better. Her shoulder had been treated and wrapped to mummylike proportions, and the painkillers she had been given made her eyes shifty and dazed. She reeked, too, a fact that Nick didn't fail to comment on.

"You also smell like a gas station."

"It's my new perfume," Kat said. "Exxon, by Calvin Klein."

"I guess that means you caught the bad guy."

"I did. And now it's all over."

She decided to spare Nick the details until morning. It

was far too late, and she had barely been able to process them herself. Besides, she had a feeling there'd be plenty of time for bedside chats in the days to come.

"Did the doctors tell you how long you're going to be here?"

"A few days," Nick said. "They want to watch my brain a bit more. Just to make sure the wheels are turning properly."

"Maybe this whole thing finally knocked some sense into you."

"Probably not." Nick chuckled, all the tubes and wires he was attached to shaking with him. "But Dr. Patel said I should be okay in time. I might have some trouble with motor skills."

"Well, you've already got the cane."

Nick nodded. "I do. The doctor said there also might be some short-term memory loss."

"Like what?"

"I can't remember."

Although he was laughing, Kat noticed a look of uncertainty flash across his pale features. He was frightened, and rightly so. She gave his hand a squeeze, letting him know that she'd be with him the entire time. He had saved her life. Twice, in fact. And she would gladly repay him by being someone to lean on whenever he needed it. A second cane, just in case the first one wasn't enough.

Kat also knew that Nick now had more than just her in his corner. Lucy Meade was there, too, and, judging from the expectant way she stood in the doorway to his room, she wanted to see Nick just as badly as Kat had.

"I see your new nurse is here," she said, beckoning Lucy into the room. "I think you're in capable hands."

The flicker of fear on Nick's face vanished when Lucy entered the room. It was replaced by nothing less than joy.

"Are you here for my sponge bath?" he asked.

"Only if you behave." Lucy moved to the side of his bed, leaned against him lightly, and placed her head on his shoulder. "Now you should get some sleep."

"Technically," Nick said, "I've been asleep all day."

Kat let out an appropriately timed yawn. "The rest of us haven't had that luxury. So, that's what I'm going to do. I'll see you both in the morning."

"Bring coffee when you do," Nick said. "I refuse to drink the swill they serve here."

Kat smiled. "Of course."

Turning to face the door, she felt a slight tug at her heart. It wasn't exactly sadness, but it wasn't happiness either. It was a kind of wistful ache as she realized that her relationship with Nick Donnelly was entering a strange and new phase. For almost two years, they had had each other's backs, through thick and thin. They still did, but now something was different. Now Kat understood that she would have to share him with Lucy.

She left the room, letting out another yawn. Christ, she needed to sleep. And soon. Even then, it wouldn't be for long. There was a lot of work to do later. Paperwork. Police reports. Meetings with the state police. At least she was no longer in charge. On her way to Nick's room, Gloria Ambrose called to announce that she would be arriving within the hour.

As for Giuseppe Fanelli and Lucia Trapani, she had no idea if they still intended to build a casino on the banks of Lake Squall. She doubted it. Even if they pressed forward, she had a feeling town officials would want nothing to do with a project tainted with so much blood.

Still, Perry Hollow had a lot of rebuilding to do. It was without a hotel. They had no rec center. Their library had been blown apart.

Yet, just like Nick, it would pull through.

Kat had no doubt about that.

Once he had reached the hospital, a nurse had kindly offered Henry a room in the maternity ward in which to take care of Adam. He didn't have it for long. Just an hour or two. Enough time to clean up and maybe take a nap.

Only Henry couldn't sleep, no matter how numbingly exhausted he was. An uncertain future gaped before him, keeping him awake even as Adam lay dozing on his chest. He was now a single father, a fact that seemed to grow more preposterous the longer he thought about it. This was not meant to happen. Fate had decided long ago that Henry was to remain alone, tied down by nothing. Yet here he was, lying in a borrowed hospital bed holding a person he would be attached to for the rest of his life.

He imagined Gia, his late wife, watching the scene in the afterlife, wherever and whatever that was. He pictured her smiling, pleased that he finally had the boy he had always wanted.

Maybe Deana was with her. Henry hoped so. It would be nice for her to have a friend in heaven, when there had been so few for her here on earth. It wasn't fair that she wouldn't be around to see Adam grow and thrive. She had deserved better, and Henry vowed to raise her child the best way he knew how. Deana's memory would live on in Adam. Henry would make sure of it.

Which meant he had a lot of learning to do. Shutting his eyes, praying for sleep to descend upon him, Henry nonetheless kept thinking about all the baffling and new responsibilities that had been thrust upon him. He knew nothing about children, especially babies. He didn't know when Adam needed to be fed or what he ate. He didn't know how to hold him properly or burp him or bathe him. He didn't even know how to change a diaper.

But he would find out. He had to.

Those tasks joined the ever-expanding list of things Henry needed to do in the next few hours. He needed to make funeral arrangements for Deana, an unenviable task, but one he had to undertake, seeing how she didn't have any family left. Then he'd need to go through her house, collecting all the things Adam required.

At some point, he also needed to call Dario Giambusso. He imagined catching his editor in mid-jog again and spilling the details about Fanelli, the casino, the fires, the deaths. And if Dario was still upright on his treadmill, the news that Henry would not be returning to Italy would certainly knock him down.

Henry didn't know where he and Adam would go after that. The possibilities were endless. Maybe Pittsburgh, where Henry had grown up. Or perhaps someplace warm and tropical, where Adam could spend his childhood splashed with sunshine.

Yet as dozens of destinations shuffled through his brain, Henry's thoughts kept stopping on one place.

Perry Hollow.

It had once been his home, and he saw no reason why it couldn't be again. Yes, he'd have to find some way to support Adam. And he knew there would always be bad memories associated with the town. But people who cared about him were here. People who could help him navigate the obstacle course that was single parenthood.

"What do you think?" he whispered to Adam, still fast asleep. "You like it here, don't you?"

His son stirred, nuzzling his head against Henry's chest. He seemed to be at peace for the first time all night. Probably dreaming, Henry thought. Maybe about the future. And from the beautiful smile on his angelic face, Henry could only assume that it was a happy dream.

"I thought you'd be sleeping."

Henry turned from his son to the room's open door, where Chief Kat Campbell now stood.

"I'm surprised you're not doing the same," he said.

"I was on my way home when a nurse told me where you were hiding." Kat tiptoed to the bed, careful not to wake Adam. "And I was thinking that the two of you might want to come along."

A half hour later, they stumbled through Kat's front door, burdened with emergency items they had picked up from Deana's house. Diapers. Baby food. Bottles. Formula.

Lou van Sickle, spending yet another night on the lumpy couch, practically salivated over the activity, so much so that it took her a while to leave. She insisted on staying until Kat could guarantee that she was feeling okay. Kat appreciated the concern but knew Lou had an ulterior motive. She wanted to get as much information as she could before starting up the gossip mill bright and early in the morning.

James, however, was simply thrilled to have surprise guests. Running downstairs in his pajamas, he repeatedly hugged Henry and cooed over little Adam.

It buoyed Kat's heart to see him so engaged and happy again. She knew her job was rough on him. She knew that it kept James from having the normal childhood she so desperately wanted for him. There had been problems in the past and there might be more in the future. But at that moment, everything was right, with James and with her. And she needed to cherish it for as long as it lasted.

Henry seemed to be enjoying the moment, too, as much as he could. His posture became less rigid as he and Kat arranged all the items they had carried in. He was relaxing, Kat knew, adjusting to the idea of staying with her and James for a while. He had been through a lot that day, and he had lost so much. But Kat knew that having a place to stay and friends nearby would make his first night alone with Adam much easier.

"Are you sure we're not putting you out?" Henry asked.

"Not at all," Kat said. "You two can stay as long as you need. Honestly. I want you to."

She meant it. She cared about Henry. She had missed him when he was gone. And now she wanted him to stay.

She thought back to their brush with death in the swimming pool earlier that day. So much had happened between then and now that it all seemed surreal and hazy, like the lingering remnants of a dream. But she remembered the way they had kissed. That was still vivid, surprisingly so. While there probably had been several reasons for the incident, Kat realized the main one was that she had really wanted to kiss

Henry Goll. She had a feeling he had wanted to do the same. And whether it ever happened again in the future was now entirely up to them.

Adam, who was being cradled by James in the living room, started to cry. It was a fraught and fussy noise that Kat remembered from when James was that age.

"He's been crying a lot," Henry said as the two of them joined James on the couch. "Is that normal?"

Kat couldn't help but chuckle at his total lack of knowledge about children. "Yes. It's very normal. He's probably hungry."

She took the baby from James and sniffed, detecting the telltale scent of a full diaper.

"And he needs to be changed."

Seeing that Henry looked petrified at both prospects, Kat grabbed a stack of diapers. She spread a white towel on the floor and gently placed Adam on top of it before cleaning him.

Henry joined her, staring at his son with a tender trepidation. "I don't know how to do this."

"It's easy," Kat said. "I'll show you."

James crawled onto the floor next to her, eager to watch and learn. With wide, curious eyes, he watched as Kat placed two diapers on the towel, one on each side of the baby.

Removing the old diaper and discarding it quickly, Kat slid a fresh one beneath Adam. She then wrapped the diaper around him, slowly, making sure Henry followed every move.

When she was finished, she unfastened the diaper and let Henry try. He was nervous, of course, and fumbled a bit. But, with her help, he managed just fine.

"See," Kat said. "I told you it was easy."

ACKNOWLEDGMENTS

I'd like to thank my agent, Michelle Brower; my editor, Elizabeth Lacks; the Ritter and Livio families; and all my friends at *The Star-Ledger*. Special thanks goes to Maura Mitchell, for patiently answering every silly question I had about witchcraft; Sarah Dutton, for literally dropping everything to read the first draft and offering valuable advice when she was finished; and Mike Livio, for telling me over and over again that I should write this book, even when I was convinced I shouldn't.